HEATHER BLACKWOOD

LUNA PARK

A TIME CORPS NOVEL

CHAPTER 1

"**L**IKE THE GROCERY STORE AND the grave, everyone comes to the boardwalk eventually," said Elliot. Astrid looked past her cousin, watching the group of girls from her high school wander past the boardwalk arcade. There were five of them, all dressed in outfits that came from expensive boutiques or high-end shops in the mall. Their shoes alone probably cost more than her whole outfit. The Luna Park Boardwalk uniform she wore consisted of a white polo shirt, khakis and a blue visor with the park logo on it. As uniforms went, it could be a lot worse. Even so, she wanted to avoid the girls.

"I just didn't expect to see them here is all," Astrid said. "Dorothy, the one in red, always makes nasty comments about my clothes. Her family has money."

"As of today, you're out of school forever," Elliot said. "You don't have to deal with them ever again."

"It's not official until graduation tomorrow," Astrid said.

"You could skip the ceremony and they'd still give you the diploma," said Elliot. "You're done. No more pencils, no more books," he sang.

He leaned against the side of Astrid's pretzel cart. The glass case enclosed rows of pretzels on metal hooks rotating slowly under a glowing heat lamp. The pretzel stand stood just outside the entrance to the arcade, so the two of them had a view of both the boardwalk and inside the building where a few people played video games. It was Wednesday afternoon and the park was not crowded.

The group of high school girls passed without noticing either of them.

"In ten years, where will those beautiful yet tragic examples of American girlhood be?" asked Elliot with mock concern. He also worked at Luna Park, and sometimes visited Astrid when he was on his lunch break, as he was now. He pulled off his visor, shoved his blond hair back from his forehead and shielded his eyes with his hand. He looked out over the Pacific Ocean, and Astrid knew he was evaluating the surf. Seagulls wheeled above them and the white triangles of a sailboat slid over the brownish green water.

The jacaranda trees along the boardwalk were dropping their lavender-colored petals, and since they were genetically modified to have more petals than their progenitors, thousands of soft purple petals blew over the planks of the boardwalk and floated over the sidewalks nearby. And when the wind blew the right way, they'd blow over the beach and into the water. People didn't seem to mind them blowing over their windshields or catching in their hair.

The people of Los Angeles couldn't enjoy the springtime cherry blossoms like those in Washington, DC or Japan, but they loved their summers and this gave them something else to enjoy. Luna Park and the surrounding businesses all up and down the street had planted jacarandas years before or had trucked in giant potted trees for the occasion. Year by year, the festival had grown into a local tradition. Of course, Luna Park capitalized upon it as much as possible.

"Those girls will probably be living in a beach house in Malibu with servants and money, and driving some car I can't even pronounce," said Astrid.

"And screwing their personal trainers and popping pills like candy. They'll be miserable."

"I wouldn't mind the misery of having too much money," she said.

She glanced at her watch. It was time to rotate her stock. She pulled out a paper bag and tongs, opened the glass door to the display case, and started pulling out the oldest pretzels.

"Ah, but you and I were born into humble circumstances," said Elliot. "And thus our ascension to the middle class will be all the more admirable. We are made of sterner stuff than those hothouse orchids, and we shall rise."

Astrid couldn't help but smile, and Elliot gave her a quick glance. "You're saving those for me, right?"

"It's either that, or throw them in the trash," she said. It bothered her to waste food, and she was glad that Elliot took the old pretzels off her hands. He didn't eat them himself, or if he did, he didn't eat many. He mainly gave them out to the homeless people who hung around the outside of the park. The rest went to the seagulls and pigeons.

Elliot lived in a trailer that was permanently parked at a nearby beach campground. He was two years older than Astrid, and was taking a few classes at the community college. But aside from working at the boardwalk, he mainly surfed and created small metal sculptures that he sold online.

A boy nearby fed dollar bills into the machine that converted cash into tokens for the arcade. The tokens poured in a jingling pile into the metal cup.

"Yeah, I wouldn't mind a little money either," said Elliot. "But you, you're going to be big. I know it."

"Art doesn't pay."

"Not now it doesn't. But after you graduate from Columbia, you could have your own exhibit at the Met."

"I seriously doubt it."

"How many applicants were there?" He had asked Astrid this question before.

She sighed. "You know already. Fifteen hundred."

"And how many got in?"

"Twenty-five."

"And you got a scholarship to boot. That's not nothing."

"It's only a partial scholarship. I'll still have loans."

Astrid knew that Columbia's acceptance of her had been a fluke. Someone in the admissions department had liked her portfolio and her teachers had written her nice letters of recommendation. She had high, but not exceptional, SAT scores and a decent GPA. But her artwork was nothing special. And though she had been offered a scholarship, her mother had refused to sign the acceptance forms. The deadline was still a week away, which left her enough time to sign it on her eighteenth birthday, mail it and hope for the best.

She folded over the top of the paper bag and handed it to Elliot. She then took out the fresh pretzels, sprayed them and dipped half of them into a shallow box of salt. The other half she left unsalted.

Elliot turned away from watching the water. "You still don't believe it, do you?' he said. "It's sweet in a way, and a pain in the ass at the same time. You're good, Astrid. Real good. You have a gift."

"Shut up. I just waste too much time drawing."

"That's your mother talking. Speaking of whom, she called me. She said you weren't answering your phone."

It was true. She had not answered when she saw her mother's name appear on the screen of her mobile phone. Today had been a good day. It was the last day of her senior year, so she and her classmates had gotten to talk and mess around in class. She knew that she wouldn't see most of her friends often, but she would see them tomorrow at graduation, so she didn't feel real sadness yet. The June day was hot without being sticky, and the breeze from the ocean had just enough coolness to feel refreshing. She had to work a boring job, but then, who didn't? At least her pretzel stand was in the shade with a view of the ocean. The Los Angeles sun was out, there weren't many people and she was going to get to move to New York in late August. She didn't want to ruin her day by listening to her mother tell her off about leaving dishes in the sink or forgetting clothes in the dryer.

"I've been busy," she said.

"I know, I know. I wouldn't want to talk to her either. She said not to bring home any of your leftover pretzels because they're making her fat."

"No worries there. I won't. Anything else?"

"Nope. But I have to go. I have to talk to Mr. Augustus."

Mr. Augustus was the manager of Luna Park. He had graying orange hair, slanted green eyes and a penchant for making the workers feel uncomfortable.

"Did you do something?" Astrid asked.

"No, he said he was going to have me work the mirror house soon."

"That guy is creepy. Something is off about him."

"An old dude who has been running an ancient amusement park for thirty years? Nah, nothing weird about that."

"That's not what I mean. When I hired on, I swear he turned away for just a second and spat in his palm before shaking my hand." Astrid didn't mention that when she had looked into Mr. Augustus's face, she had felt something more than disgust at his damp handshake. It was like she was signing onto something more than a part-time job.

"You saw him do it? You actually saw him spit?" Elliot asked. He looked thrilled with the idea. He probably wanted a piece of gossip to share with the other employees.

"No, not exactly."

"Oh." He was disappointed. "When are you off?"

"At nine."

"You're lucky you're not eighteen yet, or you'd be working until midnight."

5

"Only five more days," she said. "Are you coming to my graduation tomorrow?"

"Wouldn't miss it for the world."

"And Aunt Ruth?"

"My mom will be there too," he said.

Elliot left for Mr. Augustus's office and Astrid adjusted her visor. Her short blonde hair was getting shaggy and she needed to decide if she wanted to grow it out or cut it. She had been putting off the decision until she was in New York, figuring that living as a student and an artist would inspire her to make a choice one way or the other. She might even dye her hair, but she wasn't sure yet. She knew it was silly, but it felt like her real life, her true life, was waiting for her, just out of reach. And with every day that passed, it inched a little closer.

CHAPTER 2

YUKIKO OPENED THE MOUTH OF her green fish coin purse and placed a ten-dollar bill on the ticket counter at the entrance of Luna Park.

"How many tickets will that get me?" she asked.

The woman in the booth pointed to the sign next to her. "A dollar a ticket."

"And the Jacaranda Festival is this week, right?"

The woman slid a tri-folded map and schedule across the counter and set a strip of ten tickets on top. Yukiko put the tickets into her coin purse, snapped the mouth shut and turned to leave.

"Hey, wait a minute. Where is the ten?" said the woman.

A large yellow leaf sat on the counter. That had happened quickly. Far too quickly. Yukiko hurried away from the ticket counter, pushed through a group of people and entered the park before the woman could call her back. As she walked, she unfolded the map and studied it. Her old friend, if you could call Santiago a friend of anyone, was correct. Something was definitely off in this place.

One of Yukiko's clip-on plush fox ears came loose from her hair and she pulled it out and fastened it back on. The bright orange ears were for show. The plush fox tail she clipped to the belt of her skirt was out of necessity. She liked to make her appearance look intentional, so she wore a short gray schoolgirl skirt, a button-down white blouse and knee socks. She adjusted her appearance, just a little, making sure her eyes were as ordinary a shade of brown as she could manage. She didn't make herself look more or less attractive than her ordinary form. If any men bothered her, well, she could handle the worst of them, and had. On more than one occasion.

It was eight o'clock at night, and according to the schedule, the last of the Jacaranda Festival events had happened at sundown. Ah well, she would be back tomorrow. That was the day Santiago had asked her to arrive, but being who and what he was, she wasn't about to meet him for the first time on his turf without having a good look around beforehand.

A pair of young men were drinking sodas and sitting on a bench. Yukiko felt their eyes on her and she gave her hips a little extra swish. Let them look. She didn't glance back at them over her shoulder. She had a more important task.

She smelled the air. The jacarandas were dropping their pale purple petals, and their scent permeated everything. There was also the scent of ocean, of sand, of sunscreen and human sweat. Someone had spilled a drink and there was the woody smell of the boardwalk floor beams beneath the sticky sweetness of the soda. She paused at a booth with balloons tacked to a large flat board. Customers were supposed to throw a dart to pop them, but they looked too deflated to pop easily. There was the smell of the latex of the balloons, the musty fabric of the plush toys that served as prizes, the sickly tang of cheese from a concession stand nearby. Then there was the metal of the rides, the scent of steel and the bits of rust here and there. The fresh paint on the walls surrounding the indoor carousel, the diaper of a baby in a stroller. She walked on.

Ah, now there was a new scent. Up ahead was an arcade. It gave off the scent of wiring, electricity and plastic. Yukiko wondered for a moment if Santiago had taken the electrical things into account, but of course he had. He was old, very old, and he was not unintelligent.

He knew the ways of humans and their technologies, even the newer ones.

Electricity and metal, swarms of people, these things should have kept most troublesome things at bay. But then, Luna Park's location lent itself to trouble.

She looked over the other boardwalk games as she passed. Which one involved the least skill and the most chance? They all involved shooting or throwing something. Well, that might work. She stopped at a booth where rubber ducks floated in a shallow pool of circulating water. The ducks bumped into one another and swirled in their own little currents, their painted eyes staring into space. Five of them had red stars painted on their backs.

"Throw a ring on a duck with a star, win a prize," said the young man.

"I'll play," she said and handed a ticket to him. She took the three rings he offered her. Two other players, a mother and daughter, stood next to her. Yukiko waited until they had thrown their rings, none of which went over the starred ducks. She tossed hers, bending things slightly, arcing the light, feeling the three people, the woman, the girl and the young man's minds next to her own.

She liked them. She couldn't help but like them. When she was that close to people, effecting their perceptions, even for a moment, she felt it. It was one of the last remnants of her kind, that feeling of connection with the people.

"You got it!" shouted the little girl.

The young man checked, and sure enough, one of her rings had encircled one of the starred ducks.

"Which prize do you want?"

Yukiko looked them over. "Which one should I pick?" she asked the girl.

"I'm trying for the pink dolphin," she said. "There are real ones that color in the Amazon."

"Are there now?" Yukiko pointed. "I'll have the dolphin."

The young man pulled it down and handed it to her. She set it on the table next to the girl and stepped away.

"Is it for me?" the girl said.

"Yeah, you can have it."

"What do you say?" said the mother to the girl.

"Thank you!"

Yukiko moved down the boardwalk and glanced back. The young man was removing the rings from the ducks and looked confused. Her illusion had broken prematurely.

There were other games of chance, but none of them would reward her with money, and she knew enough about the effects of the place on her abilities. Perhaps she should use her tickets for rides. The roller coaster was of the old wooden style. She could remember when any roller coaster was considered a new thrill, even ones considered tame by modern standards. No, today she wanted something else. She wanted to get into the parts of the park where something might be lurking. The carousel. Yes, it was old and generations of children had loved it. The spinning and bobbing created just enough disorientation to make it a good place to check.

She found it on the map and headed toward it. She could smell it from a distance, underneath all the human smells and the beach smells. It was lower, like the lowest notes of a cello, like a long, drawn-out heartbeat. It was one of the places that made the park what it was. She smelled for Santiago, but he was not nearby. Knowing him, he was probably drinking at some nightclub downtown with a half-nude woman wriggling in his lap.

In his letter, he had told her something was wrong and that he could sense something coming. A difference in the air, like an approaching storm. He had asked her to come and see what she could learn. In all the years she had known him, he rarely asked for help. And when he had, she had always refused on principle. Her kind was not like him. Her kind had rules and a code of honor and nobility.

Santiago was nothing more than a swindler and teller of tales. She refused to aid him in his cons.

It must have been difficult for him to ask her for help. And it had not involved a con, at least none that she could detect. She had agreed to come, mainly out of curiosity.

She stayed at the carousel, but aside from sensing a faint remnant of an otherkind who had come through a day or two before, she sensed nothing else. She spent three tickets on a haunted house ride, sitting alone in the car as it wound back and forth on a little track through a series of dark rooms. Screams, moans and tinny music in a minor key blared over the speakers. The walls were painted with fluorescent paint and lit by black light. It hurt her eyes. She closed them and inhaled. There was something behind the back wall of the ride, a higher-pitched sensation, like a tingle in the back of her nose.

She got on the ride next door, which allowed her sit in a yellow caterpillar as it wound through a garden of giant flowers, caterpillars and insects. The feeling was fainter on this ride. When she got off, she walked around, but the area behind the rides was impossible to access.

"What's back behind these rides?" she asked the man at the churro cart.

"What, back there? There's a staff lounge, offices, stuff like that."

Yukiko circled around the rides, glancing at the map. Yes, that area would be off limits to her. She stopped at a snack stand that shared a wall with these offices and the staff lounge. There was the smell of pizza, nacho cheese, sugary drinks, the people, of course, and the other thing. It was fainter now than it had been on the haunted house ride.

"What would you like?" asked the girl at the snack booth.

Yukiko looked over the machines. "Could I have a red slushie?" She didn't know what flavor "red" might be, but from past experience, she knew it would stain her mouth and tongue a fun shade of bright red.

"Here, I'll get this one," said an older man to the girl. He was sweating and out of breath. "You take your break." The man had slanted green eyes and hair that had once been orange before it had gone gray.

"How much is it?" Yukiko asked. She wanted to get her money out on the counter and get out of there before it changed.

"Three fifty."

He filled her cup while she hunted in her coin purse for coins to make exact change. She didn't want to end up waiting for him to make change. She put the money down and found him looking at her, holding the cup in a stubby-fingered hand. His eyes were light green, almost the shade of sunlight as it passed through new leaves. She paused to smell. Nothing. Just regular human smell mixed with cigarettes and the deodorizing pads he put inside the soles of his shoes.

"I don't need a receipt," she said as she took the slushie and turned away. She had learned all she could, at least until she could discuss the issue with Santiago and learn whatever he knew. She sucked on the slushie as she left the park and walked down the block to the Seaside Inn. It was not on the seaside, of course. She would need more money than she had for a hotel on the beach. Her motel was a few blocks inland, a two-story U-shape of pink stucco with palm trees planted out in front. At the center of the courtyard sat an empty pool, cracked by age and earthquakes. She had already paid, using some of the real money she had won at the Chumash casino. She still had some of it left and needed to be careful with it.

She climbed the stairs, fished the motel key card from her coin purse and entered her room. It was a non-smoking room, and though it smelled like disinfectant and people, it was not too bad. She had certainly seen worse. Her plush tail and ears went onto to the bathroom counter and she washed off her makeup. She dropped onto the bed and flipped on the television. Why was she so tired? She could barely keep her eyes open. The voices on the television seemed so far away, like people talking through the wall. Or maybe there were people talking in the next room. She couldn't tell, and within moments, she was sound asleep.

CHAPTER 3

AFTER WORK, ASTRID SAT ON the commuter train and checked the balance on her rail pass. She had enough to get her to the next payday, but would need to buy another pass right after she got her check. She leaned back in her seat and watched the buildings flash by the window in the dark.

She loved the train, not because of the people or the scenery, or even because she wasn't at work, school or home with her mother. It was something else. The train existed to move, to travel from one place to another, pausing but never truly stopping. Naturally, it rested at stops. It parked when the trains stopped running in the wee hours of the morning or when it was taken out of service for maintenance. But at its heart, it was built to move, to exist in the undefined places, the places that were neither destination nor starting point.

She got off at her stop and walked home. It was night, and walking alone in the dark wasn't her safest choice, but what else could she do? She had to make money somehow, and without a car or anyone to drive her to Luna Park, the train was the only affordable option. She passed the quiet houses, all of them small, run-down two- and three-bedroom homes from the mid-twentieth century. Paint peeled, vehicles decayed and curtains faded bit by bit as the years passed. Only the children changed.

Astrid's front door was locked and she rummaged in her purse for her key. Her mother wouldn't get up off the sofa to unlock the door unless Astrid yelled through the door that she had forgotten her key, earning her a scolding. She unlocked the door and dropped her purse on the entryway table, kicked off her shoes and shoved them up against the wall next to the door.

"You took your sweet time coming home," said her mother. She was in sweatpants and a tee shirt and had a glass of wine on the table beside the sofa. The television was on, tuned to a talk show.

"The guy who takes the shift after mine was late. And then I missed my usual train and had to wait for the next one."

She watched her mother's reaction. If she went back to watching television, Astrid could go into the kitchen and grab something to eat. She hadn't eaten since her peanut butter sandwich at lunch and she was famished.

"What did you bring?" her mother asked. "Anything?" She took a sip of wine and the ice cubes tinkled against the glass. The wine was the cheap stuff that her mother bought at Walmart, some blend of red and white that combined into a light shade of pink.

"I thought you said you didn't want any pretzels because they were making you gain weight."

"How could you say something like that? You're saying I'm fat."

"No, no. It's just that they're unhealthy. Too many carbs. They're all white flour and salt."

"Well, I guess that's true. But there's other stuff they throw away at that park, right? Why don't you bring home some pizzas?"

"Those aren't particularly healthy either. And besides, I don't work the pizza stand."

"Well, why not?"

"Because I'm assigned to the pretzel stand. It's what they trained me for." Astrid took off her jacket and hung it on one of the pegs behind the door. Mother had gone back on her request for Astrid not to bring home any food, which meant she was looking for a reason to fight. Her mother was watching her. Astrid had to be careful. "So, what are you watching?"

Her mother glanced at the television. "I don't know, some thing." She fanned the air in dismissal. "You should have brought something home."

"But you called Elliot and told me not to."

"Never mind Elliot. This isn't about Elliot. This is about you. And I just don't want any more of those nasty pretzels you make. You're a high school graduate now, and look at you." She waved her hand up and down to encompass Astrid from head to toe. Her nose crinkled slightly, as if she smelled something unpleasant. Astrid knew that she was no beauty. She was flat-chested, her eyes were a completely unremarkable shade of blue and her nose was too big. Her blonde hair was getting too long and was starting to stick out.

"I'm growing my hair out," she said. What was she thinking earlier about cutting or dying her hair? There was no way she could afford a haircut on top of a bus pass, a plane ticket to New York and any other expenses. She'd have to let her hair grow. "It'll look better in a few weeks."

"It's not just that, sweetie. You could get free food at work, but you don't even bother to do it. And when you do, you bring home crap. I work all day to support you, and you just screw around in school, play around at work and then come home and eat all the food I bought."

"Sorry," she muttered and headed for the kitchen. There was no way to win this. She hoped she could grab something and take it to her room.

"Now just a minute," her mother said. Astrid heard the sofa squeak as her mother got up to follow her. Astrid leaned back against the kitchen counter and looked at the floor. The vinyl flooring was supposed to look like tile, but it wasn't having much success. It was torn in a few places near the kitchen table, and was worn in the areas where people walked. Like everything in their house, it was old and ugly.

"I've got a bone to pick with you," her mother said. "You need to really do some thinking about your life and where you're headed. I've been tolerant up to now, but you're going to be eighteen in a few days. You can't freeload off of me forever."

"I just finished school today, Mom."

"You're becoming a bum. I can see it. Your laziness is getting the best of you."

"What are you talking about? I'm going to college in two months and I'll be working all summer. I'm not a bum."

"It's not a real college."

"Columbia? Columbia is a real college."

"I mean the art classes. That's not a job, that's a hobby. That's something you do for fun. You'll be moving back in with me and I'll be taking care of you your whole life while you draw things in your little notebook. You need to think about moving out and learning to take care of yourself."

"I'll be moving out in two months. I leave at the end of August. I told you."

"So you have an apartment? Money for a deposit and everything?"

"No, I still have to sign the financial aid papers."

"And why are you late on those? Why did you put them off?"

"I can't sign until I'm a legal adult. And you refused to sign for the grants on my behalf. So now I'm stuck. And if I don't get the full amount of my grants, it'll be because I was late signing my papers."

"I'm not going to co-sign on any loans for you to go play with paints."

"It's for grants, not loans. We went over this."

"Don't lie to me," yelled Mother. "You're getting loans."

"But you don't have to co-sign for those!"

This was getting bad. Astrid was shaking with anger and her mother was staring her straight in the face. She wanted a fight, and now she had it. But there was no way Astrid could get away without more yelling. Or worse. Mother took a step closer.

"Don't you look at me like that, young lady," Mother said. "It's disrespectful."

Astrid knew she needed to back down or it would get bad. "Sorry," she muttered and opened the refrigerator.

"Don't you turn your back on your mother. Now you listen to me." Her mother moved even closer. Astrid closed the refrigerator and turned back toward her, avoiding looking directly in her eyes. Astrid wasn't tall, and neither was her mother, yet she always seemed so much larger. She came within striking distance.

Astrid kept her eyes on her mother's slippers. They had once been light blue, but were now a dull grayish color and the plastic soles were cracked. Her mother's calloused feet hung over the edges.

"Things are going to change, starting now," said Mother. "You look at me when I'm talking to you!"

Astrid forced herself to look up. Her mother stuck her finger in Astrid's face.

"You are going to shape up or ship out, you got me?"

"Got it," she muttered.

"That's right," said Mother. "Now get out of the way. I need something to eat, seeing as you didn't have the courtesy to bring home anything."

Astrid left the kitchen. She could go back in half an hour and see if there was any cereal that she could eat for dinner. She went into her room and shut the door. Earthquakes and the natural settling of the house had left the door frame slightly askew, so she had to push the door with her hip to get it to close all the way. She flicked on the light, a bare bulb screwed into an ancient fixture in the center of the ceiling.

Beside the bed sat a cardboard box, and inside lay her cat, Cinderella, and her three kittens.

"How are you doing, kitty?" she said, kneeling down and stroking Cinderella. The sleek, white cat lifted her chin for scratching and purred. Astrid spent a few minutes petting the kittens. Cinderella watched her, but then closed her eyes and rested her head on her paws. The kittens were three weeks old now, big enough to move around the box, but not yet old enough to venture into the outside world. One male was solid white like his mother. The other two, a male and a female, were gray and black striped tabbies.

"I still need to name you guys," she said. She thought of the smallest one, the white male, as Runt. He was tinier than his siblings, thinner and less energetic. She didn't have names for the other two.

Astrid took her graduation cap from on top of her desk and tried it on. She opened her closet and pulled the gown from the hanger where she had hung it to get out any wrinkles. She held the gown up under her chin and looked in the mirror on the inside of the closet door. Tomorrow evening, she would get her diploma. And then, a few more months and she'd be off to New York.

Cinderella climbed out of the box and rubbed against her legs. Astrid lifted the gown out of the way.

"I don't need your white hair on this," she said, and reached down to rub the cat's ears. She still wondered how Cinderella had gotten pregnant. No, that wasn't true. She knew exactly how that had happened. But she had always thought that the cat was spayed. She had found Cinderella when she was eight and had fed her in the backyard. The cat had hung around, and Astrid had named her. The cat hunted, left mice, gophers and lizards on the back steps and Mother had decided she could stay as long as she killed vermin and didn't pee in the house. But in all the years they had kept Cinderella, she had never gotten pregnant. And then one day, Astrid had seen that her stomach was protruding.

Cinderella leapt onto the brown blanket that covered Astrid's bed and sat, watching her. Astrid put the gown up in front of her again. The bedroom door banged open.

"How come you don't have any money?" her mother said.

"What do you mean?"

"I need to borrow some."

"I don't have any," Astrid said. It was a lie. She actually had a baggie of money hidden in her desk, up against the back of a drawer. She also had a twenty-dollar bill tucked into a book. In total, she had fifty-eight dollars and twenty-three cents. She had counted it twice the night before.

"Yeah, I know that. I checked just now," said Mother.

"You went in my purse? You can't go in my purse!"

"You live under my roof, you live by my rules. Now I need to borrow money for grocery shopping, and seeing as you supposedly work so hard, you ought to be able to lend me fifty."

"I can't. I get paid on Friday, but I need the money for a rail pass and my cell phone bill."

"Is that the cell phone that you didn't answer when I called you today? Is that the one?" Mother's voice was loud in the small room and Cinderella jumped off the bed.

"I was working all afternoon and all evening. I'm not allowed to take personal calls."

"And what, you don't get breaks? You can't spend two minutes to call your own mother?"

"Look, you didn't want me to bring home pretzels, so I didn't. What else do you want from me?" Astrid shouted.

"I want you to quit being a bitch! Now give me fifty. Consider it rent."

"I'm not even eighteen yet."

"So you're old enough to work, have a cell phone and graduate, but not to pay rent? Bullshit. You give me the money now. I know you have it. You hoard it like there's no tomorrow." Her eyes scanned the room, and Astrid knew at that moment that her mother had searched for it earlier. "How much did you make with your last paycheck?"

"I don't know. I need to save it for New York."

"So you lied. You do have money."

"No, I don't."

"Did you spend it on drugs? Is that it? Hanging around with that deadbeat cousin of yours? Smoking weed?"

"He's not a deadbeat, and he's your nephew."

"Elliot is a waste. He thinks he's having some spiritual experience surfing and living in that disgusting trailer."

"It's not that bad. And he sells stuff online and goes to college."

"The junior college is not real college."

"Like Columbia? How about Harvard and UCLA? Are those real colleges?"

"Don't you talk back to me! Now give me the money."

"I don't have it."

Mother slapped her hard across the face, and for a second, Astrid lost her balance and bumped into the closet door.

"Where the hell is it?" Her mother's face was inches from hers, and Astrid could smell the wine on her breath. She wasn't sure if her mother was drunk, but it didn't really matter. She'd hit Astrid whether she was drunk or sober.

Astrid shook her head. "I don't know." She knew she should just give Mother the money, but she needed it. It was her only hope of a decent future. Besides, she'd get hit either way. Might as well be hit and keep the money. She knew such calculations were probably wrong, but she had been making them for years. Clean the house and be hit for doing it incorrectly, or be hit for not doing it at all. Read a book in her room and be yelled at for avoiding her mother, or sit in the living room and be yelled at for any one of a thousand things.

Her mother looked at her, her eyes darting from one of Astrid's eyes to the other, as if trying to discern if she was lying. She hit Astrid in the mouth, hard. Astrid cried out as her lower lip smashed against her teeth.

"You are going to give me that money, right now, or you are out of this house right now. And I don't care where you go."

Astrid hesitated. She could go to the shelter, but it was almost eleven o'clock at night. She could sleep on Elliot's floor, but all her things were here. And her mother would tear apart her room and take the money anyway. Either way, her mother would get it.

She pointed at the desk drawer, her hand shaking. She tasted blood in her mouth, just a little. She didn't touch her mouth, as she didn't want to provoke her mother. Tears of rage stung her eyes.

"Oh, what?" said her mother. "Are you going to cry now too? Such an adult."

Astrid looked down. Her mother pulled open the drawer and dug through the pieces of charcoals and stubs of colored pencils that her art teacher had given her. Mother pulled out sketch pads and tossed them onto the desk.

"Back of the drawer," said Astrid. The sooner this was over with, the better. Her mother reached back and pulled out the baggie of money.

"This is it? That's all you have?"

Astrid nodded.

"You have to be on drugs. I knew it. What else would you do with all that money?"

"I had to rent my cap and gown. It was fifty dollars."

"Shit. Fifty dollars? That's highway robbery. I can't believe they charged you that much." Her mother looked at her like they were on the same side now. She had softened a little. Good.

"I know. I didn't have much left after I paid for that and bought my rail pass."

"I'll pay you back when I get paid," said her mother, walking out of the room. "Oh, and you're grounded for a week for lying." She pulled the door shut behind her and Astrid sank down on the bed. She pulled a compact mirror from her nightstand and flipped it open. It was old and shaped like a pink clamshell with a regular mirror on one side and a magnifying mirror on the other.

Damn. Her lip was bleeding. She touched it, feeling how swollen and painful it was. Something about the pain was soothing, and she sucked at the blood. She put her face into her pillow and cried. How was she going to get to New York with no money for a plane ticket or rent for an apartment? Even the dorms required a deposit.

Cinderella jumped up beside her and nosed at her hand. Astrid rolled over and stroked the cat, resting her ear against her side, letting the low rumble of her purr drown out the drone of the television outside.

CHAPTER 4

ASTRID JOLTED AWAKE. A SOUND hung in the air, like a voice. It had said her name, she was sure of it. The echo of the sound was there for just a moment, and then her head cleared and her room was just as it always had been. She thought it had been a woman's voice, but it had also sounded like her own. Maybe she had made a sound in her sleep and woke herself up.

On her ceiling, two triangles of shadow pointed toward the closet like twin pyramids. She glanced at her alarm clock, the source of the only illumination in the room. Her metal bell in the shape of an owl was sitting in front of it, the peaked feathers on its head casting the shadows. The body of the owl was hollow, and the clacker clinked against the inside as she moved the bell to the other side of her nightstand. The clock read three thirty-nine in the morning. What had awakened her? She glanced down beside the bed into the kitten box. Cinderella was awake, staring at the window, her body stiff. The cat rose, but her eyes never left the blinds. The faint light of a nearby street lamp cast yellow lines on the carpet.

Then Astrid heard it: a click-clack sound, like stones being knocked together. It clicked once, twice, paused and then clicked a third time. It stopped for a few moments, and she thought she heard some kind of scuffling in the dirt outside her window. Then more clicking. Something was outside, very close, and it was right by her window.

Then there came a second sound. *Tok, tok-tok, tok*. It was

almost like the sound of the stones, but more hollow. This sound was a little farther off.

Cinderella let out a low growl and jumped out of the box. Astrid had left the door ajar after scavenging for dinner and Cinderella snaked through the opening, her tail puffed up and hair standing up along her back. The clacking noise came again. The bell on Cinderella's collar jingled as she walked down the hall, followed by the flap of the cat door in the kitchen swinging open and shut.

The kittens mewed and squirmed, and Astrid hung her arm over the side of the bed, stroking them. Their little bodies were warm and soft. The female poked her nose into the blanket over and over, searching for her mother to nurse.

"It's okay. She'll be back," she whispered. She should get up and see what was making the noise, but she hesitated.

Tok-tok.

The sound was closer now, but the stone noise had stopped. The jingle of the bell on Cinderella's collar grew faster, like she was running. It stopped for a while, then started up again, moving closer to the house.

Astrid got up and stepped quietly to the window. She pulled down one of the blinds with her finger. There was movement off to one side, but it was not white, so it couldn't be Cinderella. It was just the bushes moving in the wind. The yard was covered in weeds and overgrown grass with a rickety, patched up fence around all three sides. A barbeque rusted near the back door, next to a cracked set of plastic chairs and a table. The yard was empty except for Cinderella at the back door. The cat door flapped and the jingle came down the hall.

Then something moved on the back fence. Astrid had not seen it before, as it had been so still. It was a giant crow, perched and looking off to the side. The thing was enormous, with a curving beak and heavy black claws. Was that the thing that had made the sound? She had heard crows make noise before, but that sound was different. But this crow was too large. She had heard of ravens and knew they were similar to crows, so this might be a raven. That was all the sound had been: a raven. It must have moved from under her window to the back fence. She relaxed.

The raven turned toward her back door and she caught the gleam of light in its black, shining eye. Then it dipped its head, pushed off the fence and flapped away, its wing beats slow and strong.

The backyard truly was empty now, with only the movement of the plants in the wind giving it life. Astrid looked down. Under her window grew a huge, gangly geranium bush. Its branches and leaves were thick, but she could also see to the ground in places. There were stacks of stones. There were three stones in each stack and she counted at least six stacks. They were set in a circle about three feet across. She recognized the stones. They had come from the side of the house, where her mother had once arranged a bunch of decorative gray, black and white river stones in a planter. But that was back when she and Astrid's father had been married. The stones had been sitting there for more than a decade.

"What the hell?" she whispered. She wanted to tell herself that a person had stacked the stones, perhaps her mother. Or maybe a neighbor kid had snuck into her yard during the day. But she had heard the sound of the stones. She wanted to think that the raven had done it, that somehow it had gotten its body into the cramped space between the geranium branches. But that was impossible. The space was too small for a bird of that size. Someone, something, had stacked them just now.

She felt someone watching her and spun around. Cinderella stood motionless just inside the door, her eyes lamp-like in the dark, watching.

"You went out there," Astrid whispered. "What did

that?" She looked back out the window, but then let the blinds snap back into position. This was too strange for comfort. Whatever was outside, she didn't want to see it.

Cinderella climbed back in with her kittens and lay down on her side, allowing them to nuzzle up to her and nurse. She glanced at Astrid, and then licked her babies.

Astrid sat on the floor beside the box, her back against the side of her bed. "Were you worried about your babies?" She stroked Cinderella, but the cat did not purr. "Is that it? You were making sure they'd be safe?"

Petting the cat made her feel a little better, but her heart was still beating hard. She got up and cranked the plastic rod on the side of the blinds to make sure they were closed all the way. Then she closed her bedroom door. If Cinderella had to go to the bathroom, she would have to wait until she got up.

The morning was only three hours away, and once it was light, she knew she wouldn't be so afraid. Things were always worse in the dark.

CHAPTER 5

ELLIOT SHOULDERED HIS BACKPACK AND grabbed the bag of leftover pretzels and day-old hot dogs from the tiny refrigerator in his trailer. He locked the trailer door and zipped up his jacket. It was June, but the morning air was still heavy with a layer of fog and the air had a crispness to it. He had twenty minutes before he had to catch the bus for his Art History class. By the time he got out of class, the sun would have burned off the marine layer and he would have to get ready for work at the boardwalk.

The bus stop was adjacent to the public parking lot for the beach and across the street from a mini mall. Elliot knew the spots where the homeless people congregated and knew some of the regulars by name. They wouldn't be hard to find. He rifled through the bag as he walked, counting up how many items he had. He gave most of the food to two men panhandling near the mini mall and continued on toward the bus stop. Sitting against the wall of a building near the bus stop was Mick. He was one of the regulars who was almost always somewhere near the beach or the boardwalk.

"Hey, Mick. Are you hungry?" asked Elliot, holding up the bag.

"You got any money?" asked Mick. Like most street people, he was wearing layers of clothing. He was in his forties, but the years on the streets had taken their toll. His brown hair had no gray in it, and though his face was weathered and his skin rough, Elliot could see that he once might have been good-looking.

"No, no money," Elliot said. "Just food. Here, take the rest." Elliot handed him the bag with the last two hot dogs and a pretzel. Whatever Mick didn't eat now, he could eat later.

"I don't need food. I'm full already. The birdman fed me."

"Okay, if you don't want it, I can give it to someone else."

"No, I didn't say that. I said I needed money," said Mick.

"Sorry. I can't help you there."

"Aww, c'mon. You have to help me. I need a bus ticket. Things around here are getting crazy. Real crazy."

"Well, I'm sure it'll be okay."

"It won't. You don't understand. You won't let me tell you."

"Fine, tell me what's happening that's crazy." Elliot wasn't sure he should be encouraging Mick, but he felt guilty just walking away. Some of the surfers who were friends with Elliot called Mick by the moniker Creepy Mick. From conversations with him, Elliot had gleaned that he had spent time in hospitals where they had given him anti-psychotic medication, but he now had nowhere to go and he no longer took whatever medication had once been prescribed. Mick also claimed that he had fought in Vietnam, but when Elliot reminded him that he would have only been a child, Mick had gotten angry and yelled at him.

"Things are changing. Like over there." Mick pointed over to the bus stop. "There was something else in the street over there, this thing with smoke coming out of a pipe on top and it made such a loud noise, like a dragon or something."

"That's the bus. It's fine."

"Jesus Christ! Listen to me. Why won't you just listen for a second?" Mick started to stand up, using the wall to steady himself. Elliot took a step backward. He wasn't normally afraid of Mick, but if the man decided to take a swing at him, he wasn't going to just stand there.

"Right the hell over there," said Mick, taking a shaky step forward. "It wasn't a bus. It had people in it, yeah. But it was different."

"Okay, I see," said Elliot, looking at the bus stop as if considering what Mick had said. There was no sense in riling Mick up. The poor guy had enough problems.

Then Elliot noticed something about Mick. He normally had a beard, but today he only had a day's worth of stubble. He must have had a shave recently.

"Did you go to the shelter?" Elliot asked.

"No, I've just been out here."

"Then how did you shave? Two days ago, you had a beard."

"The birdman helped me out."

Again about the birdman. Mick had only started talking about this person in the last two weeks and he mentioned him more and more often. Mick settled back into his spot against the wall and pulled his jacket closed. He looked at Elliot as if daring him to say anything.

"Well, it was good seeing you," said Elliot. "I have to go to class."

"I'll be here when you get back. Maybe the birdman will be here too."

"Maybe. I'll see you later." Elliot turned away.

"Wait! There's something else. It's important," called Mick.

Elliot turned back. Was this a play for attention, or did he actually have something important to tell him? He knew that some of the homeless were so starved for companionship that they'd talk his ears off if he let them. Mick usually wasn't too bad.

"My friend says not to worry too much about your girl, but keep an eye on her."

"I don't have a girlfriend."

"Shit, will you shut up? Also, that parking lot moved. It was over there before." Mick pointed.

"I need to get to class. I'll see you later."

Elliot walked to the bus stop and sat on the covered bench. The next bus would be along in eight minutes, so he had the time to chat with Mick. But he felt like he was only encouraging the man's delusions if he let him go on and on about the birdman and the strange things he saw. If only there was somewhere for him to go. But he wasn't a danger to himself or others, so he couldn't be legally institutionalized. And Mick said all of his family had died in World War II. Elliot took that to mean that he was estranged from them or they really were dead.

Mick came around the bus shelter wall and sat beside Elliot.

"Look, I'm sorry," Mick said. "I know they call me creepy, and I'm not trying to freak you out. I just get confused is all. Still friends?"

Mick's face was so childlike, so sincere. He had his hands folded in his lap like a schoolboy. Elliot put his hand on his shoulder. "Still friends."

"I'm trying," said Mick.

"I know you are. I know it's hard."

"I've been through some things."

Elliot supposed he had. He knew nothing about mental illness, but even if the traumatic things Mick went through were only in his mind, they were still hard on him.

"And I know you're trying too," said Mick. "I know. You don't live back to front yet, but you will. See, I learned things in Vietnam. There was this guy."

"Mick, you are too young to have been in Vietnam. You need to stop this."

"Not everyone lives front to back like you do."

"That's enough. Now, where are you going to go tonight for dinner and a bed? Are you going to the shelter on Third Street later?"

"You need to listen, is what you need to do. You need to understand that you can remember the past. Right? You remember the past. And you can't remember the future, you get me?"

"That's true. You can only remember the past." Elliot wondered if this was going somewhere, but maybe sorting out pasts and futures would help Mick get a grip on reality.

"So you can see your past in your mind. But not your future."

"That's true."

"And when you're walking, you can see in front of you, but not behind."

"Also true."

"So I walk, and I see what's in front of me. Just like I see the past in my mind. And so do you. So since we can only see what's in front of us, and we can only see the past, we live from future to past. See?"

"No, we live past to future," said Elliot.

"We can't see the future. And we can't see behind us when we walk. So we go from unseen to seen, from future to past. We all live backwards."

"No, Mick. Look, you need to talk to Imelda at the shelter. I think you're having a rough day." Imelda was the administrator at the shelter. She wasn't a psychologist, but she was good to the people who came to her. Elliot had once been one of them, but since he was young and employable, he had been able to find work quickly and rent his trailer from one of his surfing friends. He was one of the lucky ones and he knew it.

"I can't go there tonight," said Mick. "The birdman will be here at night. But you go have a good time. Learn lots at school and go be a great doctor."

Elliot didn't know what he wanted to be, but he doubted he'd ever manage to become a doctor. The bus pulled up and Mick retreated back to his spot against the wall. As the bus pulled away, Elliot saw Mick dig through the bag and then roll the top down and set it next to him. He must have been telling the truth about someone giving him something to eat.

CHAPTER 6

YUKIKO ROLLED OVER IN BED. Sunlight shot through the gap between the motel curtains and she heard people talking outside. The pillow smelled musty, like human hair and institutional laundry detergent. But something was wrong. There was a sort of pain, deep pain, but it wasn't physical.

Then, in a flash of horror, she remembered. It had been late and she hadn't known what time it was. She had fallen asleep while watching television and then something had awakened her. The television had cast a pale, jumping light in the room. She had opened her eyes, feeling someone in the room with her. But her head had felt so fuzzy and she had been unable to sit up or even keep her eyes open.

Then the room had twisted. Or rather, something had been twisted out from inside her. It had been so violent that it felt like she was a rag being wrung from the inside out. Her swirling vision had gone red and then black. Then something large and flat slammed against the length of her body. She had crashed to the floor. While her spirit ball was being torn out, she remembered screaming, but she did not know if it had been in her mind or out loud.

She looked to the floor. Yes, she remembered being facedown on the putty-colored carpet, its rough surface abrading her face and palms as she writhed and tried to escape or fight. But her fighting had been feeble, and after the removal of the spirit ball, she had been weak. It had been so difficult to move or open her eyes. Maybe she had passed out. She did remember that someone had lifted her, tenderly and lovingly, and laid her on the bed. Then they had pulled the blankets up over her. She could not remember the person's face, though she had tried to look.

Drugged. Someone had drugged her. It was the only possible way anyone could have taken her spirit ball. And of course, normal human drugs would never have worked, most of them anyway. She also knew exactly how the drug had been administered. Whatever had been in the red slushie had been powerful. Sleeping through the removal of her spirit ball was like sleeping through an amputation, impossible without a substance so incredibly strong that it could incapacitate her kind. She thought of the green-eyed man who had served her the red slushie. He had told the girl at the booth to take a break and that he would help her. He had made the drink. But she had smelled him, and there was nothing other about him. He was just a human.

But what did that mean? Humans could work for otherfolk. And some otherfolk could disguise themselves so well that they were nearly indistinguishable from humans. Heck, she herself was one of that kind. She knew the methods well enough. But she didn't think the green-eyed man was working alone. No.

She swung her legs over the edge of the bed and tested her weight on them. The pain was bad, but not unbearable. She would manage.

But wait. She was wearing her flannel pajamas with the jelly bean design and she was certain that she had not put them on prior to lying down to watch television. That meant that the person who had taken her spirit ball had also taken off her clothes and put her into her pajamas. He or she had even taken off her bra.

Who the hell had done this? She racked her brain, trying to remember the person who had been with her, but nothing came, only memories of pain and flashes of terrible color and sensation. She remembered the strange feeling she had gotten from some areas of the park. That might have something to do with it. But how could anyone but Santiago have known that she was coming? Well, she would be paying him a visit, and if he hadn't known before that her normally gentle kind would kill to regain a stolen spirit ball, he was about to learn.

"Damn," she muttered, "stuck in human form."

She could change, but it would drain all the remaining energy she had. So she would have to stay as a human. Of course, she spent most of her time in human form. It was a necessity in the modern world. But to have to be trapped in one shape was like being imprisoned in her own flesh. It was akin to cutting the wings off a bird but allowing it to keep its legs and walk. It was alive and mobile, but it did not exist in its proper and whole form. It was no longer truly a bird. She felt around inside of herself, but there was nothing. Residual power, yes, but not the kind she needed. Not her native abilities. Oh, Santiago was going to pay all right.

"I'm going to kill Coyote." She headed to the bathroom and flicked on the light. The fluorescent tubes flickered and then steadied and she blinked in the white light. She remembered times when an electric light was a marvel, a near miracle. But now, she just sighed and looked in the mirror. Her hair was a tangled mess and her skin was pallid. Her eyes were bloodshot and her lips were nearly white. She looked just like she felt.

She appeared to be in her mid-twenties, when she had stopped aging. She could appear older or younger if she wished, but it would use up some of her remaining power. And she needed to conserve it. She couldn't even use a minor adjustment to make her face less narrow or her eyes a little farther apart. Her face was the face she had been born to: long and thin with arching eyebrows, high cheekbones and a mouth that turned down at the corners.

If she was going to see Coyote, she needed to prepare. He had done this for a reason and she wasn't about to let him have any advantage or see her weakness. Let him think what he would but she was not helpless, no matter what had been taken from her. She peeled off the pajamas and dropped them on the floor. Then she showered, dressed and blow-dried her hair.

She wished Inari was still alive. She wished her kind were still united around their god and that her sisters and brothers could help her. She imagined them, most of them white, some grey or red, and even the few black ones, racing in a sea of fur and teeth to aid her. They would subdue and tear apart the one who had harmed one of their own. But there were none. The brothers and sisters she once had were now scattered around the world if they were alive at all. There was no one to call upon, no one to help.

She also wished she had one of her old kimonos, one of the ornate ones with the thick obi around her waist, tied in a giant bow at the back. Her face would be covered in white makeup and beads would dangle down from her elaborately styled hair. Coyote would see her power then. Or maybe she would wear a tailored suit and heels too high for comfort. Something to make her feel like her old self. Instead, she put on her schoolgirl skirt and blouse, fastening on the plush fox tail. Even without her spirit ball, she would cast her normal shadow.

Now for some makeup. Some red lipstick fixed the problem of her colorless lips. Some powder and eyeliner made her look a little healthier. She wanted to paint symbols on her skin, old symbols to give her power in battle, but this would have to do. She swiped on mascara, stepped back and looked her reflection in the eye.

"Whatever he wants, he's in for a surprise," she said and pulled her hair up, turning her head side to side. Yes, up would be more intimidating. She styled it in an old-

37

fashioned way, pinning it and then sliding two black and red lacquered chopsticks into the top. Then she fastened on the plush fox ears. Let him remember her as she was, formidable, terrifying. If he thought that by stealing her spirit ball that she would be his slave—with soft voice and eyes downcast, shuffling with tiny steps—then Coyote had another thing coming.

CHAPTER 7

I N THE EMPLOYEE BREAK ROOM, Elliot filled his Styrofoam noodle cup with water from the tap and placed it into the microwave. The break room was small and smelly, with faded wood-paneled walls and an old vending machine against the wall it shared with Mr. Augustus's office. The tables were covered in carvings and permanent marker drawings from former employees and the mismatched chairs always rocked on their uneven legs. At least the microwave and old refrigerator worked.

Astrid pulled her brown paper bag from the refrigerator, sat down and took out a cheese and pickle sandwich and a spotted banana.

"You got a couple quarters?" Astrid asked. "I didn't bring a drink."

He dug in his pocket and set the money on the table.

"Are you still coming to graduation?" she asked.

"Yeah, I requested the time off."

"We'll have pizza afterwards. I think my mom is paying, but I don't know. She's kind of broke."

Elliot saw her look down and trace one of the carvings on the table with her finger. His Aunt Carrie was often short of money, but then so was his mother, her sister. He understood his cousin's worry. Something as simple as a family pizza night could become uncomfortable if paying for it was a strain. His mother and her current boyfriend weren't much better off financially, and if anyone expected him to chip in more than ten bucks, they'd be out of luck.

He thought of other families, ones that gave cars or computers to their kids for graduation. Those kids got to go on the graduation trips and attend grad night at Disneyland and go to prom. He and Astrid had not been able to afford any of those things. They had been lucky if they had jackets that fit and shoes without holes.

"After the ceremony, we'll see if your mom still invites everyone," Elliot said. "And if she doesn't, then we'll just all go home. So I guess we'll cross that bridge when we come to it."

"I guess," she muttered, inserting the coins into the machine and taking the soda. After drinking, she set the can down and he saw the circular smudge of lipstick on the can. That was odd. He looked at her more closely. Astrid rarely wore makeup, but she had some on today.

"Have you seen the Chumash Legends show yet? It's really good," he said. The show was only going to run on the boardwalk stage for a few weeks during summer. The Jacaranda Festival events were in full swing now, with musical events, dancers and even a drumming group.

"I haven't seen the show yet. But I heard it was good," said Astrid. She looked like she was only half listening. Another employee came in, got a candy bar from the vending machine. Astrid glanced at the door after he left.

"Something happened last night," she said. "Something really weird."

"Yeah?" He stirred his noodles with a plastic fork and took a bite.

"It was late and something woke me up and the cat was staring at the window. You know how cats stare like they can see something you can't? It was like that, but she was looking at the window like something was outside. Then she went out the cat door and I looked out the window. First, there was this giant bird. I'm pretty sure it was a raven, because it was too big to be a crow. And then, right under my window, there were all these little stacks of rocks. All of them were exactly three stones high."

"The bird was stacking rocks?" Elliot had heard of crows being intelligent, and ravens were cousins to crows.

"No, no. I think ... I'm not sure. Something was out there."

"Something stacking rocks outside your window."

"It sounds stupid, I know. Never mind. It's dumb."

Astrid wiped her mouth. Most of the lipstick was gone and Elliot saw the telltale dark scab that meant her lip was split. So that was why she had been wearing lipstick. She had been trying to cover it up.

"Your mom hit you again, didn't she?" he said.

"It's fine. I don't care anymore. I really don't."

"It's not fine."

"Whatever."

"Seriously, Astrid. You can't let her do this."

"And what do you want me to do, huh? She owns the house."

"Stop her or hit her back or something."

"Like you did with Aunt Ruth's boyfriend? How did that work out? You had to go to the shelter."

It was true. His mother's boyfriend had picked a fight with him and had shoved him into a wall. Elliot had fought back. It had ended with Elliot out in the driveway with only the clothes on his back. He couldn't go to Astrid's house, since her mother didn't like him much and would have sided with his own mother, who had done nothing to stop him from being kicked out. So he had ended up at the Third Street shelter. He had gone back home the next day while his mother's boyfriend was away, collected his things and went back to the shelter, where he stayed until he had gotten a job and his first paycheck.

"It's only a couple more months," said Astrid. "Then I'll be out of the house and she can have her wish."

Elliot knew his aunt was a mess. His own mother wasn't violent, but the men she dated sometimes were. He had seen Astrid wear long sleeves in summer to hide bruises on her arms that she had gotten protecting her face from her mother's fists. He also knew that her mother had broken Astrid's finger once and that one time, Astrid had bruised her cheek when she was thrown into a wall. Of course, both times she claimed she had fallen.

Now, Astrid was looking at the table, her eyes dull and her face expressionless. He wished he could help her, but there was nothing he could do. A dark rage boiled within him, fury at his aunt, but also at himself and his inability to do anything useful. Without money, a car or even a halfway decent job, he was helpless, and he hated feeling helpless.

While other young people their age were driving new cars and had tuition paid for by their parents, he was barely able to pay for groceries and Astrid was forced to walk home at night through a bad neighborhood. It was a wonder she hadn't been attacked. He felt the flimsy plastic spoon bend in his hand and realized he had been holding it too tightly. However he might feel himself, whatever anger and frustration burned inside, he was the only person in her life who knew what she had been through. He wanted her to know that he understood.

"Hey, Astrid."

She looked up at her name.

"Don't let her get to you, okay?"

She tried to smile, but though her mouth moved a little, her expression remained miserable. "I won't."

He hoped she wouldn't. But he also knew that, in a way, it was already too late. Her mother's treatment of her had gone so deeply into Astrid's psyche that she was nearly incapable of believing that she could do anything right. She dressed and moved as if she wanted to be invisible. She had never had a boyfriend, not that he had known about, and she had few friends at school. She also had no confidence in her artistic ability, even though she had been accepted to one of the most prestigious art schools in the United States. It was like she was more willing to believe bad things about herself than good.

"And hey," he said. "She's wrong about you."

"Yeah, I know."

But he knew she didn't. And there was nothing he could do to convince her otherwise.

CHAPTER 8

"HEY KIT," SAID SANTIAGO. HE leaned against the wall just outside of the entrance to the boardwalk. His arms were crossed and he wore a self-satisfied smirk that had always irritated Yukiko. She hadn't seen him in decades, but his smile had not changed at all. His clothing had, of course. He was hatless, as was the modern style, and his tawny hair was tousled. He wore jeans and cowboy boots and she supposed some women might have found him attractive. She was not one of them.

"Don't call me that," she said.

"It's what you are."

"I am not a kit, not for at least a century." She smelled, discreetly, for her spirit ball. There was no scent of it on him, not even a residual feeling.

"Kitsune then," he said.

"I'm Myobu."

"All Myobu are Kitsune."

He was correct, of course. Kitsune, the fox spirits of her homeland, were either Myobu, law-abiding and friendly to humans, or Nogitsune, the wild foxes.

"But not all Kitsune are Myobu. My kind have a code."

He motioned toward the entrance archway to the boardwalk. Pulsating yellow and orange lights spelled out *Luna Park* in arching letters over the gate. On either side of the words hung two mermaids made of green, yellow and red neon lights. Their tails flicked up and down in abrupt flashes, and their blond hair jerked in waves, as if they were underwater.

"The god you served is dead," said Santiago. "Dead and gone."

They continued into the park, passing the ticket booths. Yukiko was not about to use any of her magic to fool a human into letting her have tickets, nor would she use her real money.

"Leave him out of it," she said.

"If you say so."

"Did you call me here to bug me about things that are not your concern? If I recall, you needed my help."

"I needed a consultant. Not help. I never said the word 'help.'"

"Oh, that's right. The legendary Coyote. Never needed help from anyone. And yet, he sends me a letter, a paper letter, in this day and age, to ask me to come and check something out."

"I didn't know your e-mail address or phone number. All I had was that old address. It's not like you kept in touch."

"And why would I?"

They had stopped at the railing that overlooked the beach. Santiago rested a booted foot on the lowest railing. No one else would have seen it, but the way he looked out over the crowds of people, the way his head tilted up slightly to catch the scents, were inhuman. She could almost see his muzzle, his golden eyes, his tongue lolling out of his mouth in a cunning grin.

"That was a long time ago, Kit."

"Only by their standards," she tipped her head toward the people on the beach.

"Two tails, I see," Santiago said, glancing at the plush tail that hung from her belt. "Wishful thinking, Kitsune."

"All you'll ever have is the one. That and the stink under it."

"Touchy, touchy."

"You're being an ass."

"No, I'm being myself," he said. "I cannot change my nature. And you didn't used to wear a fake tail."

"You know damn well why I have it. My shadow is the same as it ever was."

"So if people see the shadow, they think it comes from that thing. Cute."

"One does what one must."

She smelled and felt for her spirit ball again. Nothing. If Santiago had taken it, he had not handled it himself.

"Do you feel it?" Santiago said, becoming serious.

"Yeah. There's something. It's over there." She motioned toward the haunted house ride and the employee section.

"What is it?"

"You can't tell?"

"No. Can you?" He turned and looked at her. He was really and truly worried. Yukiko thought back. She didn't think she had ever seen him like this before.

"It's bad then," she said. "I know this place, this borderland, attracts things. But I thought all the metal, the people, all those things would keep most otherfolk away."

"If it was otherfolk, we would know what it was. This is something I've never smelled or felt before. And I've been around a long time."

Yukiko knew that he had. While she was only a little over a century old, he was practically ancient. He was still watching her.

"Shit, Yukiko. What happened to you?"

She drew back and looked away. "If it was you, Coyote, I swear on the bones of my master and god that I will make you suffer."

"How are you still alive? I mean, can your people live without your spirit ball?"

"Yeah, we can live. Not well, but we can survive."

It would be a half-life, a life like the humans around her,

an endless series of ordinary days without her abilities. Such a life would be worse than death.

"Who took it?" he asked.

She looked into his face. He was an expert liar, she knew that. He had sometimes boasted of the fact and took great pride in his so-called art, so she knew she would learn nothing from studying him. But she still tried to tell if he was sincere.

"I thought you might have something to do with it," she said.

"No, not me." He looked toward the rides and the game booths. "Do you think something here did it?"

"Definitely. It happened last night. I'd like to know what could do that. It's not exactly a common talent."

Santiago watched a couple go by. "You said there was something over by those rides?"

"Yes."

"Well, let's go have a look-see, shall we?"

"I'm not going to help you."

"What?" he looked genuinely surprised. "This is your home also. Not LA, but this part of their country. If something happens here, it'll affect you as well."

"How can I trust you? How do I know you didn't take my spirit ball?"

He seemed to be thinking it over. "You can't. You can't trust me, and I didn't take your spirit ball. But I can tell you this. If I had, would we be standing here?"

"What do you mean?"

"If I had your spirit ball, you'd be on your back in the hotel room. Or I would be. After we played naughty geisha for a few hours first." He grinned wickedly.

"You're a racist bastard."

"How can I be racist if I don't have a race?"

"You look white to me." Yukiko wondered if he had modeled himself after a modern movie star. But then, Coyote had looked this way since at least the early twentieth century.

47

"For the last couple centuries, this appearance has allowed me to do as I please. And before I was white, I was brown. You would have liked me then. I didn't used to wear so much clothing. I change with the times. How come you haven't?"

"My kind don't change like yours. Besides, by the time I got here, there were plenty of Japanese in America."

"So will you help me?"

"If you'll help me get my spirit ball back."

"I can't see that there's anything I can do, but it's a deal. I'll do what I can. First off, you can talk to Red Fawn."

"What is he?"

"She, and she's just a person. Old. Very old. But a person."

Santiago headed toward the rides and Yukiko kept pace beside him. She didn't like how he was luring her across the park, as if she had agreed to help him. But if he had any way to help her to discover her attacker, she supposed she had to take her chances.

"How could a human possibly help me?" she asked.

"She works here during the day, at the stage show. She can feel the change here too."

"How could a human feel that? They're not capable of it."

"Now who is being a racist?" He smirked.

"It's not racist, it's a fact."

"Whatever. Then don't talk to her."

"Would she know who might have taken it?"

"Maybe. I don't know."

Coyote found the only ticket booth run by a woman and started chatting with her. Yukiko knew what he was up to and left him alone to get his tickets. He might have had money, in fact, he almost certainly did. He loved cars and fancy restaurants and exclusive clubs. But he wouldn't pay for anything if he could get it by trickery. It was a sort of personal policy of his. He returned a few minutes later with a strip of tickets. He didn't offer half to her, but tore off enough for both of them to ride the haunted house and then put the rest in his shirt pocket.

"Will you introduce me to this Red Fawn?" Yukiko asked while they waited in line.

"Best not to. She and I had a disagreement. She doesn't like me much."

"That's a shock. What did you do to her?"

"It was nothing. A little misunderstanding. But she runs the Chumash show that's going on during the Jacaranda Festival."

They boarded the haunted house ride and when the car was at the back of the ride, where the scent of other was strongest, Santiago kicked at the car with the toe of his boot. For anyone else, nothing would have happened. But for him, the safety bar popped up.

"Come on," he said and jumped out of the car and into the dark.

"I can't hide myself," she whispered after she had climbed out of the car and hurried behind a plywood coffin. Other cars with riders passed by on the track. She hated asking him for anything, even if it was in order to help him. But without her regular power, she was close to helpless.

"I'll do it," he said, and before she could say anything, she felt his presence, his smell, spin around her loosely, then tighten like a coil, until it touched her skin. The sensation was both pleasant and repugnant to her. Like fatty meat fried in too much oil, delicious and sickening at the same time. She wanted to shake it away, to replace it with her own power. But she could not.

They moved through the ride and then ducked into an access corridor. An employee walked past them, oblivious to their presence. If Yukiko did anything to draw her attention, like speak or move too closely to her, she would be seen. But if there was any way for the girl's mind to dismiss the movement from the corner of her eye or the thing she thought she heard, she would do it. Humans were sweet and gullible things, most of the time.

Coyote was not. The employee passed and Yukiko looked at the back of Santiago's head as he walked on ahead. He was a liar and a thief. She couldn't let herself be lulled into any false sense of trust. And if he had taken her spirit ball, she would tear his throat out.

They moved down a back corridor, but the scent, the tingle, she had felt the previous day was still there.

"Do you feel anything?" asked Santiago.

She paused. "Yes, but not quite as much as there was before."

"You mean you felt more when we were across the park?"

"No. I came yesterday to check things out."

"Tricky, tricky," he said, pleased.

"Nothing tricky about it. You called me, I wanted to know what I was getting into. Little did I know I'd be attacked."

Coyote glanced at her. She couldn't see his expression well in the dark, but he seemed to be evaluating something. "So you couldn't smell or feel anything from across the park?"

"No. I had to get close to it."

"I can smell a little," he said, looking down the corridor. "Like an itch."

"I wonder what it is."

"And here I was, thinking you'd be helpful," he said. But his tone was joking, not cruel. She may be Myobu, helper of mankind and friend of the just, but that didn't mean she'd put up with any nonsense. She decided that she'd leave if he got to be too insufferable. Except, now she was tied to his geographical area, unable to leave until she regained her spirit ball.

The employee access corridor ended in a T shape, with one hallway going off to the left and one to the right. Both of them paused, smelled and headed left without a word.

There was a door at the end, and Santiago reached for the handle without hesitating. Yukiko almost stopped him, but then, what purpose would that serve? If they surprised some people, the worst that would happen is that they would be told to leave. Still, she was nervous and hoped the room would be empty.

Perhaps she had grown soft by living in modern times. She had heard tales of her kind, when they were strong and fierce. Was she now afraid of a few park employees?

"No one home," said Coyote.

The room was a break room, old and musty. The smell was here, but it had been some time since its source had been present.

"A person," she said.

"You think it's coming from a person?"

"Must be. It's stronger in this room than in the corridor. I'd say it's something that moves, so a person."

"Or an animal. Don't forget those."

"I include our kind and otherkind when I say 'person.'"

"How fair-minded of you," he pulled open the refrigerator and took out a half-finished bottle of soda. Someone named Kim had written her name on the label with permanent marker.

"What's fair-minded in including us?" she asked.

"No, I mean, including us, them and the otherkind in one big group. Like we're equals." He took a gulp of the purloined soda and offered it to her. She refused and opened the break room door.

"I can't believe that after living as long as you have, you still hold to those outdated ways," she said.

"Aww, now don't be like that."

They both fell silent and stood with their backs against the wall as an employee passed. He was a regular human, not the source of the scent. Once he was gone, they headed down the hall. Santiago opened the outer door and held it for her.

"I will be like that," she said. "They're not toys of the gods or anything like that. They're like us."

"You keep telling yourself that, Kit. Then you fall in love with one and see how much he's like you thirty years on, or fifty. And before you know it, your grandkids are dying while you live on and on."

"Sounds like you have personal experience."

They had emerged near the dime toss and Santiago stopped. "You want to find Red Fawn, you head down that way." He pointed. "The stage show is on a couple times a day."

"You sure you won't come with me?"

"I'm on Red Fawn's shit list. You're better off without me. But I'll be around. I'm not going anywhere."

"You'd better stick around. Because if I don't find my spirit ball soon, I'll hunt you down, no matter how far you run."

"You're so cute when you talk like that. I'll keep my ears open about it."

She had no doubt he would. And if there was any way he could get the ball for himself, he would do it. But then, being enslaved to Santiago was not the worst fate she could face. There were far more sinister beings, ones that would not simply enslave her to play naughty geisha.

CHAPTER 9

ASTRID CARRIED TWO GIFT BAGS, one large and one small, from her mother's car to the front door. Her graduation celebration had started a few hours earlier at a local pizza parlor. Somehow, her mother and aunt had come to an agreement on payment, and Astrid, her mother, Elliot, Aunt Ruth and her aunt's boyfriend had enjoyed a decent dinner. Astrid's mother had told everyone at the table how proud she was of her beautiful daughter. She had even said that she was happy about her acceptance to Columbia and how she knew that Astrid would become a great artist.

Her mother had given her high-end colored pencils from the art store. It was an extravagant gift, and her mother had kissed her cheek when Astrid had stammered out a shocked thanks.

Astrid pulled her keys out and was wishing that she or her mother had left the porch light on when her stomach dropped. There was a package partially hidden in the planter to the side of the door.

She didn't know what was inside it, but she knew from whom it came. It was a medium-sized envelope, the yellowish type that came with a layer of bubble wrap cushioning inside. She picked it up and, as expected, it was addressed to her. It had no postage sticker, nor did it have any stamps. It also had no return address.

She shoved the envelope down inside the larger of her two gift bags, the one from her aunt with the navy blue wool peacoat that would keep her warm in the New York winter. It had been a very thoughtful gift, and Astrid appreciated it all the more knowing that her aunt had probably had to scour the clearance rack to find it.

Astrid heard her mother's car door bang shut and she pulled the tissue paper up over the envelope and got her key into the lock. She knew better than to mention the envelope to her mother.

She had gotten out of her jacket and had put both bags on her bed when she heard her mother close the front door.

"You didn't get the mail," called her mother from the front room.

"Sorry, I can do it in a sec."

"I already got it. Looks like you got something."

Astrid went out to the kitchen. On top of the pizza box filled with leftovers sat a few pieces of junk mail and another envelope. This one was a regular white envelope, but it also had no return address. At least it had a regular stamp on it. Two mystery envelopes in one day. Well, she had graduated and her birthday was on Monday, so maybe she deserved two envelopes.

Her mother slid the pizza box into the fridge. There was plenty of room inside and Astrid noted that her mother had not done the grocery shopping after taking her money. She didn't want to open the envelope, not here. If it was related to the other envelope, she didn't want her mother to see it. But then, it had come in the regular mail, which none of the others packages through the years ever had.

"Well, open it up," her mother said. She moved next to Astrid, who took an involuntary step backward. Her mother looked at her sharply. "Is it from one of your friends?"

"I don't know who it's from." Astrid knew that she would have to open it in front of her mother. There was no avoiding it. If only she had checked the mail when she had gotten home from school. Then she could have opened it in private.

54

She tore open the envelope and pulled out a single piece of stationary that was folded around a stack of bills. She counted them out. Five one-hundred-dollar bills. She looked at the crisp, new bills, stunned. They looked almost fake, they were so new. She didn't think she had ever seen a one-hundred-dollar bill before. Who would do this?

"Well, don't stand there like a lump on a log. What does it say?" Her mother snatched the piece of stationary from her hand. "I'm sure you can use this in New York," she read, then looked at the money. "Who would send you five hundred bucks?"

"What, it doesn't say in the note?" said Astrid, reaching for the letter.

"Would I ask you if it did? I can read a note. I'm not stupid."

"I know, I just thought ..."

"So who sent it? Who just gives you five hundred dollars out of nowhere?"

Astrid shook her head. "I don't know." But she did know. At least, she thought she did.

Her mother took the money from her hand and thumbed through it. And before her mother could say anything, Astrid knew what would happen.

"How long until you leave?" her mother asked, glancing at the calendar on the wall.

"Two more months."

"And you expect to be staying here rent-free, don't you?"

"Please, Mom, it's for graduation and my birthday."

"From who? Who the hell sends you this much?"

"I don't know, I swear. But I still need it. I still don't have a ticket to New York or a deposit for an apartment or anything."

"Is it drugs or prostitution?" asked her mother, folding the money in half and slipping it into her pocket.

"What?"

"Are you dealing?" Her mother's eyes traveled up and down her body. "Or are you having sex for money?"

"No, no," Astrid sputtered. "Of course not."

"Then how did you get this money?"

Astrid looked again at the letter, as if its handwriting might have a clue. She had seen the same handwriting before, in other notes through the years.

"Here's the deal," said her mother. "You tell me where this money came from, and we'll talk. Until then, you're paying rent. This can be for the two months."

"That's not fair. I need it."

"It's completely fair. I'm protecting you from yourself, sweetie. You can't be mooching now that you're full grown. Everyone else has to work for a living, and you're not special. Call this a lesson in tough love. Now take out the trash. It stinks in here." Her mother turned and stalked off to her room, no doubt to put the money where Astrid would not be able to find it.

Part of Astrid wanted to wait until her mother was at work and then search her room, find the money and run. But she had enough sense to know that she wouldn't get far. She could neither rent an apartment for that amount, nor could she stay in a hotel for two months for that little. And getting her airplane ticket to New York wasn't going to be cheap. Maybe she could take a Greyhound bus.

Astrid paused outside after dropping the leaky trash bag into the outdoor can. She wondered about the stones under her window. It was dark, but it was still early in the night and she wasn't afraid. Music pounded from a neighbor's house and she heard people outside in another backyard. She pushed aside the geranium branches under her bedroom window. The stone stacks were still there, but some had fallen over. She shoved her foot under the plant and knocked over the rest of the stones. She thought about collecting them and taking them back to the planter from which they had come. But she didn't want to touch them. They were repellant to her.

She stepped back and then headed inside. Her mother

was watching television and Astrid slipped into her room, closing the door as quietly as she could. Cinderella was asleep with her kittens and Astrid gave her a pat.

Now for her other envelope. She pulled it from the gift bag and thought about her mother's room and the possible places she could have hidden the money. If she looked hard enough, would she find it? And was her mother right? Perhaps she herself was being unreasonable. Eighteen was old enough to pay rent, and if her mother didn't demand any more money, then two hundred fifty a month was a good deal. Sure, her mother had taken her gift money, but most kids, especially poor ones, were expected to help pay for the necessities of living once they were adults.

No, that wasn't right. She was still angry. The feeling came back up, no matter how she tried to excuse her mother's behavior. Her mother had stolen the money, not asked for it. But Astrid also had a plan forming in her mind. Her birthday was coming, which meant she could legally open her own bank account. And once that happened, she could deposit her paychecks, take a little out, and then "hide" the money in her desk. Her mother would find it, take it, and hopefully leave it at that. It was like the mafia, you paid a little to keep the rest safe. And once she moved out, her mother could never take anything from her again.

She tore open the padded envelope and looked inside. There was a book and a piece of paper. She took the book first and glanced at the old, faded cover with the line drawing of a water spirit woman, her hair a giant, round swirl around her pale oval face. It was an odd gift for an eighteen-year-old, but she wasn't too surprised. The package was from her grandfather, her mother's father. He had given her an identical fairy-tale book when she had turned nine. He must have forgotten about it. Either that, or he was getting a little batty.

She almost didn't open the book, but then she noticed

that something was sticking out of it like a bookmark. She pulled it out. It was a paper sleeve with an airline logo on it. There was a ticket in her name. It was dated August 20th, from LAX airport in Los Angeles to JFK airport in New York. Her hand trembled as she stared at the thing. This was her ticket. How much had it cost? It must have been hundreds of dollars, and now she had it. Her ticket out.

Where to hide it? She put it back into the book. She would figure that out later.

She unfolded the note.

My Dearest Astrid,

Let your mother have the money. She needs it.
As for you, the ticket is already paid for. Just show your ID at the airport. Best of luck in New York.

It was unsigned, but she knew from whom it came. Her grandfather had left a similar envelope for her when she was seven, and every year on her birthday she received another. They always contained a book and an unsigned note. The first letter had told her nothing about why her mother and grandfather were not on speaking terms, but he had made it clear that Astrid had to keep the packages a secret, or he would not be able to send them. Mysterious packages from an unknown grandfather? She could not resist, and so had kept the secret. She had saved every note and had read every book more than once, learning about mythology and fairy tales, wars and conquests, cultures and customs. This package was the only one that had contained anything other than a just a book.

Sending money in the mail was new, however. Her fury with her mother subsided a little as she understood what her grandfather was doing. He must have wanted to help his daughter, but how could he if they were estranged? Sending money to Astrid was one way to do it. But how could he have known that her mother would take it from her?

She looked into the envelope again, but there was nothing else inside. But wait. There was something. Down at the bottom were small bits of white. She upended the envelope and nine salt packets tumbled onto her bed. They were the type of packets one found at a fast food restaurant.

Her grandfather was not getting batty in his old age. No, this was more serious. She thought of the rocks under her window, and of someone else, years before, who had given her salt packets.

She had been about six or seven, old enough to remember things, but too young to put them into chronological order or into any meaningful context. Her memories from her childhood were scattershot and uneven. But still, she remembered.

Her mother had taken her to a Mexican grocer in Reseda, one where groceries were cheaper than the regular grocery stores. In the San Fernando Valley summer, her clothes had stuck to her skinny frame in the heat, and the single oscillating fan in the tiny grocer had done nothing to cool her off. Part of the store held a carniceria, a butcher, and the smell of the meat made Astrid feel sick. She always hated meat.

"Can I wait outside?" she asked her mother.

"Right outside the door," her mother said.

She walked out the back door and stood in the narrow strip of shade that ran along the base of the wall. The air over the pavement wavered from the heat and the stink from a nearby dumpster was heavy and choking. She moved off to the other side of the door, as far as she could get from the dumpster without disobeying her mother.

A woman came out of the shop next door to the grocer. She was dressed in a long denim skirt and a cotton shirt with the sleeves cut off, so it looked like a sort of vest. Her brown arms were soft with age, but her build made her look like she had been physically strong when she was younger. Her gray hair was in two short braids that barely touched her shoulders. She smiled at Astrid. Her teeth were yellowish, like a smoker's.

Astrid looked down at the ground. She knew she wasn't supposed to speak to strangers.

"Is your mother inside?" asked the woman, tipping her head toward the grocer's door.

Astrid nodded.

"Isn't it cooler in there?"

"I don't like the meat smell. So she let me stand out here."

"Well, meat is what hamburgers and hot dogs are made from."

"I don't like those either."

"Is that so?" the old woman had moved closer, but she had her back to the wall now, so she wasn't facing Astrid. She was looking out past the parking lot, toward a weedy yard with a chain-link fence. "What do you like to eat?"

"I like pizza."

"I like pizza too. There's a place down the street that has good pizza. They have spicy Italian sausage that they put on it."

"I only like the cheese kind," said Astrid. She glanced at the woman. She was still looking away, and Astrid felt safe in studying her a little. She wore a silver bracelet with a large oval of turquoise set into it.

"You don't like meat at all?" said the woman.

"No. It makes my mom mad, but I can't eat it."

The woman seemed to be thinking it over, which Astrid liked. She liked that this woman wasn't scolding her about it like other adults had.

"I'm sorry, but I haven't introduced myself. I'm Red Fawn."

"Like a deer?"

"Yep. I'm an Indian princess."

"A real princess? For real?" Astrid didn't think there were any princesses any more. There were no kings or queens either.

"That's right."

"Where do you live?"

"Oh, here and there. Here, I have something you can have." Princess Red Fawn reached into a pocket of her voluminous skirt and Astrid held out her hand. Who knew what a real princess would give to her? Three little white packets dropped into her hand.

"What are they?" She was a little disappointed that it wasn't a little carved animal or a jewel or something beautiful and mysterious.

"Salt. Now listen closely. You listening?"

Astrid nodded. Princess Red Fawn looked intently at her now. Her eyes were deep brown, so dark that Astrid couldn't make out her pupils. The skin around her eyes was wrinkled and crepey, but the whites of her eyes were bright.

"You keep those," said Red Fawn. "You keep them close to you. If you get scared, you can sprinkle it around."

"But ..." Astrid looked down at the packets. She did get scared at night sometimes, but how would salt help?

"There you are!" said Astrid's mother. Astrid turned and found that she was far from the doorway. She must have moved without realizing it, as she was now on the far side of the doorway of the shop next to the grocer. "I thought I told you to stay right by the door," her mother said.

She hurried to her mother's side. "Mom, she's a princess. A real live princess." She looked back at Princess Red Fawn, who was leaning against the building. The old woman bent over and rifled through some boxes that had been left outside the door.

"We need to go. Come on," said her mother. She started walking to the car, and Astrid trotted behind.

"Her name is Princess Red Fawn, and she's a real live Indian princess."

Her mother put the bags of groceries into the trunk. "Is that right?"

Astrid knew from her tone that she didn't think Red Fawn was telling the truth. Astrid knew there were no more princesses, but why would a grown-up lie? Red Fawn looked like an Indian she had seen in a movie. They had braids and turquoise jewelry too.

"Yeah, and she gave me these," Astrid said.

Her mother glanced down at the salt packets in Astrid's outstretched hand. "Throw those away. They're just trash."

"I want to keep them."

"I don't want you eating them. God only knows where they're from. You can throw them away when we get home."

"No. I'm keeping them!"

Her mother turned toward her and Astrid took a step back. "Don't you dare use that tone. They're trash, and you're going to throw them out."

Astrid felt tears coming to her eyes. All she could do was shake her head. The packets felt moist as she crushed them in her palm and held them behind her back.

"Give them to me right now." Her mother put out her hand.

It was hard for Astrid to breathe, and her voice came out choked. "But she gave them to me."

"Sweetie, she's a homeless woman. You can't take things from anyone like that." Astrid looked down, and before she knew it, her mother had grabbed her arm and tore the salt packets from her hand.

"Give them back!" Astrid cried.

"Now stop it." Her mother shoved her toward the car. "Get in."

She obeyed and fastened her seat belt. Her mother tossed the packets on the asphalt, got in and started the car. As they drove away, Astrid tried to spot Princess Red

Fawn, but the woman had gone. Her disappearance was unbearable.

"I wanted them!" she wailed. "They were mine!"

"You quit crying right now!" her mother shouted, glaring at her in the rearview mirror. "I swear to God, you are the biggest crybaby. Your father couldn't stand it."

At the mention of her father, Astrid tried to listen. Her mother rarely spoke about her father.

"You cried more than any baby I ever heard of. You cried all the time, every single goddamn day until you were three years old. You were such a difficult baby, and our marriage suffered for it. It's not your fault, but it was hard. You need to get yourself under control. You're too old for these theatrics now."

Astrid wiped her tears with the back of her wrist and tried to quiet herself. Her breath was still hitching in her chest, but she tried to keep from making any sound. She knew that she was a crybaby. Her mother had told her over and over. And she knew that her problems as a baby had made her parents' lives hard. Her mother said that her father's abandonment of them wasn't her fault, but she was pretty sure she knew better. She was a crybaby, and she knew it.

They were only salt packets. She could get more the next time her mother took her to McDonald's. But they wouldn't be the same. They wouldn't be a gift from a real Indian princess.

Astrid picked up the salt packets from where they had fallen on her bed. She hadn't thought about Princess Red Fawn in years. And now, more than a decade later, her grandfather was giving her the same gift.

CHAPTER 10

ASTRID FANNED HERSELF WITH A folded paper bag. Even in the shade and with a slight sea breeze, the day's heat was harsh. The inside band of her visor was wet and her hands were soaked in sweat each time she took off the plastic sanitary gloves used to handle pretzels. It was only mid-morning, but already the heat had exhausted her.

"Regular pretzel please," said a young Asian woman. She dug in a green fish-shaped coin purse.

Astrid slipped on the plastic gloves, got the pretzel and slid it into a paper holder. The woman placed a fifty-dollar bill on the counter.

"Do you have anything smaller? I'll have to give you a lot of change," she said.

"Sorry, no."

The woman was looking off to one side, as if studying something inside the arcade. She was dressed like the cartoon schoolgirls Astrid had seen in anime films. The woman had a fake fox tail pinned to the back of her skirt and two little ears pinned in her hair. At least her hair was pinned up in a mature style instead of pigtails.

Astrid opened her cash drawer and started to count out change. She saw in her peripheral vision that the woman was now watching her. But it was more than that. The woman was studying her. Some people were creepy, and fox girl here was a little extra creepy. She bumped the cash drawer closed with her hip.

"Where's the fifty?" said Astrid. The fifty was gone, and a shiny green leaf sat in its place on the counter. It was large and waxy, like something from the rain forest.

"I gave it to you," said the woman.

"No you didn't. It was on the counter." Astrid opened her cash drawer. She only had twenties, tens, fives and ones. No fifty. She glanced up, and just for a moment, thought she saw the woman's eyes flash topaz. But then they were brown again, as ordinary as they had been before. Astrid froze and for a moment, she didn't hear any of the ambient sounds of the boardwalk or feel the day's heat.

"Just give me my change already," said the woman. She was looking straight into Astrid's face, not glancing away or varying her expression in any way. It was completely disconcerting.

Astrid blinked. "Give me the fifty first," she said. She wasn't going to be cowed by some manipulative nutjob in a costume. The woman had obviously put the leaf there as some kind of a joke. Did she honestly expect Astrid to be so easy to bully? The illusion that her eyes had changed must have been an accident of the light. Maybe light had reflected off of something and had lit the woman's eyes from the side. That would make them look strange for a second.

"I did give you the fifty. Now give me my change or I'm going to ask to see your manager." The woman took a bite of the pretzel and chewed. The little brat, she hadn't even paid properly yet.

"Fine, we can call him. I'll do it myself." Astrid looked for signs of uncertainty in the woman, but she held her ground and even seemed pleased.

"Hey Brad!" Astrid yelled around the corner. Brad worked the counter where children traded arcade tickets for cheap plastic toys.

"Yeah?"

"Call Mr. Augustus, would you?"

"He's over fixing one of the machines."

"A customer needs some help."

Thankfully, Brad didn't ask any questions and summoned their supervisor. A few moments later, Mr. Augustus came out of the arcade. He was covered in sweat and his orange and gray hair was sticking to his forehead along his hairline. When the woman saw him, her lips parted slightly in surprise.

"May I help you?" Mr. Augustus asked.

"I gave her a fifty, and now we're having a little trouble with my change," said the woman. Her tone was different now. Whereas she had used little inflection with Astrid, now she smiled and shrugged as if this had all been a misunderstanding and she was a little embarrassed to bother him.

"So why don't you give her the change?" Mr. Augustus turned to Astrid.

"There's no fifty. She put a fifty down, and while I was making change, she swapped it for a leaf." It sounded stupid when she said it. She glanced down at the leaf, but it was gone. The counter now just had a light dusting of beach sand.

"A leaf," he said.

"Look, I can prove it." Astrid opened up her cash drawer. "See? No fifties."

Mr. Augustus looked into the cash drawer to verify and then looked back at the woman.

"Give her change for a twenty," he said.

"But my drawer will come up short tonight."

"I'll worry about that."

Astrid opened her mouth to protest, but the woman crossed her arms and looked deeply unhappy. That pleased Astrid. Let her have the pretzel and the money, as long as she got the hell away from her pretzel cart. The woman was now looking hard at Mr. Augustus.

"Who are you working for?" the woman asked him.

"I'm the manager."

"You know what I mean. And what about her? What the hell is she?"

"I'm sorry about the inconvenience miss," he said and took the money from the cash drawer and gave it to the woman. He turned and walked away, but the woman kept her eyes on him. Her expression was filled with such malice that Astrid was afraid that she was going to yell something at him.

"You said his name is Augustus, right?" she asked.

"Yeah. He's the manager." Astrid hoped she would go to Mr. Augustus's office if she wanted to cause any more problems. Let him handle her.

"How long has he worked here?"

"I don't know. A long time."

The woman looked her up and down, assessing. "When is the Chumash Legends show?"

Well, that was an abrupt change of topic. Astrid pulled out the brochure she kept under the cart. She used it to show lost people where the bathrooms were or the locations of various rides. The other side of the brochure displayed the summer show schedule.

"Noon is the next one," Astrid said. She wished the woman would go away. She thought she saw the woman's nostrils twitch.

"And a woman calling herself Red Fawn runs it, right?"

"Red Fawn?"

"That's what I said."

"Oh, um. I don't know. I haven't seen it," Astrid said.

"Thanks," the woman muttered and walked away.

Red Fawn. It had been so long since Astrid had seen the Indian princess with that name, surely it couldn't be the same person. But how many people went around with a name like that? She counted back. If she had met the woman when she was about six, that was only twelve years ago. It could be the same woman. She didn't know if she would recognize Red Fawn if she saw her, but it couldn't hurt to take a look.

CHAPTER 11

Y UKIKO BALLED UP THE PRETZEL wrapper and tossed it into a trash can. She turned a corner toward the stage and paused. The stage for the Chumash Legends show was a simple raised platform surrounded by a half circle of hay bales that served as seats for the guests. The entire area was enclosed and shaded, which was a mercy. Someone had rigged a red curtain, but from the look of it, it wasn't part of the original setup.

She hopped up on stage and parted the curtain. A hilly yellow landscape had been painted on panels that were tacked together as a backdrop. She slipped backstage. It had been a full day since she had lost her spirit ball, but her sense of smell was still good. She had needed to work extra hard to make the fifty-dollar bill, especially since her illusions broke so quickly here. Presumably the pretzel girl had something to do with that. Yukiko was furious that she had only received change for a twenty. Paying for another week at the Seaside Inn was going to be tough. But that was a minor problem compared with her eventual enslavement to the holder of her spirit ball.

The area backstage was devoid of people, but then, it was still almost an hour before the show would begin. She could wait. Her sniffing and exploration of the park had yielded nothing other than the knowledge that Mr. Augustus was the manager of the park and the person who had given her the drugged red slushie. There was still no clue as to why he had done it, or if he understood the magnitude of his deed.

The blonde girl who ran the pretzel stand was troubling. She was the source of the strange smell that she and Santiago had found, but she was human. A strange human, but human. She had no trace of the spirit ball about her, and judging from her interaction with Mr. Augustus, he was not subservient to her. Of course, that could have been an act to throw her off. But she had sensed nothing from the girl to indicate that she was malevolent or manipulative, nor that she had been in any way involved with her attack.

When Yukiko had used a little of her remaining power to make the fifty-dollar bill and convince the girl to see it, she found resistance, but not an enormous amount. It had been when the girl had opened the drawer to check for the fifty that she had given off the distinctive scent that matched the one in the haunted house. It had shocked Yukiko so much that she had felt a little of her fox nature surge forward for a moment.

Yukiko was young for a Myobu, and she was still learning about otherkind, but she hadn't run across anyone she couldn't identify in decades. The girl was trouble, and it couldn't be coincidence that she was creating a disturbance at Luna Park while otherkind were being attacked.

She opened the door to the backstage area to find it lit with a single, bright bulb attached to an ancient metal fixture on one wall. Boxes of stage makeup, colored scarves, wigs and masks covered folding chairs and tables. One box overflowed with props. Seven large paper mache dolphins leaned against a wall beside a wooden rainbow and other pieces of landscaping, including green and yellow hills and light and dark blue waves. Yukiko rummaged through things, smelling. If someone had come to the park with the performance group, they could easily leave town with her spirit ball. But what good would that do them? Its only purpose was to enslave the Kitsune to whom it was attached.

"Excuse me," said an old woman. She was glaring at Yukiko.

"I'm looking for Red Fawn. Are you she?"

"What do you want?"

"I was sent to speak to you."

"I told Augustus that I'm not taking tips from the audience. So he can back off. There's no cut for him."

"I'm not here for that. It's something else." How could she explain? She wasn't about to tell a mere human what she was or what had happened to her, but maybe Red Fawn could help her in another way as well. "Does Mr. Augustus do things, strange things?"

"What do you mean?"

"Like, does he speak with people who seem off, somehow? Like they're not normal people?"

Red Fawn's face relaxed a little, and oddly, she seemed relieved. "I don't know who he associates with. But he can be a pain in the neck. And he's been on my back since I brought my show."

"I want to see the show, but I needed to talk to you first. There's something ..." Yukiko decided to take a chance. "Do you know Santiago?"

"I've dealt with him. Are you a friend of his?"

"No. Not a friend. He's a bastard and a liar."

"Well then, we are in agreement." Red Fawn grinned.

Yukiko noticed that Red Fawn was looking at her feet. No, she was looking a little to the side of her feet, at the place where the single bulb caused her shadow to fall. Yukiko looked down, and though the shape of her skirt and the plush tail partially concealed it, if one was looking for it, a person would see the shadow of a fox's tail.

"Why don't you sit down?" said Red Fawn. "And tell me why you're here. I don't think I've had the pleasure of meeting one of your kind before."

Yukiko noticed that Red Fawn had not asked her name, but had offered her own readily enough. It was a small act of courtesy. Among some otherkind, giving your name from your own lips allowed another to have some degree of power over you. Kitsune had no such problem. Their original name was known only to Inari, their god. And he had been dead since World War II. Even Yukiko herself did not know her true name.

"Is there somewhere else we can speak?" asked Yukiko.

"There's an office down the hall. It's this way." Red Fawn led her to the office and closed the door behind them. The room had once been used for whatever administration the stage shows of bygone days had required. But now, it was empty but for an old desk with some of the drawers missing. Any chairs were long gone.

"Are you like Santiago?" asked Red Fawn. "He doesn't have a shadow tail, but I know his other nature."

"I'm Myobu. A fox. My name is Yukiko."

Red Fawn was surprised at her forthrightness. "I see."

"Do you know of my kind?"

"I know of fox spirits from Asia. Is that where you're from?"

"Japan. I am one of the Kitsune."

"So you are like Santiago, a trickster."

"No. The Nogitsune are the tricksters. My kind are lawful. And I have had something stolen from me. Something very valuable."

The look on the old woman's face was skeptical. She had no way of knowing that Yukiko was not lying. Yukiko wished she could let the woman see that she was telling the truth, but she had nothing other than her good word.

"Let me see your hand," Red Fawn said.

Yukiko put out her hand, and the old woman studied the back of it. Yukiko thought she would flip it over to read her palm, but she did not. She pressed on one of the bluish veins twice, then released her. "I know your kind have a lightning ball. Is that what was taken?"

"A spirit ball. And yes. Santiago said that you might know where it was. Mr. Augustus is involved with it."

"Is he?" Red Fawn's eyebrows shot up. "Well, well. I didn't give him enough credit. The greasy bastard."

"Do you know anyone here who would take it? Who here would know what it is?"

The old woman hesitated, and for a moment, Yukiko wondered if she wanted to strike some kind of deal. Few people, human or otherkind, would pass up the opportunity to have another being in their debt, especially one of her kind.

Red Fawn shook her head. "I have no idea. But tell me something. Will you be enslaved to this person?"

"Yes, more or less."

"But how did they do it? Did they win it in a game, guess your real name or what?"

"No. I was drugged and it was stolen while I was asleep."

"I see. I think you'll find out soon who did it," said Red Fawn. "It can't be long."

"Do you sense that? Can you See?"

Red Fawn laughed, showing yellowed teeth and dark gums. "No, nothing like that. But if someone took it to enslave you, the slave master is going to show up soon and claim you. And then you'll know who it is. Your real question is how to get it back, and as to that, I have no idea. How have other Myobu retrieved their stolen spirit balls?"

Yukiko did not know. There were tales of trickery, of bargains made and infants and maidens traded. But without knowing who stole her spirit ball, she was helpless.

"So you haven't seen or felt anything?" Yukiko asked. "You can't help me at all?"

"Well, I can help you, yes. But not with the ball."

"Then I don't require your assistance," Yukiko said and opened the office door.

"Now hold on. Your spirit ball is how you get your magic, correct?"

"Yes."

"But your kind have another source. People."

"I'm not going to kill."

"No, no. Not that way."

"I'm not going to become a prostitute either."

Red Fawn sighed and put her hands on her hips. "I have a stage and an audience. You're not Chumash, but you can work with us."

"You're offering me a job?"

"Well, seeing as your new master is going to collect you soon, it won't be a long one. And I won't pay you either."

But Yukiko understood what she meant. There was a reason that Santiago teased her about playing geisha. She had lived in Japan, but also in San Francisco. She had danced, and done other things, to survive in those early days. Red Fawn was offering her a willing audience.

"Why are you helping me?" she asked.

"It's what I do. I like lost children."

CHAPTER 12

ASTRID SAT ON A HAY bale and drank her bottled water. It was still nice and cold from being in the fridge with the rest of her lunch, and she was grateful for it. A breeze rustled through the leaves of the potted jacaranda trees on either side of the stage, sending down a few lavender petals.

"Hey, Astrid," said Elliot and plopped himself down next to her. He was in his Luna Park uniform also, and she hoped that the park patrons wouldn't bother either of them for help or directions. "Have you seen the show before?"

"No."

"I've been coming to see it as often as I can. It's amazing."

Astrid wasn't sure if he was using artistic hyperbole and liked it because it was campy and silly, or if it was truly good. Elliot loved old horror movies and low-budget science fiction, so his definition of "good" could vary sharply from her own.

"Hey, Elliot? You remember when I was a kid and I saw that homeless woman named Red Fawn?"

"Yeah. You said she was an Indian princess. It was cute."

"Well, I heard that the woman who runs this show is named Red Fawn."

"And you came to see it for that?"

Astrid shrugged. Why was she here anyway? To catch a glimpse of a woman she barely remembered?

The hay bales filled up with sweaty patrons carrying cold drinks and melting ice cream cones. They talked and laughed, and something about their noise bothered Astrid. She was there for a reason, a serious one, while they were just messing around. She glanced at Elliot. Of course they were all there for fun. Why couldn't she just relax and enjoy herself too?

A few minutes later, the curtain parted.

She felt a rush of cool air come over her, delicious and refreshing. But then she found that there was no breeze at all. She had experienced the feeling of coolness inside, not the actual physical sensation. Her skin was as hot and sticky as ever.

The stage stood empty and silent. The backdrop was of hills, yellow and green, painted on wood panels. Other panels slid forward, dropping one after another in layers, giving the impression that she was moving over the land at a fast pace. Then, the movement slowed and a hawk dipped overhead. A doe and fawn ran from one side of the stage to the other. They were painted, but it had been done so well that the animals looked half alive.

A coyote loped across the stage. Rather, it slid, as its legs were neither jointed nor independently mobile. But the movement of whoever operated the creature created the exact likeness of a coyote loping across a field.

There was a woman now, but she was large and earth-colored. *Hutash*, Astrid thought, though she didn't know how she knew the name. She must have learned it from one of her grandfather's books. Over Hutash stretched the sky snake, the Milky Way, with a tongue that flicked in and out. *Alchupo'osh.* He was made of undulating cloth, like a Chinese dragon, painted indigo with gleaming iridescent stars over his entire length. His lightning tongue touched the earth and struck tiny orange fires.

Then there were people. They emerged from the ground head-first. A man and a woman with dark skin and hair. The man wore a loincloth and the woman had a something like a skirt wrapped around her hips. The woman's breasts were bare, with nipples painted dark brown, but something about her was so comfortable, so completely unashamed, that Astrid knew that no one would complain to the park management about it. The woman did not seem nude at all, and she was far from being lewd or tantalizing. She and the man both gave the feeling of being both completely real and completely constructed.

The man lifted his jointed arm in a gesture and then left the woman alone. The man and woman must have been operated from below, like puppets, but Astrid could not see how it was done. There were panels standing upright on the stage to signify hills and grass, but they were only a foot or two in height, not large enough to conceal a grown person. There must be some kind of hidden panel beneath.

The coyote returned from the side of the stage and the woman spoke with him. It was only then that Astrid heard the drums. They were soft, like a heartbeat, but instead of a one-two, one-two beat, they had three beats. One for the man, one for the woman, one for the coyote, she thought.

And then it happened. The coyote split into two. He was still one thing, a puppet, an object. But at the same time, there was a life to him, a spirit. The same thing was true of the woman, who now was speaking with the man as the coyote watched from a distance. She was different. Astrid had to pause to think of the right word. She was—ensouled.

The grass swayed now, and swished just like real grass rubbing against itself. Astrid could even hear the sound of the surf, hissing in and out over the sand. But the sound wasn't coming from the actual beach behind her, but from the stage. The grass existed in two pieces now also, but it had no ensouled quality like the woman, the coyote and the man. Astrid stared at the grass, and saw it twice. Once, it was the painted representation of grass, and the second time, it was real grass, fragrant and alive. Both occupied the same space.

What was going on here? This was not simply a good puppet show or even an amazingly artistic one. This was different.

The woman had children, living babies with milk-sweet breath who grew into children with dirty feet and tangled black hair. Then there were more people, each unique, each alive. And they filled the land, which Astrid now saw was an island. They were loud, and there were so many of them.

Hutash appeared again, and now she was both larger and more magnificent than before. She *teemed* somehow. Like an anthill. Or the sea. Her hair was rivers, and grass, and air. Her arms were snakes and tree trunks and the strong arms of a mother, a husband, a lover. She raised her arm, and then a bridge appeared, stretching from the tallest peak of the island to a mountain peak across the sea. It was composed of every color, fading on the edges out of the range of human vision. Astrid could feel the other colors, and was filled with longing to see them, but they were just out of her reach.

Hutash wanted the people to cross this rainbow bridge, but they were afraid. They cowered. She grew smaller and spoke to them. She told them they had to cross, that they should not look down. They understood, they lost some of their fear and they stepped upon the rainbow bridge. They crossed, but of course, some looked down. Of course. For what sort of story would it be if they had not?

These people fell, and they cried out as they plunged toward the water, their voices mingling with those of their sisters, their fathers, their children who stood above, reaching their helpless arms toward them. The waves enveloped their bodies, but instead of finding death, they were transformed.

They became dolphins, and Astrid saw both the paper mache props bobbing up and down in a row, as well as the real dolphins. Their bodies were sleek and strong, knifing through the cold ocean water. She felt their power, their delight, their joy. And there was the loss, the loss of their families, their humanity, the pleasure and the comfort of being warm and dry.

They lived *between* now. The dolphins could drown, so the very water that was now their home could kill them. But they could not live on land, as that meant death as well. Water was like fire, death and life from the same source. The dolphins were two-natured now. *Otherkind.* They were the brothers of humanity, sprung from the same source.

On the shore stood the coyote, so small that Astrid almost did not see him. Or it. How she felt it was male, she could not tell. But he was watching, pondering, smiling.

The dolphins dove into the waves while the people moved over the hills and into the distance. The coyote turned and trotted away, tail high until it was only a point, slipping through the yellow grasses until even it was gone.

The drums stilled, the sound of the sea and the grass vanished, and now there were only wooden representations. Props. Nothing more.

Astrid glanced at Elliot, who blinked and then met her eyes.

"Great, huh?" he said.

What had he seen? Was it the same thing she had, or was she going mad?

An old woman appeared on stage, wearing a long pale yellow skirt and matching flowing top. Long hunks of dried grass hung from both hips, and intricate patterns of seashells were sewn into both top and skirt. Astrid studied her face, but did not recognize her. Neither could she say for certain that this woman was not the Red Fawn she had met years ago. It had simply been too long ago, and she had been so young.

"Thank you for coming to see our show," the woman said. "We have a special treat today, which is not a part of our regular show."

She left the stage without another word. She had not introduced herself or given Astrid any hint if she was the Red Fawn who ran the show. Astrid was becoming frustrated. Not only was this show strange in the extreme, which unnerved her, but the entire purpose of her visit had been to see this Red Fawn person.

And then, the Asian woman stepped out on stage. It was the woman from the pretzel cart, but now she was in a traditional kimono, all pink and white. Her face was painted white, with her lips blood red and smooth curves of black eyeliner giving her a catlike appearance. But no, it was not catlike, but it was most assuredly animal. She moved forward in tiny steps and stopped at the center of the stage.

Astrid was close enough to the stage to see the woman's eyes as they swept the crowd. They passed over her, but the moment the woman saw Elliot, she stopped. Her ruby lips parted in an expression of recognition and surprise. She pulled her eyes away and looked out over the crowd.

Astrid didn't glance at her cousin, but she felt him shift beside her. Oh please, did he think this crazy woman was attractive? If he had met the woman earlier and he had been taken in by her, Astrid would have to set him straight later.

There was music then, a soft, lilting melody played on a stringed instrument. And there was the sound of water, but it was not the sound of surf on sand this time. This was the sound of stream water pouring over pebbles. A bridge appeared next to the woman, arching and red, crossing the stream.

The woman danced. And when she did, Astrid saw things twice once more. The bridge was real, in a village in Japan. It was a fishing village with ox-drawn carts and old-fashioned clothing. The small white stone shrine with the fox god statue was real, as were the curls of scented smoke rising from the sticks of incense standing upright in a bowl of sand. They were props, she was sure, but she could not see them as props. The woman bowed at the shrine and raised her eyes to look straight into the face of the fox god. *Inari.* That was his name.

Astrid thought of something. Throughout both segments of the show, she had not heard any sounds from the audience. No one had applauded or spoken a word. The people in front of her had not moved. Ice cream melted over fingers and no one noticed. She glanced over her shoulder, and the people behind her were similarly transfixed. They blinked and moved a little, but they seemed stuck somehow. But wasn't that was how all people looked when they watched a movie or television? She was simply not used to seeing people in broad daylight so mesmerized by a puppet show or a dance.

She turned back, and now the woman was on a steamship, headed to a land far across the Pacific. Astrid could feel her anticipation, and another emotion. Fear. Then she was in San Francisco, though there was no Golden Gate Bridge then. She slipped through streets, and Astrid knew she was alone, hungry. There was a cabaret, its walls painted red and gold. There were paper pictures of women, all clothed but looking at the viewer with languid, alluring eyes. The cabaret was hiring.

The woman stood with her hand on the door. Her kimono now was simple and brown. Her sandals were worn and falling apart. Her hair was lank and unwashed, yet she was so achingly beautiful, so graceful. She was tiny and feminine, vulnerable, there and not there. And yet she was strong, ferocious as a mother animal. She pushed open the door, and then turned back, a small movement of her shoulder and head.

The light changed over her and she was back on the little bridge, dancing with the stream gurgling beneath. The cherry blossoms dropped their petals, a drift of soft pink, falling like waves, like confetti, like snow. They poured from the stage out over the people, but now they were both purple and pink. jacaranda blossoms and cherry blossoms at the same time. Places separated by a sea. Pouring over the people like rain and ocean waves and tears.

CHAPTER 13

THE HEAVY CURTAIN SWUNG CLOSED, but no one clapped. Elliot watched the sway of the fabric and he could think of nothing other than the girl, the way the light had fallen on her, or rather, how light had seemed to emanate from her, like the radiant skin of a nude woman in a Reuben painting.

"What the hell was that?" Astrid said to him.

"What?"

"What was that? How did they do that?"

"Do what?" he asked and looked down. He brushed petals off his pants. "Did you like it? I told you it was good." It had been good. He loved watching the show, but it had made him a little sad somehow. But all of the best music and books and art did that to him.

The people gradually filed out, the looks on their faces distant. Elliot knew what they were experiencing. Like him, they were satisfied at a deep level by what they had seen. But there was sadness also. The satisfaction had opened up a new longing, a deeper longing that was farther down than they had known. The beauty they had felt through the window into the puppet world had fed their hearts. But it had also brought a wound. The bitter sweetness of it demanded a few moments of silence afterwards.

Elliot and Astrid left the stage area, heading toward the arcade and Astrid's pretzel stand. Astrid looked out over the water, as if searching.

"It was good, wasn't it?" he said.

"How did they do it? I saw things there and things that weren't there."

Now that was odd, Elliot thought. "What do you mean?"

"Like the people and the grass. They were real and fake at the same time. You know what I mean?"

He didn't. He had enjoyed the show, but the people had been puppets all along. But then, when he remembered them, he thought of them as real people. The dolphins had looked real, though he knew they were props. So had the coyote.

"Not really," he said. "But the people who put on the show definitely have a talent for it. I can imagine the old plays in Medieval times being like that. If you don't have movies or TV, and that's your only way to put on a show, you'd pour all your energy and creativity into it."

"I guess," she said.

They walked in silence until she stopped and turned toward him. "At the end, when the petals were falling, what color were they?"

"They were purple."

"Not the pink ones from the cherry trees?"

He thought about it. The petals had come from the stage, where the pretty Japanese girl stood among the trees at the end. Then they had blown outward over the people. So they must have been pink. They had matched the girl's kimono. But the petals that had been caught on his pants had been the lavender ones from the jacaranda trees nearby.

"They were both, weren't they?" Astrid said. Her expression was a little wild, frightened. "They were pink and purple at the same time. See? Something is weird about that puppet show. And that Red Fawn woman and that Japanese girl had something to do with it."

"It was just a puppet show."

"That woman knew you. When she looked at you, she was surprised. Did you meet her earlier?"

"Nope," he said. "Never seen her before. She was cute though."

"She's a basket case. She came to my stand and tried to pass off a leaf as money. Then she got mad that I wouldn't give her change for the stupid thing. She's a complete bonk job."

Elliot didn't know about that. The woman on the stage had been so sweet, so delicate and defenseless, but with an edge of steel to her. He found it captivating. Along with a certain innocence about her, she had also been sensual, especially when she had been in front of the cabaret. But his hunger for her was more than a sexual desire at the thought of her performing in a cabaret. There was something else to it. It was as if part of him had been given to her, but willingly.

They continued on until they arrived at Astrid's pretzel cart. The other employee who had been covering for her during her lunch break left.

"When are you off?" Elliot asked. "I have your birthday present back at my place."

"My birthday isn't until Monday."

"It's a combo birthday and graduation present. Also, there's something else I want to show you."

Astrid glanced at him suspiciously at this last bit.

"What is it?"

"Just come by, okay? It's kind of weird." He could tell her about it, but describing it wasn't going to do it justice. She had to come by anyway to get her present, and he wanted to show it to her. Having her see it, verifying that it was real, would help him.

"I opened, so I'm off at four," she said.

"Me too. Will your mom be mad if you're late coming home?" He made sure to watch her when he asked. She wouldn't volunteer much information about what was going on at home, but he had known her too many years to be easily fooled. She shrugged and looked down, so he knew things were still bad.

"She won't be home until late, so it's okay."

Elliot returned to the mirror house, where he took tickets and tried to stand in the shade. After work, he picked up his paycheck at Mr. Augustus's office, deposited it at the ATM, picked up some groceries at the market and walked home.

The seashell wind chimes hanging beside his trailer door clicked together musically in the afternoon breeze. He unlocked his door and climbed in. The interior was cramped and old, but it had a little table, a two-burner stove, a small refrigerator and a sleeping area in the back. He had just finished putting away the groceries when Astrid arrived.

"Hold on a minute while I get your present."

He pulled a little box from the cabinet over the stove. It wasn't properly wrapped, but to do that, he'd have to go and buy paper and then store the rest of the roll somewhere, and that was too much trouble. Astrid wouldn't care anyway.

"Thanks," she said and set it on the table.

"Well, open it."

"You sure?"

"Unless you want to open it at home and listen to your mother tell you what an ugly piece of crap it is."

"It's not a piece of crap. Everything you make is good." She must already know what it was. He made lots of little wire sculptures, most of which he sold online, so it stood to reason that he would give her one. Also the size and weight of the box were a pretty good tip off. She opened it and pulled out a wire rabbit, about the size of a golf ball. It had two green faceted glass beads for eyes and its tiny triangular nose was tucked into its paws. After he had made it, he had thought of her and set it aside.

"It's adorable. Thank you," Astrid said and hugged him. She felt so small and wiry when he hugged her. She had always been slight, but working long hours and eating too little had made her too skinny. Maybe some dorm food and New York pizza would fatten her up.

She plopped down into the seat facing the table. It was almost dinner time, and he had bought some macaroni and cheese as well as some pasta, frozen vegetables, cereal and things for sandwiches. He had an awful moment where he debated whether he should offer her anything. She was thin, but then so was he. And he had to make the groceries last until his next payday. Then he hated himself for being so selfish and got out the loaf of bread and jar of peanut butter.

"Hey, could you hold onto this for me?" she asked, pulling a folded paper out of her pocket. It was her paycheck.

"Yeah, why?"

"I'm going to open up a bank account on Monday and deposit it. And if I cash it and take it home, my mom will want it."

He took the folded check and slipped it into the cabinet over the stove.

"So what is it that you wanted to show me?" she asked.

Elliot stopped making sandwiches and went through a stack of books on the chair across from her. The book he removed from the stack was old. Elliot thought that maybe it was from the 1920s or 30s. The book had no copyright page, so there was no telling how old it really was, but the cover design reminded him of some of the old art deco buildings he had seen in Hollywood. The typeface inside was different than in modern books, uneven and splotchy in places. The pages were thick and the edges were ragged.

"Metalurgy," Astrid read over his shoulder. She took it and he watched her flip through the pages, going back to see if she could find the missing copyright page, just as he had. Then after going through it, she stopped and stared, just at the same spot he had, the inner cover.

"Property of the Library of A—" she read. The few

inches of the cover that would have said the name of the library had been torn out, leaving a jagged white rip on the patterned paper. "Fines not to exceed one century." She looked up at him. "What is this?"

"I found it by my door last night."

"You think it was our grandfather?"

"He's never given me anything before. And it's not my birthday or graduation or anything. There's no reason for it."

"Was it in an envelope?" she asked.

"Yeah, but I threw it away."

"Was it empty?"

"You mean a note?" he said. "No, there was nothing but the book."

"No salt packets? I got one with salt packets."

"That's nuts. Why give you those? You guys aren't so poor that a bunch of salt packets would help you."

"I don't think they were for eating," she said. "And what's this Library of A?"

"It looks like it was a library book and part of the name just got torn out."

"The thing about the fine is weird too."

That was the oddest part of the book. Everything else about it could be accounted for. Their grandfather must have bought this old book somewhere. Of course, he must have come in person to deliver it, as the envelope had no post mark.

"He gave me one yesterday too," said Astrid. "I got a fairy tale book. It's the same as the one he gave me when I was younger."

"And you said he gave you salt packets too."

"Yeah, that too," she said. "And it's not the first time someone has done it."

CHAPTER 14

ASTRID TOSSED AND TURNED IN the heat, unable to sleep. She slept in cotton shorts and a tank top, but they stuck to her damp skin in the heat. An old fan rattled near the window, circulating the hot night air. Cinderella was out, and all three kittens lay sound asleep. Astrid went to the kitchen for a drink of water and found her mother asleep on the sofa with the television on. She turned the volume down but left the television on, knowing that turning it off would wake her.

She dropped into bed again and stared at her bookshelf, wondering if she should read the fairy tale book her grandfather had sent. Cinderella's collar jingled in the backyard. It was faint, as if the cat was on the far side of the yard. Then it grew silent.

She got up to get the fairy-tale book when she heard a low growl, long and drawn out. It must be Cinderella, getting ready to attack her prey. She pulled the book down and opened the front cover. There was no mark inside about libraries or fines. Like Elliot's book, this one had no copyright page, but it was probably an antique from some used bookstore somewhere. She flipped on the light, got back into bed and thumbed through the pages, seeing the familiar pictures and text that she had read so many times through the years. She knew all of the stories and black and white illustrations by heart. It was pleasant to flip through the book, seeing old friends.

Something was bothering her though and she closed the

book, her finger holding her place. It was something about the way the cat had growled. That was it. A hunting cat would never growl and alert its prey. They hunted silently. That meant Cinderella was preparing to fight something.

Astrid did not hesitate, but leapt out of bed and looked through the blinds. Though it was dark, there was enough light to see that there was nothing in the backyard.

Then there was a scream, so close to human that it almost didn't sound feline any more. Cinderella's collar jingled constantly now, as if she were running. Or struggling. Astrid ran to the kitchen, flicked on the porch light and threw open the back door. Cinderella stood near the back corner of the house, at the far end from Astrid's room. Her back was to the door and every snow white hair on her body stood on end. She was alone. Whatever it was had gone.

Then Astrid smelled it, the acrid reek of something burning. The cat sniffed at the edge of a small section of smoking grass.

"What the hell?" Astrid breathed as she moved closer.

Cinderella turned, seeing her for the first time. The cat's pupils were fully dilated, making her eyes look almost human. It also made the cat look wild and a little frightening. Cinderella lowered her nose again and sniffed at the smoldering grass.

The burned area was about two feet in diameter, and though it was not a perfect circle, it was close. Cinderella circled it, sniffing all around the perimeter. The smoke rising from it seemed to be getting thicker. Astrid wondered if it might catch on fire, or if it could spread. She turned on the hose and sprayed water over the circle. The grass hissed, and the smoke abated.

The smell was terrible. It reminded her of the time that Aunt Ruth and one of her old boyfriends had taken Elliot and her camping and Elliot had peed on the embers of the dying campfire. But this was even worse, with a stench like rotten eggs, like decay and death.

CHAPTER 15

Yukiko sat across from Mr. Augustus in the man's dingy little office as he talked on the phone. A radio playing a classical station sat on the desk beside a chipped mug full of coffee. He had not offered her any. Not that she would have taken any food or drink from the man if he had.

A note had been shoved under her motel door the previous night, another frightening invasion of her privacy. It was calculated. It had to be. It was a reminder that they knew where she lived and could enter her area without her knowledge. Whoever had her spirit ball controlled her. She could not leave the area without it. She had not been able to locate them. She could only wait for them to contact her.

Mr. Augustus hung up the phone and turned to Yukiko. "She says she'll be right over. So tell me, Fox, how old are you anyway?"

"Now that's a question a gentleman never asks and a lady never answers," she answered tartly.

"No, seriously. They said you only had one tail. So that makes you, what? A hundred? Or are you born with one and you get a second tail when you reach one hundred?"

"You can go to hell. I'm not talking to someone like you."

"Like me?" he leaned back in his chair and studied her. The light from the window behind him, made his orange and gray hair into a wiry halo.

"Someone who poisons other people and steals. You

are a brute and a thief and I am disgusted to be in the same room with you."

"God, you're a bitch."

"You have no idea, human." She said the final word like a curse, and in a way, it was. He was mortal, weak, unintelligent and easily manipulated. Maybe Santiago was right. These people were not like the two of them. The humans were more changeable, with less fidelity to their true natures, whatever that nature might be. They went from kind to cruel, loving to harming, with such ease.

"Well, Iolanthe will be here soon, and you can talk to her."

Yukiko crossed her arms and waited. An employee came and picked up her paycheck and Mr. Augustus marked off her name in his ledger. After she had gone, the door opened again and a woman entered.

Yukiko caught a glimpse of shining blonde hair and smooth fair skin, but the moment the door closed, the woman changed. Her body remained the same, slender and soft in a diaphanous gown belted just under her breasts. It was sleeveless, and looked like something from a sculpture from ancient Greece but also like a light summer sundress that could be purchased at a local boutique. She wore gold sandals and her fingernails and toenails were a matching shade of glittering gold.

She also had the head of a ram. Her golden eyes had horizontal slits for pupils, like sideways cat eyes, and white horns curled on either side of her face. Rams were male, and Iolanthe was, presumably, female. Gender consistency was not a trait of some otherkind.

Yukiko stood, not because she wanted to, but because she had to. It was not the compulsion of her spirit ball, but rather her old training to show respect to equals.

"You are Yukiko, the Kitsune?" asked the woman.

"I am."

"A pleasure. I am Iolanthe." The woman gave a little nod

but did not offer to shake her hand. That was a custom unique to some human cultures. Iolanthe took a chair and Yukiko sat in the other.

"The seer said that the agent is causing all sorts of difficulties, but his tracks are so well-covered that it's difficult to prove," said Iolanthe to Mr. Augustus. "Do you know anything about this?"

Either Yukiko was allowed to hear this, or the ram-headed woman did not consider her important enough to keep the conversation private. She guessed it was the latter.

Mr. Augustus shook his head, "Nothing about any agent. Sorry." Yukiko noticed that Iolanthe held his gaze for a moment too long, most likely assessing his truthfulness.

"You will find out what you can," she said.

"Look, do you have my spirit ball?" asked Yukiko. Ignoring her and slighting her were an insult, calculated to show dominance. Whatever games this woman wanted to play, Yukiko would not willingly participate in them.

Iolanthe turned those strange eyes on her. "I personally do not," she said. Yukiko could see her long, pink tongue, like a thick piece of meat, moving inside her mouth. "But *we* have it, and you will do our bidding."

"Who is 'we?'"

"I will be the one with whom you speak. Also Mr. Augustus here, who is my representative."

"So he poisoned me on your behalf. Is that it?"

"That is correct." The woman showed no tinge of shame or remorse. "You will be employed here at Luna Park, under the direction of Mr. Augustus. You will obey every instruction he gives you on my behalf."

"And if I do not?"

"Then we will destroy your ball. Either that or lock you up for a century or two. You aren't what you once were, sadly. But even so, you are bound by the rules of your kind."

"You stole my spirit ball to make me work at an old amusement park? What, am I going to clean up vomit and run the Ferris wheel?"

"You will do as he tells you. And he does what I tell him."

"And who tells you what to do?"

The woman inclined her head slightly, and if Yukiko hadn't known better, she would have said that the woman was enjoying this. "You do not need to concern yourself. You will do as Mr. Augustus tells you. If you do not, as I said, we will destroy your spirit ball or imprison you. Perhaps both." She turned to Mr. Augustus. The radio station started playing a commercial and he turned it off.

"I will be in touch," said Iolanthe to Mr. Augustus.

And with that, she rose and swept from the room. The instant before she opened the door, Yukiko saw the woman's blonde hair reappear, falling around her shoulders in soft waves. She caught a glimpse of the side of Iolanthe's face, a human face.

"Well, it looks like you'll be doing as I say," said Mr. Augustus. He was more relaxed now, which meant that Iolanthe must be some kind of danger to him. Yukiko was not terribly surprised. Humans could be conned and manipulated. They were so full of pain and longing, that they would welcome any promise to receive honor, power or love. She wondered how Mr. Augustus had come under Iolanthe's power. "I heard that some of your kind worked as courtesans," he said. "Do you—"

"Not a chance. We suck the life from the men who hire us, leaving them empty shells. And that's if they're lucky. Most end up dead, most by their own hand. Or so it always appeared."

"I was going to ask if you played an instrument."

"Are you going to order me to play?"

"I wasn't instructed to. But I thought I might ask you."

"Not after what you did to me. I won't do a thing for you except under compulsion."

"Would you kill me if you could? Iolanthe said that your kind were all noble and honorable. Friend of mankind and all that."

"Usually we are, yes. But one does what one must," she said. She looked him up and down, as if assessing a meal. Of course, she wouldn't kill him. It wouldn't restore her spirit ball, and a violation of the Myobu code would bring a punishment so terrible that it wouldn't be worth it. Not even close.

"I could kill you," she said. "And then use the power to overpower Iolanthe. She'd have to give me my spirit ball back."

"She's not the one who has it. She's like me, down low on the totem pole. And, in case you get any ideas about killing me, know this. It won't do a bit of good. They have your ball hidden, and from what I gather, it's somewhere none of us, not them and not me, would ever want to go. And having them after you for killing their servant isn't a good idea either. They can keep you for centuries and it would be like a single afternoon to them."

"Where is this place that no one wants to go? How secure can it be if they don't post guards?"

"Oh, now we're buddies and I'm going to help you?"

"If you have any decency, yes. You poisoned me and helped enslave me. You owe me."

He chuckled and shook his head. "Sorry, sweetie. No deal. But more importantly, here's what you're going to do. We need your skills at manipulating reality. You can bend time and space, right?"

"You make it sound like something from Star Trek."

"But you can do it? Better than the Seelie?"

"Yes. Is that what Iolanthe is? Seelie?"

"What, you couldn't tell?"

"There are many sorts of beings that can change their appearance."

"Yeah, she's Seelie," said Mr. Augustus. "I only tell you

so you know whose protection I'm under. You don't want to mess with them."

Then he told her what her first task was going to be. Yukiko didn't envy him. Being under the supposed protection of the Seelie brought unsavory obligations. The Seelie and their cousins, the Unseelie, were two types of sidhe. They thought of themselves as opposites and enemies, but to Yukiko, the Seelie were very bad, and the Unseelie were even worse. Being enslaved to the Seelie wasn't going to be easy. There were many types of beings that could have been her new masters. It could be worse than the Seelie. But it could also be a whole lot better.

CHAPTER 16

ELLIOT STOOD IN FRONT OF the mirror house, taking tickets and counting the hours until he was off for the day. Cartoon mermaids and whales decorated the front of the attraction, in keeping with the park's theme. And over it all leered a giant blue head, a crown atop his wild white hair. It was supposed to be Poseidon, but Elliot thought it looked like a blue demon.

It was Saturday, and the crowds were getting bigger. The mirror house was hot inside, but that didn't stop anyone from wanting to go in. By tonight, the teenagers would be celebrating their first weekend of summer vacation. He took out a bottle of water he kept on a shelf inside the wooden stand where the employees kept tickets, glass cleaner and paper towels. His water was warm, but he was just a few minutes from his lunch break, and he would refill it then.

He took tickets from customers and then stopped. The last person in the line was the cute Japanese girl from the Chumash Legends show. She wore a pink tee shirt and little white shorts that showed a long expanse of smooth thigh. She also had plush orange fox ears and a tail.

"Hi," she said. "I saw you yesterday at the show." Her voice was low and musical. She hadn't said a word during the performance, and he had imagined that her voice would be high and girlish.

"Um, yeah. Yeah, that was me. You were really good."

Really good? Was that the best he could come up with? She had been beautiful, exquisite.

"Thanks. I don't usually work with that group."

"You mean Red Fawn? That's the woman who runs it, right?"

"Yeah."

"Are you going to be performing again?" he asked. "I'd love to come."

It was a bold thing to say. And he was just a loser working at an amusement park, while she was a talented performer. She looked around his age, but she might be older and would think he was a dumb kid. He was sweaty and dressed in his stupid Luna Park uniform. He wouldn't blame her for turning up her nose and walking away.

"I'm not sure when I'll be performing," she said. "It depends on Red Fawn."

"Well let me know. I'm usually here, but I sometimes work at the arcade."

"Okay, I'll do that." She looked him in the eye and gave him a little smile. She liked him, he was sure of it. Otherwise she wouldn't say that. Or maybe she was just being polite.

She was holding out her tickets and he was just standing there like a knob. He took the tickets.

"No, no," he said, offering them back. "That's okay. Go on in. It's on me." It was a dumb thing to offer, something so small and cheap.

"Thanks, that's really nice of you," she touched his hand for just a moment longer than necessary when she took back the tickets. "I'm Yukiko."

"Elliot," he said. "Nice to meet you."

"Hey, Elliot." Astrid was next to him. He hadn't heard or seen her come up, but then, he was a little distracted. "Augustus said I have to give you your lunch break."

"But what about Rick? He usually takes the mirror house."

Astrid shrugged. "He said it, I come. It's not like it's brain surgery."

She was right. The job only involved taking tickets and keeping an eye on things. Then he noticed that Astrid was glaring at Yukiko. Oh yes, she said that Yukiko had been the woman who attempted to pay for a pretzel with a leaf.

"Well, see you later," said Yukiko and climbed the steps to the mirror house. The plush fox tail swung back and forth with the sway of her hips.

"I think you have a little drool, just here," said Astrid wickedly, swiping her finger beside her mouth.

"Shut up."

"I told you, she's nuts," said Astrid. "I don't know why she's here again."

"I think she's working for the stage show on and off."

Elliot grabbed his water bottle and was about to leave when he heard someone crying from inside the mirror house.

"Aw, man. Some kid is stuck in there," he said. A child would occasionally get scared or confused and he'd have to get him or her out.

Then he remembered saying those exact words before. Déjà vu.

"I'll get him," Astrid said and headed into the mirror house. He remembered her doing that too.

Without thinking, he followed her. He had always had incidents of déjà vu that weren't really déjà vu in the normal sense. He didn't remember doing the things before, but he remembered dreaming about doing them. This time, he remembered being in bed at his mother's house when he had dreamt of saying something about a kid stuck in the maze. But he couldn't remember the rest of the dream.

He followed Astrid, who followed the sound of the crying child. The maze was made up of tall mirrors, all packed close together to allow the entire maze to fit onto a portable trailer platform. The best way to get through was to hold one hand out in front to keep from running into the mirror walls. Astrid didn't do this, but kept her eyes on the floor, looking for the places where the floor wasn't reflected on itself.

Elliot almost ran into her when she pulled up abruptly. She had come to the end of the maze portion, and was at the back of the maze, where a series of funhouse mirrors let customers have a look at themselves as stretched, squat or distorted before they left through an exit door to the right.

They would have to go back inside and find the lost kid. They must have missed him inside. Wherever he was, he was no longer crying.

"Elliot?" Astrid said. Her voice was terrified and she was stock still, but she had not turned around. He looked over her shoulder.

The mirror, the wavy one that made a person look neither fat nor tall, but completely distorted, was moving. It was an undulating motion, then a flattening until the mirror was smooth. Then he saw a girl, as if the mirror's frame was a window and he was looking through it. Her face and shape were as familiar to him as the girl in front of him. It was Astrid. She wore some kind of long, shabby dress and her feet were bare and filthy. There was someone near her, a figure with his back to them. The girl shook her head. *No, no.*

Then the figure threw something at the girl, the contents of a bowl of liquid. The girl whimpered and pulled at her clothing, which was now hot and clinging to her body. The figure cracked the bowl against the side of the girl's head and she fell to the ground. She was not unconscious, but pressed herself to the ground, begging. The action was animalistic in its subservience.

She was groveling.

He did not think he had ever seen a human being grovel before, not with such complete lack of regard for her pride or dignity as a human being. He had never seen Astrid like this. She had always, even when cornered and crying, had a little defiance in her. An anger. A fire.

The figure kicked the girl and swept away. And then the girl lifted her head, and Elliot saw the anger in her eyes. Then she was gone, replaced by something that made Astrid involuntarily step back, bumping into him. He put his hand on her shoulder. He remembered doing this before also, this touching her, both to comfort her and to make himself feel less afraid.

There were creatures, black as cinders, some cracked and oozing, some feral and hairy. They clawed and screamed, inhuman howls that made him suddenly cold. They pressed against the mirror, furious at being held back. Sometimes a creature was torn away by others who then clawed and screamed as they bashed at the glass. And worst of all, a reptilian creature, toothless and insane in its motions, made eye contact with him. Its eyes were dead. Not blank. These eyes were not simply flat and black like those of a snake or a shark, but were instead pulling, sucking something vital from within him.

Then that creature was thrown back, and another took its place. Astrid did not move, her gaze riveted to the mirror. He also remembered this and knew he was supposed to do something. There was only one thing he could do.

"Astrid!" he shook her shoulder gently and she gasped as if she had been holding her breath.

The mirror went back to normal, returning to its wavy, warped shape. But Elliot thought he saw something fly from the upper edge. It was only a motion caught from the corner of his eye, but he poked his head around the edge of the mirror wall to see where it had gone. There was nothing, just the empty passageway to the exit from the mirror house.

"Do you believe me now?" said Astrid. "About the stones?"

"I never disbelieved you," he said. And he had a memory

of saying these same words to her in just that way. And then, the memory ended, and he recalled waking in his bed, the alarm clock beeping on his nightstand.

"I want to leave," she said.

They left through the back exit and walked back around to the front of the mirror house. As they took their positions behind the counter, the old woman from the Chumash Legends show hurried up to them.

"You two okay?" she asked.

"You're Red Fawn, right?" asked Astrid. Her voice was steady, though Elliot could tell she was still shaky.

"That's me," said Red Fawn, glancing up at the giant head of Poseidon, grinning overhead. She then looked at Elliot. "Keep an eye on your girl," she said and went into the mirror house.

"You saw it too, right?" said Astrid. "I'm not going crazy?"

"If you are, then we both are."

"That wasn't me. The girl."

"What do you mean?"

"That stuff never happened to me."

It occurred to Elliot that he and Astrid had not run into a single soul inside the mirror house. And now, no one was in line to go in. The place felt wrong, as if something evil emanated from it, but the feeling was fading with each passing moment.

A minute later, Red Fawn was back. "What did you do?" she said, pointing a gnarled finger at Astrid. "Tell me right now."

"I didn't do anything."

Red Fawn hesitated, then looked at Elliot, sizing him up. Apparently she was not impressed, as she turned back to Astrid.

"Something happened in there. Something came through. And you did it."

"Leave her alone. She didn't do a thing," said Elliot.

"Oh yes she did. Now tell me."

"First, are you the Red Fawn who gave me salt packets when I was a kid? It was in the Valley, about ten or twelve years ago."

"Salt packets?" Red Fawn looked thoughtful and a little worried. "Stick out your tongue."

"What?" said Astrid.

"Your tongue. Stick it out. Quick."

Astrid did, and the woman put her hand under Astrid's chin. "Say 'aaah.'" She looked into Astrid's mouth and then nodded.

"It was me. Now be honest. What happened? I need to know."

"We just went in," Astrid said. "And then we saw these things, these creatures, scratching at the glass like they wanted to come through." Elliot noticed that she didn't mention seeing herself being hurt. Was that some kind of vision of the future? Like his déjà vu dreams?

"And did any come through?" asked Red Fawn.

"No," Astrid shook her head.

"Wait. I think I saw something," said Elliot. "It was up near the ceiling. But birds sometimes fly in there and get caught."

"It wasn't a bird," said Red Fawn. "And you, young lady, let it through."

CHAPTER 17

"WHAT DO YOU MEAN, I let it through?" asked Astrid. "You did something," said Red Fawn. "You opened a Door. I could tell clear across the park."

Astrid exchanged a look with her cousin. She could see from his expression that Elliot agreed with her that Red Fawn sounded insane. But they had been in the mirror house with those horrible creatures, scratching to come through. Elliot said he had seen it too. That meant she wasn't seeing things. She wasn't crazy.

"So, what is it, exactly, that you think came through?" Astrid asked Red Fawn.

"It could be any of a hundred things. This place, it's a borderland. There are things from all over that could come through. And now we have to somehow get rid of it. Shit. Shit! I'm going to have to ask that stinking bastard for help."

Two Luna Park security guards jogged past, walkie-talkies bouncing from their belts. Astrid hesitated and then ran to catch up.

"What happened?" she asked them.

"Tell your boss that there's a problem with the logjam ride. He's going to have some pissed off customers."

"What should I say happened?"

"They radioed that a couple of the logs somehow sprung leaks. Bad ones. They took on water, got stuck on the bottom of the flume and other logs are piling up."

So there was a logjam on the logjam ride. She let them continue on and turned back to find Red Fawn approaching.

"Where is it?" Red Fawn said.

"There's a problem with a ride. It's nothing."

"What was it?"

"The logjam ride. Some of the logs are leaking."

"Let's head over there. If it's done with that ride, it may move on to others."

"Breaking rides? Is that what demons do these days?"

"I didn't say it was a demon. And yes, some creatures love to cause mischief. We're lucky if that's all it does."

They passed the Typhoon ride, the line of two-person cars spinning endlessly on an undulating round track, and moved past the midway games, scanning for trouble, but found none.

"I think I smell smoke," said Astrid. It was faint, but definite.

Red Fawn followed her. An employee was about to pull the window closed at the pizza counter. Astrid ran up and asked him what was happening.

"Kitchen fire. We have to close up until we clean up." He pulled the window closed.

"I'm not sure," said Red Fawn before Astrid could ask the question. "Could be the creature, could be coincidence. Let's see if that pattern holds."

"There's a pattern?"

"So far, the level of mischief is potentially harmful, but not clearly malevolent. Since we don't know what it is, we observe its behavior and see if we can figure it out."

Astrid didn't voice her thought that she would be useless in diagnosing demonic activity. Or, if the creature wasn't a demon, evil creature activity. Whichever.

"Tell me about the salt packets," said Astrid. "Why did you give them to me?"

"I don't remember. Now, don't be upset, I'm not lying to you. I really don't remember doing it. It sounds like something I would do though."

"What did you see when you looked in my mouth?"

Red Fawn waved the question away and her turquoise and silver ring gleamed bright on her wrinkled hand. "The important thing is that you opened a Door to somewhere else. Lots of dangerous beings don't like salt. So if I gave salt to you, it was for protection."

"Protection."

"Yeah, protection. It's an ancient warding measure to protect from fairies, goblins, demons and other things that go bump in the night."

Salt. She thought of her grandfather's books. Running water, knots, salt and other things all were protection against bad spirits. And Red Fawn had thought Astrid needed such protection. It was one thing to think that the creatures were real. It was another to think that she might somehow be attracting them.

Red Fawn said, "Now, you brought the thing through, so I want you to try to concentrate. See if you can tell where the creature is now."

Astrid paused and tried to concentrate, but she didn't know exactly what she was supposed to be looking for. She pictured one of the horrible creatures, but that only made her stomach clench in fear.

"Anything?" asked Red Fawn hopefully.

"No. But how come you can't feel it? I thought you felt it across the park."

"I felt the Door, not the creature."

Elliot ran up. "Over by the carousel. It was there. A horse came off."

When they reached the carousel, they found that the ride had stopped and one of the carousel horses was lying on the ground, its mouth open and its wooden mane and tail flying. A woman held a boy who was a little too big to be comfortably carried. His face was pink from crying. She spoke with a park employee.

"Rick was over here," said Elliot. "He said that the

106

horse's legs moved. Actually moved. And then the horse ran for a few seconds before falling to the ground."

"And the kid was on it?" asked Astrid.

"He looks fine," said Red Fawn. "Tell me about the horse."

"That's all," said Elliot. "He said it looked like the horse ran, but it had to be the movement of the carousel or something."

"No, he saw what he said," said Red Fawn. "Funny that he told you though. Most people would just write it off or keep quiet."

"We're friends," said Elliot. "But more importantly, where is the thing now?"

Astrid was a little surprised that he so easily accepted the existence of this creature. He had seen what she had in the mirror house, but it still seemed impossible. But the stacked stones were real, as were the burned grass circle and the salt packets. She wasn't sure what was reasonable and what was too strange to be real.

"It's going to be over that way next," said Red Fawn. "See, it's making a path. Logjam, pizza counter, here. If it continues, it'll be in that direction," she pointed.

They moved on. Astrid didn't know how the old woman planned to catch this creature once they found it. It wasn't like she could snap a leash on it. Or could she? Maybe she could sprinkle it with salt.

Astrid scanned the area. The Sea Swings twirled, the riders flying out on their individual swings as the mushroom-shaped support structure spun them around. Panels with Italian paintings of schooners, clippers and frigates flashed by. Some sailed under sunny skies, some were buffeted by storm winds and gray sheets of rain. The images blurred as they whirled. Nearby, the swinging pirate ship ride took on new riders and the multi-colored kiddie boats made a leisurely circle in their water-filled track.

"Red Fawn?" she said. "Other strange things have happened."

She told her about the stacked stones and the burned grass. Red Fawn grew more serious. "When you opened the Door today, it was accidental. If you can do that, then you might have done it before. Maybe when you were asleep or distracted. I don't know much about opening Doors like that. But there are some that can do it. Dangerous business. I'd recommend against it."

"It's not like I did it on purpose."

A man was watching them. He had tousled sandy hair, cowboy boots and was very good looking. He gave Astrid a wink and she looked away, embarrassed to be caught staring at him.

"Shit, it's him," said Red Fawn. She muttered something under her breath and then called over to him, "Come on over here you, old smiler."

He walked over, his movements loose and fluid. Astrid wouldn't have called him graceful, as that somehow implied a certain femininity. But he had an easy manner, as if he was entirely comfortable in his skin.

"What is it?" Red Fawn asked him. "What sort of spirit?"

"Well, it's no hob, Granny. It's a slaugh."

"First, don't call me Granny."

"Fine, May."

"It's Red Fawn."

"All right. Red Fawn," he said. "Since you're going by that name nowadays."

"As if I'd tell you my own. So a slaugh. Part of the Wild Hunt?"

"More than likely," he said. "But the big question is how an Unseelie came through."

"The girl opened a Door."

"Oh, did you now?" he looked at Astrid in approval. He was even more good looking close up. "That's something you don't see every day." He made it sound like she had accomplished something wonderful. "And who might you be?"

"Astrid."

"Santiago," he took her hand and kissed the back of it. She pulled it back, uncomfortable. But she had liked it too.

Then people started screaming. The sound of people having fun on rides is very different than the sound of those in fear, thought Astrid, though she had never thought of it before this moment.

The Sea Swings were spinning as usual, but one of them was askew. Each swing was secured by four metal cables, one on each corner of the chair. The riders were strapped in by seatbelts and a metal bar crossed in front of them with a connector attaching to the chair between their legs. The crooked swing held a man, and though people on the ground were screaming, he was silent as he sailed in a circle, clinging for his life. Two of the cables, the ones toward the inside of the ride, had snapped. Or had been cut. The man hung onto the two remaining cables as his inertia pulled his body outward, toward the ocean, then toward the buildings, then toward the ocean again. Any direction would be deadly if he fell.

Elliot leapt forward and yelled something at the ride operator, but the Sea Swings were already slowing.

"That's a tidy little lawsuit he'll have," said Santiago. "Loose cables coming off, two at once. Awful coincidence."

The swings slowed and the man was taken from the ride, shaken but safe.

"Can you tell where it is?" Red Fawn asked Santiago.

"There," he said, pointing. There was a bird, a pigeon, sitting on the top of a light post. It was as ordinary as any of the hundreds of its kind scavenging the boardwalk.

"You sure?"

"Yes," he said, without explanation.

Well, thought Astrid, if Red Fawn could feel Doors, maybe this guy could feel evil creatures. Slaugh, he had called it.

"Can you catch it?" asked Red Fawn.

"Probably. Slaugh are clever though. Did you know there's a Kitsune around here?"

"Yeah, I've seen her."

"This place is just full of awful strange folk," he said. "It's like the Grand Central Station of the weird."

"You ought to talk," said Red Fawn. "But could the Kitsune help you?"

"I'm not sure. Some Kitsune were tricksters back in their country. This one clings to an old code, but others of her kind were not much different than that slaugh there. Between the two of us old dogs, I think we can take care of it."

CHAPTER 18

Y UKIKO HELD THE CHUBBY INFANT against her body. He was as bright-eyed, smooth-cheeked and black-haired as the perfect child of her imagination. But that was intentional. He was a flawless specimen. He even had the milky sweet scent of a baby. He reached up a chubby hand and patted her breast.

"Quit it," Yukiko muttered under her breath and repositioned his hand on top of the fleecy blanket that she had wrapped around him.

"Gah." He grabbed a tiny handful of breast and squeezed.

She slapped his hand away, harder than she should have, and a middle-aged woman gave her a sharp and disapproving look.

"You stop it now," she whispered.

"Pah," he said with a toothless grin.

She couldn't believe she had agreed to team up with Santiago, but if they didn't catch the slaugh, she would be in worse trouble than she already was. Mr. Augustus had told her to get that girl, Astrid, into the mirror maze and had told her how it was to be done. Then, the Seelie were supposed to handle the girl. He had not said anything about any slaugh. And if Augustus was working for the Seelie, she could bet her hind leg that letting a slaugh, an Unseelie, into the park was not part of their plan. Not to mention the judgment she might incur from the other Myobu, or worse yet, The Lady, for allowing an evil spirit to harm anyone.

Yukiko detected the scent of the slaugh. It was in the arcade, and had been for some time. She shifted Santiago, and he made a little squeak of objection as she pulled him away from her chest and propped him up on her hip. She should have carried him like that before, but she could have sworn his neck had been too weak to hold up his head before. Now he appeared to be about six or eight months old. The little fiend had aged himself.

From his place on her hip, Santiago looked around the arcade with her, sniffing. Yukiko entered the arcade. The games were loud, with distorted recordings of cartoon men shouting while performing martial arts moves, race car motors roaring, and other beeping and screeching. It was horrible. So was the scent. To one side of the arcade stretched the prize counter, where children could bring tickets that some of the games dispensed and trade them for cheap prizes. Lanes of skee-ball were at the far end of the arcade next to a basketball toss. There were driving games and dancing games, shooting games and games with puzzles involving geometric shapes. The whole place was overwhelming.

The arcade was close to empty. About a third of the game screens were black, and she could make a guess why. A line of children stood at the prize desk. Yukiko figured that some of the children were asking for refunds for lost tokens or were just cashing in their tickets. Good. The fewer people here, the better.

"Up," said Santiago, very softly. He did not point.

"Got it," she said. The slaugh was in the shape of a pigeon and perched on one of the wooden rafters.

The pigeon flew toward them and landed directly overhead. Yukiko knew he was taking a look at her and the baby. The creature would be able to sense them as easily as they could sense it. And the more intrigued it was the better. She walked over to the prize counter and pointed to a few toys, talking softly to Santiago as if he were a real baby.

"See the little spider?" she said, pointing to a plastic spider ring.

The slaugh moved. It was very close, completely focused on them. Now, time to get it somewhere away from the people. She moved Santiago so he was looking over her shoulder. He could talk to her that way, and see behind her. She forced herself to move slowly, knowing the thing was behind her and could attack at any moment. She had no spirit ball, very limited power, and the only person on her side would just as soon leave her to die as get himself hurt. At least, she thought so. Coyote was unpredictable, so he could just as well stand and fight to help her. There was no telling.

"Look at the balls," she said to Santiago, pointing to a girl playing skee-ball.

"Bah," said Santiago.

"I like your baby," said a deep voice.

"Thank you," she said and looked up. She didn't have to pretend to be afraid. This creature was dangerous, more than the humans like Red Fawn seemed to realize. Santiago squirmed in her arms, and she realized she was clutching him too tightly.

"I like him very much." The pigeon alighted on the top of a video game and cocked its head to one side, then turned to look at her from the other eye.

"Leave us alone." She turned to leave.

"I will play you for him. Name the game."

"He's not for wager. I didn't know you were here. We'll just leave you alone." She hurried toward the door.

"For sale? Can I buy him?"

"Not for any price." She kept going.

"Play for him or I will take him."

"Just try it," she said. She imagined she had her full powers and glared at him.

"I will have him. A Kitsune, yes?" he said.

"We are."

"I can raise the little fox as my mount and ride him in the Hunt. What a fine thing, to have such a servant."

"You cannot take him. I refuse to wager him, and he cannot be bought."

"If the mother will not wager or sell, there is always theft."

So the vile creature did not know the rules of this world governing infants. An infant could be bartered, sold or wagered, but not stolen. Not by his kind anyway. Humans, of course, could steal their own kind.

"I can take him right now," he said.

"You can't steal him. Not here. It doesn't work that way," she said. "You can only buy or wager."

"Or kill. I can kill." Its voice was so hungry, so full of longing for death that she took a step backwards. This creature was one of the beings her kind existed to fight. And here she was, helpless, powerless.

Santiago was not acting as a normal baby would but was giving the situation his full concentration. She hoped the slaugh would not notice the pleased gleam in his eye. She was terrified, and here Santiago was, having a grand time.

"I shall kill him," the slaugh growled. "I shall dash his little round head on the concrete. His brains will stick in his fine black hair."

The pigeon fluttered to the ground, and an instant later, in its place was a middle-aged man. He was dressed like a tourist, no doubt modeled on some of the men the slaugh had seen at the boardwalk. But his eyes were off. They were a normal brown, but the pupils felt wrong, as if they pulled at something inside her. And his eyes did not move much in their sockets. He had to turn his head a fraction to look from the baby to her face. She tried not to look directly into his eyes, but focused on a spot on his forehead. He licked his thick lips, giving them a glisten of saliva.

"Death or a wager," he said. "I can kill him before you know it."

He was correct. He could kill the baby in an instant. If it had been a baby.

"No! No, please," she begged. "I'll wager. Just don't hurt him."

"Better," said the slaugh. "A game then?"

"Sure, a game. Whatever you want. Just leave us alone."

"A game. A game of skill. Not of chance. Your kind cheat."

That was rich, coming from this vile creature. Yukiko knew better than to think that the slaugh wouldn't cheat to win.

"First, the terms," she said. "I win, and you leave us alone. Me and my descendants, forever."

"And if I win, I take the boy for my slave."

"Very well," she said. "It is agreed."

"It is agreed," he said.

Now it was sealed. She had to repress a smile. Santiago grinned and made a bubbly, happy gurgle.

"We will choose a game," said the slaugh.

They needed a game of skill, not of chance. She didn't want the slaugh to go out on the midway for a ring toss or shooting game. There were too many people out there. They needed something close by.

"How about that?" Yukiko pointed toward the skee-ball ramps.

"Throwing balls," the slaugh said. "That is skill." It turned, its motions slow and alien and walked away from her. It assessed the basketball and the skee-ball games.

"That one," he said, pointing to the basketball game.

Interesting. It was the easier of the two games, at least to her way of thinking. Was the slaugh picking it because he had trouble coordinating a human body? Or could it not understand the numbers on each of the skee-ball holes, and that some holes were worth more than others? No matter, the basketball game would do.

"You can go first," she said. "I'll hold my baby while you play."

"No, fox spirit. The child will wait there." He pointed to a spot on the floor. He was technically correct. She could not hold on to the prize of the wager during play. She set Santiago on the floor, where he looked around with round, wondering eyes. Cute. Now just hold still for a few minutes, she thought.

"Now, we play." The slaugh looked the game up and down. Did it not know that it needed tokens? Yukiko was about to dig in her purse.

"Bah!" Santiago slapped his chubby thighs. Three balls rolled down and bumped up against end of the chute, ready for the slaugh to toss them. The slaugh missed his first shot, but then the second and third ball went into the basket. He was more able to control his body than she had thought.

Then three more balls came down the chute. The slaugh didn't seem to notice how strange that was. Perhaps he thought she was using her magic. She wished Santiago had let her pay tokens for playing so they didn't arouse the slaugh's suspicions. But this would make a better story later, when he would regale others with it for a glass of whiskey. To have him sitting there as a useless baby would not. He was showing off.

Yukiko tossed the first ball, holding her breath as it bounced against the rim and fell outside the basket. The second ball went in. The third ball was the key. She threw it and it went wide, bouncing off the backboard.

"I win," crowed the slaugh and grabbed Santiago. The baby whimpered.

"Wait, please!" cried Yukiko. "Give me another chance!"

The slaugh pulled something thin and silver from the air, fastened it around his own wrist and around Santiago's little ankle. He then turned to leave.

What was Santiago waiting for? She had no magic of her own, not even enough to affect a stupid basketball machine. And now Santiago was sitting placidly in the slaugh's arms, sucking his fingers as the monster carried him off.

She trailed behind, and just as the pair crossed the threshold of the arcade, Santiago reverted to his true form. The slaugh dropped him and Santiago looked up at him with a canine grin.

"Hello, friend," Santiago said.

"What manner of fox are you?" the slaugh said.

Yukiko had forgotten how small coyotes really were. Of course, her form was even smaller, but Santiago looked almost tiny compared to the slaugh in man's form.

"Not a fox, you halfwit. I am Coyote."

Santiago was an egomaniac. He couldn't be satisfied to catch the slaugh, but had to revel in doing it, making sure his name would be remembered and cursed by the creature forever.

"You tricked me!" the slaugh cried, turning on Yukiko.

"Your argument is with me," said Santiago. His tawny fur was bristling all up along his back.

But the slaugh grabbed Yukiko by the elbow and put its hand around her throat. The hand was cold and reptilian, not soft and warm as it appeared. She clawed at it. He put the other hand around her waist and squeezed, lifting her. By the gods, the thing was strong. Yukiko ripped at the hand choking her, and then her old lessons returned to her. The thing's hands were busy, leaving its vile face unprotected. She went for its eyes.

The hands jerked away, clawing the skin of her throat, and Yukiko fell to her knees when it dropped her. Santiago was a snarling, insane creature. The thin silver chain wrapped around Santiago's hind foot tied him to the slaugh's wrist. Coyote yanked it, pulling the slaugh's arm backwards. He clamped his jaws around its wrist and savaged it, snarling in fury. The slaugh kicked at him.

Yukiko did not waste any time, but dashed for the pretzel cart. Astrid was there, as planned, and was waiting with a metal box, filled with salt. Yukiko was about to take it, but Astrid rushed forward. Yukiko stopped her.

"You have to wait," Yukiko said. "It's still a man."

Coyote and the slaugh were still fighting, and the slaugh was mostly staying as a man, beating Coyote about the head. Now and then, it changed into a bird to fly away and Coyote jerked it back by the chain. They had gotten lucky. A slaugh that could become a bear or a tiger would have been impossible to subdue.

"Let me do it," said Yukiko. "If it hurts me, it won't be so bad."

"Thanks," said Astrid, and Yukiko heard the note of surprise in it. She supposed after the leaf incident that the girl had no reason to like her. Fair enough. She took the box of salt and the matching metal lid.

The slaugh was a man again, but it was tiring from changing back and forth. It turned into a bird, and then the chain slid from its body. Ah, so it had caught on that it could release its prisoner, but too late. Coyote grabbed it by the neck and shook it senseless. Yukiko slid onto the ground in front of him and Santiago dropped the slaugh into the box. She smashed the lid down and put all her weight on it. The slaugh inside screamed in an incomprehensible language and bashed its body against the sides of the box.

"Here," said Santiago, slipping the chain from his foot. Yukiko took it and tied it around the box four ways, like a ribbon on a Christmas present.

"Astrid, grab a couple magnets!" called Santiago.

The girl stood confused for a moment, but thankfully, she obeyed. She pulled some magnets from the wall of the prize counter where they advertised Luna Park, Los Angeles and the Golden State. She slapped them onto the outside of the box.

"Will that help keep it in?" Astrid asked Santiago.

"It'll help. They hate cold iron and magnets."

The slaugh was quieter now, but Yukiko could feel it

118

moving in the box. Santiago panted, his pink ribbon of a tongue lolling out of his mouth. He was happier than she had seen him in years.

Astrid glanced around nervously. "I think you should become human. You don't exactly look like a normal dog." There were only a few people, and Santiago must be doing something, because they were passing as if nothing had happened.

"He won't have clothes if he changes," Yukiko said. "So no, he really shouldn't."

Yukiko watched Astrid's cheeks turn a little pink. Poor girl. Santiago was handsome, if erratic, and had been charming ladies since before Astrid's grandmother was born.

"Go find Red Fawn," said Yukiko. "We'll need to get rid of this thing."

Astrid left and Yukiko brushed herself off with one hand while holding the box.

"I heard something about your spirit ball," said Coyote.

"Why didn't you say something before?"

"What, and ruin our fun time?" He scratched his ear with his hind foot. "One of the seabirds said something about dark water."

"That's it?"

"That's it. It was kind of garbled actually, so you're lucky I could make that much sense of it."

Yukiko looked out over the ocean, but the water looked as it always had.

"Aren't you going to thank me?" Coyote said.

"Thanks."

She was still shaken from the slaugh attacking her. She touched her neck and looked at her fingers. No blood. The whole area felt tender though. It would probably bruise.

"Sorry I didn't get him in time," said Santiago.

"Goes with the territory," she said.

"We make a good team, Kit."

"No. We really don't."

CHAPTER 19

"JUST CONCENTRATE," SAID RED FAWN.

"I'm trying," said Astrid. She stood in front of the same mirror in the mirror house through which she and Elliot had seen the horde of angry slaugh. She tried to make the Door open again, imagining the mirror as water smoothing out, as a sliding door, as a window, but nothing happened.

"Concentrate harder," Red Fawn said.

"What does that even mean? What am I supposed to be concentrating on?"

"I don't know. I never opened a Door."

"So why did you say it?" said Astrid.

"I was trying to be helpful."

Astrid sighed, pushed her hair behind her ears and tried again. Elliot stood to one side, waiting. They had tried to recreate the conditions under which Astrid had accidentally opened the Door, but it hadn't worked. It seemed that she had opened the Door entirely accidentally, and was unable to repeat it.

"You called me?" Yukiko said, tone as icy as she could manage. She held the magnet-covered metal box and felt the slaugh slide along the bottom as she shifted the box from one arm to the other. Mr. Augustus sipped his coffee, which must be six hours old by now. The radio played a soft piano concerto.

"We know about the slaugh," he said.

"I gathered, seeing as you asked me to come in and bring it."

"You weren't supposed to bring a slaugh through," he said.

"It's not my fault you and the Seelie had a bad plan," Yukiko said. "I did my part as instructed. No more, no less."

"And yet, we have a slaugh."

"It's not really my problem, is it? The illusion of the lost child was there, I bent reality a little. It's not my fault that the girl is what she is. And besides, you should be thanking me. I helped catch the evil little thing before it could kill someone and bankrupt your park."

She set the box on the desk a little too hard, infuriating the slaugh within. It cursed and scrabbled inside its prison. Mr. Augustus pulled away from the box.

"How are you going to send it home?" asked Yukiko. "Are you going to call the Unseelie to come pick it up?"

"I have called Iolanthe. She'll handle it."

"Yeah," she sighed. "I suppose it's best to let the sidhe manage the sidhe."

"Can't argue with you there, sister."

She wasn't his sister, not in any way. Except both of them were under the command of the Seelie. And both of them were helpless regarding their own destiny.

"Don't release the knots on the chain," she said.

"I'm not stupid."

"So will I be freed? I did as I was asked."

"Unlikely."

"How long will they keep me?"

He shrugged. "They'll keep you as long as they keep you. It's not like you're a djinn and they only get three favors."

"They could keep me forever then."

"Until you die, yeah. Why don't you sit down?"

Yukiko paused, considering, and then took the seat. Mr. Augustus took another sip of cold coffee.

"Look, I'm sorry I poisoned you," he said. "I didn't have any choice in it, just as you don't."

"How are they holding you? Can't you get free?"

He shook his head and glanced at the clock. "I can't get free any more than you can."

"Maybe I could help you. And you could help me? My word is good. I honor my agreements."

"So I've heard. But there's nothing you can do for me. The Seelie have many in thrall to them, many slaves. They don't get free."

"Well, Mr. Augustus, I am not them. I am a Myobu, an ancient and noble race. And we do not take kindly to being enslaved."

"Maybe not a few centuries ago. But now, you're all freelance, from what I understand. No family, no god, no nothing. So who will stop them?"

He was correct, of course. There was no one to stop them. She was completely on her own to help herself. But she had spent most of her life on her own, so it was not a new feeling. Later today, she would dance again in Red Fawn's show and gain more power.

And then she would see about getting her spirit ball back.

CHAPTER 20

"YOU SHOULD GO HOME, SWEETHEART. There's really nothing for you to see." Red Fawn gave Astrid a grandmotherly pat on the shoulder.

"No way. I saw those horrible things, and I want to see the thing that can stop them."

"He isn't their master and he doesn't fight them."

"But he can take them away from here and send them back to hell where they belong," Astrid said.

"Oh, the slaugh don't come from hell."

"It's almost sunset. I'm going, and you can come or not."

Astrid didn't give Red Fawn time to answer, but hurried down a cement staircase, the bottom of which was buried in the sand of the beach. She pulled off her sneakers and stuffed her socks inside. There was no way she was going to miss seeing the slaugh taken away. She had opened the Door, and she wanted to see the being who could undo her deed. Red Fawn had said that the slaugh would be fetched by someone called the Piper, but she wouldn't give any more information other than to say that he was strange, fearful, and the sight of him drove men mad.

She had to see him. Red Fawn pulled off her sandals. There was a shady place under the pier, the perfect place to see and not be seen. According to Red Fawn, the Piper would come to this place because it was the borderland between sea and earth, and he would come at sunset, as it was between day and night. It was poetic, Astrid thought, if a bit literal. But these things had rules, she had learned.

"Is he scarier than the slaugh?" Astrid asked.

"Scary? Oh, not really. He's ... himself. And that's enough to scare the britches off most people."

"So why are you afraid of him if he's not evil?"

"Don't be a fool, child. My friend Rattlesnake isn't evil, but he'll coil and strike if he's surprised or threatened."

"But we're not threatening."

Red Fawn gave a snort. "I'm not."

The sun touched the horizon and a woman walked down the beach, holding the metal box. It still had the colorful magnets attached and looked like a tacky souvenir. But she held it like it was a treasure.

"Who's that?" Astrid asked.

"Iolanthe."

The woman's movements were graceful and slow, as if there was nothing worth hurrying for in all the world. She wore a filmy gown that blew around her legs and exposed her bare feet. The ocean wind swept a tendril of her blonde hair across her face, but she did not push it away. She kept both hands on the box.

Then, her face changed. It was the serene human face, and it was also the face of a ram.

"What's wrong?" asked Red Fawn. Astrid realized she must have gasped.

"She has a ram's head."

Red Fawn didn't seem surprised. The ram woman stood stock still, waiting. No human ever waited with such composure and serenity. She looked out over the water, and Astrid looked too. The waves rose, broke and hissed on the sand, the gulls wheeled overhead and the people on the pier above passed without noticing a thing.

Astrid understood that things happened in the world that were just outside of regular people's senses. It wasn't that they weren't paying attention. It was that they were incapable of seeing most of it. Red Fawn had told her as much, but she had not believed it completely. It was difficult to believe that she could see what other people could not.

The waves were a few feet high, not big enough for surfers, so the water was empty on this side of the pier. That in itself was odd, but she figured some weird creature or person probably put the whammy on it to make it unappealing to visitors. The waves came in and out, soothing and rhythmic. The next wave was high, rising in a giant swell of foam and brownish water, and when it broke, emerging from the crash of the water came the Piper.

He was tall, at least eight or ten feet high, with a face that looked mostly human. The eyes were too far apart, too slanted, too black, and his nose was too flat. His mouth was wide and sensual, and though he was monstrous, he was also appealing at some level. Like Iolanthe, he had horns, but his were not ram horns, but the curving horns of a bull, black, shining and sharp. His torso was bare and covered in a light covering of curly brown hair. His body seemed to be partly made of water, not just covered in it. It was brown, green, full of life. The water poured from his curly brown hair, his beard, his shoulders.

And then, he moved forward through the surf and Astrid saw the lower half of his body. It was hairy, with thick, powerful legs that bent backwards at the knees. He was half goat. Then, his cloven hooves touched the sand, and he changed. He still had the same appearance, but now he was solid, harder, of the earth and the things below the earth.

"Is that the devil?" Astrid whispered. There was no way anything could hear her above the sound of the waves, the people and the rides, but she didn't want to take any chances.

"Of course not. Like he'd make an appearance." Red Fawn was keeping her voice low as well.

"Then what is he?"

"Like I said, he's the Piper. Master of None. A bit of a celebrity, really."

The Piper took the box from Iolanthe, and said something to her for a few moments. Then he turned and moved back into the water, the surf swirling around his ankles. Astrid watched as he went from being of the earth to a being of water as he passed from the sand to the sea.

He paused, and Astrid stopped breathing. He turned his head toward them, slowly, deliberately, as if giving her the chance to run or look away. She did not. Red Fawn gripped her arm hard. It hurt, but she did not move. The Piper's gaze met hers, and she felt the scurrying wild things of the forest, the movement of leaves, the music, pulsing and tearing into her heart, elevating it and breaking it at the same time. She felt the hunger, the desire, the pulsing need, and just beyond that, the madness. In his being was the brink and the place beyond the brink, where thought did not matter and where reason was useless. She could not look away.

Then, the feeling pulled back, and she felt him assessing her. He wondered about her, and there it was. It was gone as soon as she thought she had seen it. The flicker of fear.

The Piper turned away and kept moving, and his hips, chest and shoulders vanished under the water. A wave crashed down, and his head was gone as well.

She looked out over the water, and far off, on a slick rock that barely broke the water's surface, she saw a woman, dark-skinned and still. She must have been sitting on an inner tube, as a dark, thick coil hid her hips and legs. A wave washed over the rock, and the woman was gone.

CHAPTER 21

A STRID DIDN'T EVEN TRY TO sleep. There were too many thoughts and too much anxiety for her to allow herself to relax. She read by flashlight, knowing that if she turned on her bedroom light, her mother might see the glow from under her door and come in. The sound of the television through the wall was reassuring, a familiar irritation.

When the TV turned off, she glanced at the clock. It was almost three in the morning. She heard her mother walk down the hall and the bedroom door closed. That was a good sign. When her mother stayed up all night or fell asleep in front of the television, it meant she was upset about something, usually unpaid bills.

Cinderella had left the kitten box before midnight and had not returned. The kittens liked to eat regularly and now and then, one of them would squirm and make tiny mewling noises. Astrid stroked them with the back of her fingers. Soon, they would be old enough to walk around, and then she would have to find homes for them. Looking at them all together, the size difference between Runt and the other two was significant. He was a good deal smaller and his fur was not as thick. She should name the other two, but if she named them, it would be even harder to get rid of them.

There was a hard lump under the old towel that covered the bottom of the box. Astrid pulled it back and found her metal owl bell. It must have fallen into the box from her nightstand. She was lucky it hadn't hit the kittens. It was old-fashioned looking, like an antique from the ancient world, and its expression was stern and watchful. She set it back in its place on her nightstand.

She waited for the sound of Cinderella returning, the jingle of the collar, the sound of the cat door. It didn't come. She thumbed through the fairy tale book, half reading, half pondering what she had seen. The slaugh in the mirror were horrible, worse than the creatures she had imagined under the bed or in the closet when she was young. And unlike the monsters of her imagination, these creatures were completely real. And then there was the Piper. She had sensed the instant of fear in him. What exactly was happening to her? The ability to open Doors to other worlds was terrifying. Red Fawn had not seemed to think that the slaugh was the worst thing that could come through. So what else was there, waiting, and how could she keep from letting it through?

Maybe she could learn how to summon the Piper. If he could clean up any stray creatures, then he could help her. She felt warm at the thought of him. He was masculine in the extreme, almost to the point of a caricature. But goat legs. He had goat legs. There were satyrs in Greek mythology, goat men who seduced nymphs. Now she understood that part of the stories at least. Then there was Santiago. She was inexperienced with men, but she knew he was bad news.

The cat flap opened and closed, and Astrid opened her bedroom door to let Cinderella in. The kittens squirmed in the box and Astrid waited. Cinderella didn't come down the hall. She must be in the kitchen, maybe eating her kibble.

No. She knew differently. Something was off. Whatever senses she was developing, they were setting off alarm bells now. Or maybe it was plain old intuition.

She went to the kitchen and sighed in relief. Cinderella was in the center of the floor, chewing on whatever she had killed outside. It was going to be a mess to clean up, but at least it was nothing serious.

Then the cat looked up. The thing in front of her was no bird or lizard. It was a small fetal thing, a homunculus, gray and humanoid. Its head was too large for its body and it had long, spindly arms with three fingers on each hand that ended in bulbous tips. The feet were similar, but with short toes. Its rounded stomach and large head gave it an almost infantile appearance. Huge, black eyes without pupils, like the aliens she had seen on television, watched her.

Thank God it was dead. For a moment, she feared that it might still be alive, but it was covered in black blood and it did not move. Part of its hip and thigh were gone. Cinderella had been eating it. Oh God, that was disgusting.

The way Cinderella was looking at her now was almost as horrifying. There was intelligence in her eyes, though her face, being covered in fur, was not readable. She was expectant, and also looked like she wanted to tell Astrid something. Astrid wished the cat could talk, and would tell her where the hell this monstrosity had come from. But she thought she already knew. Red Fawn had said that she could open Doors unintentionally, even in sleep. She had not slept that night, but she had slept every other night.

Cinderella puffed up and shot toward the cat door, stopping a few feet short of it. Then, Astrid heard it too. Something scrabbled outside at the door.

The cat growled a warning, high and loud, and the scrabbling stopped, only to begin again. Then Astrid understood. That's why this vile little monster looked like an infant. It was a baby. And it had a mother.

She yanked open the drawer, looking for the slide-in panel that had come with the cat door. It had to be in here somewhere. She yanked out another drawer, but it was nowhere to be found. She opened a cabinet, pulled out a cookie sheet and held it against the cat door. The thing stopped its sniffing outside and she felt it push experimentally against the cookie sheet. Then it banged on it hard.

"The chair," Astrid whispered to herself. She held the cookie sheet with her foot and pulled over a kitchen chair, laying it on its side so it held the cookie sheet against the cat door.

Cinderella stayed a few feet away, every hair on end and every muscle tense. Her eyes were so dilated that her irises were just a thin strip of yellowish green around her giant pupils.

"Another slaugh," Astrid whispered. "You killed a slaugh baby."

The baby was still on the floor, oozing a slow flow of black blood. The smell coming from the thing was awful, the same death and sulfur smell that had come from the burned circle in the grass.

"What are you doing?"

Her mother was behind her, blinking in the light of the overhead kitchen light. She was in her pajamas.

"Um, there's a raccoon," Astrid said, but stopped. The dead slaugh lay in the middle of the kitchen floor. "No, it's not a raccoon. It's something else, trying to come in. It's the mother of that." She jerked her chin toward the corpse, keeping pressure on the chair, and thus the cookie sheet.

"The mother of a rock? What the hell is wrong with you? Go to bed."

"No, that thing. That baby thing, right there."

Her mother looked straight at the dead thing, but was unfazed. She put her hand around Astrid's upper arm and pulled.

"Come on, sweetie. You're sleepwalking or something. I thought you had outgrown it. Let's just go back to bed, okay, baby?"

Astrid stood, astonished. She glanced back at the twisted

little corpse. It was still there, stinking and dripping. Was she imagining it? Was she really going crazy? Then she glanced at Cinderella. Black blood smeared the white fur around her mouth.

"Here," said her mother, setting the chair upright.

"No, no. You need to leave it. There's something there."

"No there's not," her mother said. "Here, look."

And before Astrid could stop her, her mother removed the cookie sheet, pulled open the door and flicked on the porch light. The back porch was empty and so was the yard.

"But Cinderella, she killed it. Look at her mouth, there's blood. She killed it." But even as she looked at the body, she saw it twice. She saw the rounded gray stone and also the dead creature.

"That cat isn't good for you," her mother said. "When we first got her, you would go on about weird stuff she did. Something about that cat affects your mind. Now, let's get rid of this thing."

Her mother picked up the dead thing. She held it as if it were a rock and tossed it outside. Her hands had no blood on them afterward.

"It's bedtime. Come on," her mother said.

She let her mother lead her back to bed, and she crawled under the covers. Cinderella stayed in the kitchen. She was guarding the house. Astrid knew that now. Guarding her babies and maybe Astrid as well. Good kitty.

Her mother turned off her light, closed her door and went back to bed. The moment her mother's door closed, Astrid sprang up and grabbed her grandfather's salt packets from her desk drawer. She tore one open as she rushed down the hall. Cinderella stood to one side as she sprinkled it along the inside of the door and on the kitchen windowsill.

She made the rounds, making a ward. Just like in the fairy stories, she sprinkled each threshold and windowsill with salt. When she ran out, she got the salt shaker and kept at it. The bathroom window, the living room window and door, her bedroom window. She stood in the hallway outside her mother's room. She couldn't go in, but she sprinkled the base of the door with salt. It would have to do.

She went back to her room and put salt around the entire perimeter, putting so much on the windowsill that her mother was sure to notice, if she looked. Then she sprinkled a rectangle around her bed.

Cinderella watched all of this and followed Astrid into the kitchen when she put away the salt shaker. The cat stood in front of the cat door, and Astrid knew that she was about to do something she did not want to.

"Don't go," she said.

Cinderella came forward and bumped against Astrid's legs, and she knelt down to pet her and kiss the top of her head.

"You don't have to go."

The cat gave a last nudge with her head and then jumped through the cat door. Astrid heard the jingle of her collar grow fainter until she was out of range. Maybe she would be all right. Maybe she would kill that horrid thing.

Her mother had left the porch light on, and Astrid wasn't about to turn it off. She made sure the back door was locked and then looked through the kitchen window into the backyard. The mother of the thing stood with her back to the window. She was bigger than a cat, about eighteen inches high, gray-skinned with a thick, powerful body. And Cinderella had already gone.

The thing turned in a flash and made eye contact with her. The feeling was unspeakable, like looking at the things in the mirror house, but worse because this thing was in her world, outside her own house.

And then the thing opened its toothless, wet mouth and grinned.

CHAPTER 22

YUKIKO LOOKED HERSELF OVER IN the motel bathroom mirror. She looked much healthier than she had when her spirit ball had first been stolen. There was more color to her cheeks and her eyes were clear and bright.

She put on a light blue sundress and white high-heeled sandals. Thank the gods she purchased a few nice things with her casino money before losing her powers. At least she wasn't reduced to wearing ugly souvenir tee shirts. She fixed her hair and put on a little makeup.

She looked at the plush tail, and for a moment, she wanted to clip it on. But it looked too eccentric, and she wanted to look normal, or at least as close to normal as someone like her could manage. She hoped that the fullness of the skirt would hide her tail's shadow. She thought she could pull it off. Maybe. And if not, then so what? She had nothing to lose.

Now, about this Elliot. She had met him before, long, long ago, by human terms anyway. She had been surprised to see him again at the show. He had not recognized her because he had not met her yet. He had been older then.

In the mortal world, time was roughly linear. True, it was faster at some points, slower at others. Her kind were not time-sensitive, so she did not notice these things herself. The Kitsune lived one day after the other, just as mortals did. Most of them anyway. Elliot must be an exception.

Now, what sort of man was this Elliot? She knew little about him, but she was sure that he was young, and was from this era. She had dealt with men before, so many men. But that had been back decades ago, and male sensibilities had changed. No longer was a sweet, docile girl who would cook and be of service to her man the ideal. Modern men wanted something else, and she was not sure she could pretend to be it. With her powers, she would be able to make a man see and feel what she wished, to an extent. And though she had danced at Red Fawn's show again, she didn't want to use up too much of the power she had gained.

Augustus had given her orders. They had come from Iolanthe, who reported to a governor or a duke who reported to the queen. You had to give the Seelie credit for organization. One knew exactly where one stood. It had been that way once with the Kitsune. The Nogitsune, the wild foxes, had their ways, wild and wicked. And the Myobu had theirs. They had Inari, the rice god, and they had order.

It was all gone now. Where were her brothers and sisters? Now and then, she could feel one passing by, on a train, or a ship. She supposed some traveled by air, but the planes were so far overhead that she did not feel their presence. She had traveled back to the old temple in Japan once and had visited the old shrines, but they had fallen into disrepair. Their decay pained her. She had done her best to clear away creeping plants, to upright the statues. She had swept the hidden temple, cleared the leaves and dirt and scurrying creatures. She had burned incense and wondered if she was the only one who had done so since Inari's death.

Maybe her kind were almost extinct. Maybe the last one she had felt truly was the last, and she was alone in the world. And what if she was? How was that any different than her life for the last century? Where had the Myobu been when she had been forced to take a ship to a strange land or when, in desperation, she had taken work in a cabaret? Perhaps her dream of a reunion with her siblings was the silly notion of a young girl. As far as Kitsune went, she was still very young.

Things had changed. Many of the old gods had died. The dragons mostly worked on Wall Street. For years, the Unseelie had been sealed away from the mortal world. The Seelie world was closer to the human world and they came through rarely. The humans were little troubled by the ancient things, the things of the deep water and the dark. They were safe. Mostly.

She walked to the boardwalk. It was mid-morning, Sunday, and the crowds were still thin. By afternoon, more people would come and fill the park with their noise and smell. Mr. Augustus had told her that Elliot would be working at the mirror house with the strange grinning head on the front of it.

Her instructions were clear. Ask this Elliot man on a date. Go on the date. She was supposed to take him to a falafel shop in the strip mall across from the park. She had eaten at the shop once and was familiar with it.

"What are you going to do to him?" she had asked Mr. Augustus.

"I don't run anything outside of the park. So I don't know what they have planned."

"Will they poison him, like they did me? What do they want from him?"

"I don't know. I really don't. I follow orders, and you will too."

She hated that he was right. If she disobeyed, she would be locked away for a few centuries or killed. By obeying, or giving the appearance of obedience, she bought herself time to locate her spirit ball.

"What use is he?" she said. "The man seems perfectly human. Or is this because he's the cousin of that Astrid girl?"

"No, he's a totally normal, totally unremarkable human. An underachiever and a beach bum. And for some reason, you're supposed to get him over to the falafel shop."

She found Elliot at the mirror house, taking tickets. She used a little of her power to make her cheeks a little rounder and rosier. Her face was naturally long and a little angular, so softening it a bit made her prettier. She slowed her movements a tiny bit, and stood up straight. Confidence was sexy. She had read that in a modern women's magazine.

"Hi, Elliot."

"Oh, it's you. Hey. Sorry I couldn't make it to your performance last night. I heard you were great."

She wished he had come. He provided such good power for her. Then she scolded herself. It was wrong to view humans as food. Only the loss of her spirit ball had brought the thought to her mind. She was not fundamentally changed.

"Don't worry about it," she said. "There will be other opportunities. I'm going to be working at the park for a while."

"That's good. Really good."

Now, she had to somehow get him to ask her out. But the magazine had said that men liked a woman who knew what she wanted, whatever that meant. What she wanted was her spirit ball and a plane ticket out of this hot, stinking place. Half desert, half beach, and all noise and cars and humanity. That was Los Angeles. She longed for a snowy place, where she could change into a white fox and run with the brisk, icy wind in her fur. But here she was, in the sun, trying to get a date with a man who was only two decades old.

"I was hoping we could get to know each other better," she said.

Elliot's face lit up, and then he tried to hide it. It was endearing.

"So, what are you doing later?" he asked.

Good! This was it. This was the lead-up to asking a girl out.

"Nothing. Would you like to do something?"

"Yeah. You want to hang out?"

Hang out. That meant to spend time with someone doing an informal activity, such as watching television or playing video games. It was not a date. It would not do.

"No. I would not."

"Oh, well, okay." He turned and took tickets from some park guests. "So, how do you like working at the boardwalk?"

This was not going well. She did not want to chitchat about work. It was also humiliating. She could make men fall down and adore her, but getting one to ask her on a date was now too difficult? She used a little more magic, and smiled sweetly.

"You were really brave around that slaugh. Most, um, people, would be afraid." Damn. She had almost said "humans" instead of people. But maybe it would work. Men liked admiration, even modern ones.

"It was nothing. You and Santiago were the ones who caught it. How did you do it anyway?"

"Oh, Santiago did most of it. I just did a little bit."

"Oh," he said. He looked a little disappointed.

Men liked to think that women were sweet and gentle, right? But the magazine had said that they liked confidence and strength. She had lived among mortals for centuries, but they were still confusing.

"Your cousin was great," she said. "She is very brave."

"Astrid's a tough little bird."

There was an awkward pause. So now they were talking about the girl Astrid. She needed to take control of this situation.

"Elliot, I would like to have dinner with you on a date."

"Oh, I thought ... um, sure. Yeah."

She waited. Now he would tell her when he would pick her up.

"Want to meet somewhere?" he said.

"Why don't you pick me up instead? Then we can go somewhere nearby. Do you like falafel?"

"Sure, that's good."

Excellent. They had a date. She gave him her room number at the Seaside Inn and they agreed that he would pick her up at seven. She was about to leave, when she thought of something.

"Will you be paying for our meal?"

His surprised look told her that she had made a social mistake, but it hardly mattered now. She had secured the date and determined the location and time. Now, she needed to know if she had to get money for it.

"Sure, no problem," he said.

She said good-bye to him and walked toward Mr. Augustus's office to report in. She hadn't mentioned to him that she had recognized Elliot, nor would she. If Elliot was able to do something like appear in the past, perhaps he could help her. She had to play her cards right and make friends with this supposedly ordinary mortal.

CHAPTER 23

"**G**ET IN HERE RIGHT NOW!" yelled Astrid's mother from the kitchen.

Astrid got up from her desk where she had been working on a drawing and went to the kitchen. She found her mother scowling over a pile of something on the kitchen floor. It smelled like vomit, but with a sulfurous reek.

"Your cat puked all over the floor," said her mother. "You need to clean it up."

"Aww, jeez. It smells horrible," she said.

It wasn't the reddish color of the cat kibble and it didn't look like a white hairball. She leaned over it to get a better look. The vomit was partly liquid with many chunks of black meat. A few pieces had a thin coating of grayish skin on one side. The hunks weren't very large, and they looked if they had been ripped off and bolted down.

"Is Cinderella okay? Have you seen her?" she asked. She looked out the kitchen window, but the cat wasn't outside.

"She was well enough to come in here and barf on the floor."

"I need to find her. She might be hurt."

"Don't you dare. You're cleaning that up, right now."

"But she obviously got in a fight with something horrible. She could be dying somewhere."

"You're going to do as I say. That cat isn't good for you. And that barf stinks. You're cleaning it up before you do anything else."

"Wait, you can see that? You can see the black meat?" asked Astrid.

"Of course I can see it. Astrid, look at me."

Astrid did. Her mother grabbed her chin and looked into her eyes.

"Your eyes look red. What are you on?"

"Nothing! I just have had trouble sleeping." She wouldn't tell her mother that she had not slept at all.

"Why can't you sleep? Are you on speed or something?"

"No, of course not." Astrid tried to pull away from her mother's hand, but she gripped her jaw harder.

"You quit lying to me, damn it!" Her mother's fingers pressed painfully into her face.

"I'll clean it up," she said, and her mother released her.

She grabbed a roll of paper towels. Her mother leaned back against the kitchen table. "Make sure you use Lysol on it afterward. I don't want to be smelling that shit all day."

Astrid doubled up a few sheets of paper towels and scooped up as much as she could. She dropped the sickening wad in the kitchen trash. The stench was horrible, even worse when it was close up, and she felt like she was going to vomit.

"You're taking that trash bag out afterwards," said her mother. "Don't try to get out of it."

"I won't," she choked out. The stench filled her mouth and nose, and her stomach heaved. Think of toast, she thought. It always helped her when she felt like vomiting. Eating meat made her feel the same, and her mother had gotten used to her vomiting if forced to eat it. If she thought of toast, nice, dry, plain toast, her stomach sometimes settled.

She knelt down to get more of the vomit when she saw something. It was two long, bulbous fingers, joined by a piece of skin or tendon, she couldn't tell which. Oh God, it was part of a hand. She heaved, and felt the vomit coming up into her mouth.

"You get back here right now!" screamed her mother as Astrid bolted down the hall and vomited in the bathroom toilet. "Don't you ignore me!"

Astrid wiped her mouth with a tissue.

"What the fuck was that?" said her mother from right behind her. She put her hand on the back of Astrid's head, and before she could react, yanked her head up. "You are going to clean up that shit right now."

"I got sick. It smelled so bad."

"Bullshit! You did it on purpose. You're making yourself sick." Her mother shook Astrid's head back and forth by the hair until Astrid reached behind her head and clawed at her hand. It was difficult and she had to wrench and claw, digging her nails in to get free. She rubbed the back of her head.

Her mother was astonished. "How dare you attack your own mother!"

She was in full rage mode now, and there was nothing Astrid could do to stop it. If she was yanking hair, there was no going back.

"I'm sorry. I'll clean it up. I just got sick. I didn't mean to hurt your hand."

"Don't you fucking attack me!"

Astrid managed to dodge the first slap, but she was backed up against the sink, and her mother got a good hit into the side of her face before she could get away.

"Leave me alone! I said I'd clean it!" Astrid screamed and managed to get past her mother. She grabbed Astrid's arm, raking it with her nails, but Astrid got free. "Look, I'm doing it now!"

Astrid ran to the kitchen and got another handful of vomit in some paper towels. If her mother hurt her, she could drop it on her feet, or hold it between them as a deterrent. She imagined mashing it into her mother's face, but the thought made her stomach heave again. She stood numbly, looking at the remaining smear of black and gray liquid on the kitchen floor.

"You are a sick person," said her mother from the entryway, her voice soft. "You are violent and disobedient and you need to learn a lesson. Who the fuck attacks their own mother?"

Astrid stopped and looked up. She expected more screaming, more hitting, not this. Sure, her mother had accused her of attacking her before. If Astrid put her arms up to shield her face, and her mother hurt her hands, she would be accused of fighting back. And naturally, tearing her mother's hands out of her hair or off her arm was a punishable offense. But it had always been punished with hitting.

"Something is wrong with you," her mother said. "You have a problem, and there's only one thing I can do. You're going to learn. You're going to get rid of that cat."

"What? I can't get rid of her. We've had her for years."

"She's a stray that you took in. And she's affecting your mind. Finish cleaning that." She gestured toward the smear on the floor and Astrid hurried to grab the Lysol and more paper towels.

"Just don't do anything to Cinderella," Astrid said.

Her mother watched her clean up the last of the vomit, and then Astrid took out the trash. She found Cinderella lying by the side of the house. She had black blood on parts of her and her own red blood was crusted around her muzzle, her throat and on both ears. One eye was mostly shut and oozed fluid.

"Oh, sweetie," said Astrid as she dropped to her knees. The cat's breathing was rapid and shallow and her good eye looked unfocused. In the distance, a trash truck roared and then stopped to pick up someone's garbage. The garage door banged shut and then her mother was beside her.

"Put her in now." She held out a white cardboard cat carrier. "She's going to the pound."

"No! You can't take her. She's hurt. She needs to go to the vet. Look at her. C'mon, please."

Her mother had a look in her eye, a mix of pleasure and determination. "We can't afford a vet. You're going to put her in the carrier right now. We're taking her to the pound."

"I'm not going to. You can hit me all you want. Come on," Astrid put her hands behind her back. "Go ahead and hit me all you want. I won't even move."

"You are so screwed up. Something about that cat is messing up your mind and making you act out. And it's my job to teach you to obey your mother. Now do it."

"No." Astrid glared at her. The trash truck was closer now, maybe even on their street.

"Then I'm taking the kittens." Her mother didn't move to get them, but watched her. Astrid looked at Cinderella, whose eyes were closed now. She looked almost dead.

"Please," she begged. "I'll be good. I'm sorry, okay? I'm sorry." Tears stung her eyes and she tried to breathe in and out, but a sob escaped her. "Don't take my cat. Please."

"Then the kittens. They'll all go."

"They're too little. They're still nursing."

Her mother smiled then, and Astrid's blood ran cold. Her mother enjoyed this, had always enjoyed it. She loved the hurt, being able to do harm and also to end it whenever she wished. She controlled it all, the hugs and kindness, the viciousness and cruelty. And Astrid could do nothing about it.

If she did not make a choice now, her mother would get Cinderella and her kittens and take them all to the pound while Astrid was at work. Astrid could maybe call in sick, but she'd eventually lose her job.

"Put her in right now, or I'll take those fucking kittens and put them all in the trash can right now."

"No! Please."

"Now."

"You evil bitch!" Astrid screamed, tears sliding free from her eyes. Her nose was snotty, and she swiped it with the back of her hand.

Her mother slapped her, hard, but it didn't matter. None of it mattered. Her mother liked hurting her, hitting her, tearing out her heart. And now she would take away Astrid's friend. Cinderella's good eye opened again, and she watched Astrid with a glazed look.

"Fine," said her mother and dropped the box. She turned to go inside.

"Wait," said Astrid. Her mother stopped and turned, satisfied. She had a little smile as Astrid lifted Cinderella into the box and fastened the lid. The cat gave a weak meow and Astrid murmured an apology. But Cinderella would want her kittens safe. Even if her mother didn't manage to get the kittens in the trashcan or if Astrid screamed for the trash truck driver to not take that can, her mother would find another way.

As long as there was something Astrid loved, there would be another way. Art school or the money to get there, the cats, the little girl who had lived down the street. Her mother had told the girl's parents that Astrid had mental problems, and they had never let her come over again. There would always be something.

"Come on then. Glad you're learning." Her mother led the way to the car, and Astrid stopped at the open door. She didn't want to get in the car.

Her mother slipped into the driver's seat and leaned down so she could see Astrid through the passenger window. "You want me to get the kittens?"

Of course she wanted to see the reaction. When Astrid shook her head and climbed in, her mother pressed her lips together and nodded once in satisfaction. She started the car.

Astrid reached her fingers through the air holes in the box. She found a spot on Cinderella's side that was not injured and she stroked her.

"I'm sorry. I'll take care of your babies," she whispered through one of the top air holes.

Astrid cried the entire way to the pound, and when they stood at the desk inside, she held the carrier to her body as her mother filled out the forms. The man behind the desk asked her questions. He was tall and thin and had an Irish accent.

"Put it down," said her mother.

"Please don't do this," Astrid cried. The uniformed man gave her a sympathetic look.

Her mother tried to take the box, but she pulled away. The man came out from behind the counter and reached for it, gently, not forcing her.

"She'll be all right," he said. His voice was gentle, and his accent gave the words a sweet lilt. He was trying to be kind. Astrid let Cinderella go.

"Please take care of her. She's hurt. She got in a fight. She needs a vet."

"She's a stray," said Astrid's mother. "And she might have rabies or something."

"She doesn't!"

But Astrid's mother took her hand and crushed it so hard that it felt like the bones were rubbing together. It might bruise, but Astrid just left her hand limp. She wouldn't give her mother the satisfaction of pulling away or seeing her hurt.

"Come on," her mother pulled her toward the door.

"I'll be back tomorrow," said Astrid to the man. "I'm turning eighteen and I can take her. Can you keep her that long?"

"She's very upset," said her mother.

"Just until tomorrow!"

"The kittens," hissed her mother, and Astrid followed her through the doorway. She could still hurt the kittens. There was nothing stopping her. She could get rid of them one by one if she wanted to, stretching it on for months.

Astrid got into the car. Her breath still came in sobs, but there were no more tears and her nose wasn't running any more. There was exhaustion, sadness, and a serene sort of acceptance. She knew what her mother was. There was no more illusion.

It was almost like seeing twice, like the jacaranda and cherry blossoms and the dead baby slaugh that her mother thought was a rock. But this was deeper and worse. She knew what her mother was, and would always be.

"Quit carrying on," said her mother. "I'm hungry. Want to get something?"

"You killed my cat. And no."

"Oh, come on. I can't be expected to take care of your strays. If you weren't going away to that hippy art school, you could have taken care of her yourself. It's your own fault she had to go."

"You wanted me to get out of the house. Now you want me to stay?"

"No, I've done all I can. I've spoiled you, that's what. I've given you everything, worked my fingers to the bone, and you're ungrateful and filled with so much hate that I just can't deal with you anymore. I have to let you go."

It didn't matter. None of the words hit their mark, because none of it mattered. It was over. She watched the neighborhood fly by outside the window and hoped Cinderella wasn't already dead.

CHAPTER 24

AFTER WORK, ELLIOT WENT TO his trailer, took a quick shower and dressed in clean clothes. He couldn't believe that someone like Yukiko would want to go out with him. Well, at first she hadn't wanted to, but then she had. Well, he understood that. He worked at a boardwalk and lived in a trailer. He was no catch.

He walked the few blocks to the Seaside Inn. It was a lucky thing it was close, as he had no car and would hate to take a girl out by riding the bus.

When Yukiko answered the door she was still wearing the pale blue sundress from earlier in the day, but she had put on a white cardigan to ward off the night chill. It made her look smaller, a little different. It was odd, because each time he had seen her, she seemed just a little bit different. Then he remembered thinking that thought before. It was déjà vu, seeing her in her blue sundress and standing in the half-twilight of the summer evening. The moment passed, and he remembered that he had dreamt of this recently. It had only been a few weeks ago, but before he had ever seen Yukiko.

It was odd. Since he was a little boy, he had experienced these times of déjà vu that didn't conform to the true definition. And the incidents seemed to be getting more frequent as he got older.

They made small talk as they walked, but Yukiko didn't seem like she was having a good time. Come to think of it, he hadn't seen her smile often, and had never heard her laugh. Well, some people were more serious than others. She was a dancer, an artist, and they were entitled to be a little temperamental.

The Falafel Hut was close by, and wasn't too crowded for a Sunday night. Elliot held the door for Yukiko and she murmured a thanks. The menu was up over the registers and while Yukiko looked it over, Elliot studied the mural on the side wall. It was of Prometheus, the Titan who carried a stolen torch from the world of the gods to give fire to mankind. The Titan bent over a group of huddled humans, offering them the flame. What an odd choice for a restaurant mural. He could imagine lots of nicer scenes for a Greek restaurant, even one in a strip mall. The other side of the room was better. It had an image of graceful nymphs dancing in a clearing. He paid for their meals and they picked a table.

"So how did you end up as a performer?" Elliot asked.

"Oh, I've done various types of work. Nothing steady. I just pick up things where I can."

"So how did you end up with the Chumash show anyway?"

"Red Fawn decided to help me out. So she let me do my bit at the end of the regular show."

The food came, and Elliot worked on his falafel wrap and soda. His soda tasted sweeter than normal, but maybe it was just because the tzatziki sauce on the falafel was so tart. Or maybe they had put too much syrup in the soda machine. He set down the cup, and experienced déjà vu again as he took another bite. The moment passed.

"Doesn't yours taste good?" he asked Yukiko. She looked as if she wasn't enjoying her food and was glancing at his plate occasionally.

"It's fine." She looked away.

Then he glanced at the mural behind her. Prometheus was now chained to a rock by wrists and ankles and a giant, sharp-beaked eagle perched on a twisted tree branch just above him. The Titan's mouth was opened in a scream of terror. Elliot knew the story. As punishment for stealing the sacred fire, the Titan was chained to a rock where an eagle came and ate his liver daily. Being immortal, it grew back each night.

"What the hell?" he said. "That painting. It's different."

And as he said it, he remembered dreaming that he had said it. He spun around to look at the other mural, but the nymphs were still dancing in the clearing. He hadn't remembered that one of them was looking out at the viewer. Her eyes were large and black and her dark hair was full and curly.

"What's wrong? Are you okay?" asked Yukiko. He caught her looking at his food again.

"That painting of Prometheus," he said. "Did you see it when we came in?"

"Yeah." She turned to look at it.

"It's different now."

She turned back. "It's always been that way. I've been in here before and I remember it."

"I mean, it's still Prometheus, but it was different before."

Oddly, she looked as if she believed him.

"Let's get out of here," she said. "Don't eat any more of that." She stood and glanced from person to person behind the counter, as if one of them was going to leap over and attack them.

Her dress was light purple now. He knew it had been blue before. He remembered it. And he remembered this, the feeling of disorientation and noticing her dress, the look she had, like a hunted animal, but with a touch of ferocity. Elliot got up, and as they left, he glanced at Prometheus, with the eagle overhead. It had not changed. Across from him were the nymphs, all of them blonde and blue-eyed.

They left the shop and started walking, not toward the Seaside Inn, but toward Luna Park. Yukiko was leading, but without really seeming to. She did not look like she was having a fun time, and why would she? Her date was seeing things. Maybe seeing those horrible monsters in the mirror house had been another hallucination. But Astrid had seen them too.

"I didn't imagine the slaugh, right?" he said softly.

"No, that was real."

"Your dress used to be blue."

"No, it was lavender. Always has been."

As they walked, he studied the shops, the cars, the street signs. All of it was as it should be.

"Do you have any enemies, Elliot?" she asked.

"That's a weird question. No."

"Is there anything special about you? Anything strange?"

"No. I'm nobody."

"I'm wondering if someone would want to poison you, make you hallucinate."

That had to be it. He had been thinking too much of his weird déjà vu dreams and not enough of ordinary causes. He had dropped acid once with some of his friends at a beach bonfire, but it had been nothing like this. But there were other drugs, weird things that could alter the senses. But all he had eaten was the food from the Falafel Hut, and no one else had been affected. Before that, he had eaten his packed lunch, cereal and milk for breakfast, water, a soda. There would have been no opportunity for anyone to give him anything.

They got close to the pier, and the wind whipped up. Yukiko pulled her arms tight around her middle, and Elliot wished he had worn a jacket so he could offer it to her.

Things here were normal. But he would not have noticed if a shop or someone's shirt had changed if he hadn't seen them before. At the end of the pier, Yukiko looked him straight in the face.

"Feel better?"

"Yeah."

"This place, out by the water is a good place," she said. "It makes it easier to think."

He had a feeling there was more to it, and he remembered how Astrid had asked about the cherry and jacaranda blossoms. They leaned out over the railing and watched the sea foam swirl around the thick, barnacle-encrusted pilings that supported the pier. At Luna Park, the Ferris wheel turned, its orange and yellow lights flashing in a starburst pattern. The other rides lit up, green and blue, white and red.

He wanted to take Yukiko somewhere fun, a movie or maybe even Luna Park, if she wanted to. He was sick of it, but if she was new in town, she would probably like it.

"Where are you from? Originally, I mean," he asked.

"Japan. I thought you could guess."

"Well, I guessed you were Japanese, but you sound like you were born here."

"No, I was born there." She lifted her eyes to the horizon, and just as it had been when he had watched her on the stage, he felt a tinge of longing in her.

"You came here really young then?"

"Why do you say that?"

"You don't have an accent."

She was still looking out over the water, and something about the light made her face look a little longer, a little more angular. She glanced over at him, and her face regained its regular contours.

"Yeah, I was young."

"Look!" he said, pointing. "See the dolphin?"

A triangular fin cut through the water and then disappeared. Yukiko had missed it. An oil rig in the distance turned its lights on and glittered white, like a warm beacon out on the water.

"Which island is that?" asked Yukiko.

In the distance stretched the grayish green shape of one of the Channel Islands. After asking for the location of the restrooms, the second most commonly asked question from tourists was if the island was Hawaii. Elliot could never keep a straight face when they asked that, but he didn't tease them for their ignorance.

"That's Santa Maria Island. There are more islands up north toward Santa Barbara."

"And out that way, I see an area of dark water," she said. She sounded almost excited about it.

"Yeah, it's a giant submerged rock. I've taken my board out there."

"Oh," she sounded disappointed.

"Do you want to go walk up the beach?" He supposed a walk on the beach wasn't too bad for first date entertainment. They went down the concrete steps, took off their shoes and headed up the beach.

"When I was young," said Yukiko, "there was a spot of dark water. I was swimming with some other young ones. Playing in the water, pretty far out. And then one of the children yelled that the dark spot below us was a dead whale. I hadn't noticed it before, and it was right under me. I was terrified. Knowing that this huge dead thing was under me, decaying, and that the water touching it was also touching me. And then I thought of its huge mouth, and what would happen if I sank down into that mouth."

"That's messed up," he said, unable to repress a smile, but she just looked out over the water.

"Probably," she said. "It's probably messed up. I mean, the whole ocean is filled with dead things, ocean things being born and mating and dying and decaying. I had just never thought of it before."

"You're an odd girl," he said. He didn't mean it as an insult, and her indifferent shrug told him that she hadn't taken it as such.

"I think the thing that got to me was that one moment, I was safe and happy and having fun. And then the next moment, I saw this danger just beneath." A minute later she asked, "Do you have family out of town?"

"My dad lives in San Diego."

"You should go visit him. Things here, with the slaugh, with your cousin, it's not safe."

"If it's not safe, then I'll get Astrid and my mom and aunt out."

"But what if Astrid was the center of it?"

"You mean with the slaugh? Then I'd stay and stick those things in metal boxes or do whatever I had to."

"You're like that, aren't you?" she said. "You wouldn't leave?"

"I guess." He was uncomfortable. He wouldn't leave, but that was just basic decency, nothing to be commended.

"Just think about it, okay? Things might get bad, and no one would blame you for getting out."

"If it's bad enough for people to leave, then all the more reason for me to stay."

"I thought you'd say something like that," said Yukiko and kissed his cheek.

CHAPTER 25

ASTRID WALKED THROUGH THE AFTERNOON heat, carrying the box of kittens. She had taken her last twenty dollars from its hiding place in a book in her room and had grabbed her purse as soon as she and her mother arrived home. Of course, she had taken the box with the kittens with her. She couldn't trust her mother with them, not now and not ever.

She stopped to rest at a park, set the kittens down on a picnic table and pulled the towel off of the top of the box. She got out her phone to text a few friends, asking if anyone could take the cats. Even if someone could only keep them a few weeks, she might be able to find an apartment that allowed cats in New York.

For today, the main concern was feeding the kittens. Little white Runt was listless and slept most of the time. The other two, the striped male and female were more active. The little female had very dark stripes just over her eyes, like eyebrows. Astrid decided to name her Frieda, after the artist Frieda Kahlo. And the boy would be Diego, after Diego Rivera. There, now she had named them. Now she was emotionally attached.

"Your mama was a hero," she said as she pulled the towel back over the box to shade them and continued on.

She turned a corner and took the kittens inside the pet and feed store. An employee helped her find kitten formula mix and a plastic bottle with a specially shaped rubber nipple. Astrid also learned how to wipe the kitten's rear ends with a washcloth to simulate their mother's tongue. They wouldn't urinate or defecate otherwise. It was disgusting, but Astrid would do it. Their mother had saved all four of them, and Astrid had made a promise. She would not allow kitten butts and poop to stop her.

After paying for everything, she filled the bottle with some powdered formula and got some water from the drinking fountain near the restrooms. She shook it and shoved it into the waistband of her pants. Right now, it was too cold, but her body heat and the hot summer air would warm it up soon enough.

On the way back home, she stopped at the park to feed the kittens. When she arrived home, her mother was talking on the phone in the kitchen. If Astrid got around the corner quickly, her mother wouldn't see her.

Her mother left her alone the rest of the evening, and Astrid fed the kittens and wiped their bottoms again before lying down in bed. She didn't want to sleep, but she wasn't going to be able to stay awake forever. If the slaugh and its baby were gone and the salt wards held, then that was all she could reasonably hope for. She read until late, fed the kittens one last time, and eventually slept.

The next morning, she got a text from Elliot and one from a friend wishing her a happy eighteenth birthday. Before she even brushed her teeth or got dressed, she signed all of the student loan and grant paperwork and slipped it into the enclosed envelope. She would go to the pound, stop by Elliot's trailer to get her paycheck, open a checking account at the bank, take the envelope to the post office and get it sent certified mail. Then she would go in to work for the evening shift. Maybe she could leave the kittens in the staff room or hide them behind the pretzel cart. She headed for the kitchen to grab something for breakfast.

"Happy Birthday, sweetheart," her mother said and kissed her cheek. She tried not to flinch.

"Thanks."

"I got you something. Wait here."

Astrid got a glass of orange juice and made a quick peanut butter sandwich for lunch. A glance at the interior of the refrigerator showed that her mother had picked up a few things from the store. With that and the fact that she had bought a gift, it looked like she had been paid.

There were two packages for Astrid to unwrap. The first was a how-to book on figure drawing. The second was a coffee table art book with glossy photographs of various pieces of modern art.

"I thought you'd like it," said her mother. "It's kind of weird and ugly and no one gets it. It's kind of like the stuff you draw, modern and everything."

Astrid's work would be classified more as surrealism, sometimes dark surrealism, but was not technically modern art, but she didn't expect her mother to appreciate the distinction. And she wasn't going to rise to her mother's bait of calling her work ugly. A lot of it was ugly. That was sort of the point. She couldn't draw a pretty angel to save her life. They always came out with wings feathered with knife blades or with twisted skeletal bodies. Sure, she had done some less dramatic stuff, but on the whole, her work was dark.

"There's even an artist in there who uses her own blood," said her mother.

"I think I'll stick with paint and pencils, at least for now."

"Yeah, who knows what they'll teach you at that crazy school in New York. You'll be smearing dog crap on a picture of the president in no time."

Her mother smiled, and Astrid couldn't help but smile back a little. Her mother was a mess, but today, she was trying.

"I can't believe my baby is all grown up."

"I guess," Astrid said and finished packing an apple, a

pack of cheese and crackers and a soda for her lunch.

"Oh, I looked up how much your room would rent for," her mother said. "It would be close to five hundred a month. And I'll let you know how much half of utilities will be. Probably close to $200. You got paid Friday, right?"

"I was hoping I could save some for New York," Astrid said, but she knew this conversation was futile.

"Well I need to pay the mortgage and electric bill."

"Fine. I'll get you a check by the end of the week."

She wasn't going to fight. Besides, once she had Cinderella back, her mother might not allow her stay at all. If Elliot was willing to take Cinderella for a few months, that might work.

"But you got paid Friday," said her mother.

"Yeah, but it's not much. And you have the five hundred you took from me the other day. Speaking of which, you took the money in my desk and said you'd pay it back. You got paid Friday too, right?"

"I did, but I had bills."

"You said you'd pay it back."

"I paid it back right there!" Her mother pointed to the two books. "And those expensive pencils I got you last week."

"Those were gifts. You can't charge me for gifts."

"I can't believe you. I buy you these really nice things that are much better than anything I ever got, give you a pizza party, let you stay here, and all you can think of is getting money from me. I swear, you're just like your father."

Astrid was about to walk out of the room with her lunch, but she just couldn't.

"You stole my money and now you're refusing to pay it back. Keep the money if you want, but admit that you stole it."

"You little witch," her mother took a step toward her and Astrid bolted from the room, grabbed her purse and the kitten box and opened the front door.

On the doorstep sat an envelope with no return address and no postage. Well, it was her birthday after all. She set everything down and opened it to find a tiny blank sketch book, no bigger across than a credit card, and a letter.

Astrid,

I am so proud of you. Happy Birthday.

Love,
Grandpa

"Who sent you that?" asked her mother. Astrid jumped at how close her mother was. "Who is this grandpa person?" She grabbed the letter. "This is sick, Astrid. Is this one of your johns?"

"What?"

"I said, is this one of your johns?"

"No. No, of course not. I'm not a hooker."

"Aren't you? How many have you slept with?"

"Stop it."

"I don't see any regular boyfriends coming around. You must get around."

"It's not like that."

"No? Then tell me, how many have you slept with. Was it under my roof?"

"None, okay? None." She hadn't ever slept with anyone, hadn't dated, nothing.

Her mother looked surprised. Then her look grew knowing.

"Well, I guess I can understand that. No wonder you're a virgin. Look at you. You've always had problems. Even when you were a baby, we took you to doctor after doctor, trying to figure out why you wouldn't stop crying. Nothing was ever wrong with you, but you screamed like you were being poked with a hot iron. Then, we took you to a shrink when you were four to find out what was wrong with you. You were talking to yourself and drawing all this scary shit. You need to go get psychiatric help."

"What I need is to get to the pound."

"Don't bother. I'm sure that filthy thing died. It was disgusting."

"She was not. And I'm going to get her back."

"If you do that, then don't bother coming back."

"Then give me my five hundred in rent money and I'll go."

"You little bitch. You ungrateful little bitch. I gave up my whole life for you, my marriage, everything. And this is how you turn out, a lying, ungrateful little bitch."

Astrid grabbed the kitten box, the financial aid envelope and her purse, pushed open the screen and backed out.

"You know what?" her mother yelled. "You're sick. You're fucking sick. Don't bother coming back. I don't ever want to see you again!"

Astrid headed down the driveway, and spun around as the screen door banged shut. Her mother was following her.

"And another thing," she shouted. "Don't you call your aunt. I'm telling her what you did. You're on your own from now on."

"Fine," said Astrid.

"You going to call this grandpa guy?" she held up the letter. "He's the one who sent that money too, right? Who is this guy?"

"It's my grandfather. Your father," said Astrid.

Her mother looked at the letter again.

"Astrid, my father died a year after you were born."

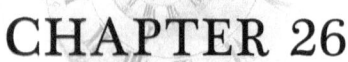

CHAPTER 26

"Shit, Astrid, there's barely enough room for me," Elliot said. Once again, Astrid sat at his little table, this time with a box of squirming kittens. She mixed up a bottle of kitten formula and fed them.

"It's either here or the homeless shelter, and they don't allow animals."

"No, no. You can't go to the shelter," he said. He had stayed there, and though it wasn't dangerous, it wasn't a place he'd feel all right sending his young female cousin. He had wondered how long it would be until Astrid left or got kicked out of her mother's house. It looked like she hadn't been able to hold out until August after all.

"Thanks. It's only for six weeks. Then I'll be out of your hair."

"Just don't clutter up the bathroom with all your girl stuff."

"Deal, I just need to get my paycheck so I'll have money to get Cinderella out of the pound. I have to be back by three for work."

A cat and kittens, on top of Astrid staying in the trailer. The place was going to be crowded, but what could he do? It wasn't like his mother would take them in either.

"I'll go with you to the pound," he said. "I'm off today."

Astrid stroked the kittens and spoke softly to them while Elliot washed his breakfast dishes.

"So, what did you do to get kicked out?" he asked.

"She tried to get Cinderella killed, stole my college

money and she's crazy. And I got another package from our grandfather."

"Yeah? What was it this time?"

"A really small blank sketch pad."

"That's a bit of a letdown. No grand inheritance upon your attainment of adulthood?"

"Sadly no. But my mom said that our grandfather died a year after I was born."

"I wouldn't know about that. My mother won't talk about either him or our grandmother. But getting packages from a dead guy is kind of cool. Maybe he set something up with a lawyer to send you things each year after he died."

"You watch too many weird TV shows. If he had enough to hire a lawyer, then where's the inheritance for us? Aside from our mothers, we're his only living relatives."

"Well, I'm sure we'll get a telegram any minute now," said Elliot.

"Wouldn't that be something?" she said and looked out the window. "We could have cars and get apartments and shop at nice stores."

"Forget about apartments, we could buy houses."

"I guess we could. But not anything too big, because they're too much work to clean."

"We'd get maids."

"Oh, yeah. A maid."

She was still looking out the window, but he could tell her mind was elsewhere. Then, he heard her sniffle and she wiped her eyes.

He went to the bathroom and got a handful of toilet paper. "Here." He handed it to her.

He hated it when she cried. She rarely did, but when it happened, it opened up something old and deep in him. He couldn't help her. He couldn't help his mother, or his aunt. He could barely help himself, and he hated it.

"Don't be sad about getting away from her," he said. "She's not healthy. There's something wrong with her."

Astrid shook her head. "It's just, everything didn't turn out how it was supposed to. I was supposed to go to New York."

"And you will. You sent in the papers. Now they'll give you money and you go. You can apply for a credit card and use that for whatever you need until you get on your feet."

"I know. I just ... I guess I just wanted her to be proud of me."

Elliot sighed and looked out to see what Astrid was watching outside. A few surfers were out, and he wished he could join them. A man threw a Frisbee for a wet dog.

He didn't know what to say. He refused to tell her that her mother was proud of her deep down. Even if it might be true, he didn't want to give Astrid false hope. The farther she was from the craziness here, the better.

"And I have to wipe their butts," she muttered. "It's disgusting."

"What?"

"The kittens. I need a washrag."

After Elliot had sacrificed his rattiest washrag for the kittens, they took the bus to the animal shelter. Elliot held the box of kittens while Astrid rushed inside.

"There was a white cat dropped off yesterday," she said to the woman inside. "She was in a fight and was hurt pretty badly. I'm here to claim her."

"A white cat?"

"Yeah, she would have needed a vet."

The woman checked the computer. "I'm not seeing anything like that. You sure it was yesterday?"

"Definitely. It was about noon or so."

She checked again. "Still not finding any drop offs yesterday matching that description. Go ahead and look through the cages."

They passed through a door and into the cat area of the shelter. The long room smelled of air freshener and cat litter. They each looked through the cages, and then looked again. No Cinderella.

"Where is she?" asked Astrid, panic rising in her voice.

She stormed out of the cat area and into the front office. Elliot followed.

"Did she die?" she demanded at the front desk. "She was injured."

"I didn't see any record," said the woman.

"Maybe she was never checked in correctly. Maybe they took her straight back to whatever medical area you have."

"We have a vet tech here," said the woman. "Let me get him."

She left the two of them in the front reception area. Faded posters encouraging pet adoption and some watercolors of dogs and cats covered the walls. Astrid shifted her weight from foot to foot, her arms wrapped tight around her body. She adored that cat, and after Elliot had heard the story of the gray baby slaugh that Cinderella had killed, he knew Astrid would be a wreck if they didn't find her.

A man came through the door. "I was here all day yesterday, and I didn't see a cat like that. Are you sure it was surrendered at this pound?"

"Yes, I'm sure. I came in myself. My mom made me get rid of her. We stood right in this spot."

"Who was here when you surrendered the animal?"

A split second before the man had said it, Elliot remembered hearing this before. But this time, something was different; he could anticipate the conversation a few words ahead.

"There was a man here who took her," said Astrid. "He was tall and skinny and he had an Irish accent."

The vet tech and woman exchanged a look.

"I'm sorry, but we don't have anyone who works here like that," said the woman. "There are three of us who work the front desk."

Elliot and Astrid double- and triple-checked the cat cages, and the woman at the desk called the county shelter. Cinderella was nowhere to be found.

Elliot put his arm around Astrid's shoulder as she carried the kittens to the bus stop.

"We'll take the train up to the county shelter tomorrow," he said. "Their records must have gotten messed up. They won't adopt her out or anything for at least a few weeks. They wait for someone to claim the animal first."

"She won't be there," Astrid said. "She probably died and they just didn't do her paperwork."

"Cinderella was a tough cat. She might have survived."

They sat on the bus bench and waited, watching the passing pedestrians and cars.

"Elliot, is that you?" Creepy Mick waved as he came toward them.

"Hey, Mick. You're a little far from the beach, aren't you?"

"I got word from the birdman."

He didn't want Mick to go on about the birdman or Vietnam or anything else right now.

"Where have you been staying?" Elliot asked.

"No, no. That doesn't matter. I talked with the birdman again. He said that she was going to be okay." Mick glanced at Astrid.

"She's fine," said Elliot. He didn't want Mick bothering Astrid.

"Oh, good," said Mick. "I heard there was a ruckus and she'd been hurt."

The bus pulled up and Astrid climbed on board.

"I have to go," Elliot said.

"Oh, sure," said Mick. "I just heard she was bloodied up real bad. But I'm glad she's all right."

CHAPTER 27

I T WAS CLOSE TO SUNSET, and Yukiko leaned on the wooden railing, face into the cool ocean wind. She had to do this before it got dark, but she dreaded it. She had danced in Red Fawn's show, collecting as much energy as she could, and now she was as powerful as she could hope to be.

Out in the distance swirled the dark water, the spot where a rock barely broke the surface and where there seemed to be some kind of large shadow. While she had stood at the pier earlier that day, she had seen something out there, just for an instant. It was a being she feared and needed, a creature that in some ways was more dangerous than Coyote, and one that was nearly impossible to bargain with. If the Seelie had entrusted her spirit ball to this creature, then she would go to it, no matter how much it terrified her.

She knew that the Seelie would not let her go willingly. She had heard tales of Kitsune being enslaved by the theft of their spirit ball, but she had never experienced it herself, nor had such a thing happened to anyone she had known. It was a thing that happened in old stories, not to real people. But here she was, at this vile borderland, a half-being.

She went down to the beach and walked under the pier, as far back against the land as she could. Then, she whispered an ancient prayer to Inari, asking for his strength, and to The Lady, requesting her protection. There was no answer. There never was.

Lowering herself into the sand, she changed into a fox. Her limbs felt lithe and quick, her teeth and jaws ready to snap. The wind ruffled her fur, and she felt every inch of the sensation, from the tip of her moist nose to the end of her tail.

She licked her muzzle and inhaled. The action of smelling was so much easier in this form, so much more natural. There was the ocean smell, the woody scent of the pier, the remaining smell of her human body clinging to the clothing that lay in a pile. No Seelie. And no spirit ball.

She trotted out into the water and jumped in, paddling out with a quick, steady rhythm of her paws. She was only an average swimmer, and now and then a wave slapped into her face. The salt water stung her eyes and nose, but she kept on.

If anyone had seen her, they would think she was a stray dog. It had happened many times before. So few people had ever seen a live fox, and never a snow white one. She wouldn't use any of her power to disguise herself. As long as no Seelie saw her, she was safe.

She swam out past the pier and turned in the direction of the rock, keeping her muzzle high, moving slowly and steadily. The farther she went, the less turbulent the water was, but the more tempting she would be to the things that lived in the sea. She felt a few things, moving in the deep, but none were interested in her.

Swimming with the dead, she thought. The ocean was full of dead things and, worse, live things. There was always something down there, in the dark, waiting. And going into the water in her human form would attract them. Regular humans were usually safe, but a creature like her out of its natural form would be like a beacon in the dark to the things of the deep.

She scrambled up onto the slick rock and shook her dripping fur, sending droplets flying. She paused to catch her breath. The rock was cold and slippery, worn by centuries of waves and sand. She had not checked the tides, but even if the water rose, she would have enough time for her bargaining.

Then she sat back on her haunches, lifted her head and called out in a language older than the human languages. She did not know the name of the creature, naturally, but there was a word for all sentient ocean-dwellers, and she used that word.

The instant the word left her mouth, she felt the creature's presence. It was far out in the water, and deep down, almost as far out as Santa Maria Island. She waited, sensing its approach. She breathed fast and hard, and not from exertion. The thing was coming, it was large, and it could kill a little animal like her so easily. One blow, and she would be a meal, or perhaps only a snack. She was out of her element, powerless, young and alone. She shivered as the wind whipped at her body. It was coming, stirring from its place below, moving closer.

But she was Myobu. Her kind had stood before the thrones of emperors and at the altars of gods. Her kind did not run, and they did not cringe from other beings, no matter how terrible and powerful. She forced ears forward and her tail up and away from her body. She would not greet this creature like a frightened kit.

The creature did her a courtesy, by surfacing about ten yards away. It was black and smooth, a whale, or rather, it took the appearance of a black and white whale. It was diseased and rotted, and as it came closer, she saw the ripped black dorsal fin and smelled the stench of the creature. A dead whale. The thing was appearing as a dead orca whale. A killer whale, the Americans called it. Its face was closer now, huge under the water, and as it drew close, she saw that it was missing an eye. The socket was ragged, bloody and partially blackened with rot.

This was good. It was trying to frighten her by picking something from her past that she would fear. It had gained the knowledge when she had summoned it, but that was the price one paid when one summoned creatures from the deep. You saw them, and they saw you. It was never pleasant.

Yukiko did not back up as the great head of the dead whale surfaced. She gave a brief nod, an acknowledgement of meeting an equal. It turned to regard her with its good eye.

"Greetings deep-dweller," Yukiko said. "May I speak with you?"

"Leave now, or you will die," it said. Its mouth was filled with sharp, meat-ripping teeth and its tongue was like a giant pink ham. It could eat her in one bite.

"I surely will not die. Please now, let us not play games. I appeared to you in my true form. Would you not do me the same courtesy?"

"You must go."

Yukiko sniffed now that the thing's head was out of the water and close to her. Her spirit ball. She felt the sparkling honey scent of it. The creature had been in contact with it recently.

"Please, dark-swimmer. You are in possession of my spirit ball, and I would speak with you."

"You will not take it."

"I know. I could not force you to give it to me, even if I wished to. But if my guess is correct, you are not keeping it of your own free will. Neither of us is free."

The eye moved but the whale did not speak.

"I can make an offer," said Yukiko. "I will give you a year of my service, if at the end of that year you free me."

The whale laughed, the sound of rocks rolling at the bottom of the sea, of waves moving deep in the dark.

"Little fox, I am under a contract that would not allow it."

"How can one as old and strong as you are be imprisoned? I do not understand."

"You should leave."

"Please, Lady of the Sea, help me. For both of us are prisoners to the same masters."

"We are."

The whale changed then, and became a woman with a fish's tail. But she looked nothing like the pretty mermaids from children's books or the neon signs at the entrance to the boardwalk. This creature was dark-skinned, a woman of Africa before white men came and raped or took willing wives, lightening the skin of their descendants. Her curly hair hung in tight dripping coils as she climbed up beside Yukiko. Her tail was powerful and grayish black, with two short pointed fins on its length and a vertical scimitar of a tail, like a shark.

She seated herself beside Yukiko and curled her fearsome tail until she was completely out of the water. It was another little courtesy, this one merely symbolic. She was removing herself from her element, just as Yukiko was out of hers. Of course, the sea woman could simply leap back into the water, but Yukiko noticed the gesture and appreciated it.

This creature was old, even for her kind. Plenty of silver streaked the black of her hair and her breasts were flat and pendulous, her stomach soft, and the skin of her face had lost its firmness.

"I have never met one of your kind," Yukiko said. "You are beautiful." And she was. She was a centuries-old creature of the dark places where humans and Kitsune had never gone and never would. She was alien, and yet, they were sisters, of a sort.

"And I have never met one of yours, though I summered off the Japanese coast a few times in my youth."

Yukiko thought then of the humans on the pier, and how any of them might see a mermaid woman and a white dog sitting on a rock in the water. The sun was almost gone, but there was enough light for someone to see. By

HEATHER BLACKWOOD

nature, otherkind were reticent to be seen. Perhaps the sea woman was too old to care. Or perhaps, as a prisoner, she also had nothing to lose.

"You wonder why I come to you," said the sea woman. "I come to tell you that now is not the time for your escape."

"What do you mean?"

"The Seelie are cunning and the plan that you have fallen into has been in motion for a long time. The Seelie, unlike your kind or mine, have long-seers, and they heed what they say. They work in groups and have leaders. We are, perhaps, too individual, too independent. Too catlike."

She smiled at Yukiko's little huff of protest. The sea woman's teeth were small and pointed.

"My advice to you, little fox, is to wait. Bide your time. Then use your trickery to escape."

But she had no trickery. No plan. She felt nothing like her powerful ancestors.

"This is slavery," Yukiko said. "It is monstrous."

"Well, you are young yet. It is the way of humans and some otherkind to enslave. The last century saw the death of your emperor and your god. And the century before that saw the end of slavery on this continent. But that is only a small part of the grander picture."

"You are enslaved also. How did the Seelie do it? And why can't you get free?"

"I was captured fairly, though through trickery, of course. I am theirs for a century, no more. They will keep you for longer."

"They'll keep me forever."

"Not necessarily. Your kind always get free. It may take a century or two."

"I can't wait that long."

The woman shrugged, a strangely human gesture. "Time passes. We live on."

"How did you come here? To California?"

"We are, both of us, far from home, are we not? I was

170

brought unwillingly to the Caribbean, on a slave ship. I lived off the Western coast of Africa, moving up and down the land with the seasons, sending fish to the humans, who are, after all, my kin. I sent shells and smooth rocks for the children to find, and I enjoyed watching them. One day, I was on shore, as I can change and take human form, just as you can. I had gone inland, visiting with some of my grandson's family."

"Your grandson was human?"

"More or less. But yes, human. And the slavers who came were human. We were captured, some of us, taken to a ship, chained together in a fetid, stinking hold. Packed together so tightly that I could feel the people on either side of me breathing when they slept. Being out of contact with the sea, I could not change back or escape.

"The men who took us were doing business, nothing more. We were cargo to them. Those of us who tried to starve themselves were beaten. They would smash out a man's teeth and force-feed him. If you tried to leap overboard, they would lash you. Then they would run a rope under the boat, tie it tightly about your waist, drag you under the boat from one side to the other. The wood and barnacles tore your skin and if you lived, you might even lose a limb."

"Keel hauling," said Yukiko.

"Yes, that is their word. I had ... forgotten it. They beat us or raped us when they got bored. If someone became too ill and they thought he or she would die, they would toss the person overboard. Well, this was bad for the humans, but good for me. I did not have to feign sickness. The problem was, I wanted to be thrown overboard before I died, not after. There were others who were sick, and when I was tossed in with them, I found a young man. He had been beaten so badly that he was almost dead. By the time morning came, we were the only two left alive. I clung to him as they tossed us overboard. I changed, became strong. I decided to carry him to shore, wherever that was.

"I spoke with the intelligent creatures of the sea, asking where I was. It was in what you call the Caribbean Sea. I headed for land, keeping the young man's head out of the water. Still, he died and I let him sink down into the water, where his bones lay even now.

"I lived in the Caribbean for a while, but my kind are restless. I swam south around the land, through the cooler water, up the coast, and found this place."

"And now the Seelie own you."

"No, they only own my services. And only for a time."

"And one of those services is guarding my spirit ball."

"That is correct."

"Then take my offer of a year of service in exchange for it. I can help you get back to Africa or wherever you like. I can get you human money, and you can give it to your descendants."

"Those things do not interest me, little one. And even if they did, I cannot give it to you. Not because I am unwilling, but because I am unable."

"Please, sea-spirit. Please, give it to me. Or tell me how I can find it or steal it. Do you keep it under water somewhere? On this side or the sidhe side? Please." She was desperate now. She could not swim down and fight the sea woman for it. If it could not be bargained for, she was without hope.

"Bide your time. I have heard your cries coming through your spirit ball. I know your suffering. But you must wait. Once events have played out, it may be your time."

"I can't just wait! By the time they're done with me, they'll have had me kill and perform atrocities."

"Your god is dead, there is no accounting for your deeds anymore."

"But there is! And if you help the Seelie, you are aiding in slavery and cruelty."

"Do not speak to me of cruelty or slavery!" the sea woman boomed. Her eyes flashed fury and she uncoiled her tail.

"I will speak of it." Yukiko stood and put her ears back. "You aid the slavers."

"Go now!" shouted the sea woman, and Yukiko was slammed by a wall of water so cold and hard that she didn't even have time to gasp for air. She was tumbled by the water until she couldn't tell up from down, and she thrashed against it, struggling to find the surface.

Then there was sand, scraping the length of her body, and the water pulled back. She was on shore, cold, wet, and no closer to finding her spirit ball. She pushed herself up and looked out over the water. The sea woman's head poked up from near the rock. Yukiko stood and glared. She would not be caught whimpering on the ground.

The sea woman watched her for another moment and then dipped below the water. Yukiko understood that she had wanted to make sure that she had been safe on shore. She had wanted Yukiko to know that she was not a killer.

CHAPTER 28

ASTRID CRADLED RUNT AGAINST HER chest. The little cat was lethargic and had refused to eat since that afternoon, and even then, he had only taken a tiny bit of milk. His breathing was slow. Too slow. She had wiped at his bottom again and again with the warm, wet cloth, but to no avail. He refused the bottle, even when Astrid manually gently pried his mouth open and pushed in the nipple. He needed his mother, and she had failed in finding her. If he suffered, it was her fault.

"We need to take him to the vet," she told Elliot. He sat across from her at the trailer table, reading.

"It's almost midnight. Nothing will be open until morning."

"Isn't there an emergency vet somewhere?"

"There's one on Sepulveda, but the buses won't be running until morning."

"Do you know anyone with a car?"

"Not one we could borrow." He took a look at Runt. "He looks bad."

"I know. I'll walk." Astrid put the bottle into the kitten box, set Runt down between Frieda and Diego and put on her coat.

"It's the middle of the night. It's not safe," said Elliot.

"He's really sick. I don't think he can wait." She'd walk all night if she had to.

Elliot brightened. "Wait, we can call a cab."

She hadn't thought of taking a cab. She had never even

ridden in one and didn't know how much they cost. Elliot flipped open the old laptop he used to sell his little metal sculptures, called the cab company and they waited. Astrid picked up Runt again and stroked him. Every time she got him to open his eyes, he immediately went back to sleep. His little limbs were limp.

"Please be okay," she whispered.

"He doesn't look so good," said Elliot.

"I know that! You think I can't see that?" She glared at him. She caught the hurt in his expression a moment before he concealed it.

Fifteen minutes later, Elliot called the cab company again, and they insisted that a driver was on his way.

Astrid grabbed the phone. "Hurry, please. It's an emergency."

Elliot hung up his mobile phone and reached to turn off his laptop. Then Astrid saw him glance at the spot just behind her and jump back. He grabbed her arm and yanked her toward him. She turned to see and just behind her, touching the floor, hung a disk of what looked like bright white fog. The disk parted in the middle, like a misty doughnut, and the center moved, like water disturbed, or a rippling mirror. The area in the center was reflective, showing bits of the trailer and the two of them.

Then, Runt lifted his head and looked at the thing. It was a Door. Runt leaped out of her hands. The instant his paws hit the carpet, she saw him twice. Once, there was a little white body with its eyes closed and its tiny torso without breath in her hands. And the second time there was a kitten on the floor, healthy and alive.

The Runt on the floor looked up at her, and then said, "Dime?" His voice was high and clear, like a note on a flute. His expression was intelligent, as if he fully expected her to answer. She had seen the same look with his mother.

"What?" she said.

"Go?" he said, his word elongated and lifting at the end.

175

"Go where?" But she already knew what he meant. This Door was different. It was not like the Door in the mirror house, full of terrors and monsters. This Door was peaceful, or at least neutral. The fog around the mirror-like center was holding steady. It was just the right size for a cat to pass through. The mirrored surface was still in motion, showing a flash of her blue jeans, then the red of Elliot's shirt.

Runt looked up at her and then butted his head against her leg, but she did not feel it. The action was so much like his mother's that it hurt to watch it. Astrid dropped to her knees and reached out a hand. The kitten lifted his head under her palm, but when she tried to touch him, her hand passed through him. Of course. The little body in her other hand was solid and real. The little spirit on the ground was not.

Elliot crouched down beside her. "He needs to go through," he said.

"How do you know?"

"I had a dream about this. It's important that he goes through."

Astrid looked from Elliot to the Door to Runt. She knew he was right. The little spirit had to leave.

"You should go." She pointed. "Go on."

Runt turned to regard the Door, but did not budge.

"Your mother is there," she said.

Runt considered, and then moved toward the Door and stopped just short of it. He turned back for a second, and Astrid waited for him to say something. But just as quickly, he turned and leapt through. The fog pulled inward until the mirror-like center was gone, and then the fog dissipated into the air of the trailer.

Astrid felt dizzy, and put her free hand against the cabinet to steady herself. She no longer saw two of Runt, but the world seemed less steady, less real. It wasn't in her mind, it was a physical sensation.

"Do you want to ... you know, put him down?" Elliot asked.

She was still clutching Runt's body.

"We need to bury him properly," she said.

"We can do it in the morning."

Elliot took a dish towel and laid it out on the table and she set the little cat in the center. He folded in the sides and made a tidy little bundle.

"I promised her," Astrid said through tears. "I promised I'd take care of her babies."

Elliot set a glass of tap water in front of her and she drank. It made her feel better, more a part of the real world. Diego and Frieda mewed in their box, and she picked them up and petted them. They were both strong and healthy. She fed them and they sucked greedily at the bottle.

"I'm scared, Elliot."

"I know."

"I'm not sure if I'm dangerous."

He picked up Diego, who was crawling toward the edge of the table. The kitten gave a hearty squeak.

"I think you are," he said.

It startled her, but he didn't look angry or upset, just matter-of-fact.

"What do you think is happening?" she said.

"I don't know, but I think you're some kind of doorway. A doorway to other places, like death."

CHAPTER 29

ELLIOT WOKE THE NEXT MORNING to a headache and a feeling of nausea and unease. Well, he was hosting talking ghost kittens and a girl who could inadvertently open Doors to hell and/or the afterlife. And he was hallucinating while on dates and his dream déjà vu was now strong enough for him to believe that it might actually be real.

Actually, a run-of-the-mill headache might be a welcome change of pace. There was a small bottle of Tylenol in the bathroom, where Astrid was now showering. He tossed back his covers and paused. The blanket had always been a dark red, and now it was solid navy blue. Oh no. Yukiko had insinuated that he had been poisoned at the Falafel Hut, but he had not eaten there or anywhere else since their ill-fated date. He always packed his lunch and prepared everything himself. It kept him from any potential, if unlikely, danger. Also, it was cheaper.

He dressed, heated two cups of water in the microwave and got out a jar of instant coffee. When he set the cups on the table, he saw that Astrid had tossed his red blanket onto the seat. So there it was. But he didn't remember ever having a navy blue blanket at all. And last night, the blanket had definitely been red, or he would have noticed.

He got down a box of cereal, but there wasn't any milk. There was a mini mart on the corner where he could get some. He shouted through the bathroom door to tell Astrid where he was going, grabbed his keys and wallet and headed out. The sunlight hurt his head and he rubbed at his eyes. He stood still for a moment, breathing in the cool air, trying to calm his stomach. Even if he got milk, he probably couldn't keep down any food.

He hadn't gone two blocks before he saw the changes. One of the stores that used to sell tee shirts, sunglasses and souvenir key chains was gone, and in its place was a realtor's office. An ice cream shop now had yellow upholstered chairs instead of pink. The three-tiered fountain that stood in the center of a sitting area used to be smooth and white with pale blue tiles lining the interior. Now, the tiles were in a pattern of yellow, white and cobalt blue and the fountain itself was orange terra cotta.

Falafel Hut was now called Falafel Shack and the mural on the wall inside now pictured Athena with an owl on her shoulder and the dancing nymphs now all had dark curly hair.

The people walking down the sidewalks were the same. Mick sat on a bus stop bench, and he waved hello as Elliot passed. Perhaps Mick's clothing had changed, like Yukiko's dress. But he wouldn't notice if it had. The mini mart was unchanged, except he thought that it had more California lottery posters in the window. He couldn't be sure.

He grabbed milk and a package of powdered doughnuts. His head hurt so much that he felt dizzy, and he needed painkiller. Now. He grabbed a bottle of Tylenol, set everything on the counter and opened his wallet. His driver's license was visible through a little plastic window, and he froze. The picture was different. He pulled out the license for a better look. In the picture, he had long hair that fell in blonde waves down to his shoulders. He looked like a girl. Or someone in an 80's glam band. It was horrific.

He touched his hair. Short as ever. Sure, sometimes it got scruffy and longish if he didn't cut it, but he had never in his life let it get that long. Then he noticed the birthday on the license. His birthday was January tenth, but this said it was the eleventh.

"You going to pay for that?" asked the man at the counter.

Elliot paid and took off for home, opening the Tylenol as he walked and dry swallowing three tablets. Mick was still at the bus stop.

"Hey, Mick, can I talk to you? I think something's wrong." If anyone would understand seeing things, it would be Mick.

"Sure, Elliot. What is it?"

They were a few yards from the fountain.

"Was that fountain always like that?" Elliot asked.

"You mean was it always right there?"

"I mean the color. Was it ever blue and white?"

Mick shielded his eyes with his hand and gave the fountain a good look. When he turned back to Elliot, his gaze was as clear and sane as Elliot had ever seen it.

"You remember it differently than it is now?" said Mick. "Does that mean you can remember forwards and backwards? Like the White Queen?"

"No—I mean, I'm not sure."

If he could dream the future and have little snippets of déjà vu ahead of things actually happening, then wasn't that exactly what Mick meant? Remembering forward?

"I just know that the fountain is different," Elliot said.

"Nope. It's always been just like that. That orangey color with the colored tiles. But I remember other things being different. Stuff moving. Things like that."

"When you started seeing changes like that, when did it start? What was it like?"

Mick rubbed his chin and Elliot noticed again that Mick looked like he had shaved recently.

"Well, it was little things at first. Like you seeing the fountain. It would come and go when I was a teenager. Then, when I was in Vietnam, I'd see things that the other men said weren't there. I had to go to the medics and they were talking about sending me home. And one day there was this shimmering spot, right up close to me. And, well, the change thing happens all the time now."

The bus approached and Mick picked up his old rucksack.

"But who knows?" said Mick. "Maybe you slipped a groove. Happens to the best of us. You should talk to Imelda at the shelter. She's really nice; she might be able to help you."

Mick climbed onto the bus and it pulled away with a roar and a puff of smelly black exhaust. Well, when the crazy people thought you were crazy, you knew you were in trouble.

By the time he got back to the trailer, he felt like he was going to vomit. Astrid had left a note saying she was going to get a few things from her house while her mother was at work. Well, so much for buying milk for breakfast. She had asked him in the note to keep an eye on the cats. Fine. He could do that much.

Runt's little body was still wrapped in the kitchen towel on the counter. They needed to bury the little guy, but he wasn't sure where. Stray dogs would dig him up if they buried him on the beach. Maybe they could go to a park and hope the cops didn't bother them. Or they could bury him at sea, off the end of the pier. Whatever Astrid wanted to do, it needed to be soon or the body would start to smell. He took the tiny bundle and put it in the freezer. Wasn't that what they did with human bodies at the morgue? So it wasn't really disrespectful.

He pulled the curtains closed in the tiny sleeping area at the back of the trailer and lay down. He wasn't due at work until that afternoon, and he needed a nap. The light and sound were so painful now, and the Tylenol wasn't helping. He dozed, passing in and out of sleep, until he heard words. They were part of a half-dream, the sort he had when he was just falling asleep.

"You gave this time and date," a voice said.

CHAPTER 30

ASTRID WENT THROUGH HER ROOM, stuffing clothing into an old duffle bag and a reusable grocery tote she found in the kitchen. An old stuffed dog, her favorite pajamas, two pairs of shoes, they all went into the duffle bag. So did pants, shirts and her work uniforms. She paused at her bookcase where the newer fairy tale book sat beside its older twin. She pulled down both and put them into the grocery tote. She wrapped Elliot's wire rabbit and put it in also.

Then she went through her desk, taking all of her new colored pencils and markers, her sketch pads and charcoals. A few minutes later, both the duffle bag and the grocery tote were full, and she turned, looking over the room in which she had spent so many years.

She wondered if she'd be able to come back. Maybe her mother would want to speak with her again before she left for New York. Her mother had not called her mobile phone, but it had only been a day. Astrid was still angry enough to avoid her mother, but enough time had passed that she felt a little sad about it. Elliot had told her the name of that feeling was Stockholm Syndrome.

She looked back through the closet and pulled out her new jacket from her aunt. She wouldn't need it now, but New York was cold, and she wouldn't have much money with which to buy a new one.

On her nightstand sat her alarm clock, and right beside it was her metal bell in the shape of an owl. She picked it up. It was heavy and had a faint metallic scent, even a foot away from her face. This was the bell that Cinderella had let fall into her kitten's box. Looking back, she got the feeling that Cinderella had put it close to the kittens on purpose.

Astrid had owned the bell her entire life and it had always been on her nightstand. She had no idea where it had come from. For the first time, she thought of it like a talisman. Its small face was stern-looking, perhaps a bit fierce. It reminded her of Cinderella in that way.

Her bags were full to bursting, so she shoved it into her purse. She pulled open her nightstand, making sure she hadn't forgotten anything. Along with various odds and ends was her old pink clamshell mirror. She stuck it into her purse. She might be poor and technically homeless, but she could still make sure she looked halfway decent.

She stood in the doorway. The room didn't look too much different, especially with the closet and drawers closed. Would her mother notice right away that she had taken her things? Had her mother come in here after she had gone, wishing she had her little girl back? Or was she still sulking in her madness, deluded into thinking that her daughter was a prostitute or a drug addict or whatever strange things her mind had concocted?

She had a strange impulse, reached into the bag and pulled out the first colored pencil her fingers touched. It was Sulphur Spring, a bright acid green. Well, at least that was somewhat appropriate. She crawled back under her desk until she could reach the base of the wall, back in the corner. She wrote, "Astrid's Room Forever."

It was silly and juvenile, but the moment she had finished, she felt better. She pulled her house key from her key ring and slapped it on the kitchen table. She would not leave a note.

When she was sure she had everything, she locked the front door from the inside and pulled the door closed.

CHAPTER 31

YUKIKO CAUGHT A GLIMPSE OF her reflection in one of the mirror house panels. It was humiliating. She wore the same khaki pants, polo shirt and ugly blue visor as the rest of the miserable park employees. She couldn't wear her plush fox tail, so she kept to the shade where she wouldn't cast a shadow.

It seemed that not only was Mr. Augustus in charge of relaying messages from the Seelie dictating how she was to use her powers in their service, but he also was allowed to dictate how the rest of her time was used. The bastard had decided that she would work at his boardwalk for minimum wage.

Maybe it was a blessing that the other Kitsune were few and far between. Had one of them seen her, she would have wanted to go into hiding for a few centuries in shame. Either that or murder her captors in a bloody rage. Right now, she preferred the latter.

She took tickets, gave directions to visitors, and waited. If she wanted to cheer herself, she could tell herself that she was biding her time. But she was old enough to know that self-deception was a worthless path.

"No food or drink inside, please," she said to a man who held a paper-wrapped Polish sausage with limp green peppers.

"I'll be careful with it."

"Park policy, sir. I'm sorry." It wasn't that she particularly cared about park policy. She didn't. But she would be the one to clean up spilled drinks and wipe down mirrors smeared with greasy handprints. A dropped sausage would make a mess.

"Well, I'm not throwing it away, so too bad," he said and went inside with it.

She had a little power left. Mr. Augustus was allowing her to dance so she did not become useless to him. And she would be performing again this afternoon. Was it worth using just a little? She needed to decide. Would she make the sausage man see himself in a mirror covered in oozing boils? Or would he see a horrifying monster from his nightmares? Perhaps something more subtle. An image so brief he would never truly be sure he had seen it, one depicting his girlfriend with another man. Or an image of hopelessness, that things never would really get better for him in his dull job and he would work in his gray cubicle forever.

To hell with subtle. She concentrated for a moment and then waited. As she took tickets from other customers, a short yell of terror came from inside the mirror house. When the man emerged, he no longer had the sausage. Damn. Now she would have to clean it up. But he was shaking and white. It was worth it.

Astrid walked up. She was wearing her uniform, but had her purse over her shoulder. From the tired, sweaty look about her, she was going home instead of arriving.

"Augustus told me to tell you that Elliot called in sick," said Astrid. "So you're going to be on for a couple more hours until he can get a replacement."

"What happened to him? Is he all right?" If Elliot was suffering from whatever the sidhe had given him at the falafel restaurant, then she bore responsibility, at least partially.

"Just a migraine," said Astrid. "He gets them sometimes."

"Oh, good." She hoped a migraine wasn't a side effect. More importantly, perhaps she could use Astrid's presence to her advantage. This could be turned into an opportunity to find her spirit ball, but she had to think quickly. The sea woman had been in contact with the spirit ball, but Yukiko hadn't sensed the ball anywhere nearby. That meant that it was probably on the other side. And if the Seelie wanted access to the ball, which they needed to keep her enslaved, then it had to be in their world. Astrid could open Doors to Unseelie, and the Seelie world was closer to the human world than Unseelie. But how to get Astrid to open the Door to the correct place?

Yukiko said, "Can I ask you something? About when the slaugh came through?"

"Sure."

"Can you show me where it happened?"

Astrid looked at the mirror house like something terrible was going to come out of it. Yukiko couldn't blame her for being afraid. But thankfully, Astrid had not connected the opening of the Door for the slaugh with the tiny illusion of the crying child that Yukiko had planted in the maze.

"I'm not sure I should go inside," said Astrid. "Whatever I did, well, I don't think I should be anywhere near that place."

"I need to know so I can perform the necessary steps to keep it from happening again."

"You can do that?" Astrid looked hopeful. "You can keep those things out? Can you show me how to keep from opening Doors again? Red Fawn can't help, and I'm so scared I'll do it again."

"I think so," Yukiko lied. "But I'll need to see exactly how it was done the first time. Little details matter."

Astrid looked again at the mirror house, and Yukiko saw her take a deep breath. Poor thing. She was frightened. But the girl walked on ahead, straight into the maze. Yukiko followed, pulling together the threads of her power. She had to be ready.

Astrid stopped at a warped mirror at the back of the

attraction. Yukiko thought of her spirit ball, not the image of it, but the feeling of it. A sweet, sparkling scent came from the mirror in front of Astrid, and the girl looked up as the feeling of a cool, fresh breeze brushed against them. Perfect.

Yukiko watched the mirror's surface, waiting. The girl was not in control of her powers, and all it had taken before was a little nudge.

Astrid told her what had happened, about the child stuck in the maze and how she and Elliot had gone inside. Yukiko was barely listening.

Nothing happened to the mirror. Why wasn't it working this time? Yukiko put more power into the illusion, adding something else, the sensation of the Seelie, the way that they smelled when they were close. She didn't want Astrid to see anything, or she would flee, and rightly so. But the scent, the feeling, it might be enough.

Astrid was describing what she had seen inside, a girl who looked like her twin and the hideous slaugh that had come after.

"Have you ever heard of the Seelie?" Yukiko asked.

"They're the opposite of the Unseelie, right?"

"Exactly. Well, not really. No. They're cousins, more like brothers, but they like to define themselves as opposites."

"Yeah, I read about that in a book once."

The scent and feeling coming from the mirror were strong, pulsing, alive. The girl needed some time, perhaps. And a little extra push.

"Well, the Seelie world is very much like our own," said Yukiko. "The worlds exist side by side, and humans have been known to visit Seelie and vice versa."

"So why did I open a Door to the Unseelie world?"

That was a good question. An excellent question. But Yukiko did not know the answer.

"So the Seelie world, is that where someone might go when they die?" Astrid asked.

"What? Die? I didn't say anything about dying. And no, it's not any land of death. No one comes back from there. Well, it happens sometimes in old stories." The last thing they needed was for Astrid to open some Door into death. She needed to get Astrid to think of Seelie again.

"A week ago, I thought things like the slaugh were just in stories," Astrid said.

"Well, people have been telling stories for slightly less time than they've been able to speak. But we were talking about the Seelie world."

She changed the illusion she was projecting, just a little, including Astrid in it instead of just the mirror. It was riskier, as Astrid might feel the change. Yukiko added in her longing for the spirit ball and a stronger feeling of the Seelie world. And now that she was including the girl, she felt something inside her now, loss. The intensity of it was shocking. The girl was young, but she had experienced loss, great loss that cut into her heart. And it wasn't heartbreak from some high school boy either. It was the loss of love, mixed with the pain of betrayal. And more than the loss itself, there was the absence of hope. That was the worst of it.

No time to dwell on it. Her feelings could be used as fuel, as a tool. It was against the Myobu code to use a human like this. But she was in a desperate situation and it called for action, not noble passivity. Besides, if she stayed as a slave to the Seelie, they would have her commit deeds far worse than tricking a girl into making a Door.

She paused then. The Myobu did not harm innocents, and this certainly would qualify as harm. The lying, the manipulation, they could be used in some cases, but not in a self-serving way against innocents. She thought then of World War II, how she had been in California while the humans of Japanese descent had been interred in camps. Her ability for speaking any language flawlessly had saved her then, as she could pass as Chinese, Korean, whatever she wished. She remembered the confusion among the Americans at the kamikaze pilots, and she had understood the confusion. To commit suicide for a cause seemed alien to her then. And it still did.

She did not wish to die or wait for centuries for her chance to escape the Seelie. She would fight, and she would live.

Yukiko saw the mirror flicker. Astrid's pain was good fuel. And there it was, the Door she needed.

But she needed more. She needed a way to get back. And there was only one way she could get a Door back to the human world, to her world. May The Lady help me, she thought. She glanced at the mirror and gasped as if she had seen something. Astrid turned toward mirror and Yukiko slipped behind her.

She wouldn't push her, as Astrid would feel it. But she could do something. She made Astrid feel dizzy, and then she used more power to give her the illusion that wind was pushing her, that she was falling backward, away from the mirror. Astrid overcompensated and staggered forward, putting out her hand for the wall to steady herself. Yukiko moved space, just a few inches, so Astrid leaned on the mirror. It bent, tore, and opened. The girl slipped through.

Yukiko leaped through behind her, and as she passed the threshold, her body transformed into its natural shape. The Door blinked shut behind her, ripping a few white hairs from the tip of her tail.

CHAPTER 32

THERE WAS A BANGING SOUND and Elliot rolled over, pulling some of the covers with him. The blanket was still dark blue, and he closed his eyes. His head ached, but it was a duller pain than before. The banging came again. Someone was at the trailer door. Astrid would have just come in without knocking, so it couldn't be her.

"Just a minute!" he yelled and then immediately regretted it as pain spiked through his skull. Maybe it was the trailer park manager, but he had paid his rent and was reasonably sure his check wouldn't have bounced.

He dragged himself out of bed and pulled open the door. Outside stood four people, two men and two women. At the front was a tall, thin man with black hair curling wildly in every direction. He wore an old-fashioned long brown coat over suspenders, a vest and striped pants. His odd appearance was only matched by a younger woman, about Elliot's age, wearing loose pants, knee-high leather boots and a white blouse with a patched vest over it. A small capuchin monkey perched on her shoulder and blinked at him.

The other two people, a man and a woman, were more sanely dressed. The man was in black jeans and a long black duster, like something from the old West. He was of average height and build with medium brown hair. The other person, a Latina woman with light brown eyes, wore jeans and a sweater.

"Hello, Elliot," said the man in the black duster. He looked happy to see him. "May we come in?"

"I'm not interested in theater tickets or whatever it is you're selling." Elliot started to close the door.

"Wait!" said the woman in the loose pants and vest. "It's about the things you're seeing. The changes." The monkey on her shoulder scratched at its ear and then watched him as if waiting for him to answer.

"What do you mean?" Elliot said. He wasn't about to talk to any strange people about anything. And who knows, perhaps these people were figments of his imagination as well. "And who are you?"

"I'm Neil," said the man in the black duster. "Neil Grey. This is Felicia Sanchez." He motioned to the woman in the jeans and sweater. "And this is Hazel Dubois." The young woman with the monkey bowed, actually bowed. The monkey managed to cling to her shoulder without falling off.

"And I'm Seamus Doyle," said the tall, thin man. He had an Irish accent.

"We can help you with what's happening," said Neil. "We know what it is. May we come in?"

"We can talk out here." Elliot closed the door behind him, climbed down and leaned back against the side of the trailer. He couldn't imagine who these people were or what they would want with him, but he wasn't about to allow them inside his home.

"If you prefer," said Neil. "So, how have you been?" The way he asked it seemed forced, as if he was not used to making small talk.

"You're the ones who want to talk to me. So talk." Elliot's head hurt, he was tired and had a dead cat in his freezer. He was in no mood to indulge anyone.

"Very well," said Neil. "You are experiencing time slips. You've slipped time streams a number of times now. It's mostly harmless, but disconcerting. The changes in buildings, décor, clothing, are all symptomatic of someone with an unusual sense of time-sensitivity. You've met Mick, correct?"

Elliot nodded.

"He is partially time-sensitive, but there are other things that have happened to him."

"Are you the birdman?" Elliot asked.

The two women exchanged a look.

"No," said Neil. "But we know someone who is friends with Mick and talks with him. He helps him sometimes."

"And I'm going to be like Mick?" said Elliot. "Seeing things?"

"Not unless you stay here like this. You could also choose to come with us."

"And go where? Are you people like Mick too?" He looked pointedly at Seamus's green and brown striped pants. Maybe they were a little mad as well. "Are you time sensitive?"

"No," said Neil. "We are not. But we have experience with things like this. You yourself told us to come and get you. You gave this time and date."

And then he remembered them, the dreams here and there. He couldn't remember any details, but there was a strong feeling of friendship with this man Neil, and an affection for the other three, touched with annoyance with the Irish man. The Irish man stuffed his hands in his pockets and looked around at the outside of Elliot's trailer like a tourist.

"Fine. You can come in," Elliot said.

The inside of the trailer was crowded with all five of them and the monkey. It stayed perched on Hazel's shoulder, but looked around, taking everything in.

"The babies!" cried Hazel and picked up the box of kittens. Then her smile changed to a look of concern. "Where is the other one?" She had a Southern accent.

"You know Astrid?" Elliot said. "Are you friends of hers? Did she put you up to this? Are you from some artist's group or something?"

"What happened to the other baby?" Hazel asked, and

she leaned down to glance at the floor under the table.

"Well, he died. The mother died. At least, we think she did. And that kitten was the runt."

"Oh God," said Felicia. Seamus touched her shoulder and she pressed her fingers to her mouth. "We didn't get here in time."

Then Elliot remembered. "Was it you at the pound?" he said to Seamus. "My cousin said there was a tall skinny Irish man there. And he took Cinderella."

"She is alive and well," said Seamus. "And she will want to be reunited with her children. So what happened to the other little one?"

Elliot explained what had happened to Runt, including the weird door that had opened. If these people wanted to talk to a crazy man, then he'd give them what they came for.

"My cousin will want to see Cinderella," Elliot said. "She was so worried about her."

"We can worry about that later," said Neil. "For now, we are here to take you back to your own time stream. It's not good to wander too far afield time wise."

"And how do you plan on doing that?"

"We have a machine. It can get us back to the main time stream."

"Sounds nifty, but why would I go with a bunch of crazies who show up on my doorstep? Yukiko or Mick or Astrid could have told you about all this. I mean, you didn't even blink when I talked about foggy doorways and crazy things like that. I probably had some bad stuff at the bonfire a couple months ago and it's just flashbacks."

The woman named Felicia said, "Elliot, what is happening to you is not a medical problem. Drugs won't help you, and neither will therapy or anything else. We know you in the future, your future. The machine allows us to travel in time, between universes, although in a limited way, and through parallel time streams. And it allowed us to come to this portion of this time stream to bring you back. This is your only chance to return to the world you know."

"So this is some alternative universe?"

"No, of course not," said Seamus. "If it was an alternative universe, you wouldn't see any of the people you know. Each unique portion of the multiverse contains unique people. But a time stream slip means you'd see little changes, but the people would be the same. You've simply experienced a minor level temporal dislocation. In fact—"

"Not now," Felicia said softly to Seamus and then turned to Elliot. "What we came to do is to help you. To bring you back with us, where you can learn to use your ... talent."

"It's not a talent. It's some kind of chemical imbalance or something."

"Not necessarily," she said. "Sometimes, things are just weird. Really weird. I've questioned my sanity after dealing with something like this. But in your case, the concoction that the sidhe, the Seelie, gave you at the falafel shop enhanced the ability you already had and you slipped time streams as a result."

"Why would they do this to me? Astrid is the one who has the scary abilities."

"We need to get them home," said Hazel, who picked up the box with the kittens. "You can talk about this all back at the house. Pangur Ban is waiting."

Seamus pulled out a pocket watch on a chain. "She's right, we don't have long. I'll see to it." He left the trailer.

"Now," said Neil. "You are wondering why you should listen to a bunch of strangers who appear on your doorstep. We don't have long, so I'll be brief. You and Astrid are in danger. The four of us and some of our allies are no friends of the Seelie. The Seelie are trying to use Astrid because of her abilities, harm you for other reasons, and some of their brethren, the Unseelie, have even more nefarious plans. We want to stop them, and we need you. Your cousin and everyone else in this world depend on it."

"Where is this machine?"

"Just outside."

"Well, let's see it then."

Neil pulled up his sleeve and checked his watch. "It has already done its work. We're here. Check your wallet."

How had he known about the wallet? He hadn't mentioned it to Astrid or anyone else.

At Elliot's concerned look, Neil said, "You told me about it. Go on."

Elliot went to the bedroom and grabbed his wallet from the built-in night table beside the bed. The blanket crumpled at the foot of the bed was now back to red, and his driver's license was back to normal.

He turned to find Neil standing in the doorway.

"You people shouldn't be here," said Elliot.

"You told us to come get you, to use the machine," said Neil. "You gave us this exact time and date."

"Yeah, so you said."

"And we came, just as you will ask us to do. We work together. You trained me, and I'll train you."

"Train me? For what?"

"The Time Corps."

The words brought another memory, one of fear mixed with exhilaration, of danger, and fun. And with some sadness, there was also a sense of meaning and purpose. Was this was why he couldn't choose a major or figure out what career he wanted? Why he was without direction or purpose? He had been waiting, unconsciously, for something to come along.

"What's the Time Corps?" he asked.

Neil smiled. "Back at the house, I'll tell you everything."

And Elliot knew that he would. Seamus and Neil loaded a huge wooden trunk into the back of a dented SUV. So far, Elliot was not impressed. The five of them, plus the kittens and the monkey all squeezed into the vehicle. Neil drove, Seamus rode shotgun and Elliot sat in the back between Felicia and Hazel. It was a tight fit, but things could be much worse than being crammed between two nice-looking women. He caught Hazel looking at him twice as they drove.

"What is it?"

"You just look so young." She smiled. "And I haven't seen you in a while."

"So we're friends or something. In the future."

"Well, your future, my past. Our present." She stopped abruptly as if listening to something. The monkey's face was near her ear. She leaned toward Elliot so no one would hear her over the noise of the car and whispered in his ear. "You and Neil were, are and will be partners. You've worked together for years. Listen to him. He's going to give you training to help you. You can trust him. And don't be angry with the Professor. He can't help how he is."

They got off the freeway and drove down suburban side streets until they were in an older neighborhood full of restored Craftsman-style houses from the early twentieth century. The car turned down a street lined with old pepper trees, their foliage hanging down in thick curtains. They pulled into a long cement driveway beside a yellow and white two-storied house. It had no garage, but the driveway stretched all the way to the back of the house, ending at a large shed. The house itself was neatly kept and had a broad front porch with thick rectangular columns on each end, both with lower halves covered in gray stones. A matching stone chimney rose up on one side of the house, and though Elliot had seen a kitchen door at the back of the house, Felicia and Hazel led him around to the front steps which were wide and painted white. Seamus and Neil got out the big trunk and took it around the back of the house.

Felicia let them inside through a wooden front door

topped with stained glass. The house had dark wooden floors and matching wooden beams framed the doorways. In the living room sat an ordinary sofa, chairs, a large television, a computer and bookshelves crammed with books both old and new. There were a few items other than books on the shelves, including a cat-shaped golden sarcophagus, a stack of thick wooden sticks tied together with a leather thong and a squat stone head that looked like it was from ancient Mexico.

He already knew the rest of the house. It was familiar, though of course, he had never been there before. He remembered bits and pieces from dreams. The kitchen was at the front corner of the house, the dining room to one side. He knew where each of the bedrooms upstairs would be, and that the place had a decently sized attic. Strange things happened in the attic, he knew.

He lingered near a built-in bookcase, looking over stacks of medical textbooks, romance novels, physics books and some yellowed science fiction paperbacks, all crammed together.

"She's upstairs," said Hazel. "You should come. It'll be easier, coming from you."

He followed her upstairs and into one of the bedrooms. On the windowsill sat Cinderella, looking out over the backyard. The window was open, and the cat moved aside as a giant black bird flew in and landed on top of an antique full-length standing mirror. It was a raven, and it made little rattling noise in its throat as it looked Elliot up and down.

"I'm sorry," said Hazel, putting down the box. Cinderella leapt down and came to examine her kittens. "The little one died. They did the best they could."

"I'm sure they did," said the cat. Her voice was low and smokey, and it was full of sorrow. "My children," she murmured and jumped into the box. The kittens mewed and squirmed as she licked them.

Now he knew this had to be a dream. The cat had spoken.

"This is Pangur Ban," said Hazel. "And the raven is Huginn."

"Nice to see you again, Elliot," said the raven.

"This is his first time here," said Hazel. "Ever."

"Oh, I see. Well, pleasant to meet you for the first time then."

"We've met before, at Astrid's house, but we've never been properly introduced. I am pleased to meet you," said Pangur Ban.

"I'm sorry about your baby," said Elliot. "We tried. We really did."

"I knew the risks," said the cat. "And I've known Astrid since she was a little girl. She promised to care for them, and I know she tried."

She looked up at Elliot then, and the ferocity of her look was frightening.

"Were you there?" she asked. "When my son died?"

"Um, yeah. She tried to save him. She tried to take him to the vet. But he died so quickly. I saw his spirit. It went into a Door she made. To the place of the dead, I think."

The cat lowered her head and closed her eyes. She licked Diego's ear absently. Elliot thought he heard the cat whisper something to the baby.

Huginn flapped down and hopped to the edge of the box.

"Do they understand?" he asked.

"They know their brother is gone," said Pangur Ban. "They feel sorrow, though they can't speak yet."

"Your son, he talked when he died," said Elliot. "He could speak a little. I thought ... I don't know what I thought. But he could talk a little."

The kittens nursed, and Pangur Ban stared at the side of the box.

"This is awful," said Huginn. "The death of the young is a terrible thing."

"You have seen worse," said Pangur Ban. "You have seen death before. You were Guntram."

"Was I? A war raven?"

"We should go," said Hazel. "Huginn will look after her."

As they left, Elliot thought he heard Pangur Ban singing a lullaby to her babies.

"You did well," said Hazel as she poured them each a glass of iced tea in the kitchen. "Not everyone takes talking animals in stride."

"It seemed rude to make a big deal of it in front of a grieving mother."

"Well put," said the monkey on Hazel's shoulder.

CHAPTER 33

"WHAT DID YOU SAY?" ASTRID asked. She stepped back from the white fox at her feet. The little animal had spoken, and was now looking at her for a response.

"I said, we should get out of the mirror house," said the fox. It had the voice of a woman, a familiar voice. "They might not feel my presence, but they'll feel yours and be here soon. We need to make this quick."

"Okay, this is too much. I'm going home." Astrid pulled up her purse strap and headed out of the mirror house. "I need to lie down."

"Astrid, wait!" said the fox. "It's me, Yukiko."

The fox trotted along beside her as she climbed down the metal stairs at the back of the mirror house and headed around toward the front. Astrid stopped dead when she saw the employee taking tickets. He wore no uniform, but some sort of tunic made of tight-woven ferns. And he had scales on his arms and legs, like a fish. His hands were webbed, as were his bare feet, although his face was that of an ordinary man.

"Hang on a minute," said the fox. The animal lifted her nose to the wind. "Come this way, or they'll find you."

Then Astrid noticed the sky. The light in this place was completely different than normal, more golden. The sky was a pale apricot, but it was not just along the horizon as it was at sunrise or sunset. The entire sky was pale orange. The ocean was greener than she had ever seen it, and parts of it were so dark they looked black.

"This is Seelie," explained the fox. "Please come along now. I'll explain everything as we go. I promise."

The little fox looked earnest and concerned, her head cocked to one side. Since she was headed toward the exit anyway, Astrid allowed the fox to follow her down the boardwalk. No one looked twice at the fox or at her, but most of the visitors looked like regular people, albeit dressed in either too little or too much clothing. One man wore nothing but tiny white fur shorts, another man was wrapped from head to foot in billowing crimson and orange silks with only a tiny open slit from which peered two reptilian eyes.

As they walked, the fox explained that Astrid had made a Door into the Seelie world, and that they had fallen through. She was Yukiko, the same person Astrid had known. She also said that they had to stick together.

They passed a pretzel stand, very much like her own, but this one sold only straight stick-like pretzels, finger-sized, with honey dipping sauce. None came with salt. The only beverages available were spring water and small beer, and the old man behind the cart had tiny fluffy koala ears poking out from under his bowler hat.

The rides here were similar to the ones at her own boardwalk, but there were some differences. The Sea Swings were called Dragon Swings, and the carved seats had some kind of long, pointed faces at the ends of the armrests. As the chairs swung outward, they seemed to lift, so the cables, or rather, silver chains, went slack, as if the seats were flying outward on their own. Only children rode, and they screeched in delight as the chairs went up and down, pulling at the ends of their chains.

And some things were the same. The Break-a-Plate game still had rows of white plates and baskets of balls to be thrown at them. Two identical boys played ring toss, and it was only when she got closer that she saw they had pink fleshy tails, or rather, a single tail that was part of both of their bodies but was fused together at the tip.

Yukiko told her how she had lost something, a spirit ball, and how it was here, in this world. They would find it and then Astrid would open a Door and take them back to their own world. The fox seemed apologetic about it, and insisted that they would be safe.

"Then why are you telling me to hurry?"

"These people, the Seelie, are mostly harmless. Humans visit them now and again, usually by accident, but it's not a common occurrence. They can tell a human from their own kind very quickly."

"Then why aren't they coming after me now? We've been here a while."

The fox pondered this. "I'm not sure." She glanced around, as if some of the Seelie might turn and grab the both of them, but the people around them continued walking, talking, eating, just as humans did at their park. "Let's take advantage of it. I think the stairway to the pier is this way. You can wait on the beach. I think she may be easier to bargain with on this side. Perhaps, if I learn about her binding, I can help her break it and she'll give the ball to me."

The fox was talking to herself and Astrid had no idea with whom she was going to bargain. But this place was Seelie. That was the name of the people, and of their world. And a strange and beautiful world it was. The colors here were more vivid, the scents more delicious and the temperature of the air was perfect for a nice stroll on the boardwalk.

"Why do the Seelie have a park like ours?" she asked.

"Their park was first, and then your people built a similar one on your side. The Seelie, most otherfolk, are attracted to borderlands, places in-between. This place is ideal, a place between sea and land, amusement and fear, reality and the imagined. It's also right on the San Andreas Fault. They like instabilities like that, both literal and metaphorical. So this place was where the Seelie park grew."

"What's it called?"

"Luna Park, like yours."

"So the humans named it after the Seelie park?"

"It happens more often than you'd think," said Yukiko.

"What about Disneyland?"

"There was no person by that name in Seelie, so it has a different name here. But it exists."

Astrid paused at the glass and wood building enclosing the carousel. In her world, the building's beams were metal, but here, they were wood painted a gaudy aqua blue with gold-painted seashells fastened on here and there. Inside, the ride had no horses, at least nothing that resembled a horse as she knew it, though there were horse-like creatures, some feathered or scaled. A tiger with iridescent green and blue stripes stood mid-stride, a giraffe with a flame-colored fish's tail smiled a secretive smile while a panda with an Asian man's face laughed. There was a pair of pale jellyfish with saddles, a beetle covered in silver fur and a seashell chariot pulled by two fat winged cherubs with four arms each.

The riders were mostly human in appearance, though a few had body parts that looked like animals. A woman and her son stood in line, both with the lower body of a squirrel.

"Is the Piper Seelie?" Astrid asked.

"The Piper? No, of course not."

"Well, he's half goat and he has horns."

The fox made a little snorting sound. "Your own goats have goat parts and horns, but they're not Seelie. Any more than you are Seelie because you look human."

"But humans don't open Doors to other places."

"That's not true. But you might not be—" Yukiko stopped in her tracks. "Turn around!" she hissed. "We have to go back. That Iolanthe woman is here."

"The ram-headed woman? I don't see her."

"I can smell her. Let's go."

Yukiko turned and trotted back the way they had come, toward the mirror house and the arcade.

"How did you know Iolanthe had a ram's head?" asked Yukiko. She sounded wary.

"I saw her on the beach, returning that slaugh in the box to the Piper."

"But she always looked human in your world."

"I saw her differently. And you too, when you were dancing. I saw the cherry blossoms and the jacaranda blossoms falling at the same time."

"Did you see that I was a fox?"

"No."

Yukiko looked satisfied. "You seeing things like that is most likely a side effect of you being a Door. Maybe Doors come with that ability. They are rare, so I don't know. Some other beings can do it as well."

They slipped into the arcade and stopped in the back corner. The games did not run on electricity, but rather had brass wind-up cranks. Yukiko mentioned that the Seelie were modernizing, but to Astrid, everything looked like something out of a clockwork exhibit in a museum. One game involved shooting mouse skulls into tiny baskets using a little mechanical catapult. Another played strange music while tiny dolls attached to a post by multi-colored ribbons spun in a dizzy dance. The goal was to guide the dancers around the post in such a way that the ribbons wrapped around the post in a braided design.

"She's coming this way," said Yukiko. "She's near the front door."

Yukiko led the way out the other exit, toward the stage where, in the human world, the Chumash Legends show played. Here, the play depicted the Civil War and various Seelie crowded the hay bales, which here were soft and a bright, verdant green. Yukiko jumped up on a hay bale and whispered that they should wait there awhile. The magic they used during the play would help conceal the two of them.

The play was a little like Red Fawn's show, with wood, plaster and paper-mache props. Humans in the play fought and died, while the Seelie characters, who appeared to be in some kind of humorous love triangle, caused various romantic entanglements between a prostitute and two men, one a general and the other a private. The general was in love with the private, while the private loved the prostitute who was sleeping with the general, who was married to a woman somewhere in what the Seelie players called Sud Caroline. Astrid presumed that it meant South Carolina. The soldiers wore gray, so they must have been part of the Confederacy, but the Seelie version of American history was very different from the one she had learned in school. In this version, the war was a grand game, with sides to manipulate, strong emotions to feed from and many lost and suffering souls. The purpose of the war was completely lost on them and soldiers switched sides now and then.

The general in the play sent one of his weaker regiments into battle, keeping the regiment with his beloved private out of the way of harm by sending them to a more remote area. But the Seelie tricked the troops by making noises in the night, leading them on a merry chase and bringing the Union and Confederate soldiers face to face. Fighting ensued, and though the private's regiment managed to recover their sanity and emerged victorious, the private was killed. The general wept into his hands when he was honored for his strategic skills and pulled a wooden prop gun from his desk. The prostitute pleaded and screamed in horror as the general put the gun between his teeth. The Seelie in the audience laughed and cried, sometimes both at once. The general thudded to the floor, the prostitute knelt beside him, and then inexplicably kissed a Seelie man who appeared and tried to get her to eat some kind of yellow fruit. The curtain fell.

"Time to go," said Yukiko. They were caught up in the throng and pushed toward the exit.

"There you are," said Iolanthe. Astrid didn't see her twice this time; she had only the ram's head. She waited off to one side, and took Astrid's hand in hers, pulling her out of the crowd and into the shade beneath a fluttering canopy that sheltered a few benches.

"Don't eat anything!" yelled Yukiko, and Astrid strained to see her, but she was gone. Had the fox abandoned her, or had she been captured? She tried to push through the crowd, but she could not find her. The advice to not eat was sound. If the Seelie were fey, fair folk, then any human who ate anything in their world could become trapped there forever.

"Don't worry about the Kitsune. She will be cared for," said Iolanthe. Astrid was close enough to detect the faint smell of the fur on her face, which was not unpleasant, and to see that her horizontally slitted eyes were gold. The skin of Iolanthe's hand was warm and soft, and her grip was so delicate as to be almost imperceptible. "We need to speak together, Astrid."

"I want to find Yukiko."

"She will be all right without you. And you without her."

Astrid wanted to say that she would not be all right without Yukiko, but it was the fox who had the spirit ball to retrieve. Astrid simply wanted to return home. She dreaded having to return to the mirror house to try to open a Door to her world. There was no certainty that she could do it, and there was no telling where she would end up. She had, so far, opened Doors to Unseelie, Seelie and Death. There had to be another way.

"You belong here," said Iolanthe. Astrid discovered that they were walking and were yards away from where they had started. She looked back over her shoulder, but Iolanthe gently led her onward. "This is your home."

"No, it's not. I belong in my world."

"Do you? I have a car waiting. There's a house in Malibu waiting for you."

"No, I'm not leaving until I find Yukiko. And I'm not going to Malibu. Unless it's Malibu in my world. Not yours."

Iolanthe stopped and fixed her with those gold coin eyes. "Astrid, dear. I have gone to great lengths to obtain a lovely home for you in order to help you. And now, you must come with me. I can answer some of your questions. This place is not safe for you. Surely you know that."

"Then you can answer my questions here. I'm not going anywhere."

"Come now, be reasonable."

"And do what? Let you take me off to some weird fairy house, never to return? Or I'll return in fifty years and my friends will all be old? Or in a hundred years and they'll all be dead? I know how this works." She turned and headed back to the main boardwalk. She would find Yukiko, get this spirit ball thing and go home.

"I wouldn't do that if I were you."

The last thing she felt was Iolanthe's hand wrapping around her own, like the twining of vines, and squeezing gently. Then the world wavered and she felt like she was falling, air and color flying past.

She awoke in a bright, high-ceilinged room. A bed was beneath her, a plump circular cushion on the floor, with fat silken pillows in shades of pale blue and sea green. There was no blanket. The wall-hangings were of similar colors, all of them woven tapestries of abstract shapes, some crafted with metallic thread. Three windows ran along the wall, all of them floor length, their white wooden shutters propped open to admit a soft breeze from the ocean. It carried with it the scent of fresh-mown grass and a sweet scent, almost candy-like. It looked like she was up high, on the second or third floor of a building.

She got up. She still wore her Luna Park uniform which felt dirty and sticky. In the distance she saw Santa Maria Island, but from a different angle than the one she was used to. That meant she was a little north of Luna Park. This must be the Malibu house. The nerve of that goat woman to force her to come here.

She rushed to the window, hoping to catch a glimpse of a way out. If she was a captive, then perhaps they didn't know she was awake. She could get away.

The window was too high up to jump from safely, and with no sheet or material with which to make a prison-style rope, a slower escape was out. There was only one door in the room, and it was closed.

A gust of air rushed in the window and she scanned the horizon. The air was so clear here. In her world, she could only see Santa Maria Island through haze. It was never as clear as this.

She pulled open the door, which had no proper doorknob or latch, but simply a round glass knob screwed into it. It led into a smaller sitting area with a cushion like her bed, but smaller. Open windows looked out over a yard with a lawn that ran alongside the house. In a corner of the little room she spotted a rectangular hole in the floor where a ladder with large, flat rungs led to a lower level. The room below looked like a kitchen. Seeing as there were no other doors on this level, she descended.

She stopped near the bottom of the ladder as she caught sight of the person waiting below. A centaur, she thought, as it rose from its reclining position on the floor. The centaur woman had a stocky russet-colored pony's body and the upper body of a woman. She was short, only about as high as Astrid's chest. Her white hair was piled high on her head with beads woven through, some dangling around her powdered face. A ruffly pink and cream dress was cut low over her generous bosom and the skirt was of uneven length. It stopped above the knees of her front legs and was long in back, spreading out over her body and ending just at her rump. Her thick white tail was styled with intricate braids and interwoven strings of beads and pink flowers that matched her dress.

"Well, which way is out?" Astrid said, taking in the rest of the lower floor. There was a kitchenette, or the Seelie approximation of one, complete with a wood-burning stove, a squat wooden chest and shelves filled with white china plates and cups as thin and translucent as rice paper.

Two sofas circled the living area, or rather, cushions with wooden frames that propped up the backs. On the floor in the center sat a flat wooden circle, like a legless table.

"The door is just there," said the centaur woman, pointing to the end of a short hallway that ran off the kitchen behind Astrid. "You may go if you wish, but it will do no good."

"What, are they going to haul me back?"

"Perhaps. Probably. But you are not a prisoner."

"Sounds like being a prisoner to me." Astrid found her purse on the table next to the door and picked it up.

"They're doing it for your good, so you can learn how to control making Doors. Otherwise, you're dangerous. You know this."

It was true. She was dangerous, frighteningly so.

"You know how I can control it?" Astrid asked.

"Oh yes! That's why I'm here—to teach you."

"Can you do it? Open Doors?"

"Well, no. But I've taught others, and I can teach you. I have experience. My great-grandfather helped people in your world. He lived just outside of Athens. But that was centuries ago by your reckoning."

"And after I learn, I'm free to go?"

"As a bird."

Astrid considered. She could stand to spend a few hours and then go home. Then perhaps she could pack some food and return here. But there was something else.

"Iolanthe said that this was my home. What did she mean?"

The pony centaur took down two translucent plates from the shelf and opened the trunk. It was an ice chest, complete with a slick block of ice at the bottom. Inside sat chilled glass bowls of flower petals and cold sliced vegetables, cheeses and fruit. The woman removed them all.

"What do you think?" she said.

So suddenly now the little woman wasn't so eager to talk. She kept her eyes on the plates in front of her as she arranged the flowers and food. Or perhaps the flowers were part of the food. It didn't matter, as Astrid wouldn't be eating any of it.

"I don't know. Obviously something is wrong with me," she said.

"Not wrong, no."

"Are there other Door people?"

"They crop up in most sentient species. They're exceedingly rare. But I have some experience with them."

"So the centaurs train Door people?" said Astrid. "Like your grandfather in Greece?"

"He trained heroes, not Doors. But my family has helped a number of humans. And non-humans."

Her hands paused at the last phrase and then she poured two glasses of some red liquid that looked like tea. She sat two yellow flowers into the glasses.

"Is that what I am?" said Astrid. "A non-human?" She wanted to leave, to bolt out the doorway.

"What do you think?"

She didn't know what to think, not really. If she was some kind of terrible creature and her ability could not be controlled, would she have the courage to allow herself to be imprisoned for the safety of others? She set her purse beside the floor cushion and took a seat. The centaur worked silently. After a minute, Astrid looked up to see the woman watching her.

"Well, I have the Door problem," Astrid said. "And sometimes I see things twice. Like Iolanthe. I saw her with her human head and the ram's head. Can the Seelie do that? See twice?"

"Yes." The centaur finished arranging food on the plates and set them both on the legless table between the cushions on the floor. The food looked delicious, especially the white cubes of cheese and the soft fresh bread. The centaur handed Astrid one of the glasses, but Astrid did not drink.

"And do the Seelie eat meat?" Astrid took a seat across from the centaur, who folded her pony legs beneath her and arranged her dress.

"Never. It makes us ill."

"And how would one tell a Seelie from a human?"

"An excellent question. Well, if I were classifying the two, aside from physical differences like my own, there are a few ways. One," she held up a finger like a schoolteacher, "they become ill from being exposed to cold iron."

"What's that?"

"Iron from a meteorite. And that is where your tale becomes very, very interesting. Because that little owl bell in your purse was made of cold iron. Rare in your world. It made the rest of us feel sick and we had to have it taken away."

Astrid pulled open her purse. Everything else was in order, including her wallet, sketch pad and other items. But the owl bell was gone.

"But it didn't make me feel sick, and that's not what you expected," said Astrid.

The centaur grinned. "They told me you were intelligent. I am pleased."

"You think I'm a changeling?"

"As you say. Albeit one who has forgotten her manners. You have not asked me my name."

"Sorry. What should I call you?"

"Ghislaine. Though sometimes I will be my brother, Gerard."

"How can you be your own brother?"

"There are many ways of being. When you are with your friends, are you not different than when you are with a teacher or your mother? Some of us are a little less apt at concealing ourselves."

"My mother, did she know that I wasn't hers?"

"It's very sad," said Ghislaine, popping a plump berry into her mouth. "You were born here, though do not ask me who your family is, as I do not know. And the infant girl whose place you took was sick, withering. She was in a hospital. It was an act of mercy as well as bravery for the Seelie to put you in her place."

"But don't the fey hate electricity and metal? Hospitals are full of that stuff."

"As I said, an act of bravery."

"And the baby?"

"Sadly, your little doppelganger died."

She thought of the girl in the mirror. If the human girl had died, then had she seen her own future? Or was it simply an illusion, frightening and meaningless?

"I think my mother knew," Astrid said. "She knew I wasn't hers."

Ghislaine nodded sadly. "She knew. She would have known it in a place inside herself that she would not have understood."

"Subconsciously?"

"That sounds like a good word to describe it."

"So, the presence of a changeling could cause a mother to become something different?" She almost couldn't bear to say it. "Cruel? Hateful?"

"Yes, and I am sorry. It is not uncommon for parents to hurt or kill changelings. They can feel that the little one is not their own. They hate themselves for it, and yet they are unable to stop. But you are here now, and the woman you called your mother has been spared the grief of a lost child. So all in all, things worked out well."

Astrid would not have said that.

"And what about my parents here?"

"Iolanthe told me that they will be told of your presence. She said that they always wanted to see you."

"So they didn't willingly give me up?"

"Oh no! No, your parents wanted you. But you were born a Door, and so the Council took you to be raised in the human world."

"But why?"

"Can't you guess?"

Astrid shook her head. She lifted the cup of tea to take a sip, but then set it down.

"You are tired," said Ghislaine. "So I will explain it to you. You are Seelie, blood and body and soul. You can blend with humans perfectly, having been raised on their food and air and water. And yet, you belong here. Once you are able to open Doors, you can be like an ambassador between the two peoples. Our kinds can live together, in peace."

It was a pleasant thought, but only for a moment. The Seelie were not known to be good for humankind. She thought of the Civil War play and how the fey had delighted in tormenting the humans, even driving the general to suicide. And the stories, so many stories, tales of people being lost, seduced, robbed. Stolen spouses, trickery, stolen children. There were stories of love too, of Seelie falling in love with human men and women, bearing children together, but the stories did not end well.

There was more to this, she was sure of it. But Ghislaine simply sipped her red tea and watched her.

CHAPTER 34

ASTRID SAT AT AN EASEL. The drawing in front of her was of a Door with a mirrored surface, sketched in pencil but not colored. She saw it flicker, move, just for a second. But there was no doubt in her mind that it had done so. The movement startled her out of her dreamlike state. She couldn't remember how she had gotten here, to this room where she had been drawing.

She did not remember putting on the scarlet and gold silk pants and sleeveless top that she wore. The fabric was cool and soft and soundless as it rubbed against itself as she walked across the smooth, birch-white floor. A beaded sash wrapped around her waist, and her toenails and fingernails were painted gold. None of it was familiar.

She had to regain her sense of place and time. She was in Seelie, was herself Seelie, and was supposed to be learning how to be a Door. Working on art was supposed to help her. This was the little sitting room off of her bedroom, and Gerard was downstairs, singing some opera in a language that sounded nothing like Italian. She and Gerard had practiced, she remembered, at opening Doors. Or rather, she had practiced while he tried to instruct her. The thing was, the ability was more an art than a skill, and it depended on feelings, intuition and other unquantifiable things. The entire process was frustrating. He had told her to take a break and draw something.

There. Her mind was clearing and she went downstairs. Like his sister, Gerard was a centaur, though he wore a ruffled shirt and tailored navy blue jacket with gold buttons that ended at the bottom of the human portion of his body. He also had white hair that he wore high on his head. Unlike his sister, he had a mole that was so perfectly placed above his lip that Astrid was certain it had to be fake.

"Afternoon, sweetling. Are you ready to try again?" he said.

There were drawings on the walls, so many drawings, at least twenty. And she remembered drawing them all. Gerard was hanging one in a blank space.

"How long have I been here?" she asked.

"Now you know that question doesn't really work here."

She had eaten here, yes. But she now understood that she was Seelie, and that her choosing to eat or not would have no effect on her leaving. Either that or the Seelie had fooled her. But no, once they had explained things, she understood what she was: a Door into other worlds. It was not only a skill she had, but was a part of her very being. Her fondness for in-between places, like busses and trains, her love of the quiet and the dark, they were part of being a creature that was neither here nor there, of one place or another. The thought was comforting and disconcerting. She knew what she was now, but was uncertain exactly what it entailed.

And she understood that she was a prisoner. The Seelie could pass through the gate at the front of the house which was opened and closed by an elaborate mechanical lock. Gerard or Ghislaine were the only two who came to see her, and they always arrived in an old-fashioned car that had no electrical parts. The car even had a crank at the front that Gerard or Ghislaine would turn over and over to start the engine when it was time to depart.

She wanted to leave, but they did not allow it. This memory was fresh. Cold iron waited around the house, in pieces, embedded underground, except near the high front gate, which was always locked. The yard may as well have had an electric fence around it, for even approaching the boundary was intensely painful for her. She had wondered if other fey people had been imprisoned here. Or had the house been built for her specifically?

Her parents, whoever they were, never came.

She took a breath to ask what time it was, and then sighed. Another useless question. She poured herself a glass of strawberry tea and gulped half of it down in the kitchen. Gerard shot her a disapproving look. She was supposed to learn etiquette, as she might one day be summoned to see the queen. He was offended by the very notion that one of their kind had been raised by barbarian humans and he insisted that she dress appropriately, and learn her people's customs.

But she had not learned enough. Not enough to find a way to get free. And she would get free. Even if she never learned to control her abilities as a Door, she would not remain a prisoner forever. She concealed her desire from Gerard and Ghislaine, though how could they not guess at it? They encouraged her abilities in Door-making and tried to keep her company, one at a time, seeing as they shared a body. But they were not what she would call friends.

"Is there anything you need before I go?" asked Gerard.

"No thanks."

The apricot sky was a darker shade. Sunset. She had tried to leave before and had failed, but her knowledge of making Doors was improving. The drawing upstairs had moved, and it gave her an idea.

Gerard finished up, and cranked his mechanical car out front. She listened as the engine popped and banged, and then rattled down the road. In her world, he rode on the Pacific Coast Highway, though she had not asked what it was called here.

The sun was lower now, and there wasn't much daylight left. She hurried up to her room and found her purse, full of reminders of her past life. The tiny sketch book inside was partly filled now, and she took it out with the pink clamshell mirror.

Ghislaine had brought mirrors for her to work with, but she had not been able to do any more than make the mirrors flicker or bend. Ghislaine had been delighted and had clapped her manicured hands, but Astrid was not satisfied. Later, she noticed that both Ghislaine and Gerard refused to leave mirrors at the house with her.

And then she had gone into a period of quarter-sleep, unaware of time passing, hunger or any desires at all, simply of following instructions from her tutors, eating, sleeping, bathing outdoors in a little spring beside the house. An outhouse stood outside too, though nothing like the ones in her world. This was a little hole in the ground surrounded by a narrow silken tent, pegged down, at the far corner of the property.

And now, the drawing had awakened her. She felt like she was becoming more accustomed to the Seelie world. Ghislaine had told her she would, eventually. Or was her rebellious human nature surfacing? She didn't feel Seelie, but still felt like herself, a girl, a young woman. And there were differences, immunities beyond cold iron. She could eat salt, for instance, with no ill-effects and be near magnets. The human world was still very much a part of her.

She found her shoes and put them on without socks, laying the socks to one side. Then she slipped her purse strap over her head so the strap ran diagonally across her body and ran her waist sash through the strap and retied it, securing it to her. The socks were too thick to tie easily, but she worked at them until they hung from her sash with three knots tied in each. They looked ridiculous and lumpy, but she wasn't finished yet. Taking the long piece of sash that hung down at her side, she tied three more knots. Three sets of knots with three knots each.

Of course, the knots did not bother or confuse her. Immunities indeed.

She kept the clamshell mirror, her sketch pad and a pencil in her hand as she closed the front door behind her and cut around to the back of the house. She faced the sea now, deep green with white foam while the evening sky was a deep autumnal orange. This place, this world, might be a prison, but it was a beautiful one. It always seemed to be summer at night and springtime during the day. The temperature was remarkably consistent, and unlike in the human world, no thick fog moved in and out over the ocean. Their sea, she had learned, contained no salt, and she wondered what creatures might live in it.

She walked to the edge of the lawn, where the property tapered off and joined the golden sand of the beach. Just as she started to feel ill, she crouched down. This was going to be tricky.

Mirrors could be Doors, and similarly, Doors could be mirrors. She had figured that out herself, having drawn so many of both. She held the clamshell mirror and inched forward, squinting as the pain in her head increased. The cold iron made it hard to breathe, but she forced air in and out of her lungs. She aimed and tossed the mirror. It landed in the sand, its two mirrors facing upward, glinting in the last rays of the sun.

Then she backed up, away from the painful barrier. After she caught her breath, she opened her sketch pad to a drawing she had made of the compact. It was as detailed as she could make it and she had even made a little mark so she would know which side was the magnifying mirror and which was the normal one. She got to work, sketching the sky and the beach in the blank white spaces that were the mirror's surfaces. She looked at a white gull overhead, and included that. She tried to imagine she was inside the compact in the sand, looking up. What did the mirror see? She drew.

And then she stood and started toward the barrier, keeping her eyes on the sketch she had made. It was time. She ran, and the pain increased, blinding in its intensity. She could not breathe, and her vision blurred, but she ran, keeping the image of the mirror in her mind even when she could no longer see it clearly.

She leapt, and though she had no breath to scream, her ears filled with sound, like a blasting train whistle shrieking one long note. This would kill her. It had to. Nothing could be this painful and not kill.

The mirror. The sky. The birds. The green water. Gold sand. Hiss of waves. Scent of the sea. She tried to think, but the pain seared her mind. There was only the pain.

She fell then, and kept falling. It took a few moments, and then she was on her knees, and the ground was sand. She grabbed the compact through which she had just come and crawled away from the barrier. She kept moving on her knees, even after the pain abated, until the sand became smooth and dark with water. The knees of her pants were getting wet. A wave slid up the beach and swirled around her wrists, knees and feet before retreating back, pulling at her. The sketch book clutched in her hand was now soaked and ruined.

Had it worked? Or had she just traveled through the barrier, her own momentum carrying her through? No, it had worked. The drawing of the mirror had become like a mirror, a Door. She had felt the falling sensation, like when she had entered Seelie from the mirror house.

Now, she had to get back to Luna Park and that mirror house. For though she may have been able to transport herself a few feet, she could not yet make a Door between worlds on purpose. And the only person who was on her side was a little fox who had vanished, who knew how long ago?

CHAPTER 35

ASTRID HURRIED DOWN THE BEACH in the direction of Luna Park. She put the clamshell mirror and the soggy sketch book into her purse. The pencil was lost, probably still on the other side of the cold iron barrier.

The city of Malibu existed on a tiny promontory, more of a bump really, that pointed due south. The coastline around it faced south also, and it would be miles before the beach curved and became westward-facing again.

She looked back at the house in which she had been imprisoned. It was rectangular, white and without trim or embellishment. The rectangular windows and flat roof gave it a box-like, geometric appearance. It was not what she would have expected from a sidhe house at all, either Seelie or Unseelie. It looked very modern, like some of the architecturally experimental homes from the 1980s. Perhaps they thought she would have been happy in a house like those from her own world? Or maybe there was another reason. It didn't matter. She was free.

An oil lamp shone in the upstairs window and she wondered if she had left it on. As she watched, a second light blinked on downstairs. The Seelie knew about her escape, they had to, or they would not have sent anyone. In the distance ahead were other lights, these also non-electrical.

She ran, which was exhausting in the soft sand, so she ran along the water where the sand was harder, pausing to walk now and then to catch her breath. She had already known that there were no neighboring houses close to her own, but as she went, she found that she only passed one house in twenty minutes. In the human Malibu, there were plenty of houses. Could it be that there were fewer Seelie than humans? The thought had not occurred to her until now. Or perhaps the fey preferred not to live in houses. That would make sense as well.

She found that the lights in the distance surrounded a small marina. As she drew closer, she saw that some of the boats had sails, others had oars, and some had both. None had motors and all were small or medium craft, suitable for only a few passengers.

She passed through the place, spotting only two other people. They would not sense her humanity, as she was not human, she reminded herself. No one had bothered her on the boardwalk, and no one bothered her now. With luck, the knots in her clothing would confuse them enough to allay any of their suspicions. A little lawn ran along the far end of the marina near a few benches and a group of six swan-shaped boats tied up to posts. She was reminded of the flat, open boats at human lakes that two people could rent and then peddle around in the water.

The swan boats had no such peddles, nor did they have oars or sails. From close-up, they looked lightweight and floated high on the water, bobbing and bumping into each other as they tugged at their ropes.

"You want to rent one?" said a man to one side. He sat on a little stool and his skin, hair and clothing were all a brownish color that made him blend into the dark.

"How much?" She had no Seelie money. Did they even use money?

"You make the offer."

Ah, so she must offer something in trade. She unzipped her purse and rummaged through. She had a little pot of cantaloupe-flavored lip balm with a cheery orange lid with cartoon fruit on it.

"How long could I get it for this?"

The man took it and unscrewed the lid. He sniffed it, dipped his finger into it and put it in his mouth.

"Odd jelly," he said, skeptical. "And too little of it."

She explained how lip balm worked, and extolled the virtues of having a pleasant scent and taste available for many hours.

He sniffed again at the pot. "Four hours. Then you bring it back."

"Great," she said and glanced back along the beach. The sand was empty, but if Iolanthe, Ghislaine or Gerard were coming for her, they wouldn't be walking along the beach. "Which one should I take?"

"Are you new to this?" he said. "You never had one before? There's one that wants to go already."

One of the boats bumped against its post while the others floated at the end of their ropes.

"I need to learn how to operate it," she said. "How do I steer and make it go faster?"

He laughed. "You tell it, love."

"They're alive?" She thought of the Dragon Swings at the boardwalk that seemed to fly on their own. Were there other objects here that were alive?

He looked at her as if she had asked if the boats were made of green cheese. "Just tell it."

He held the rope for the closest boat and Astrid climbed in, sitting down on the wooden plank that served as a bench. It sunk lower in the water and the man untied it.

"Four hours," he said. But he spoke to the boat, not to her. A little necklace of white lights lit up around the swan's curving neck. They were neither electrical nor fire, but they were bright.

She felt bad stealing, but maybe the boat would be able to find its way home after she no longer needed it. The boat glided out into the water and the man went back to his stool.

"Take me to Luna Park," Astrid said, and the boat

started moving. The craft bobbed up and down as it got farther into the ocean, but kept upright, and she held onto the brass railing that ran along the inside.

The sky and water grew dark. She thought she could see the boardwalk in the distance, but there was also the Seelie version of Los Angeles. If they like illusions, luxury and madness, then she could see the attraction. Yukiko had said they liked instability, and there was plenty of that as well.

The water grew choppier, and the wind grew cold, colder than she had ever felt it here. It felt like winter, a biting chill, and the wind grew stronger the longer she rode.

"Faster," she said to the swan. "Go as fast as you can. I think a storm is coming."

The boat sped up, and she tried encouraging it, telling it that it was doing a great job and was very beautiful. She wasn't sure if it would help.

Behind them, little spots of light appeared on the water, spreading out, following her.

"Turn off your lights. We're being followed."

The lights stayed on, but then after a few seconds, they blinked off.

"Thank you. You're the best."

The swan's painted eyes stared out from its immobile wooden face. She put her hand on the base of its neck and stroked it.

The storm came up over the next few minutes, first a light sprinkling and then getting harder. She was within sight of Luna Park and rain pelted down, soaking her to the skin. Some of the waves washed over the sides and filled the bottom of the boat, soaking her shoes and making her feet numb.

She thought she caught sight of something in the water. It looked like a head, but as soon as she focused on the thing, it dropped out of sight. She caught sight of it twice more, then a slick hump, like a sea serpent with a pointed fin broke the water's surface and was gone.

"What's out here with us?" she said to the swan and then held on to the railing tight as a wave tipped the little craft sideways. It teetered upright, and dark water sloshed in. The waves were getting higher, and the boats behind her were getting closer. She could hear the shouts of the riders, calling to one another. Lights or no lights, they knew exactly where she was.

There was a bang and the boat lurched, as if it had been hit from beneath by something large and strong. Oh God, a shark. She had heard of sharks attacking boats. She hung onto the railing and knelt on the bottom of the boat, begging for it to hurry. The thing bumped her again, and the side of the boat shot so high up that she almost fell out.

A wave crashed over her, and cold water slammed her body and face, filling her mouth and nose. It tasted like murky lake water, and she spat it out. The sky was completely black now, as were the waves, and the rain came down in needles, stabbing at her skin while the freezing wind tried to push her into the water.

The Seelie were doing this, she knew. It was how they were going to stop her. That was why it was always pleasant and warm. The Seelie kept it that way. And now, they were using the weather to stop her.

She hung on as the thing beneath the water slammed her boat again, and the swan dipped sideways, wavered there, and then continued a slow, agonizing tilt. She scrambled to climb up the boat, to shift the center of gravity and force it upright, but the waves lurched hard, the boat was too slick for her to grip, and she slammed into the freezing water.

Something slid up behind her. She felt a tail, muscular and sleek, slide against her legs. She grabbed at the boat, which now floated on its side, trying to get a purchase. And then she felt something strong, like the tail, but thinner, wrap around her waist and pull her under.

CHAPTER 36

ELLIOT SAT IN THE LIVING room across from Neil, who leaned back with his hands clasped behind his head, and Hazel who chatted with Mr. Escobar, the capuchin monkey.

Neil was Elliot's partner in the Time Corps, in Elliot's future and Neil's past, present and, presumably, future. And since Elliot knew nothing about time travel or the work of the Time Corps, Neil was training him.

So far, he had met Seamus and Felicia, who tended to work together and who had been there to take him from his trailer. Seamus Doyle was an Irish inventor, born in 1825, and had created the machines that they used to travel in time. Felicia Sanchez, who was born sometime in the late twentieth century and had been in medical school, had somehow fallen through a time rip of Seamus's creation and was hoping, some day, to find a way home. Hazel, an orphan from the mid-nineteenth century, was Seamus's ward.

Seamus and Hazel were from the same home universe, and their evolution had taken a slightly different course from that of people in other worlds. Their feet were too wide in the front, with apelike big toes. Felicia was from a different universe than they were, but also a different one from Elliot's own. She looked just as people in Elliot's world did, though her eyes were a shade lighter than average.

Hazel and Neil were good friends and sometimes partners, although Hazel sometimes worked with Seamus and Felicia. Hazel's monkey, Mr. Escobar, was also her first mate, though Elliot still wasn't clear on what sort of ship she captained.

Huginn, the raven, and Pangur Ban, the mother cat, were the other team, though with Pangur Ban taking care of the kittens, the two of them stayed around the house, going out only to hunt and prowl and do whatever ravens and cats liked to do at night. Huginn had some sort of problem with his memory, and Pangur Ban helped him remember things.

Neil didn't say which universe he was from, when he was born, or what had happened to him before he joined the Time Corps. No one else seemed to mind his reticence.

Lastly came a stout, white-bearded man named Julius, the owner of the Time Corps house here in Los Angeles. There were other safe houses, places that had been owned for decades or centuries, where Time Corps members found shelter or stayed for as long as they needed. Julius mostly stayed in his room, but he wandered the halls sometimes in his pajamas. He lost his reading glasses frequently, though he otherwise seemed mentally sharp. He said he was a researcher, and liked to read technical manuals, historical records and romance novels.

"So stable time lines are good. Time loops are bad," said Elliot.

"That's about the size of it," said Neil. "Our job is to make lines out of loops, straighten things out and to stabilize the unstable time lines."

"You make it sound simple."

"Well, sometimes it is. Your first assignment shouldn't be too complicated. Just make something and deliver it."

"And I can't go back to my trailer or see Astrid until I do this?"

"Right. You gave this time and date, and it corresponds with your future statements—"

"Which I am not allowed access to."

Neil gave a little nod. "Which, for now, you are not allowed access to. And we know that you'll need to return there soon, so you shouldn't be in the area of Luna Park for a while. You need to keep a ten-mile radius. Technically, you could go back today and stay until the time Astrid returns, but you need to be here for training."

"But I need to go to work tomorrow."

"Not anymore," said Hazel, smiling. "You're with us now. You'll get a yearly salary and paid expenses. Not that it matters that much. One little piece of gold, invested a century or two back is all it takes. A little compound interest and your money worries are over."

"Believe me, you'll earn every ingot," said Neil.

Elliot looked out the window. No money worries? It was hard to imagine. Bills paid, all the groceries he wanted, a place to stay. He could buy a car. A new car, maybe even an Aston Martin or something ridiculously expensive. A convertible maybe. And maybe a house on the beach, the best surfboard money could buy, a high-end entertainment system. But none of the members of the Time Corps seemed to have much in the way of material things. Neil was fond of his black duster, and Seamus was protective of whatever laboratory equipment he had in the attic, but no one had an expensive car, and their clothes were just normal clothes. Well, normal if you considered Hazel's pirate queen outfit and Seamus's ugly striped trousers as normal.

"Wait, what did you say about a ten-mile radius?" Elliot asked.

"There's something about traveling as we do that does not allow anyone to be within ten miles of themselves," Neil said.

"Except for Neil," said Hazel. "He's the only one of us who can do it."

"So the radius keeps you from meeting yourself?" said Elliot.

"Essentially," said Neil. "But not because it would cause a paradox and end the world or anything. That doesn't happen. It's just, we can't go that close to ourselves. No one knows why."

"So how come you can meet yourself?" said Elliot. "Why can you do it and no one else?"

"Don't know," said Neil, but he didn't look at Elliot as he said it.

He had so many questions, and Neil and Hazel were trying to be patient with answering them. Why were the people in each alternative universe unique? There weren't infinite Elliots running around in other worlds, only him, living one lifetime a day at a time, even if they wouldn't be chronological. And how could they interfere in time without causing paradoxes? And there were other difficulties.

"I have a question," Elliot said. "If you truly travel in time, and the Earth is moving through space constantly, each time you traveled you would end up freezing and suffocating in the vacuum of space. So you're not only traveling in time, but through space as well. How do you make sure you end up on Earth and in the right spot?"

"That's a question for the Professor," Hazel said.

"Okay. And another thing, you said my ability to sense time slips is useful to you."

"It sure is," said Hazel. "There aren't many people who can sense when time lines are off. Some people who can do it remember little fragments of things as they would have been or they have a vague sense of unease. Not the regular feeling all people have, but something more. Most of them never have a clue why that is. But you, you can identify time slips. It can be useful."

"A useful idiot?" said Elliot. He wasn't a brilliant scientist like Seamus, a doctor like Felicia, a ship's captain like Hazel or stealthy like Huginn and Pangur Ban.

"A little bit of practice, some training missions, and you'll be ready to go," said Neil.

"He would know," said Hazel. "You've saved his life more than once."

"And this thing I have to deliver, it will make a stable time line?"

"Precisely," said Neil. "Right now, the existence of the thing is a loop—it has no origin. It appears in one place, vanishes, and reappears back in the first place. A normal object has to have an origin, a lifetime, and then it decays or falls apart. This one doesn't do that, and we have to fix it."

"And one little thing like that matters? What happens if I fail?"

Neil and Hazel looked at one another and Mr. Escobar looked down at the floor.

"What?" said Elliot.

"Well," said Hazel. "This thing is critical to keeping this world safe. It could be overrun with slaugh. We've seen the potential results, and they're bad. Very bad. This world is what is known as a hub world. If this world becomes unusable, much of our travel between worlds will be jeopardized."

"What about Astrid and her letting slaugh through? Will this help Astrid with her problem making Doorways?"

"The Time Corps are sort of specialists in Doorways, although not the kind she makes. And yes, it will help her," said Hazel.

"And what is this object I'm supposed to make and deliver?"

"A little bell. In the shape of an owl."

CHAPTER 37

ASTRID STRUGGLED AND FOUGHT AS she was pulled backwards through the water. She clawed and tore at the arms that wrapped her body like iron bands, but they did not loosen, even a little. The arms pulled her down, under the black water and then she was yanked so quickly that her shoes slid off and the rest of her clothing felt like it might go with it.

Then she was above the water, gasping, but still the arms did not release her. The thing waited for her to take a few breaths and then pulled her down. Again, she was pulled through the water, and again raised to the surface to breathe. Then down she went. This time, she tried to pay more attention. Though everything was black and she couldn't see a thing, she felt the body behind her along with the arms. The body was strong, so strong, and it moved rhythmically in a side-to-side motion, the lower and upper parts of the body moving opposite from each other.

The next time she surfaced, she looked for the Seelie. They had gathered around the swan boat, but they were far off. She was pulled down before she could take in anything else. The person dragging her through the water was saving her, allowing her to breathe and then pulling her away from the Seelie.

After a while, it stopped pulling her under and simply towed her along the surface. They were far away from the Seelie now, far enough that there was no chance of being seen. Astrid couldn't make out any of the fey creatures, and only knew their position by the lights on their boats. The lights on shore were farther away than ever. The creature had pulled her away from Luna Park.

And just as she started to feel glad that she wasn't being drowned and had eluded the Seelie, she gave in to fear of this creature pulling her. She reached down to feel the arms, not to pull at them, but to explore. She also stretched down her bare feet. The thing had arms and fingers, albeit long and webbed ones. The lower legs moved as one, side-to-side, like a fish or a shark. It was a tail. And then, she understood exactly what it was that had her. For how could she be in the ocean of the fey, in a storm, dumped overboard, and then be saved by anything else?

But wait. The creature had intentionally capsized her boat. The thing had rammed her. She could have died. And now she was helpless in its arms. But it did not seem intent on harming her, or it already would have. She hoped this was true, that it was not dragging her away to kill her at its leisure.

"Where are you taking me?" she asked, turning her head sideways. The thing's face was so close, right behind her ear, but she had not heard a sound or felt a single breath in her ear. Even in the dark, she could see the flash of small, white pointed teeth when it opened its mouth to speak.

"Somewhere safe. Away from our captors."

And then, the creature released her and she was able to stand up in the water. She waded the rest of the way out, the mermaid swimming up to shore, pulling herself out, and then changing her lower body into that of a human.

She was not pretty, at least not by the standards of modern beauty. She was not thin or young, and her face and body were those of an ordinary older black woman. But that body had been so strong and so fast in the water. And those eyes were keen enough to spot her so far off.

The woman was entirely alien and strange and she was now studying Astrid.

"Thank you," said Astrid. "For saving me."

"I am pleased you survived." She sounded like she was reciting words from a book, and she had an indefinable accent.

The mermaid looked out over the water, toward the Seelie. The lights were staying put. They must have thought that Astrid was under the water somewhere.

"I must go. They summon me."

And like that, the mermaid rushed into the water. Her legs fused and grew longer, ending in a dark crescent of a tail, and she slipped beneath the water.

Astrid took in the beach and the hills behind it. If Luna Park was in the distance, then this was Santa Maria Island. And though she was free of the Seelie, she was still far from Luna Park and her only hope of returning home.

And when she did get home, what then? Wouldn't the Seelie come again for her? Or did they need her to get to her world? Gerard and Ghislaine had spoken of meeting humans, but it was always in the distant past. But the Seelie surely were able to enter the human world, or Iolanthe would not have been able to come through. So why keep her captive? They already had a way to get to the human world without her.

Unless they wanted access to other worlds. There was Death and Unseelie, but surely there were other places as well, places stranger, and perhaps more dangerous.

Our captors. That is what the mermaid had called the Seelie. And what had happened to Yukiko? Was she also kept as a prisoner?

The water lapping at her feet looked dark, and not simply due to its normal murkiness. Even in the moonlight, she couldn't see the skin of her feet when even a few inches of water covered them. What else hid in the depths of the dark water around here? For surely there were other mythical creatures, leviathans, sea serpents, and others that, unlike mermaids, were not kind to drowning sailors.

Her two socks had, amazingly, stayed tied to her sash and her purse was still intact. She walked up and down the beach, searching, but there was nothing but rocks and scrubby plants. Astrid waited, and eventually the mermaid returned. She changed and walked up the beach, as naked as a newborn babe, and just as unconscious of her nudity.

"I have a cave. You should come, as the Seelie will search here soon."

The lights floated closer with each moment, and the mermaid led her down the beach. Then, she stepped back into the sea and beckoned.

"It is underwater, but you can hold your breath long enough. There is air inside."

Astrid hesitated. The last thing she wanted was to be dragged to this creature's lair where she could be killed or left to die and no one would be the wiser.

"The Seelie do not mean you well. Like the fox, they can keep you forever."

"You know about Yukiko?"

"They are her captors. They are my captors as well. And I despise them."

She understood, but she was frightened of being dragged down, of being lost, of not knowing where she was going or how she would get out. She made herself step into the surf. Then, the mermaid seized her and yanked her down beneath the water.

She tried to keep her eyes open, but it was no use in the black. She was pulled along, down deep where the pressure hurt her ears, and then into a tunnel. Then they moved upward and the mermaid's strong arms pushed her to the surface. She filled her lungs with air, held onto a rocky bit of wall and then wiped the water from her eyes.

The grotto was beautiful. Bioluminescent algae clung

to the walls, giving the place a bluish green cast. The light reflected on the water and wavered on the walls, making the whole place look like it was under water. A submerged ledge jutted out beneath a foot of water, and the mermaid gave her a gentle push toward it. She used it as a step and climbed out onto the rough, rocky floor of what looked like a cave. A dark hole opened at the back, large enough to crawl through, leading back into the interior of the rocky island.

"Stay here. I have to go speak to the Seelie," said the mermaid, and she was gone.

The room was about ten feet across and just tall enough for Astrid to stand. The jagged rocks made a sort of dome overhead, marred by a long crack where white moonlight poured in. A little gust of cool air blew from the tunnel. There must be a hole that provided fresh air in that direction also.

She took a few paces toward the tunnel. The rock under her feet was rough and craggy, like volcanic rock, only more solid and less porous. It cut into the soles of her feet. The bioluminescent algae lined the tunnel, and she lowered herself down, trying to see into the dark, but the tunnel made a sharp twist a few feet in and she could not see beyond it. She crawled into the tunnel, past the twist and then climbed as it sloped upward. It hurt her knees and palms and she had to move slowly.

It was then that she heard the crying from up ahead inside the tunnel. It was Yukiko. She went on, and the tunnel opened enough for her to stand in a kind of craggy hallway. Water collected in little pools between the rocks, and the algae colonies were larger here, giving more light. Mats of tightly woven sea grass cushioned her feet. It was almost homey.

A few things hung on the walls, just as in a human hallway. One was a life preserver with a ship's name printed on the side. Another was the skull of a sea creature, narrow and long-toothed, its empty eye sockets extraordinarily large, as if it lived deep under the water. It was mounted like a trophy.

Covering two doorways were curtains of seaweed, dried and woven with bits of rock and shell. The crying sound came from behind one. She parted the seaweed curtain and entered.

A treasure cave, she thought. Though most of the items were far from treasures. There were no crowns or cups or chests full of gold doubloons. On the floor and tucked into crannies in the walls were objects of all sorts. There were plastic toys, like the sort that came in fast food meals for children. And there were shoes, both sneakers and flip-flops. A deflated volleyball sat on the floor beside a gigantic pearl-white nautilus shell, perfect and unbroken. There was a bowl filled with smooth sea rocks, all of them white, and a water-warped photograph of a child. It was black and white, and the little boy posed in front of a suburban house beside his tricycle.

The sobbing came from one side, and she found a cloth, a hunk of burlap from an old coffee bean sack, tossed over something. She peeled it back and put her hand to her mouth.

The voice, it was Yukiko's, and this was her spirit ball. It could be nothing else. It was a perfect glass sphere, or something like glass, clear and smooth and the size of a softball. Inside were white light, and lightning, and something like the glitter inside a snow globe mixed with sorrow and weeping and beauty. It was power, both strong and subtle, and illusion, and the very soul of a person. A non-human, most certainly, but a person.

She didn't want to touch it, but she wanted to comfort it. The thing was in pain. This thing, it was immortal, she knew, or close to it. Something in her felt kinship with it. The ball was, she understood, a soul. A soul without a body. She had never encountered such a thing, as it was unnatural, grossly unnatural. And yet, here the thing sat, beside a silver fork with a monogrammed S on the handle and a piece of driftwood in the shape of the moon. Somewhere far away from her spirit ball, Yukiko cried, alone and frightened.

All remaining resentment from the ridiculous leaf incident vanished, and she felt sorry for the little white fox who had been robbed of that which made her who and what she was. Astrid decided to take it to her, give her the ball and restore the girl. To have one's soul removed was worse than death. For though death separated soul from body, the soul remained intact. Yukiko was wandering the world with part of her soul, conscious and aware, but separated from the rest of her own being.

The spirit ball gave off light, and the little room was brighter now, revealing more of the things that the mermaid had collected, some things from the human world like toys and hair clips, some from the Seelie, like hairsticks made of moving wood and a red-cheeked painted doll under a glass dome that danced, clasping her tiny hands to her chest, smiling and spinning, dancing forever.

Behind the spirit ball, she noticed two points of shadow on the wall. The shape was familiar. It was her owl bell, sitting upright and staring forward like a guard. And perhaps it was. For this was a piece of cold iron, the only one in the world to which she was immune.

She dropped the owl into her purse. Then, she took the spirit ball, put it into the burlap coffee sack and went to sit at the edge of the water to wait for the mermaid.

Stars were visible through the crack in the top of the dome, and she watched them move, slowly. The Earth turned, in the Seelie world as in her own. The moon was the same as well.

The mermaid's head surfaced and she climbed out of the water. "You have something of mine."

"The spirit ball belongs to Yukiko. You mentioned it

before, that she is the Seelie's captive. She told me she needs the ball, and I'm going to give it to her."

"And another thing you have taken also." She looked at Astrid's purse.

"The owl bell is mine. I've had it my whole life. The Seelie took it from me and gave it to you."

"They did not give it to me. I found it over fifty years ago."

Had that long passed? Had she been in the Seelie house for so many years?

"Look, I need to go home," Astrid said. "The bell is mine, and Yukiko needs her ball. It's a part of her, not just a pretty trinket."

"I know what I possessed. And you have stolen things from me fairly. You have entered as a guest and stolen from your host, which the Seelie most definitely frown upon. I will not be punished, by their own laws."

"So, I can have them?"

"You have stolen fairly."

The look in the mermaid's dark eyes told her that the loss of these things did not bother her. She could have taken them back easily. With her strength and her wicked little teeth, she could kill Astrid in a moment. She was allowing this, though for what purpose, Astrid did not know. If she hated the Seelie, then giving Yukiko back her spirit ball was a small act of defiance.

"Where is Yukiko?" Astrid asked.

The mermaid pointed at the wall of the grotto.

"Are you pointing at Luna Park?"

The mermaid bared her teeth and made a rhythmic hissing sound. Laughter. "Yes, at your park."

CHAPTER 38

YUKIKO CURLED UP NOSE TO tail on her thin, filthy blanket and snuggled down into it, but not because she was cold or tired. There were no more tears for her to shed, no more cries and pleas for mercy from the Seelie. Even her hate for them was fading into a kind of resigned indifference. She was theirs, not her own. She existed for their purposes. They had spoken with her, made her offers to become Seelie, which she had naturally refused. But time was on their side. It was only a matter of time now until she became weak enough to be forced to do their will.

A breeze blew in from the water. The smell! The smell of her spirit ball was more potent. That meant they were bringing it. What could that mean? Were they going to let her have it and then enslave her in a different way? Or perhaps they would allow her to draw a little power from it.

She leapt up and rushed to the front of her cell, a little caged area built into the rock beneath the Luna Park pier. It was wet and damp and cold. Other creatures had been kept here before her. She had found their bones and had collected them in the back of her cell, like a little burial mound. They were not Kitsune bones, but she felt they were her brothers and sisters.

She was afraid, for if the Seelie were bringing her spirit ball to her, then she would be asked to do something for them. It was not as bad as being held captive by the

Unseelie or some other creatures, but whatever they asked of her might not be good. It might violate the Myobu code, and then, when she got free, she would be in even more trouble than she already was.

She sniffed, trying to feel what was coming. Was it Iolanthe? Or one of the guards? Or perhaps the governor of this region? Was she important enough for that? The Seelie were hierarchical, and there might be many layers of bureaucrats who might want to come and assess their prize.

The wind now carried the scent of the person, and she was getting closer. It was the girl, Astrid, and the sea woman. There was only a hint of feeling from the sea woman, a remnant from the connection when Yukiko had summoned the creature before. She felt her presence as well as smelled her. Now the sea woman was moving out to sea, swimming away into the deep, and she could feel her no more.

But the girl drew closer. Was she a fool? There was a guard posted outside the cell, a small frog-faced man who liked to eat pineapple and sing to himself when he was drunk. Yukiko had gotten used to him. Of the guards, he was the least odious and cruel.

The spirit ball was close now, but not close enough for her to draw any power from it. Only a little nearer, and she could. But could Astrid get close enough without the guard spotting her? Right now, he sat on a three-legged stool, bottle in hand as he watched the waves. Funny, almost all sentient creatures could watch waves and fires and be fascinated. He was bored, that was clear, and was halfway through his bottle of blackberry wine.

Yukiko started to pull power from the spirit ball. First it came in a tiny trickle, not enough to do anything, and she pulled harder. A small stream now, though it was exhausting to pull it at that rate. The ball protested in its silent way, and the scent went slightly sour. No matter, for if Astrid was caught, then it would never be restored to her. She drew more power from it.

The frog man glanced down the beach, in the direction from which Astrid came. She must be far enough away to still pass for a Seelie. Maybe her being a Door would help disguise her. But Yukiko would not take the chance.

She almost had enough power now. She pulled more, and her head hurt, a sharp pain behind her eyes, but she kept pulling. Almost there. Just a small bit more.

"You there!" shouted the frog man, and Yukiko was out of time. She poured her power into the illusion, to hide Astrid, to make an image appear on the other side of the beach, the image of something pleasant, a female who the guard fancied. She slipped reality a bit, making him unable to see Astrid, and made the illusion of the female call out to him.

Then, she held her breath as the guard stared into space. He blinked and turned around, looking up the beach in the opposite direction of Astrid. He waved to the illusion and stepped away. Yukiko sighed in relief. The illusion was small and brittle, but it was all she could manage.

Astrid appeared, holding a burlap sack with the spirit ball inside. She glanced at the guard, and thankfully had the sense not to say anything. Then, she pulled out the spirit ball and held it out. It was too large to fit through the bars, but that was no trouble. Yukiko shrank it and Astrid pushed it through the bars and held it in her open palm.

Yukiko reached to take it in her jaws. How trusting this woman-child was. Didn't she know what she held? What she could do with a slave like a Kitsune? And yet she so willingly offered the spirit ball to her. She could smell the girl's pity at her captivity. She knew she looked bedraggled and starved, though she had been fed. She would have continued to wither over time, but would not have died. Death would have been a mercy.

The girl felt sorrow and wished to help her. Yukiko

was the reason she was in this world, and she was so completely ignorant of it, most likely blaming herself for accidentally opening the Door. She trusted Yukiko to help her, not to trick or harm her. It made her feel like an honored being, a true Myobu. She did not deserve it.

She swallowed her spirit ball. It burned a fiery path down her throat. She closed her eyes in ecstasy. It was back, back inside her, flowing like electricity through her cells, through her blood. She was whole, and alive, gloriously alive. She was fully herself.

The lock wasn't a problem for her now that she had her ball. She pointed her tail at it and it clicked open. She pushed open the door with her paws and she and Astrid ran up the beach, heading away from the guard and past Luna Park. They climbed up the rocky embankment that separated the land from the beach as soon as they were past the park.

As they went, Yukiko used her power to shield them from Seelie eyes and senses. Her fur felt more lush and thick, and she felt her eyesight and hearing becoming keener. The feeling surged through her. Yes. This was what she was, what she was created to be.

They stopped just outside the side gate to Luna Park. Luminous white birds, each four feet high, sat on perches on either side of the gate, welcoming people and chatting with guests and each other. It was only a matter of time before the birds were informed that there were two fugitives matching their description.

"We need to get to the mirror house," said Astrid.

"Can't you make a Door any other way?" whispered Yukiko. "This park is the worst possible place we could be at the moment."

"No, I've tried. I managed a small Door, but only managed to travel a few feet. I can't do it without the mirror house. That's the only place that will work."

"Well, if we move soon, I can get us there without

being caught," said Yukiko. "They have guards in both worlds, both in the human world and here. But that's not what's worrying me. I had some time to think while I was imprisoned. They might also have what you would call a magic tripwire to tell them if someone traveled from Seelie to the human world or vice versa. And if we trip one of them, they could send someone strong enough to catch us both. I don't think my magic can conceal us from those."

"How can they plant a tripwire in somewhere insubstantial?"

"Well, it's not like a mechanical device. They would have to attach it to the far edge of the human world and the far edge of Seelie. But they can create such things."

"So even if you used your magic and we got through on this side, they'd catch us before we reached the human world?"

"That's correct." Yukiko considered. "Since you have consistently used the mirror house, it's sure to have an alarm attached. But there might be another way."

"And what is that?"

"It's dangerous, and most likely terrifying, but I'm completely sure the Seelie won't have guards or sensors there. They would never risk it. We would set off the tripwire leaving Seelie, but they wouldn't know where we went to, as it wouldn't be the human world. The Seelie couldn't follow us."

"Well, let's go." Astrid headed for the entrance.

"It means we enter the Unseelie world," Yukiko said, softly enough not to be overheard.

The girl paused, but then kept on, either ignorant or foolish. "Let's do it. I've had enough of being forced to stay where I don't want to be. I'm a Door, and I'm going to go where I want to go."

Yukiko had no argument with that. Luna Park was as it had been before, full of tourists, travelers and locals, though Yukiko would have been hard-pressed to tell one kind from the other.

"As long as we don't get too close to whoever is at the mirror house, the illusion will hold," said Yukiko. "Just stay right next to me."

"I'm not sure I can open the Door."

"I think you can. You're scared, right? Weren't you scared when the slaugh came through?"

"Yes."

"And when you opened the Door to Seelie, what then?" She knew the answer, the sorrow and hopelessness and heartbreak the girl had felt. But Yukiko could never admit to knowing such a thing.

"I thought I saw the mirror move," said Astrid after a pause. "It startled me."

"Another strong emotion. And you said you made a small Door to move a few feet."

"That was in the house in Malibu where they held me captive. I got near the cold iron barriers and I was in pain."

"So fear and pain help you with the Doors," said Yukiko. "That's good."

"It's a real barrel of monkeys."

They passed the stage show and the arcade. Astrid glanced down at her.

"You're looking better already."

"I'm feeling much better. I'm not fully restored, but it won't be long."

"Why did they starve you and leave you in that place if they need you so much?"

"They fed me, but without my spirit ball, I can survive, but I will wither. They offered to give me back the ball if I would become Seelie and serve their queen. But I refused."

"How long were you there?"

"I'm not sure. A few days, I think."

"How long will have passed in our world?"

"I have no idea."

They walked in silence for a short time before Astrid spoke again.

"Yukiko? I have a question. I have a bell made of cold iron in my purse. How come they aren't affected?"

"You're moving, so they're only exposed for a moment or two. They probably feel nauseated, maybe a little headache, and then it passes. Also, you have all those knots. That'll throw off their perception of the source."

"And I'm immune to it."

"Well, naturally."

"Not so naturally, really," the girl paused. "As it turns out, I'm Seelie by birth, a changeling. A baby died and I took her place."

Yukiko was surprised, but then things fell into place in her mind. Something had been off about the girl, but she had smelled and felt completely human. She still did, except for the strange Door scent. But her ability to see things in their real form and as illusion was not human at all. And the Seelie had not felt her come through into their world. They had not had any tripwires then. But any human entering their world would have drawn attention, perhaps attraction, perhaps hostility. Anything but being ignored.

Well, now. A changeling, in this day and age. The more things changed, the more they stayed the same, as the humans said. And now this changeling girl wanted to go home to the human world.

The mirror house waited ahead. Two employees, both large and male, stood near the front and rear entries. They were undoubtedly guards, but not conspicuous ones. Yukiko headed toward the one at the rear entrance and changed reality a little, making him hear the call of the other guard. He went around to the front of the mirror house.

"How do you do that?" asked Astrid.

"There's a reason they wanted my spirit ball. It lets me bend reality and time, create illusions. I'm burning through its power quickly, but hopefully we'll be home soon. Assuming you can open two Doors in succession, one into Unseelie and one from there to the human world."

"I'm not sure I can."

Yukiko thought Astrid could do it, but mostly because she would use her magic to make an illusion that would help the girl. They went inside and headed straight for the mirror they had used as a Door previously.

"I'm going to make an illusion to help you," said Yukiko. "It's not real." She used her magic to create an image of slaugh, scratching and snarling. They clawed over one another and wailed in their eerie voices. "Is that how they were?"

"Yeah, that's it," said Astrid, breathless.

"They're not real."

"I know."

Astrid kept her eyes on the slaugh and stepped forward. Yukiko kept close, remembering how quickly the Door had closed behind her before.

"Unseelie," Astrid whispered. "Unseelie."

The mirror flickered and Astrid put her hand through. Yukiko leapt through beside her. There was the falling sensation, dizzying and swirling, and then she was on the floor of the mirror house once more. Astrid was on her knees beside her.

"It didn't work," said Astrid, looking around the mirror house.

"No, it did. Look." Yukiko pointed her nose out the back exit from the mirror house. The light was more blue here, like twilight.

"It's purple. The sky is purple," said Astrid. It was the light purple shade of the jacarandas that the humans planted around their boardwalk. "Do they call this place Luna Park also?"

"I've never been to Unseelie, so I don't know," Yukiko said. "Now, let's go to our world." She summoned her magic and made an image of the human Luna Park, blue sky, ocean-scented air, the distant music of the carousel.

"Home. Home," whispered Astrid.

A breeze rustled Yukiko's fur, but it was not the illusion of breeze from the image she had made. Then, the air grew unbearably strong, pulling at her, dragging her away from the Door. Astrid yelped as she fell and slid behind Yukiko. They were being pulled to the exit by something unseen, but strong. Yukiko bit at it, but there was nothing there.

"Release us immediately!" Yukiko shouted in her most commanding voice. "We are not under your jurisdiction! We have free right of passage!" It wasn't true, but she wasn't going to let anything or anyone know that. Perhaps the Unseelie had an ancient treaty with the Myobu. One never knew.

"You heard her. Release her," said a woman's voice. The force pulling them released them and Yukiko spun around, teeth bared and magic flaring. The woman before her was lithe and graceful with curly dark hair. She wore a blue dress and a blue and gold silk scarf tied around her neck. Matching faceted blue gems glittered from her earlobes and from a pendant around her neck.

Yukiko would use every ounce of her power, even causing her own death, before she was taken again. She drew power and prepared to attack. Electricity crackled the air.

"No need for that, Kitsune," the woman said. "I simply wish to speak with my daughter."

CHAPTER 39

ASTRID STOOD UP, BRUSHED HERSELF off and took in the elegant woman before her. There was no resemblance between them at all.

"You don't believe me," said the woman. Her voice was soft and gentle.

"No, I don't."

"And yet, here you are. Home."

"I am simply passing through. I'm Seelie. They explained it to me. Now we're going to leave."

"Then why did they keep you captive?"

Astrid wasn't sure what to say. The Seelie had kept her captive to train her so they could control the use of her powers. But she didn't want to reveal that she was a Door to this woman, this Unseelie.

"What I mean is this," said the woman. "If you were Seelie, then you are subject to their queen. If she summoned you, you would have to come. I am sure they did not tell you this. Why would they? It would reveal them for what they are—liars. They kept you because it was the only way to keep you from your own people, your blood relations."

"Don't listen to her," said Yukiko. The little fox's fur stood on end and though she wasn't crackling with electricity anymore, Astrid thought that she looked ready to do something dangerous with her magic. "She's Unseelie," the fox growled. "They are liars and cheats."

"And the Seelie?" said the woman to Yukiko. "They have been truthful, honest and compassionate to you? I heard rumors that a Kitsune had been captured. I heard that there might not be any of your kind left. I am honored to make your acquaintance. My name is Bogdana." She gave a little bow and clasped her hands together in what Astrid supposed was a formal greeting gesture.

Yukiko returned the bow by lowering her head. It should have been a cute movement from the little animal, but instead it looked very grave. "Yukiko," she said.

"How did you know I was coming?" asked Astrid. "We didn't even know." If the Unseelie knew she was here, would the Seelie know also? She needed to know what she was up against.

"Both the Seelie and Unseelie have far-seers, and some of us actually listen to them, unreliable as they can be. I hired one shortly after I lost you, to learn if I would see you again and where and when. I visited a few others, and they gave conflicting times, so I simply went to each indicated place at the indicated time, hoping."

Her expression was warm, sincere and a little unsure. Bogdana was polished and lovely, but there was a little vulnerability to her, a sort of deep pain. She was taller and curvier than Astrid, her hair dark instead of blonde. But if Astrid was a changeling, that meant that her appearance was made to match that of the baby that her human mother had lost.

"How do I know you are telling the truth?" Astrid asked. Yukiko made an exasperated noise.

"You cannot. You have no birthmarks or identifying traits that link you to me. And since you are a Door and are incredibly valuable, what world, what people would not do anything to have you join them? I have nothing but my word."

"Why would you think I'm a Door?"

"Would you come with me? I give you my word that neither I nor the spirits who attacked you will do you any harm."

"No, I need to go back home. Sorry, lady," Astrid said.

"You can test the theory that you are Unseelie," said Bogdana. "You will always be drawn to this place and the things of this world will always be drawn to you. They are your brothers, and you are their sister."

She thought of the slaugh, coming to her house at night, coming to her place of work, attacking her cat, stacking rocks. The Unseelie had indeed been drawn to her. And opening a door to Unseelie had been so easy.

Bogdana continued. "Our king or queen will summon you, and you will come, willingly or no. Wouldn't you prefer to know about where you came from before you are forcibly dragged before our sovereigns?"

"The Unseelie are enemies of humans," said Astrid. "The slaugh I met wanted to hurt people. They're evil."

"The slaugh are only one kind of Unseelie. Do you not have evil people among humans? Terrible criminals who delight in harming the innocent?"

She could not deny it.

"It is the same here," said Bogdana. "And among our cousins, the Seelie, it is the same. Even among the Kitsune it is so."

One of the guards glanced at them. They needed to get back into the mirror house. But what if what this woman said was true? She had to know.

"You have five minutes," said Astrid.

"There is a place here that serves sweet goat milk where we can chat."

The Unseelie version of Luna Park was very similar to the Seelie one. Most of the people appeared human, though here and there walked strange beings. Instead of resembling mostly mammals, they were more likely to be reptilian, insectoid or arachnoid. They were not ugly or frightening, most of them anyway, but they were unsettling. The Unseelie seemed to like similar games to humans and Seelie, like breaking plates with balls, tossing rings onto pegs and throwing balls at stacked bottles. A game caught her eye, one involving shooting needlelike darts at cats and dogs. She thought of Cinderella with a pang.

The logjam ride, which in her world was a soaring construction that was one of the tallest in the park, was mostly underground here. The water ran red, and howls of delight came from passengers as they plunged into the darkness beneath the earth. A fine mist that smelled like toasting marshmallows rose from the underground tunnel.

The window serving food was similar to the one in the human world, and the Unseelie man behind it was human-looking. The menu, just as in the world of the Seelie, had no meat, but included cloverseed rolls, mushroom paste rolled in grape leaves, sweet hibiscus cakes, sweet goat milk and cattail juice. Astrid and Yukiko asked for water, in a wooden cup and dish respectively, while Bogdana ordered goat milk, served in a wooden cup with an orange paper umbrella. They found seats at a table under a shady tree covered in thousands of heavy, dangling blue blossoms the size of Astrid's fist.

"You asked how I knew you were a Door," said Bogdana. "I knew from your birth. When you were born, the court took you from me. They tore you from my arms. A member of the court had won a bet with the human father of the infant girl you replaced. One of our kind went through on the appointed day, and somehow convinced the man to wager the child. I opposed it, of course. A dreadful business. But the Unseelie have been trapped for so long, only able to slip through one or two at a time on certain nights of the year. Our brothers and sisters longed for freedom. So they took the only Door born to us in a thousand years and changed you with another infant. You were raised in the human world, are almost completely human, except deep in the depths of your very being, where you will always be Unseelie. Once you were of age, according to your own internal perception of such, you started to be called home."

Her father. Her mother had spoken of him now and then. They had stayed married for a few years after Astrid's birth, but then her father had disappeared. Sometimes her mother had spoken of him fondly, but mostly she talked about how he was a drunk and a gambler. Her poor mother, first stuck with an unreliable man, and then to have him actually gamble away her infant daughter.

"And I was made to look like the baby?" asked Astrid.

"You were. It is permanent, though there are glamours you can learn to employ if you wish. But I do say, you do not look bad. You were beautiful as a babe also, all rosy cheeks and tiny cupid's bow mouth. It broke my heart to lose you. Tell me, was your human family kind?"

Astrid nodded and sipped spring water from her wooden cup. Yukiko was not drinking at all, but was scowling as much as a canine could scowl. Her ears were not back, nor was she baring her teeth, but her physical posture was one of wariness.

Perhaps she should trust Yukiko. She had stayed by her side and helped her as much as she could under the circumstances. Something was bothering her though, something about the mirror house when she had slipped through to the Seelie world. Yukiko had been there, and she had been there when the slaugh came through the first time. But so had Santiago and she didn't blame him for the chaos. Indeed, there was no one to blame but herself for any of it.

"I have a house not far from here," said Bogdana.

"We're not interested," said Yukiko.

"You would be guests, and under all of the protection that your status offers."

Astrid looked at Yukiko. She knew that in some cultures, a guest was fed the best food, given the finest bed and treated with more honor than any member of the household. To harm a guest was a grave offense. And the mermaid had said that the Seelie frowned upon stealing from a host. There were rules.

Bogdana rose. "I will leave you if you wish to discuss it between yourselves."

"I can't leave without you," said Yukiko once Bogdana was out of earshot. "And I wouldn't if I could. I will see you safely home."

"Do you think she's telling the truth?"

"It's possible. You said the Seelie kept you contained with cold iron. If you were truly theirs, then you would be subject to their queen. She would call, and you would come."

"So they would have had no need to forcibly contain me."

"I had not thought of it, but it's true. However, there are many types of otherfolk. You could be so many things, and each one would want to claim you. Our own god, Inari, would have offered to make you a Kitsune, if only you would use the power in his service."

"I think she might be telling the truth. That first Door I opened in the mirror house was to Unseelie. And at my house, while I was asleep, I let another slaugh through, a mother with a baby. My cat killed both."

"Well, that's one point in favor of Bogdana telling the truth," said Yukiko. "Tell me, what were you thinking, that first time in the mirror house, when you first saw the slaugh?"

"Nothing really. I was tired and I was thinking of going home, eating dinner, resting."

"Going home, you said."

Astrid drank the rest of her water. "Yeah, there's no place like home, right?" She looked up at the yellowish clouds floating in the lavender sky.

"I'm sorry," said Yukiko. "I really am. If this is your home, then I am sorry."

"How bad is it? You said you had never been here."

"I've only heard things secondhand. But the Unseelie are brutal, cruel and lawless. Where the Seelie have order, the Unseelie have chaos. Their only loyalties are to themselves, and they'll use murder, trickery and cruelty to achieve their ends."

"Like your wild foxes?" asked Astrid.

"Yes, but often worse. There's the Wild Hunt, and the members of the Unseelie Court are absolutely vicious."

"Are some of your wild foxes good, or at least neutral?"

"Well, yes. Some are decent enough people."

Perhaps not all hope was lost then.

"We'll just stay for a few hours, then we'll go home," said Astrid. "If I'm going to be pulled back here, then I need to know what I'm in for."

Astrid waved to Bogdana, who stood a bit off, looking out over the water. She returned to the table.

"We'll come with you for a few hours," said Yukiko. "But I stay by the girl's side every moment." At Bogdana's surprised look, Yukiko said. "I am bound to her. She freed me from captivity, and I am her bondservant."

Astrid had no idea what this meant, but Bogdana nodded in understanding. Yukiko must have a reason for what she said. Perhaps it was just a precaution against them being separated again. Sensible enough.

They left the park by the main entrance, passing the carousel. She was disappointed when it looked very much like the one from Seelie, although this one had a few wolves mixed in among the other creatures. Where the parking lot should have been, there was a wide open space, dirt-covered with patches of weeds. A stable stood to one side. Bogdana paid a fee and hired two ponies. Yukiko jumped up onto the rump of Astrid's pony and balanced there, looking grouchy and imperious.

"Just a few hours," muttered the fox.

As they rode, Astrid half expected her pony to turn and speak to her, but he never did. They took a wide dirt path toward the hills, then a thinner one that circled a round hill. The large house was built into the side of the hill with ivy-covered stone walls and steep rooflines ending in conical towers on the corners. Astrid loved it on sight. The back of the building cut straight into the hillside, and diamond-paned glass windows covered the front, presumably to let in as much light as possible. A few tiny birds fluttered out from a hiding spot under the eaves.

It was almost like a castle, though smaller, and here, under the lavender sky, with the strange plants and the odd, tangy smell to the air, it fit.

They arrived at a large door at the front corner of the house and dismounted. The ponies turned back, winding their way back down the hill, presumably back to their master.

The front door was huge and arched with no knobs, but rather two heavy metal rings. There had to be a latch or some mechanism to hold them shut, but as Bogdana pulled the door open and they entered, Astrid did not see one.

Servants stood here and there, all of them hooded figures who kept their faces downcast. They vanished as soon as Astrid saw them, slipping into other rooms or down hallways. The house itself was beautiful, filled with antiques, ornate rugs and historical pieces. Some light came through the front and side windows, and brass sconces held flickering torches that created no smoke or smell, but only light.

Each room contained differently colored torches. In the main living areas, they were white and yellow, while the library had a greenish light illuminating its shelves of books and scrolls. The sitting room, filled with soft couches, had a friendly pink tinge. And bright yellow illuminated the dining hall with its giant stone-topped table, large enough for twenty, and matching high-backed chairs carved with bird and dragon heads on the armrests.

Art filled every room, from sculptures in little niches or on tabletops to giant tapestries depicting elaborate stories covering entire walls. There were charcoal drawings and paintings in oils, watercolors and other mediums which Astrid could not identify. She paused often, examining them. In her world, some of them would have been worth a good amount of money, so skillfully were they executed. One particular painting of a horse and dismounted rider climbing a winding path up a mountain caught her attention. The horse seemed alive, as did the man, though his face was turned away from the viewer, his gaze looking up the path ahead of him.

"He is one of our ancestors. Would you like to see the gallery?" said Bogdana. "We have many other pieces."

"Are you a collector?" asked Astrid.

"I haven't purchased any of the pieces, if that's what you mean. I draw. My brother sculpts. My father liked to paint, as did my mother. My mother's mother wove tapestries and my grandfather was an expert musician, still renowned throughout the Unseelie world."

"Your family made all of this?"

"Our family," she said. "Do you think you would like to try your hand at some form of art?"

"I already like to draw. I'm actually going to art school. At Columbia. That's in New York."

"Indeed?" Her mother turned to her with a look of pure pleasure. "I would not have thought the humans would have nurtured any talent you possessed. They do surprise me sometimes."

Astrid did not consider her upbringing nurturing, but she hesitated to say so. "Well, I had the materials and took some classes in high school."

"And your mother, she must have been so proud of you. Is this Columbia a good school?"

Astrid vacillated between being modest and telling the truth that yes, Columbia was one of the top schools in the country. She partly wanted to tell Bogdana that her mother had not liked her "scribbling" but she felt oddly protective of her mother as well. The poor woman had lost her daughter and raised a changeling. It was Astrid herself that had driven her to become what she was. Elliot would have disagreed, but he wasn't here to argue with her.

"It's a good school," said Astrid. "It's hard to get admitted, so I was shocked when they accepted me."

"Do not be shocked. What you are and what you can do means that your creations are so far superior to the work of the humans that they will marvel at it. And if they do not, it is because they are so blinded by their ape nature that they are incapable of recognizing the worth of the things you create."

"That's a little harsh. There are marvelous human artists."

"Many of them otherkind," said Bogdana.

"But not all," said Astrid, eager to defend humankind. "And humans are innately curious, innately creative."

"As are we, except we are even more so, sometimes to our folly."

Bogdana led Astrid and Yukiko to an upstairs series of rooms connected by arching doorways. The light was better here, coming in through windows along the front of the house. Statues and sculptures, tapestries, vases, paintings and drawings filled the room. Another room housed taxidermied birds: crows, owls, pheasants and other winged creatures she did not recognize.

A clock chimed three times somewhere downstairs.

"Are you hungry?" Bogdana asked. "I'll order us some refreshments for after we enjoy the rest of the gallery.

She swept out of the room.

"I'm tiring," whispered Yukiko. "I'm using my power to shield your bell so she doesn't take it. But I'm getting worn out."

"We'll leave soon. How long can you hold out?"

"Another few hours, enough time for tea and then for us to leave."

Astrid forced herself to hurry through the rest of the

gallery. All of the art was unsigned, but Bogdana, upon her return, told her which of their family had created each piece.

After they finished, Bogdana showed them into a sitting room downstairs. A hooded figure, this one slight and thin, brought in a tray of sugar-sprinkled lemon cakes, sliced white cheeses, fruit and glasses of iced tea the color of daffodils.

A bell rang in the hallway and a minute later, another servant leaned in to whisper something in Bogdana's ear. Astrid tried to catch a glimpse of the servant's face, but the hood was full and concealed it. The other servant, the smaller one, was off in one corner, rearranging curios on the shelves. Astrid got the distinct impression that the servant was trying to steal glances at her and Yukiko.

"Excuse me," said Bogdana. "The court knows you have arrived and wishes to speak with you. Shall I admit them?"

Yukiko bristled and Astrid scooted to the edge of her seat, ready to rise. "No," said Astrid. "I don't want to speak to them. I need to go."

"After your experience with the Seelie, I do not blame you for being wary," said Bogdana. "I will inform them to come another time."

"You can do that?" asked Yukiko.

"Astrid is not property, but a citizen," said Bogdana. "And citizens have certain rights. If they want to formally summon her, she cannot refuse. But my servant told me the rank of the man at the door. This is not a formal summons. I will handle him."

Bogdana left and the slender servant moved closer. It looked like a girl, at least from its build. Astrid put a piece of cake on a plate and lifted it to her mouth when the figure leapt forward and snatched the food and plate from her hands. The person's face was still downcast, but maybe she could see through the fabric of her hood. The figure shook her head vehemently and pulled the tray to the far end of the coffee table. Her fair hands were scarred on the backs with crisscrossing lines and a shiny pink mark, like an old burn. The girl raised a finger and waved it back and forth, telling them "no."

Astrid understood then what she was doing.

"It's fine. I'm not human. I won't get trapped here. I'm sidhe." She couldn't quite bring herself to say she was Unseelie, not yet.

The figure pulled her hands into her sleeves and hesitated. Something about her hands was very familiar. Astrid pulled her plate back toward herself and picked up her glass of tea. The girl jumped forward and pulled the glass from her hands. She shook her head violently.

"Is it poisoned?" Yukiko asked the girl. Then she hesitated. "Oh, wait. No. Gods, no."

"What? Are they trying to poison us?"

"This girl. Her smell. I didn't catch it before because it was so familiar, because of you. But you have the Door scent as well."

"What do you mean?"

"Girl," said Yukiko. "May we see your face?"

The girl shook her head and backed away, almost to the door. She turned to run. Quick as a shot, Yukiko was up and grabbed a mouthful of the hem of the girl's robe. The girl let out a strangled cry of dismay and tried to pull the fabric from her teeth.

And then Astrid knew what was wrong with the hands. She went to the girl, took the edges of the hood in her hands and paused. The girl stopped struggling and held still, the tilt of her head rising so she was looking at Astrid from behind the fabric. Astrid pushed the hood back.

She was looking into a copy of her own face, but this one had scarred cheeks and a freshly bloodied lip. Her nose was slightly crooked, though her eyes, the exact color and shape as Astrid's own, were clear and bright with both fear and a touch of defiance.

"The changeling," said Astrid. "I mean—the human child. You didn't die. It was you that I saw in the mirror."

The girl did not answer.

"What have they done to you?" demanded Astrid. "They hurt you?" She grabbed the girl's hand and examined the scars, the newer cuts. The sleeve slipped back to reveal a purple bruise on her wrist. The girl's collar now hung loose and Astrid saw a thin silver chain around her throat, tight enough to stay above the collarbone, but not choke her. "What happened?" Astrid said. "They told me you were dead."

The girl still did not speak.

"Tell me!" Astrid said.

The girl shook her head and opened her mouth. The space inside her lower teeth was empty. Her tongue had been cut out.

CHAPTER 40

E LLIOT'S SHOVEL HIT SOMETHING.

"It's here! I can't believe it's still here!" He looked up at Neil who leaned against a rock a little ways off, resting after his turn with the shovel.

"Of course it's still there," said Neil, heading over. "That's where we put it, isn't it?"

Elliot was warm from the exercise, but the cool Mediterranean breeze kept him from being uncomfortable. They stood on a windy island off the coast of Turkey; tiny, rocky and uninhabited.

"Yeah, but to think, it sat there for a thousand years," Elliot said. "We forged it, hid it, and it's still there."

"You did all that. I just watched," said Neil.

"Technically, yes. But you helped. I couldn't have done it otherwise. Without you, I'd still be stuck wandering in the Syrian Desert."

Elliot knelt, pulled the box out of the earth and opened it. Inside, wrapped in the remains of what had once been a cloth, was the small owl bell that they had buried over a thousand years before. It was covered in a layer of rust, but it could be cleaned easily enough.

Neil and Elliot had arrived in Syria in the year 798 AD, searching for a piece of cold iron. Wandering for weeks, they grew discouraged. The meteorite was scheduled to fall at any time, and they kept their eyes to the skies night and day while searching the ground in case the prediction had been off a little and the thing had already hit the earth.

As it turned out, it had fallen before they arrived and they eventually found it, lying in a small crater. It was heavy, the size of a baseball. They took it to a renowned smith in Cairo who would make it into an owl bell, for the right price. His fee was exorbitant, but they had paid gladly.

Neil and Hazel had not been joking about money, for the Time Corps had money in banks and hiding places from Egypt to Reykjavik to Shanghai, and in the New World as well. Most of it was in gold which could be converted to currency or simply traded throughout all human civilizations in all time periods. What wasn't in banks was left in hiding places like caves and remote rock crevices. Sometimes the Time Corps employed law firms who held on to trusts for generations, and other times they simply abandoned money they didn't need. Each Time Corps member was supposed to memorize where safe houses were as well as where money could be found to purchase transport to them. Elliot tried his best.

After paying the smith in Cairo, they had taken the bell, put it in a protective box and buried it off the Turkish coast, on an island that they knew would remain undisturbed for centuries. Elliot had been skeptical and had wanted to keep the bell with them. They had gone to such trouble to create it. But Neil had explained that it was better to leave the bell to have a continuous existence on earth instead of taking it with them through time. It wasn't strictly necessary, as the bell would have a continuous existence either way, although one asynchronous to the rest of the planet. But Neil had explained that with an object that was going to move between worlds, the more stability, the better. They had buried it. And now, in 1895, they dug it up.

"The ship is going to leave soon," said Neil. Their next step was to board a steamer that would stop in Athens and then take them across the Atlantic to New Orleans.

Neil wore his black duster, black jeans and a shirt

and waistcoat. The effect was at once anachronistic and effective. He blended in well enough. Elliot had wanted to wear his regular clothing, but after considering how much he would stand out, had opted for a workman's coat, trousers and heavy boots. Of course, in Syria he had purchased native clothing so as not to be cooked alive by the brutal sun. Pangur Ban, though Irish originally, was well traveled and had given him information on Syria. Hazel, who had been born in 1846, gave him a primer on Victorian culture. She had even taught him some of the dances.

They rowed their small boat back across the water and returned it to its owner. Their ship was waiting and they started the long walk back to civilization, stopping on the way to retrieve their time machine. Elliot still thought it was strange, ridiculous even, how a device the size of a trunk could allow them to move through time, but he had done it enough to now believe it.

The device was homemade by Seamus in his disaster of a laboratory, long before the Time Corps was even an idea. But for all that, it was beautiful. It consisted of a rectangular wooden base, set on end like a pedestal upon which sat a paneled brass dome. There were dials and knobs and even a little book of dates and coordinates that slid into a compartment on the side. It was not the only one of its kind, but it had been the first.

The whole ability to travel in time and between worlds was dependent upon synchronicities, though there were exceptions. It was a critical weakness. The fabric, the walls between worlds, were thicker and thinner at points. And to tear a hole between them required things on both sides to be happening in a similar way. For example, Felicia had come through a hole into Seamus's world because a twenty-first century bus she was on was traveling down Saint Charles Street in New Orleans at the same time as an omnibus in 1857. Seamus had accidentally created the conditions for the hole to appear, and the synchronicity triggered the rip. He had spent years trying to learn to control the holes, to find a way to get Felicia back to her world, but so far he was unsuccessful. Her world was one of the more difficult ones to break into.

Elliot's world, however, was fairly easy. Seamus was hoping to use his time here to work more of the kinks out of his device. For Felicia's sake, Elliot hoped he would. The other members of the Time Corps had little or no family and seemed content, or at least adjusted to the fact. Felicia had family from which she had been separated, and it pained her.

Neil hired a cart to carry them and the trunk with the machine to the docks. Neil had insisted on paying extra for a nicer cabin, telling him that steerage was not pleasant, not even as a historical study. They boarded and went to their tiny quarters to change for supper.

"Why can't we simply use the machine to travel one week into the future and show up in New Orleans?" said Elliot. "I don't see why we have to take weeks on this ship."

"We only use the machine when necessary, not as a way to avoid unpleasantries. Besides, I paid extra for the nice cabin and so we can dine on the upper deck. We get better food that way. Think of it as a vacation."

"I'm just worried about Astrid. I haven't seen her in more than a month. I hope she's okay."

"When we get back, it will only be a few days after we left."

While waiting for supper, they stood against the railing as the last light of day faded from the sky. Elliot thought about the Time Corps, how he had not officially joined and could leave at any time. Just because his colleagues told him that he had decided to join in his future didn't mean he had to. It was still his choice. But traveling, seeing the world, not only in his own twenty-first century, but in so many centuries, was delicious and irresistible. He knew he would stay.

Supper consisted of herb-crusted beef, wilted greens and roasted potatoes. The two of them dined at their own table, though a few of the younger women cast appraising glances at them. Neil was oblivious to this, or seemed to be. After supper, they went out on deck.

"I have another question," said Elliot.

"You usually do," said Neil.

"You're the one who wanted to train me."

"Just returning the favor."

"That's what you said, that I trained you," Elliot said. "Did you learn everything from Seamus and Hazel?"

"Some of it. But a lot of it was from you."

"That means that the information passed between us forms an unstable time loop. The information has no origin. I told you in my future, you tell me now so that when I'm older, I can tell you."

"I try not to think about that too much," said Neil, shielding his eyes with his hand as the last rays of sunlight glittered on the dancing water.

"But you do think about it."

"I suppose that one of us watched a lot of Doctor Who reruns as a kid."

Perhaps, in time, Elliot would figure it out. Maybe he and Neil would be old men in the Time Corps retirement home on Mars and figure out who had learned what information and at what point in time. Nothing could really be an unstable time loop. Everything had an origin. Paradoxes could not exist.

The owl bell now had a stable origin, as a meteorite in Syria, forged in Cairo and buried for a thousand years. Now, they were taking it to New Orleans where it would be held by a shopkeeper and his son until the 1960s when it would be put up for sale. Then, Astrid and Elliot's grandfather would buy it. Elliot knew that their grandfather had given it to Astrid as a baby and that she had kept it her entire life. So all they had to do was ensure that it arrived in their grandfather's possession.

Pangur Ban and Huginn were taking care of the rest of the bell's lifecycle. From what they told him, Astrid had given them information in her future. As they were not human, the cat and the raven could travel to the Seelie world without being detected. They would steal the bell that had been stolen from Astrid when she was in Seelie. Then, they would use their time travel devices to travel into the past within Seelie to leave the owl bell on a beach.

The light was fading, and a dolphin swam off the bow, rising to the surface and then dipping below only to rise again, its dorsal fin splitting the churning waves.

"You're not kidding me that a mermaid is going to find the bell," said Elliot.

Neil wasn't watching the dolphin, but was looking straight down into the water below. "There are more things in heaven and earth, Horatio, than are dreamt of in your philosophy."

"I get that, but a mermaid?"

"That's what Astrid said. Will say. So unless she's playing a joke ..."

"She's not. I've never known a more serious person. Except for you, perhaps."

Neil turned around so he was leaning back against the railing, looking across the deck. "I find humor in some things."

"You don't think having talking ravens, cats and monkeys as colleagues is funny?"

"Mr. Escobar works for Hazel on her ship. He's not Time Corps. But yes, on some level, it seems funny. But I'm so used to it that it's no longer amusing."

"Fair enough," said Elliot. "I'm going to go inside. Some of those young rich girls were cute, and I think they may be in need of a dance partner."

Elliot left Neil on deck and found the dancing hall where he got a glass of punch. He still didn't fully understand the workings of the Time Corps. For the most part, they were open and friendly, though they refused to answer questions now and then.

That was another thing. Neil told him that the Time Corps members did not withhold information from each other. They did not fear time paradoxes, as they did not exist. The only information they would ever willfully withhold would be the time and place of someone's death or other life-changing information. He supposed no one had told poor Pangur Ban that her son would die.

Seamus was the de facto head of the Time Corps, but he listened to Julius and made phone calls or visited other safe house keepers, including September Wilde in New Orleans and a woman named June in San Francisco, for advice.

The Time Corps had a research department somewhere, and Neil had told him that they both had spent time there doing research and investigative legwork. Or, rather, they would spend many years there in their future. Neil looked young, but he had crammed a lot of living into those years, judging by the stories he told.

Elliot made eye contact across the room with a girl of about eighteen who was sitting with her mother. He introduced himself, learned her name was Anne and that she was British. He asked her to dance and she accepted.

The steps were easy enough after his practice with Hazel.

"Will you be staying in New Orleans?" he asked the girl. "Or taking another ship elsewhere?"

"We'll be staying there, my sister and I, with a maiden aunt. And you?"

"Staying there briefly, then moving on. Heading west to Los Angeles." He didn't mention that it would be twenty-first century Los Angeles.

"Are you a businessman?"

"Something like that. I'm traveling to New Orleans after some time in Syria, Egypt and Turkey."

"How fascinating!" she said with more enthusiasm than was necessary. "You sound like quite the adventurer."

He supposed it was true.

CHAPTER 41

"**T**HIS IS DISGUSTING!" SAID ASTRID to Yukiko. "Look what they did to her!"

"I see it," said Yukiko. She saw the wounds and old scars and also that the two young women were identical in appearance.

"Can you tell us what happened?" Astrid asked the girl. "Can you write it down? Are you trapped here?"

The girl shook her head, but Yukiko saw that Astrid was peppering her with too many questions and she was too flustered to answer. Then, she picked up the sound of footsteps. Astrid and the servant girl hadn't heard them yet.

"She's coming back," said Yukiko.

"Find us later," said Astrid, and the girl rushed out of the room.

By the time Bogdana stepped through the door, Yukiko was sitting beside Astrid, both of them eating lemon cake.

"He will be back tomorrow," Bogdana said.

Yukiko watched Astrid hesitate, and then look her mother in the eye. "When tomorrow?"

"In the afternoon."

"I think we'd like to stay until then."

"Would you?" Bogdana looked surprised. "I'm not sure if he'll have an official summons for you. Even if he doesn't, they can summon you in other ways. Leaving here won't change that."

"I'm starting to understand that," said Astrid. "If this is my home, my family, then I'd like to get to know it better."

"I'm so glad," said Bogdana, smiling and clasping her hands together. "I'll arrange some rooms to be made up."

"One room," said Yukiko.

"If you wish. I will have some clothing brought up." Bogdana looked pointedly at Astrid's clothes. She still wore the gold and red silk outfit with her purse slung across her body and the two socks tied to her sash. The outfit was filthy, wrinkled and wasn't the freshest thing Yukiko had ever smelled.

Before supper, Yukiko and Astrid were shown to their room. As they passed through the corridors behind a hooded servant, Yukiko smelled and looked for the servant girl. She could not find her. Astrid closed the door to their room, a spacious round chamber at the top of one of the front towers. The view stretched all the way to the sea. A plush four-poster bed with piles of deep purple pillows stood at the center, and there was a smaller bed, also covered in purple pillows, for Yukiko. A pile of soft cushions cluttered a nearby chair. What was it with the fey and pillows? Yukiko's own people were not so obsessed with luxury.

In a tiny adjoining room waited a tub full of steaming water, a wash basin and a jug.

"We're going to get her out," said Astrid.

"Impossible," said Yukiko. "She belongs to them. Did you see the chain around her neck? Remember how that slaugh bound Santiago to him with a silver chain? It's the same."

"So we cut the chain."

"It's not just a chain. It's a bond, an unbreakable bond."

"Unbreakable?" said Astrid. "But Santiago broke it."

"The slaugh broke it when he changed his mind about having Coyote tied to him."

"So we get Bogdana to change her mind about the girl. We get her to give her up as a servant."

"And how do you propose we do that?"

"I was hoping you'd have an idea. You're the clever fox, remember?"

She was not nearly as clever as she wished she could be. She had worked her way out of sticky situations numerous times, certainly, but freeing a girl enslaved to the Unseelie was madness.

Astrid dug through the armoire, pulling out dresses, trousers and tops made of cotton, silk and other fine fabrics. The girl settled on a pomegranate red cotton dress. She took it into the adjoining room and took a bath, leaving the door ajar.

"Tell me about the Unseelie. About the court and the Wild Hunt," Astrid called from the tub.

Yukiko sat next to the door, her back to the bathing girl. "Imagine the most corrupt human royal court with intrigues, murder, entrapment, lies and brutality, all beneath a façade of civility and refinement, and you have it. Don't get involved. Not that you could. Even if the king and queen summoned you, they would never ask a girl who was raised in the human world to be part of their court. You're too ... uncivilized."

"If that's their idea of civilized, then I'll take that as a compliment."

"Now, the Wild Hunt, that's something else. I've never seen them myself, but I had some Irish customers back in San Francisco. They'd drink and talk and tell tales their grandfathers told them. When the west wind blew off the ocean, they'd talk about the Wild Hunt. Some said that the slaugh were the souls of the restless dead, souls not welcome either in heaven or hell."

"They seemed hellish to me," said Astrid.

"The Wild Hunt flew, filling the skies, like a flock of birds, coming from the west. They would try to find the dying and claim their souls. So people would cover their west-facing windows. That pigeon slaugh that got into the park wanted to have my baby Kitsune, thinking he could ride it in the Wild Hunt."

"Kitsune can fly?"

Yukiko laughed. "No, but the slaugh could manage it somehow."

"Okay, so the court is evil. The Wild Hunt is no picnic. And my mother is worse than my—I mean my real mother is worse than my human one. I'm still not seeing a whole lot of difference between the Seelie and the Unseelie. They're both terrible."

"They both have codes that they live by. The Seelie code is the opposite of the Unseelie, or so they claim. Seelie, as hard as it may be to believe, have a code of honor. The Seelie would believe in sacrificing themselves for others, while the Unseelie code is one of selfishness. Of course, they call it self-preservation, but for them, no sacrifice is too great if it achieves one's ends. The Seelie will always repay a debt, but the Unseelie may or may not, as convenient to them. Notice that the Seelie may have caged us, but they did not torture us or starve us. They caught me fairly, according to their own rules, but they did not mistreat me by beatings or starvation. They did the same with you. And never forget this: The Seelie believe in order and honor. The Unseelie love chaos and domination."

Astrid did not answer, though Yukiko heard the soft splashes of water that indicated that she was still bathing. She jumped up on the windowsill and looked out over the hills, Luna Park in the distance and the sea beyond that. The water had a bluish cast, more of an indigo color, perhaps reflecting some of the purple of the sky.

She thought of the poor servant girl, gambled away by a father who probably couldn't even remember doing it. Gambled. Human children could be gambled. But this girl was not a child. She was a slave, free and clear, and an adult. Bogdana could lose her by gambling, but she would only agree to any sort of game if Yukiko put up something of similar value. That would mean either herself or Astrid. And Bogdana would be wise enough not to play a game of chance that Yukiko could influence with her magic, which meant that she would be risking Astrid or her own freedom. There had to be another way, but she couldn't think of it.

"Yukiko?" Astrid called. "When I let the slaugh through near my house, it stacked stones in a circle near my window. And another time it burned a circle into our lawn."

Yukiko thought about it. "I'm not familiar with the ways of the slaugh, but my guess is that making stacks with the stones was an attempt to get you to make another doorway, perhaps to get the slaugh home."

"What do you mean?"

"Do you know about fairy rings, made of mushrooms?"

"Yes, I've heard of those," said Astrid. "If a human goes to dance in a circle with the fairies, they might never return."

"Precisely. It's a kind of Doorway. I think the stones and the burned grass might have been the slaugh version of circles, attempts to get home."

Astrid didn't say anything, and Yukiko wondered if she felt bad for the slaugh, trapped in a strange world without its kin.

Astrid left the owl bell in their room so Yukiko would not have to use her power to conceal it. After a supper of spiced chickpea patties in dill sauce, greens with pine nuts and a dessert of bluebell custard, Yukiko and Astrid chatted with Bogdana, toured the library and finally, were able to head upstairs to go to bed. They did not sleep, of course, but sat up, talking and waiting for the servant girl to come. Astrid told Yukiko everything about what had happened to her in Seelie from being held in a house in Malibu, escaping, meeting the sea woman, whom she called a mermaid, and visiting her cave. The oddest thing was the bell, which the sea woman claimed to have had for over fifty years.

It made Yukiko think of Elliot. She had seen him decades

before, in San Francisco. He clearly had not recognized her, which meant that either he was an amnesiac who aged backwards or that he really had not yet met her. And then here was an object which appeared earlier than it should have. Odd.

The bedroom door opened and the servant girl slipped in, silent as a shadow, and closed the door behind her. She had a quiet, sneaking way of moving, almost blending into the room. It wasn't simply a physical quality. She seemed less there, smaller in spirit, as if she took up less space than other people.

The girl pulled her hood back herself, which pleased Yukiko. She liked that the girl, tortured and mutilated as she was, was brave enough to look them in the eye.

Yukiko watched from the windowsill as Astrid pulled out her sketch pad and tried to get the girl to write, but she could not. She stood with her hands folded and no way to communicate other than nodding or shaking her head. Through asking yes or no questions, they discovered that she could not read, she did not know how old she was or how to get out of the Unseelie world. She cooked, cleaned, did laundry and worked in the gardens. She also had no name.

"But what do they call you?" Astrid asked.

The girl shook her head.

"Do you want a name?"

The girl shrugged and Yukiko considered. What good was a name to someone who barely had any existence? Her life was a series of tasks, not one of affection or having any sort of identity or belonging. If she didn't understand how relationships between people worked, she wouldn't understand that she would need a name. Perhaps they had a word they used to summon her, but she couldn't write it down.

Astrid took her duplicate's hands. "We're going to be leaving soon, but I am going to get you free and take you back to the human world where you'll be safe. Your mother lives there. Your real mother. And we have a cousin. Well, I guess he's really your cousin." Astrid got a pained look.

Yukiko said, "He's still your cousin. You were adopted, just unknowingly."

"I suppose."

"And you humans make all sorts of families. The accident of your birth does not interfere with it. You haven't lost your family, only added a member to it. A sister."

The servant girl lifted her chin and made a little grunt.

"Is it all right that I call you my sister?" asked Astrid.

She nodded, eyes wide and tapped her chest.

"You're my sister, yes," said Astrid.

The girl looked frustrated and shook her head, then tapped her chest. Then she made a little hand sign and Yukiko understood.

"She wants you to call her Sister," said Yukiko. "Like a name."

"How do you know that?"

"I can speak any language, and interpret most forms of communication."

"Why didn't you say so earlier?"

"She wasn't signing before," said Yukiko. "I didn't know she could. I'm not a mind reader." She looked at the girl. "Can you sign other things?"

She did and Yukiko translated.

"Kitchen. Food. No. Yes. Cook."

The girl pointed to herself.

"Sister," said Yukiko.

The girl was elated. She signed a few other things, but they quickly discovered that her vocabulary was limited. There simply weren't signs for many of the things Yukiko wanted to ask her about.

A clock chimed and Sister moved toward the door.

"Do you have to go?" asked Yukiko.

Sister nodded.

Astrid said, "I'm going to speak to Bogdana and see if I can get her to free you."

The girl gave a hopeless little shrug.

"I will. And if that doesn't work, I'll find another way to get you out of here."

Yukiko didn't know of any way to accomplish that, but maybe Astrid would be able to make a Door to swallow up Bogdana, thereby freeing the girl. Sister left, and Astrid flopped onto the bed and looked up at the ceiling. She stayed that way for a long time. Eventually Yukiko curled up on the cushions of the smaller bed and went to sleep.

The next day was filled with a tour of the garden and Bogdana showing Astrid records of their family history. Yukiko sat on the library rug, waiting for Astrid to be finished. She understood the appeal of family and genealogy, but she also understood that one could be alone in the world, without relations, and still find contentment.

She listened to Astrid ask her mother about Sister and what had happened to her. Bogdana said that the girl had been disobedient, had spoken out of turn, and like other servants, had been kept under control by whatever means were necessary. The girl was troublesome. Each scar was a remnant of an act of Sister's defiance, and Yukiko felt a hot anger as well as a deepening admiration for Sister. What little acts of independence had she engaged in to bring on the punishments? To fight and continue to fight in the face of injustice and hopelessness when the only result was pain made Yukiko proud that she was a friend of humankind. They were not all cowardly and easily manipulated.

Astrid was remarkably calm throughout the discussion, though there was a certain tightness to her voice and posture. Yukiko had to admire her self-control. To become angry and demand Sister's freedom would accomplish nothing.

"I was told that the baby died and I was put in her place," said Astrid.

"More Seelie lies," said Bogdana. "I have not lied to you. The child was of no consequence. Oh, I took her in, and I even tried to love her. She was like a pet. But blood will out. And you, my daughter, have bested the Seelie and learned to open Doors to your homeworld without assistance. You are intelligent and resourceful."

Yukiko watched Astrid pause and compose her thoughts. She knew what the girl was thinking. Sister might be intelligent and resourceful as well, but being tortured and mutilated tended to put a damper on expressions of either trait.

"If she is nothing, then give her to me," said Astrid. "As a gift. A maidservant."

"You would keep a slave?" said Bogdana, skeptical. "No, I think you would free her."

"And why not?"

"Because, it would be a waste. Like tossing good food into the rubbish heap."

"If she cannot be freed, then at least let me visit with her. Let her come and see us off at the mirror house."

"I don't understand your attachment to the girl," said Bogdana. "She is only a human."

"I happen to be attached to a few humans in my world. So what's one more?"

"You like her that much?" Bogdana said. There was a calculating look about her, though Yukiko wasn't sure Astrid would catch it.

"Yes."

"Then you may come visit her as often as you like."

Ah, and there it was. An inducement for Astrid to return to the Unseelie world. A hook. It was more subtle than the Seelie's overt imprisonment. But a subtle hook was a hook all the same. But why? Did Bogdana want to see more of her daughter and fear that she would not return to Unseelie except when forced? Could Bogdana truly love her? It seemed so unlikely, but Yukiko had to admit to the possibility.

An hour later, three ponies were brought to the front door and Astrid, wearing pale green pants and a matching blouse, mounted one. Bogdana took the lead and Sister took the last pony. Well, at least Bogdana wouldn't force the girl to walk. She must be currying Astrid's favor. Yukiko jumped up onto the rump of Astrid's pony.

"Where is the bell?" she whispered once they were on their way down the hill and Bogdana was about ten yards ahead. Astrid had her purse with her, but Yukiko could not detect the bell's metallic scent.

"It's fine," whispered Astrid.

"What are you up to?" asked Yukiko.

"It'll be fine. I'm a Door, remember?"

"You can't steal the girl. The moment she goes through the door, the chain will tighten and strangle her."

"I'm not going to steal her."

Yukiko tried to get Astrid to reveal what her idea was, but the trail reached the bottom of the hill. A few moments later, they were almost nose to tail with Bogdana's pony and could not speak without her hearing. They rode on to Luna Park, gave their ponies to the stable groom and entered the park. Sister trailed behind, and Yukiko slowed to walk beside her. She had never been fond of anyone having to walk a few steps behind anyone else. It was another symptom of her modernity, she supposed.

Astrid and Bogdana talked together, and both of them seemed animated and intense. When they arrived at the mirror house, Bogdana spoke to the person who was running the attraction and the four of them entered, Astrid at the front.

Yukiko followed Sister, who had the ends of her sleeves balled up in her fists as they went through the maze. Yukiko smelled the fear and frustration pouring off of her.

"Are you ready?" Bogdana asked Astrid when they reached the back of the mirror house.

Astrid motioned Sister to her side. "She's going to take off your chain."

Sister's mouth popped open and she shook her head in disbelief.

"She's freeing her?" said Yukiko. "But how?"

"An exchange," said Bogdana. She had a delighted and chilling smile as she lifted the chain over Sister's head. Sister cried, both in joy and in fear. She pulled Astrid's hand and shook her head. She signed "No" over and over, but Yukiko did not need to translate.

"It will be fine," said Astrid. "Yukiko will take you to our cousin, Elliot. He'll look out for you. I'm tied to the Unseelie world whether I like it or not. But you can go free. You were never meant to be here."

Sister put her hands over her face, still shaking her head.

"You've lost too many years," said Astrid. "Now it's your turn to live."

"Don't do this!" Yukiko said to Astrid. "How can you help her if you're a slave here?"

"That's just it. It's the only way I can help her. Take her to Elliot."

Bogdana placed the chain around Astrid's neck and it tightened until it pressed into the skin. Yukiko watched Astrid gasp and pull at the chain. Then she swallowed, took a few calming breaths, turned to the mirror and muttered something under her breath. The mirror wiggled in its frame.

Sister uncovered her face and looked at the mirror. She backed up until she bumped into a wall of the maze.

"Go through. It is already done," said Astrid.

Yukiko changed into her human form, complete with the illusion of clothing, not because it was necessary, but because there was no other way Sister would go through the mirror. Yukiko took her hand.

"I'll take you to Elliot," she said. If he had found a way to be in San Francisco decades ago, then he may yet be some help. Iolanthe had mentioned an agent, and if the

Seelie had poisoned him, then he must be of some threat to them. That might be a good thing.

She would lose her tail for certain, she knew. The girl she had tricked into the Seelie world was now a slave to the Unseelie. There was little she could imagine short of murder that would have been a greater crime to the lawful Myobu. But it didn't matter. She had to help Astrid and Sister no matter what the consequences. Her fate was already sealed. But Astrid, Elliot's and Sister's were not.

CHAPTER 42

ASTRID WOKE UP ON HER thin straw palette in a small room at the back of the house that she shared with Foon, one of the other maids.

As soon as they had returned home from the mirror house, Bogdana had taken Astrid to Foon for instruction and integration into the household. Foon was a humanoid raccoon. She was bipedal and had somewhat human features, but with a pointed snout and triangular ears high on her head. Thick gray fur covered her entire body. Her face was pale gray except for the black mask around her eyes and though her tail was concealed under her robe, Astrid had seen it when they had changed clothing in their shared quarters. It was thick, striped and luxurious. Her nimble hands were black and slender and ended in thick dark claws. Like everyone in the house, Foon went barefoot, and her claws clicked on the stone floor.

"Get up," said Foon. "It's the big day."

Their room was dark and windowless and though there was a window in the hallway outside, no light came from it. Astrid supposed it would be around four in the morning if they lived on human time. She forced herself out of bed.

During the weeks of her imprisonment, she had mopped, dusted, hauled wood and water and had occasionally served meals to Bogdana and the small staff of the house. Her mother had not acknowledged her or spoken to her the entire time, except to give brief orders. So much for being the favored child. But she had not expected anything more. Taking Sister's place was worth it.

Even when she had been beaten for spilling a tureen of soup, it had been worth it. Somehow, being beaten by the cook, a tall lean man with a short temper and hair like fir needles, was easier than being struck by her human mother. Perhaps it was because there was no pretense of love or attachment. When she was beaten, she noticed that the chain around her neck grew tighter, then it loosened later. It happened at other times as well. She tried to pay attention to when it loosened or tightened and found that it corresponded with her moods. The angrier or more upset she got, the tighter it became. Perhaps it did so to punish any angry thoughts of escape. Or perhaps it was simply another way to torment slaves.

For all her exhaustion from work, Astrid was not idle in her quiet moments. She tried opening Doors whenever she got the chance. At first, she tried to use the mirrors that hung here and there in the house. She could make them waver more often than not. But she knew that if she went through, the chain would choke her to death. Then she tried to make Doors on blank walls and found that Yukiko had been correct. When she was frightened or upset, she could occasionally do it. After that, making Doors with mirrors became even easier.

Occasionally, Bogdana entertained houseguests and Astrid was called to serve them food and drink. Tonight, a giant group of Bogdana's friends, or more accurately, her political allies, were coming.

Foon and Astrid made the preparations in the gigantic dining hall, cleaning and scrubbing, then moving tables and benches in from other parts of the house. Once she, Foon and some of the other staff had finished moving the furniture, Astrid hauled in wood for the giant fireplace at the end of the dining hall. Then she went to the kitchen to peel potatoes, fetch water and wash and dry an endless series of beer steins.

At sunset, the guests began to arrive. More than half of

them were men, giant, bearded and hairy. The women were large and strong. Everyone wore leather and metal, axes and swords. They were like the giants from Celtic myth, but these people came in all colors and races, including a few who did not look human at all but had reddish fur. They were not Unseelie or Seelie, as they ate meat, and Astrid wondered what they were.

They filed into the dining hall, where Astrid filled and refilled their steins with mead, ale and beer as they talked and ate. One man strode into the dining hall with a beautiful buck draped over his shoulders. He hefted its body onto a table and motioned to Astrid.

"Take this to the kitchen for cooking. My brothers are hungry!"

The animal was huge, at least two hundred pounds. There was no way she could move it. Foon appeared, squared the buck upon her shoulders and carried it away. How anyone expected the staff to skin and cook it for that night's meal was beyond her, but it was not her problem. One of the tables shouted for food, and Astrid grabbed a tray of mutton, venison and broiled rabbit and hurried over. Within an hour, the entire room was drunk, shouting, singing and, in some cases, flirting. Astrid kept her hood down, though she could see easily through it, and hurried from table to table.

Bogdana made the rounds, speaking with various people. Whatever political alliances she was hoping to forge seemed to be going well, as the guests were all in a fine mood.

"Sister!" shouted a man to Bogdana. He looked nothing like her, but then Astrid had noticed that some of the other guests called each other brothers and sisters. "A fine gathering!" he said.

"Thank you," said Bogdana with a polite smile.

Astrid set a heavy platter of pig with roasted potatoes and carrots on the table.

"And excellent food," he said. "Is this human a new servant? I do not remember her."

Astrid had to stop herself from glancing up at her mother, but instead took a few steps back, head lowered.

"She's not human," said Bogdana. "She's Unseelie."

The man looked at Astrid, appraising, and Astrid took another step back. She did not want to draw her mother's attention and be punished.

"If you say so, sister. But she's made a choice."

Bogdana shot her a look so venomous that Astrid spun on her heel and rushed to the other side of the room where she busied herself collecting empty dishes. She took them to the kitchen and when she returned to the dining hall, she snuck a glance at Bogdana. She was sitting and talking with some of her guests, looking relaxed and happy.

A choice. He said that she had made a choice. But how could one choose to be human? One was born human, Seelie, Unseelie, Kitsune, or a host of other mysterious beings. But then, the Kitsune could be either a Myobu, like Yukiko, or Nogitsune, a wild fox. She wondered if it was a choice for them or if they were born to it.

The next morning Astrid was summoned to Bogdana's breakfast table.

"You have been summoned by the governor to meet with him in five days. I told him that you can only open Doors at that mirror house, so we will meet him there. He wishes for you to open a Door for him as a demonstration."

Astrid dipped her head to acknowledge that she had heard and then backed out of the room.

The governor. At the mirror house.

She climbed the stairs to the unused upstairs room where she had hidden her owl bell. Bogdana had never come to her quarters, and so there had been no risk of it being discovered, but Astrid had not known that when she arrived. She returned to her room and slipped the bell into her purse with her clamshell mirror, the pencil and water-warped drawing pad and then shoved the purse under the head of her palette. Later that evening, Foon sat cleaning and filing her claws, unbothered by the presence of the bell. Astrid considered asking her where she had come from, but decided against it.

The next five days passed slowly, and she had plenty of time to think as she scrubbed floors on her hands and knees, climbed and dusted. There was no vacuum, so heavy rugs had to be dragged outside and beaten. And with no gas for the stove, she chopped and hauled wood. She was beaten twice more for breaking a cup and for allowing a fire in the stove to go out. Her back was a mass of burning welts, but even without the injuries, she would have been sore from work. The welts forced Astrid to lie on her stomach that night. In the dark, she saw Foon's black eyes gleaming, watching the ceiling.

She turned her head away and thought about Sister. Was Elliot taking good care of her? Had he taken her to meet her mother? She hoped not. As much as Sister may want to meet her real mother, it was a bad idea. She would take one look at the mutilated girl and call the police. No, Elliot would have to keep her safe on his own. She hated to burden him, especially without even asking, but she had had no choice. Perhaps Yukiko could use her magic to help them somehow.

The next morning was her meeting with the governor. She knew this would not simply be a demonstration of her abilities. No. It would be the day she was forced to create a Door that released the Unseelie into the human world.

CHAPTER 43

THE NEXT MORNING, BOGDANA SENT a midnight blue dress with a full skirt and silver trim for Astrid to wear. She also included silver bracelets and anklets. The links were the same size and shape as her slave chain. Interesting. Perhaps Bogdana wanted to downplay the fact that Astrid was her slave by making the neck chain look like a decoration. But who would be fooled? No one. No, this was Bogdana's way of reminding her of her position. Astrid would either willingly wear chains around her wrists and ankles or she would be in defiance of her owner.

Astrid bathed, dressed and put on the ankle and wrist chains.

"Did you know the girl who looked like me?" Astrid asked Foon as she combed her hair.

"You took her place," said Foon softly after a glance at the door.

"Was she troublesome, like Bogdana said?"

"She was."

"How old was she when her tongue was cut out?"

"I do not know how old. But she was this high." She held up her slender black hand a few feet off the ground, at about the height of a six- or seven-year-old child.

Astrid felt her skin flush hot with anger, and her chain pulled tight around her neck. She forced herself to be calm, to think of Elliot, of school, of anything other than the torment Sister had lived through. There was just so much pain, all because of her. Cinderella was dead or an injured stray somewhere, Elliot was stuck being a caretaker to a mute, tortured girl who probably had emotional damage, and her mother had been driven to violence and the brink of mental illness solely because of her presence.

Then she thought of the kittens, Diego and Frieda, and how Sister would like cuddling them, how she would sleep with them curled beside her. She was safe now. No one would hurt her again.

After Foon left to work, Astrid pulled out her purse. She found her clothing from Seelie and dug out her socks, turning them both inside out. She filled one of them with her few belongings, shoving her empty purse back under the palette. Then she hiked up her skirt. She took the Seelie sash from the outfit she had brought from Seelie and tied the sock to it and tied it around her waist, letting it fall low to the top of her hipbones. Then she took the other sock, the empty one, and tied three knots in it. That was one knot in the sock with her things, three knots in the other and one in the sash. Five. She took the end of the sash and tied more knots, for a total of nine. Then she turned her underwear inside out. That made three pieces of inside out clothing, nine knots, a bell made of cold iron. There was no salt here, so she was out of luck on that score.

She let the dress fall and tugged at the sash and sock until they were hidden under the skirt. She looked at herself in the mirror in the hall. Her hair was getting longer and hung into her eyes. She looked weary and older, but she was not meeting the governor as a beauty contestant.

It was almost noon, and the Unseelie sun was white, small and hot in the sky. A horse-drawn carriage stood outside, and Astrid wondered if Bogdana had hired it or if she had kept it somewhere. She wasn't going to ask. She rode straight-backed and silent to Luna Park across from Bogdana who wore rich purple and gold in a dress similar to Astrid's. Neither of them had shoes, but Bogdana's feet were adorned with gold toe rings and rows of anklets. On the drive, she saw her mother touch her stomach and her neck, as if uncomfortable. The bell must be having some effect on her. The knots might dampen its effect somewhat, but she was still suffering. Good.

The carriage dropped them at the front entrance of Luna Park and Astrid passed beneath the arching gateway and walked to the mirror house silently behind her mother. There were only two outcomes for her. Either she would die, or she would succeed. But she would not be opening a Door for the Unseelie to invade her world. For whatever she was, she was not one of them. She was a human being at heart, no matter what world she had come from. And she would live like a human or die like one.

They waited in the hot sun for half an hour before the governor and his entourage arrived. The man wore a fitted coat, tight breeches, white men's hose and shiny black shoes.

"Bogdana, duchess of Dreen," said a man beside the governor by way of introduction. Bogdana curtseyed low and the governor nodded acknowledgement.

"Governor Platt," she said.

"Astrid, Door and slave," said the man.

Astrid curtseyed. When she rose, she saw the governor swallow hard. Sweat glistened on his upper lip and she wondered if he felt the effects of the bell also.

Instead of wandering through the mirror maze from the front, the governor led the way to the back entrance. Well, it wouldn't do to have him get lost inside and make a fool of himself. Before she entered, Astrid caught a glimpse of something in the sky to the west. She stepped back, bumping into Bogdana, and took another look. The purple sky was full of black things, birds, a flock so thick and so fast that it was blotting out everything behind it. She went cold.

"The Wild Hunt," murmured Bogdana.

Astrid now could make out the closest of the slaugh. They were twisted beings mounted on panthers, vultures, undulating serpentine dragons and skeletal horses. The slaugh themselves varied even more than their mounts, from skeletal humanoid creatures with fingers and toes as long as their arms to thick-bodied creatures with four or even six powerful arms. These were not small creatures like the ones she had seen in the mirror, though there were smaller slaugh scattered in among their larger brethren. These were the things of nightmare and legend. And they were utterly focused on their destination, the place where she now stood.

Then she heard their cry, an undulating sound, a mix of voices both high and low, wailing, screaming and bellowing. A sound of starvation, fury, the sound of beings so hungry to kill that it was their sole desire. Death. Chaos. Torment. Domination. They howled their song, and then horns blew, resonant and bone-shaking.

"They come!" cried Bogdana, and Astrid saw the eager look in her eyes. Other Unseelie pointed at the sky, some with shouts of triumph, some with wild-eyed looks of pure delight.

"They come!" the people cried.

Over and over they said it, like a summoning. Now Astrid understood. She understood everything.

She understood that in times gone by, human beings possessed a greater sense of evil, of something dark in the world. Something hungry. The rituals of salt and knots, of prayer and holy water were like a flame, held up to ward off what the people knew waited just outside the circle of light. These beings were the things that waited.

The humans today were like wandering youths in the fairy forest. "Let's explore the cave!" one cries. "I have wine!" says the other. And they go, and drink, and make love, and on their blanket, they fall asleep in each other's arms, oblivious to the eyes that watch. The things that their ancestors knew all too well. Things that mean them harm. The babes sleep. As even now, in the human world, they slept.

She knew that long ago, people did not leave the confines of home at night, and the wall and the city gate kept the things of the black at bay. But what happened when the evil breached the walls? When it rode through the streets? When it destroyed the world in fire and blood? Or would it be more subtle, as in the days of old, where the dark things waited in the lonely places, the quiet places, to ensnare their prey?

When had the Unseelie been barred from the human world? Was that when the fear of the dark started to fade? Once there had been old men and women who made a sign with thumb and forefinger, whispering words to ward off the spirits, but they had gone, and their children and grandchildren after them, until the modern people simply smiled and shook their heads at the quaint ways of their ancestors.

But the knowledge was not completely gone, was it? Astrid thought of the stories that people still told of aliens coming from the dark of space to capture and kill, of vampires and zombies rising from the grave to feast, of men driven mad by evil until they themselves became the very blackest hunger for violence. The stories, however banal or silly, were stories of evil. Fairy stories.

Astrid knew that there had been times when these creatures had names, and how rituals of knots, water, salt, mirrors, magnets and beads could repel them, even defeat them. And she was about to attempt just such a thing.

Her mother's hand clamped around her upper arm and she forced her forward into the mirror house. The governor's two servants stood behind them, and they moved to stand on either side of Astrid as they stopped before the exact mirror that she had used before. Someone must have told them which one it was, and the only one who would have known would be Bogdana. It was another secret, another betrayal, meaningless.

Her heart pounded in terror as the song of the Wild Hunt grew louder. The chain around her neck was comfortable, and that would not do.

"Make the Door," said the governor. He did not attempt to explain or cajole. It was an order, and he expected her to obey.

She thought of Sister, the little girl of six or seven, crying and fighting as they whipped her soft skin, or burned her little hands. She thought of her screams as they held her down to cut out her tongue, the blood, the pleas for mercy. She now had no words. No name. The screams of the Wild Hunt became the girl's screams. The chain tightened, and yet she thought of Sister more. Crying on her palette. Blood on her skin. Blood in her mouth, on her teeth, her lips.

She was choking, and she pulled at the chain. "I can't," she gasped. She fought to pull off the chain, but the more desperately she fought, the tighter it became.

"Take it off," said the governor to Bogdana.

"She's my slave," she said.

"And now she is mine. You will give her to me."

"I most certainly will not!"

The cries of the crowd grew louder and Astrid heard the sound of people running. Then there were several heavy thuds outside followed by shouts of jubilation. The slaugh were landing, and she could not breathe.

"That is an order," said the governor quietly. "Give me the chain." Bogdana, with a look of pure hatred, touched the chain, which loosened. Astrid gasped and pulled in the sweet, clean air. She doubled over coughing, but at least she could breathe.

The mirror house lurched as slaugh landed atop it. They tore in through the front and back entrances and Bogdana screamed. The governor backed up and his servants flew to his side. Gigantic black arms wrapped around Astrid from behind.

She did not fight, but instead whispered one word, over and over. And then the floor flexed, and bent, and she fell through, clutched tight in the arms of the slaugh.

CHAPTER 43

"I
T IS FINISHED," SAID PANGUR Ban. She was sitting on the kitchen windowsill when Elliot came down to have breakfast. Seamus had already made coffee and was sitting at the table while Huginn perched on the baker's rack against the wall. "We stayed until the sea woman found the bell," said the cat.

"You two are amazing," said Elliot, giving a nod to Huginn.

"They're the best infiltration and retrieval team we have," said Seamus.

"You are too kind," said Pangur Ban, squeezing her eyes shut as she turned her face into the beam of sunlight.

"Tell me about Mick," said Elliot. "He kept talking about the birdman. Is that you?"

Huginn made a croaking sound in the back of his throat. "Mick is time sensitive, like you, but he can't get back to his original time stream, and I'm hoping we can help him. He slipped sideways, into a different time stream, but he also moved forward along the time line. And now, he keeps slipping into different time streams, but thankfully, not between worlds. It's an interesting case."

"I'm working on it," said Seamus, flipping open the morning newspaper.

Elliot had just poured a cup of coffee when Neil came in through the kitchen door, bringing a gust of warm morning air with him. "We're not finished," he said to Elliot. "There's a problem. Julius was at the library all night, looking up old records."

Elliot wondered how Julius had managed to stay in the library without being caught, but he didn't have time to ask before Neil continued.

"He said that Astrid's grandfather, and yours, died three years before she was born."

"But that's not what Astrid told me," said Elliot. "She said it was a year after she was born."

"She wouldn't know if she was a just baby," said Neil.

"So it's what her mother said. That's almost the same thing."

"How do you not know when your own grandfather died?" asked Neil.

"Neither of our mothers will talk about him. It's like they agreed that he never existed. I think there was a letter when he died, but neither of them went to his funeral."

"So you and Astrid only know of his death from your mothers?" asked Neil.

"Yeah, but they have no reason to lie. And what does that have to do with Astrid and the bell? He delivered it to her, so he must have died after she was born. Simple."

"I don't know," said Neil. "Julius says that we no longer have a time loop with the bell any more, but we do have an unstable time line."

"But we did everything just as we were supposed to. The bell went to the shop in New Orleans, and our grandfather will buy it and give it to Astrid."

Neil leaned against the kitchen counter. "How can he deliver the bell if he died three years before she was born?"

"How do you know he died?"

"There was a death record, but no record of next of kin. They were never notified."

"How did he die?"

"Train accident," said Neil absently. It was a good thing Elliot hadn't known his grandfather or he might have been offended by the thoughtless way Neil delivered the news.

"And he's certain?" said Elliot.

"Julius is a researcher," said Neil. "He can obtain almost any record, either from our library or almost anywhere else. So yes, he's certain."

Hazel came in with a cardboard box. "I think I got everything you asked for," she said. "And there was a note taped to your trailer door."

Elliot was still staying away from his trailer, giving Luna Park a ten-mile radius in case he needed to enter the area to help Astrid. So Hazel had brought him a few of his belongings. He took the note from the box and opened it.

"It's from Yukiko, that girl I told you about," he said. "She says it's urgent."

"Why didn't she just call you?" asked Neil.

"We just had the one date. We never exchanged numbers. I don't think she had a phone."

"Wow, she didn't give you her number and you didn't want to call afterward," said Neil. "It must have been a good time."

"Considering the Seelie snuck something into my food and I began noticing the time slips and seeing things, yeah, it was horrible. I thought I was going insane. She probably thought so too."

"And yet, she wants to see you."

Elliot remembered her kissing him on the cheek, but the note didn't seem like any kind of romantic invitation. Neil and Seamus had both assured him that Astrid was in Seelie, but she would return safely. But there was no way to know for certain, which was why he was staying away from Luna Park. That way, he could intervene if needed. Besides, if the time line was unstable, anything could happen.

"I'm going to see her. It may have something to do with Astrid."

"I'll come along," said Neil, pulling a set of car keys off of a hook by the kitchen door.

Twenty minutes later, they were at the Seaside Inn.

Elliot knocked on Yukiko's door. When she answered, he thought he caught a flash of movement behind her.

"I'm so glad you're here," she said. "I wasn't sure you'd get the note, and Mr. Augustus said you quit your job."

"I did. So what's wrong?"

Yukiko glanced at Neil, and for a moment, Elliot thought he saw recognition in her eyes. He also thought he saw Neil shake his head a fraction, but he couldn't be sure.

"Where's Astrid?" he asked. "You said it was urgent."

"Astrid is alive," she said. "I will be blunt. There's someone here you need to meet. It's your cousin."

"What do you mean, meet her? Where is she?" Elliot pushed into the room.

"Wait, it's not Astrid," said Yukiko and Elliot felt her touch his arm. But he pulled away from her. Astrid was in the back of the room, looking at him with wide, terrified eyes. She wore pajamas and her hair—her hair was much longer than when he had seen it last.

"How long was she there?" he demanded, turning to Yukiko, then Neil. Yukiko was flustered, and Neil was unreadable. "How long was she stuck there?"

"It's not her, it's her doppelganger," said Yukiko.

Then he saw Astrid's skin, the scars, and he closed the distance between them. She shrunk away from him and skittered sideways, toward Yukiko.

"What happened to her?" he yelled. "What did you do to her?" He rounded on Yukiko.

"Elliot, listen to me!" Her voice was louder than it should have been, and he saw a light, like a flash of lightning. It forced him to stop, just for an instant. "This isn't Astrid. She's a changeling—Astrid, I mean. This girl was the human baby she replaced."

"What are you talking about? That's Astrid!" But another look at her told him otherwise. Everything that he normally sensed in his cousin wasn't there. She had a different feel to her. Yukiko put a protective arm around her shoulders.

"What happened to her? Who hurt her?" asked Elliot. Yukiko would get about one minute to explain why his cousin was covered in scars and was so damaged that she didn't seem anything like herself. And then he didn't know what he was going to do.

"Listen to her," said Neil. He was standing too close, as if he was ready to hold Elliot back if he tried to grab Astrid or hurt Yukiko. Elliot hadn't noticed him approach.

Yukiko explained it to him. How Astrid was born to the Unseelie people and how this girl was the human child she replaced and who was then kept as a slave to the Unseelie. How Yukiko and Astrid had fallen through a door into Seelie, then escaped to Unseelie. Astrid had allowed herself to become a slave to free this girl who had chosen the name Sister. How he had to take care of the tongueless tortured girl. How Astrid was now trapped.

He looked into Sister's eyes, the exact color and shape of Astrid's, but the person behind them was different. The girl signed something.

"She says that she is your cousin, but Astrid is your cousin too. They are sisters."

"How did you get all that from her making that sign?"

Yukiko said, "I can translate for her until she learns regular sign language."

"But how can you do it now? How do you know Unseelie sign language?"

"It's not that. I can just—" she glanced at Sister. "I can just tell what she means."

"Tell me the truth," said Elliot. "You were there at the puppet show and when the slaugh came through and you and Santiago were the ones who captured it. You were there when Astrid went to Seelie. And you were there when I was poisoned and thought I was hallucinating. Now you come back with this girl. Tell me the truth. All of it."

Sister was signing something over and over.

"What is she saying?" asked Elliot.

"She's asking if you're family," said Yukiko.

"Yeah, of course," said Elliot. "Of course we're family. We're cousins."

The girl eyed him with a mixture of assessment and wariness, but there was also a gleam of defiance to it. It was strange, to have two identical cousins, one of whom wasn't really related to him. But he didn't care if Astrid was the daughter of the devil himself. She was still his cousin. He had now simply gained another family member.

Sister signed to Yukiko.

"No, I won't leave you. Not until you want me to."

Sister signed more.

"I told you I won't leave you. Not unless you want me to."

As Sister continued to sign, Yukiko got a strange look. Sister stopped, and the two women stood looking at one another.

"What is she saying?" said Elliot.

"She says I'm her cousin too." Yukiko paused and Sister put her fingers to her lips in some sort of sign.

"I said I would look after you for a while," said Yukiko.

Sister got a stricken look and Yukiko sighed. "I don't have any family. I'm not even—I'm not related to you."

Sister signed something and then pulled her hands into her sleeves and crossed her arms. She looked like she was about to cry.

"Fine," said Yukiko. "I'll be your cousin too if you want."

Sister looked satisfied. Neil was almost smiling. As touching as it was, Elliot wanted answers.

"Now tell me the truth," he said to Yukiko.

"Seeing as we're both responsible for our cousin," said Yukiko. A moment later, a snow white fox stood in a pile of Yukiko's clothing.

A few minutes later, after Yukiko had explained what she was and why she had come to Luna Park, how her spirit ball had been restored and how she could create illusions, Elliot turned to look out the window. The bright summer sunlight beat down on the pink stucco walls and the empty pool. Outside, they had work to do.

Astrid's mother had seen his grandfather when he delivered the bell. There was an eyewitness. But eyewitnesses could be unreliable.

"I'll tell you what we're going to do," he said to Neil. "First, call Julius and get Seamus to buy back the bell from the shop in New Orleans. The records showed a man buying it, so it's either one of us or him. Then, Yukiko is going to help me with an illusion. And then we're going to Luna Park, and I'm going to save my cousin."

"You'll want to stay close to me," said Yukiko. "Just to make sure the illusion holds. It's not just changing your appearance. I have to make her think you're her father, which means I have to affect both of you at the same time."

They stood on the sidewalk outside of Astrid's house. They waited there until Astrid's father left for work so her mother would be home alone with baby Astrid. Yukiko studied an old photo of his grandfather that Julius had somehow obtained. Elliot had never seen him. They looked a lot alike.

Neil was back at the safe house with Julius. Julius should have been almost twenty years younger at this point in time, but he looked just the same to Elliot. He had been working on fabricating a death notice to deliver when Astrid was a one-year-old baby. Now Elliot had to do his part. The little owl bell waited in his pocket.

"Ready?" he said and at Yukiko's nod, they crossed the street and rang the doorbell.

His Aunt Carrie looked so young when she opened the door. Her eyes went wide with shock and then she composed herself.

"Hi sweetie," he said. "I came to visit you and the baby."

"And who is this?" she said, looking Yukiko up and down.

"This is my girlfriend, Sally."

Yukiko offered her hand, and Elliot wondered if it was a way to make the magic more potent through physical contact. But maybe it was just a handshake.

"I brought a little present for the baby," said Elliot.

His Aunt Carrie hesitated, and Yukiko must have been applying her magic, because she then welcomed them in. She led them to Astrid's room, where the baby lay sound asleep in her crib.

"Your baby is beautiful," said Yukiko.

Carrie looked down at her daughter. "She is, isn't she?" She had a wistful smile that Elliot had never seen on her. She was so young now, happily married with a brand new baby who had survived a hospital scare. She glowed with contentment.

He tried to imagine what a regular grandfather would do, even an estranged one.

"May I hold her?" he asked softly.

Carrie hesitated and then picked up Astrid and placed her in his arms. She stirred a little, and then fell back asleep, her tiny pink mouth slightly open. She had a faint smell to her, not of diaper or baby powder, but of sweet soft skin and milk. He kissed her forehead. She squirmed awake, and he knew what was causing her pain. The bell in his pocket was cold iron, and this little baby was a changeling, a cuckoo in the nest of her human twin.

Astrid's face screwed up in pain and she opened her mouth. Her chin quivered, but no sound came out. Then she drew breath and let out a hearty cry. Carrie took her and soothed her.

"I brought this for her," said Elliot, pulling out the bell. "It's a good luck charm. Been in the family for generations. It's an antique."

Astrid screamed, and he found his hand shaking. The bell hurt her. She was a tiny, helpless baby, and he was going to put this bell next to her crib where it would hurt her constantly. But it was the only way for her to develop immunity to it. It had to be done, and yet he wanted to take it away, to take Astrid away where she would be safe. But things had to progress in this way. He set the bell down.

"She's a little young for it now, but maybe when she's older she'll enjoy it," said Carrie.

"Yeah, when she's older," said Elliot, hating this, hating himself.

Astrid arched her back, wailing louder. He was hurting a baby, and there was nothing he could do about it.

Yukiko touched his arm. Carrie was studying him. This was bad.

"I should go," he said. "And Carrie. I'm sorry. About everything."

He didn't know what he was apologizing for, but it felt like the right thing to say. Carrie's face relaxed into a beautiful smile. He kissed her cheek, quickly, and he and Yukiko left. His hands were still trembling as he put the key in the ignition.

When he had first joined the Time Corps, he had thought it would be fun and adventure. It had been. But there was an ugly part. Runt had died because his mother was a Time Corps member. He didn't know what had happened to Huginn, but his memory was complexly shot and he relied on Pangur Ban to remember even the simplest things. Felicia was trapped in a world not her own. Sister had been tortured, and if they changed the time line to save her as a baby, then Astrid would never come to the human world at all, but would be raised Unseelie, or perhaps swapped with some other baby. As it was, Astrid had to spend eighteen years with her mother. If he wanted to save both Astrid and Sister, then he had to allow them both to live through hell.

CHAPTER 44

A STRID FELL. THE SLAUGH'S ARMS stayed around her, and though she felt the slaugh loosen its grip, it then grabbed onto her even harder once it realized it was no longer inside the mirror house. They were in the void. The place between. It was cold and scentless, soundless and black. And yet, she was not afraid. The falling sensation was almost pleasant, like being weightless. Never had she stayed so long in the void when she made Doors, but she found she liked it.

The slaugh made a low, throaty sound. She had to rid herself of it, or she would carry it with her into the human world. It gasped and gurgled and she understood that it was choking. There was no air here. How had she not realized it? She was not breathing, but she felt no discomfort. This must be part of being a Door, being comfortable in this void.

Then she heard a different sound. More slaugh, they were coming, even here. The Door in the Unseelie World was still open, and they were coming through, following her. She willed the door to close, but nothing happened. She felt their approaching presence, hostile and angry.

The Door to the human world hung just before her in space. Though she could not see it, she knew it was there in the black. But she couldn't allow the slaugh to enter into her world. She had to protect it.

She thought about closing the door to the human world. It shut immediately. Interesting. So a Door not in use could be closed with a thought. But the Door from Unseelie could not, presumably because it was in use.

A pressure built within her. She wanted to allow the slaugh to come into the void and then leave them here to choke and die, but something was not allowing it. It was like a pressure inside her, growing almost painful. She had to open another door to allow the slaugh to pass through. The slaugh clinging to her was losing its grip, but before it released her, she made another Door, this time to the mirror house in Seelie. The moment her feet hit the floor of the mirror house, she ducked down, slipping out of the slaugh's grip. It gasped, and with its next breath it roared. The sound vibrated through her, terrifying in its volume, and she had to stop herself from cringing.

She made a Door to the human world through a mirror, and felt the roaring slaugh pressing behind her. The other slaugh raced on its heels. If she got through to the human world and closed the door quickly enough, then they would have to go back through the open door behind them, wouldn't they?

She raced through the void, flew through the door into the human world and the instant she was out of the black, she thought of shutting the door. But it was too late. The slaugh behind her had reached a terrible clawed hand through and dug into the metal floor of the mirror house. The door remained open, and then the slaugh passed through, followed by two more.

"Close!" she shouted, but the Door remained open. The sky was blue outside the exit, and she scrambled out of the mirror house. "Close!" But the mirror door remained open, stretching to accommodate the slaugh and their mounts. More came, dozens of them, all looking around with delight. They scrambled through the maze and out the back exit as she fled. She staggered out onto the middle of the boardwalk and turned back. My God, what had she done?

Humans screamed and ran, and Astrid did nothing to stop them.

Yes. Run. For the Wild Hunt is here. They come.

The slaugh poured out, taking to the skies or racing in all directions along the ground. She had to escape before they noticed her and caught her. She had to find a way to send them back.

She ran, dodging in and out among the humans, but most of them were running in the same direction she was, away from the slaugh. The arcade was up ahead. The little slaugh that had come through before had not seemed to mind electricity. Aside from mildly repelling the slaugh, the arcade would afford her no protection. But something else might.

Her pretzel stand stood just outside the arcade, and whoever had been on staff to run it was long gone. Salt. Knots. She slid behind the stand, hoping the slaugh had not seen her. She grabbed the box of salt and poured some of it over herself, letting it stick in her hair. Then she took a paper bag and filled it with pretzels and dumped the rest of the salt into the bag. There were only a dozen magnets at the prize stall in the arcade, but she dropped those in also. It would have to do.

The humans yelled and ran, but the slaugh seemed to be leaving them alone, for now. None of them seemed to be searching for her, but instead they ripped up games in the arcade and shattered windows, bellowing to one another.

She ran back to the mirror house. The Wild Hunt still poured through the Door and the sky darkened with slaugh as they whooped and screamed through the air. The building that housed the carousel burned, flames licking at its roof, and the swinging pirate ship crashed to the ground, cracking down the center. The few people inside scrambled out, helping the injured.

"Hey, Wild Hunt!" she yelled. "You're missing a Door!"

The closest slaugh looked at her, then spoke with

another slaugh and they ignored her, rushing to shatter a glass display case in the souvenir shop. Within minutes the humans were all gone, except for the few that were trapped on rides. Now and then, she saw a person running to help others. Astrid yelled and waved her arms, trying to catch the attention of the slaugh. They either ignored her, delighting in the destruction, or glanced at her and then moved on.

She was Unseelie still, and the queen and king could summon her at any time and she would have to obey. They had no interest in catching her. She wasn't going to work as bait. Or perhaps the thing preventing them from attacking her was her makeshift method of confusing fey. She hiked up her dress, unknotted the socks and sash and tossed them aside, keeping only the owl bell and the clamshell mirror. She threw away her sketch pad and pencil. There would be no time for drawing a Door. She dropped the bell and mirror into the pretzel bag.

She kept moving through the park, but the slaugh still took no notice of her. When she reached the Sea Swings, she found they were slowly coming to a stop. A human man was on the ground, injured but moving, and the others had somehow managed to cling to their seats despite having claw marks on their flesh. She helped them down and was about to check on the injured man when she saw another person kneeling beside him. It was Elliot. He looked up at her and smiled.

"Welcome back!" he yelled. "You have to go. We'll keep clearing the park. You have to stop the slaugh."

But she had no idea how to do it. Within a quarter of an hour, the slaugh had the park in shambles. The midway was now a pile of rubble with rings, rubber ducks and darts strewn across the ground. A hunk was missing from the highest point of the logjam ride and a tiny trickle of water poured from it. Empty logs lay in a chaotic heap below. At least the humans had managed to escape. There were no bodies, no people anywhere. How could Elliot have done this on his own? But he had said "we." He had help.

The arcade was dark and the flames of the carousel building were growing brighter. Or perhaps, it was that the sky was growing darker. It was sunset, and once it was night, she knew that the slaugh would head east, across the continent, bringing waves of destruction with them. The night was their time.

But in the old stories, they had not burned cities to the ground. So why now? Were they more evil than they had been then? Or was this the result of their pent-up destructive impulses all being released at once? The Unseelie had been imprisoned for at least a hundred years, she guessed, around the time of the industrial revolution. That was when superstitions and stories of bad spirits had started to wane. A hundred years, seething and waiting, and now they were free to destroy the world which they had been denied for so long.

And why were they not killing people? Was it true that they simply loved mischief? Or were they keeping people alive for another purpose? Did they want to toy with them?

She returned to the mirror house, which was still standing, slaugh tearing out the front and the back. The last slaugh that came through sat astride a giant warhorse that leapt down the metal steps and came to a snorting halt. Gold fringed epaulets decorated the slaugh's uniform and he wore a sword on his hip. An enormous curving bone horn hung from his saddle. He must be a general of some kind. She felt the Door through which he had come and was able to close it now. The general surveyed the destruction and turned to another slaugh beside him and spoke. This slaugh must be his second in command.

When the general turned toward her, she shrank back. His face was white, corpse-like, and his pale silver eyes were round and lidless, giving him a piercing, staring look. He must have had a mouth, but she couldn't see one.

"Excuse me," she said, approaching him. She was terrified and her heart was pounding, but she would master herself. She was not going to be dragged back to Unseelie and she was not going to allow the Wild Hunt to stay in her world. She knew what she was and this monstrosity was not her brother.

He turned to look at her, and his eyes, though staring and unnatural, were like the slaugh she had seen in the mirror maze. They were empty. They pulled at her inside, but she did not break eye contact. Instead, she stood straighter, moved closer and tipped her chin up. She would not be cowed. His mouth opened, a tiny lipless slit.

"Yes?" he said, and his voice was as smooth and dark as liquid chocolate.

"I'm the Door."

His head tipped an inch and his eyes rolled up and down in their sockets as he studied her from head to toe. She stepped back, ready to run, to lead them away and open another Door. If she could lead them into the void, maybe they would die there. Perhaps despite the pressure she would feel inside, she could stay there indefinitely until they were all dead, and then find a way home. It was a flimsy hope.

"If you are the Door, then we have you to thank," he said.

"No, you don't. Because I'm not going to open a Door back to the Unseelie world. You are trapped here."

"The king and queen will summon you and force you. You have already obeyed by opening this Door."

The slaugh general got an uncomfortable look, as if he smelled something unpleasant.

The salt, the magnets, the pretzels. And the bell.

He turned back to his second in command. Astrid pulled out the owl bell and held it aloft.

"How about this?" She rang the bell and the two slaugh cringed. The general's mouth opened wider as he grimaced, but the inside of his mouth was empty and toothless. "You like that?" She rang it harder.

"Stop her," said the general, and a nearby slaugh turned and grabbed for her. But she was ready and dodged away.

"And you know what else? The king and queen can't summon me. I made the choice!"

She watched the general exchange a worried look with his second. It was true then. It was a choice to be Unseelie. Was that why Bogdana had originally been kind to her, or her version of kindness anyway? Was she trying to get Astrid to stay willingly? She tried to remember what Yukiko had said about the Unseelie code. Selfishness, using people, doing anything to achieve one's goal.

And she had freed Sister. She had made a choice, a very human choice. A sacrifice. She had not thought of it as any kind of great deed. It was only her attempt to repay a debt to Sister that could never truly be repaid. The girl had suffered the life that Astrid should have had. And if Bogdana would not have beaten and burned her own real daughter, then Sister had still lost a life in a loving human family. Astrid had only been trying to help Sister, but it must have been enough. She had broken the Unseelie code and had chosen humanity.

"That's right. I'm not Unseelie anymore. I'm human. I chose!"

The general seemed to be thinking, but Astrid didn't wait to see what he would do. She turned and fled, opening a Door. The horn sounded, deep and reverberating. She got a glimpse of the Wild Hunt, all turning in the sky or on the ground, flying toward her at terrible speed. She leapt through the Door and soared into the void.

She opened another Door inside the mirror house, went through and opened another. Mirror after mirror became a Door, and the Wild Hunt followed, pouring from mirror to mirror in a stream of solid black with the sound of pounding hooves, wings, shouts, screams, and over and over, the peal of the horn. Now and then, as the closest slaugh drew too near, she dropped a salted pretzel or a magnet behind her. Then the slaugh fell back with a shout.

When she was sure she had a good lead on them, she opened a Door through a mirror at the front of the mirror house. Then she poured out the last of the salt and pretzels just at the mirror's base, grabbing her bell and clamshell mirror. She snapped the mirror in half. Inside, the Wild Hunt completely blackened the interior of the maze. They were not in the spaces between the mirrors where people would normally walk, but were inside each and every mirror, moving from one to another, on and on.

She had never tried moving a door before, but now was the time. She concentrated, trying to move the last Door she had made in the mirror house to the half of the clamshell mirror. It was like moving a boulder, and while it dragged aside, she heard the shouts of the slaugh as they encountered the pretzels and sprinkled salt. She pulled the door, the pain in her head stabbing as it had when she crossed the cold iron line in Seelie, then worsening. She kept pulling. Then, it snapped into place. The slaugh were still flying into the first mirror entrance, but now the exit had moved to the little clamshell. She pressed the clamshell into the salt, facedown.

Now she just had to wait for the last of the slaugh to go through the entrance, and then she could move the entrance to the other clamshell. Then, she would hold them together, making an endless loop in which the slaugh would be trapped. But the line of slaugh entering the mirror maze was too long. She couldn't wait. The first of the line would break through the salt barrier before the last of the slaugh were in the maze.

"Elliot!" she screamed. She saw a cat out of the corner of her eye, a white one, but when she tried to spot it again, it was gone. A minute later, Elliot ran up.

"What?" He crouched beside her.

"See these mirrors? I need you to hold them together," she said. "Then if you can get some rope or a thin chain, then tie them together. Nine knots in three groups of three."

"What are you planning to do?"

"Just do it, okay?"

"Tell me!"

"I'm going to move some Doors and trap them between these two mirrors. The exit is already here," she nodded toward the little mirror that she held into the salt. "But there are too many. I need to get in there and make a door into the Unseelie world so they'll go there. Otherwise, they're just going to break through this mirror," she nodded toward the clamshell.

"And then you'll make another Door to come home?"

"Yeah," she said. But she had no idea how she would accomplish it. Because as soon as she entered the mirror house in the Unseelie world, she would be captured. And all of the mirrors in the human mirror house would be in use, save two, the one she had just moved to the clamshell as an exit and the one she was about to move, the entrance . But how would she find either of those two mirrors once she was in the void? Her abilities were in no way specific enough to manage it.

It didn't matter. People would die, and if it meant she was trapped in the void, then so be it.

"I have to move the entrance to the other clamshell mirror," she said. "Or you can't hold them together."

She forced herself to do it, through the pain, and moved the entrance door. A flying slaugh crashed into the mirror that had been an entrance a moment before and shattered it. He backed up, dazed. Others came behind him, bumping into one another in their haste. One of them crashed into the last mirror, the one she had moved to the first clamshell mirror, shattering it as well.

"This way," she said softly to the slaugh and leapt into the clamshell mirror and into the void.

For a while, it was only her and a single slaugh, and then others joined them. She moved away from them, finding that she could manipulate the direction of her movement in the void. She wasn't fast or nimble. It was more like moving underwater. But the slaugh were helpless and could barely move at all.

She made a door into Unseelie right beneath them and then tilted it. It was easier to move Doors in the void. She moved it until the slaugh moved slowly into the Unseelie world. But Doors opened in both directions, and now and then, a slaugh or another kind of Unseelie would travel through into the void, hoping to find the human world.

Elliot must have seen the last of the Wild Hunt go through the entrance that she had moved to the second clamshell mirror half and must be holding the two clamshell mirrors together, because the Wild Hunt starting pouring into the Void in much greater numbers. Most of them went straight into Unseelie, but some hesitated.

Backing up, she enlarged the Door, making it easy for each and every Unseelie to pass through. She wished she could move them, but she could not, and some choked in the void until she moved the Door up to them and they slipped through to Unseelie. She would not have been sorry to see them die in the void, but if she could trap them for eternity, then she would do it. Let them tear up their own world if they so chose.

With a little practice, she learned to bend the door into a kind of funnel, pulling the line of slaugh and sending them howling back into their own world. At last, the line ended and after waiting to make sure, she closed the door to Unseelie.

It was done. The Unseelie were back in their own world. She hung in the Void and whispered, "home." Nothing happened.

The mirrors in the mirror house would be empty now, but each of them was still an open Door without her there to close them. She could not pass through them. She tried again with no success, and then again.

That was it then, she thought. She was trapped here, in the cool and the quiet, with no way home. She hung in the void for a long time, perhaps twenty minutes, perhaps forty. It was quiet here. How odd, that she would enjoy this place.

She caught movement from the corner of her eye, and there was a sound, like a soft thud. Something was with her in the void, something alive. She tried to catch a glimpse of it again, and in the distance was something bluish-white and luminous. Then she made out an eyeless head, serpent-like. The thing was moving toward her.

She fled in the opposite direction, willing a Door home. But there was only the black empty space, stretching on forever.

Home. Home. The human world.

Nothing. Only the black.

She was going to die here, hanging in space, alone.

Home!

And then another flash of something. It was not white on the black, but rather an absence of the void in one particular place, like a tiny pinprick in a piece of black paper. Not a Door exactly, but more of a keyhole. But instead of light coming through, there was a sound, a ringing sound. A bell.

She moved toward the tiny hole. It was as black as the rest of the void, and she was unsure where it led, but it was her only hope. The thing behind her was getting closer, and somehow, she knew it was hungry. She pushed through the keyhole, like pushing through a membrane. Then she willed it to close behind her.

This place was not the regular world. She was in the air, up high over Luna Park, but it was wrong. The ocean was to the east. It was the Atlantic, not the Pacific and she was in New York. She looked down. Coney Island. Luna Park.

Another Luna Park in another world, in another place. And then she heard the bell. She followed it through another tiny door and found herself at another park, another instability. It was Luna Park in Rio de Janeiro. And other Luna Parks in Athens, Osaka, Haifa, Sydney. All of them on the coast, the border between land and sea. Others were in other places in other worlds, with languages she did not know.

They were in-between sort of places, and she knew they were other versions of her own Luna Park, spread throughout various times and places, some real and some she had never heard of.

They were the places where people gathered, where real and imagined things met, where couples courted and children were delighted and frightened. All of these places were Doorways, and that, in a way, made them hers. She knew that was not really true, that she was not master of any of them, but she was connected with them all the same.

The bell rang, and she followed. Now she was beside a sleeping woman on a cross-country bus. She heard the bell from inside the woman, and she touched her. Then she was inside, where the woman dreamed, where everyone dreamed. It was all one place. A rabbit warren of people and places and thoughts and dreams.

And she flew, and followed the bell, through swamps and grocery stores, an elderly Korean man, down waterfalls and through hospital corridors, into a dreaming Chilean girl, past classrooms and cemeteries, fog-covered green hilltops and down into the cool depths of a lagoon that existed in the mind of an elderly Japanese pearl diver.

She followed the bell. Through the dreamers and the dying, the comatose and the feverish she hurried, careful not to disturb anything, for she knew that their minds were fragile, that she could harm them. Then there was a boy, age two. He was dozing and she heard the familiar sound of American-accented English in his dream. She entered his mind, slowing, as the bell was stronger here. He dreamed of his house, his enormous fluffy dog that towered over him, and there was more. Now that she could pause inside him, there was so much more. Worlds and more worlds, infinite space, twitching and teeming with thoughts and life, all inside this child. And then she was beside him.

How remarkable.

He was so much bigger on the inside.

His mother was turned away, paying for a smoothie. Astrid backed away, out the glass door and onto the street. She was across from Luna Park. She couldn't hear the bell from here, but she knew exactly where to go. She ran.

And when she found him, he was kneeling in the pile of salt, holding the clamshell mirrors together, ringing the bell.

CHAPTER 45

ELLIOT HAD MISSED THE MOMENT when Pangur Ban introduced herself to Astrid after the chaos at Luna Park, and for that, he would always feel regret. He wished he could have seen his cousin's face when her beloved Cinderella spoke to her and revealed that she had been keeping an eye on her for the last decade. But he had missed it. He would miss so many things now.

"How can they have sentenced you to death?" Astrid demanded. She paced back and forth in front of the hearth in the safe house living room. "You're not sidhe. You're not Seelie or Unseelie. You're human. They have no jurisdiction over you." She paused. "Do they?"

"No, not strictly. But you're Unseelie. Or you were. And when the Time Corps interfered—when I interfered—in your life, I broke an agreement between our two groups. By watching over you, Pangur Ban interfered. And by placing the bell with you, I did the same. I essentially hijacked you. You would have been theirs."

"I made the choice to escape, to be human, to defy them."

"But if I hadn't put that bell next to your crib, if you never had immunity, things would have been different. And if Pangur Ban hadn't looked after you, she never would have killed the slaugh mother and child. And if you never had the fairy tale books, would you have known about the ways to ward against the fey?"

"Those were from our grandfather."

"Our grandfather died before either of us were born."

"But my mother—"

He explained how he had posed as their grandfather to deliver the bell and how Julius had delivered a fake death notice to both of their mothers a year after Astrid was born.

"But the books and the airline ticket and the sketch book, was that you too?"

"No," Elliot said. "But someone did it. And it wasn't our grandfather."

"Forget the books and things," said Astrid. "I'm more concerned about the sidhe sentencing you to death."

"It's done. The trial is over, evidence was presented. I'm guilty. I violated our agreement with them and cost them a Door. We're lucky I was able to convince them that Pangur Ban acted on my orders, or they'd insist on punishing her for killing two slaugh. They don't know about Huginn and the others. The Seelie knew there was an agent at work, but they had trouble figuring out who it was. But in the end, they found me."

"Because it was you ringing the bell."

"Yeah."

"But we have to do something!" she said.

"There's nothing we can do. We're lucky they're not imprisoning you and taking back Yukiko as a prisoner, let alone executing Pangur Ban next to me. And what about Neil, Seamus, Julius and everyone else who helped? It's a small price to pay." How could he make her understand that this was the best possible outcome?

"It's not! I mean, I don't want them hurt either. But your life is not a small thing."

Elliot could tell she was trying hard not to cry, and he felt miserable and helpless in the face of her tears. He tried not to think of what he would miss, the adventures, the Christmases, the hope of finding a nice girl who didn't mind living asynchronously from her boyfriend.

"Astrid, I'm no one. I'm a beach bum who just happens

to have this weird and mostly useless ability to identify time anomalies. No one needs me."

"You're not no one. And I need you. You and me, we lived through our family. We kept each other sane. We survived."

"And you'll keep on surviving. You're a Door. You get to discover what exactly that is."

She was turned away and put her face in her hands. He put his arm around her shoulders and she collapsed into him, sobbing silently.

"I need you to do it for me," he said into her hair.

"Do what?"

"Open the door to Death."

"What?" she looked up at him. "I'm not sending you to Death!"

"It's either that or I have to let them kill me as they see fit. Your way is painless."

"I can't do it," she whispered.

"You have to. Please. For me."

"Time travel away!" she said. "Go a hundred years back, a thousand. Just run!"

"There are some events that have to occur. Like you being raised with your mother and that bell. And this is one. Julius verified it over and over."

"But I can't kill you. We're family. They have rules about killing family. The furies descend on the killer or something."

"We're not really related. Not by blood."

"That doesn't matter!"

"Not to us. But to them, it does."

"I don't care about them. We're family and I love you."

"And that's why I need you to do it."

CHAPTER 46

Y UKIKO WAITED. THE LADY WAS coming. Yukiko heated water in the little motel microwave, where it waited, steaming. She opened a box of tea bags from the nearby supermarket.

There was a knock at the door. She opened it, and looked into the face of a middle-aged woman who was thousands of years old. She wore a white silk kimono with gold threads woven throughout and her perfect, delicate hands were clasped one upon the other in front of her. The late afternoon sunlight poured in through the door behind her, casting a shadow on the carpet. The shadow was tall and elegant, slender and beautiful. It had a thousand tails.

"Little one," The Lady said with a nod.

Yukiko bowed low. "Lady."

Behind The Lady stood a man, a warrior, wearing ancient Japanese armor. A helmet with a black, red and white mask ended just above his mouth. It was painted to look fearsome, with heavy black eyebrows, red and black striped cheeks and eyeholes that were round and staring. Yukiko was afraid, but not because of the mask. He also wore a katana.

"Please come in," Yukiko said. She set out three paper cups with tea bags and poured in the hot water. She was ashamed. She had no fine teapot, no delicate tea fit for royalty, no proper table or ceremony. Only paper cups and teabags in a cheap human motel. She deserved no better, but they did.

They drank the tea in silence, sitting on the floor, feet tucked under them. When they were through, Yukiko said, "I am ready."

"Little one," said The Lady, her expression full of affection, "you do not have to do this. You can become a Nogitsune. Many others have."

"With all respect, Lady, I am a Myobu. I will live a Myobu and, if necessary, die a Myobu."

"We are not here to kill you. You will survive."

"But it will be a century before I grow another tail."

The Lady nodded once in assent. "That is true." She turned to the warrior. "State her crime."

He spoke without looking at either of them. "Yukiko, a Myobu, has chosen to aid the Seelie rather than die with honor for refusing them. She has used her power without regard for others, taking a human man to be given mind-changing substances and fooling a young woman into entering the sidhe worlds where she was enslaved. She has betrayed the Myobu and their code."

"I also allowed myself to be robbed of my spirit ball, potentially giving the Seelie a Kitsune slave," said Yukiko. If her crimes were being recounted, let them be complete.

"That was not your choice, little one," said The Lady. "You were poisoned."

"I understand why they poisoned me, but why did they drug Elliot?"

"They knew that a time agent was interfering with their plans, and they supposed it was him because he was close to the Door. He was interfering, but there were others also. The Seelie poisoned him, hoping he would slip through time, go mad and be a lost man. He would not interfere further."

"What about Iolanthe and Augustus? They have wronged our kind. Will they be punished?"

"I spoke with Mr. Augustus, and he has committed no crimes against us willingly. He poisoned you, but

317

against his will. He has even acted against Seelie orders, though indirectly and in ways they would not suspect. He assigned the Door to a pretzel stand to work, where she would be surrounded by wards. It kept most of the Seelie from getting too close to her most of the time."

"It didn't do much good. The Door had a distinct scent and her presence mixed with Iolanthe's and whatever things are always at that park. It threw off the way our powers work. My illusions broke too quickly, and the place felt strange. Even Coyote felt it. He had called me into town to figure it out."

"Coyote," said The Lady with a fond smile. "He still lives?"

"I think he refuses to die. But tell me about Iolanthe. She deserves punishment for taking my spirit ball."

"I am still in negotiations with the Seelie. I speak to them again in a few days, after the human man is dealt with. She will be punished. I will see to it."

"So you defend the Kitsune still? Are there others of us left?"

"Not many, but yes. There are others."

"And Inari, is he still dead?"

"Yes."

"I will not be able to see my brothers and sisters," said Yukiko. "Not in my state of disgrace."

"A hundred years is not long."

"It is to me."

The Lady smiled indulgently and kissed her forehead. She smelled of cherry blossoms.

"Are you certain?" The Lady asked.

"I am." Yukiko knelt and placed her hands, palms down, on her thighs.

She did not cry or let her face or body betray her feelings in any way. She was a Myobu, and she would meet her fate with serenity and strength. She changed.

The katana blade sang as the warrior pulled it from its sheath.

CHAPTER 47

"I'M NOT SURE WHAT YOU expect me to do," Astrid said to Elliot as Neil drove them to Luna Park. "I can only open doors to Seelie, Unseelie, Death and here. If the sidhe of either court get hold of you, they'll kill you, staying in the human world leads to them killing you and going to Death is, well, death."

"I'm sure something will come up," said Elliot.

He was uncomfortably confident, and Astrid knew that she would be expected to do something, just as he and the Time Corps had known that she would be able to send the Wild Hunt back to Unseelie.

It was three o'clock in the morning when they arrived, and Luna Park was officially closed. But the boardwalk was far from empty. Otherkind of all sorts walked in one direction, toward the Chumash Legends stage. Astrid walked beside Elliot with Neil trailing behind them, hands in his pockets, until they reached the performance area. They stood to one side and watched.

They came alone and in groups, Seelie and Unseelie. There were other beings as well, including Santiago, Yukiko and perhaps others. Astrid was not able to discern who was and was not otherkind.

All of the decorations for the Chumash Legends puppet show had been stripped and the stage stood empty and dark. All that remained from the show were the hay bales which filled with chatting otherfolk. Aside from Elliot, Neil and herself, the only humans present were Mr. Augustus and Red Fawn, and Astrid wasn't sure about them anymore. Some of the other people could have been human. There was no way of knowing.

"How much longer?"asked Elliot under his breath.

"Don't tell me you want your execution to come sooner?" said Neil.

"I'm just sick of waiting. If they want to do this, I would rather it happen without an audience."

Neil looked over the crowd as if assessing if he could fight them all off. It was his partner's execution, and yet Astrid knew that something had to happen differently for the personal history between Elliot and Neil to play out. Elliot was supposed to be Neil's partner for years, and according to Elliot, he would later train Neil as Neil had trained him. Her cousin had assured her that time paradoxes could not exist, so this execution had to work out differently than the sidhe meant it to happen. But she could not see how. The Unseelie and the Seelie had come to an agreement that the offending Time Corps member had robbed them of a Door. It was more than an interference. It was a grave offence, punishable by death. It was probably the only thing the two courts had agreed to in centuries. It was no wonder there was an audience.

"The Piper is coming," said a tiny wrinkled woman the size of a toddler.

"Yes," said her companion, an enormous green macaw.

The crowd murmured and turned in one direction. They must feel the approach of the Piper. A little thrill went through Astrid. He was coming.

She saw the bobbing of the tips of his shining black horns over the top of the panels that enclosed the stage area and his hooves made a deep reverberating sound as they struck the wood of the boardwalk. He rounded the corner, and he was just as he had been the first time she had seen him on the beach, huge and intimidating. He seemed even larger now that he was close, and she caught the faint scent of leafy trees and loamy earth, smells that were alien in this place of ocean and sand.

The Piper did not pause, but walked straight up the center aisle to the stage, bent his powerful goat legs and leapt onto it. Then he turned and looked out over the crowd. Iolanthe of the Seelie and Governor Platt of the Unseelie came forward and stood to one side of the stage. No sidhe kings or queens were present, nothing more than small time bureaucrats.

"I think we're supposed to go up," whispered Neil.

The three of them climbed up on stage, and Astrid wondered how she and Neil somehow were in the places of authority corresponding to Iolanthe and the governor. She was necessary, but Neil was not, except as moral support. She appreciated his presence.

"The sentence has been passed," said the Piper. His voice was impossibly low and there was a guttural, growling sound to some of the words. "This man, Elliot Van Dorn, has violated agreements held with the Seelie and Unseelie courts and the Time Corps. The sentence is death."

He turned his wide-spaced black eyes to Elliot then to her, and Astrid felt her blood run hot. The scent of him was stronger here, and there was a warm male scent beneath it, utterly primal and attractive. His arms were human and well-muscled and his shoulders were broad and strong. And she felt the presence of life, plants and animals, fertility and growth. She broke eye contact. She could not allow him to distract her.

"Door," the Piper said. "Elliot Van Dorn has chosen you as his executioner. You will be sending him to Death."

She felt Elliot's hand seek hers and give it a squeeze. He still believed in her, that she would save him. But every existing option would send him to his death.

Well then, she would have to find another option.

Two identical men in green brought out a large mirror and hung it on the back wall of the stage.

"Make the Door," said the Piper.

"Ready?" she asked Elliot.

He nodded. Astrid glanced at Iolanthe and Governor Platt. Both of them wore satisfied expressions. Red Fawn had her fingers to her mouth. Yukiko stared, unblinking, at Elliot, as if trying to memorize his features. Coyote sat with his legs crossed, ankle over knee, looking bored. He winked at Astrid when she made eye contact, but after a moment of surprise, she knew it was a gesture of support, not of mockery. He had not wanted the slaugh in his region, and he could only be pleased that Astrid had banished the Hunt. But otherkind politics was still politics, and he could hardly leap to Elliot's defense.

"Make the Door," the Piper repeated.

She stepped to the mirror. If this was going to work, she had to put on a good show. Doors were rare, and this would work to her advantage. Only one person present had seen what a Door into Death looked like, and Elliot wouldn't betray her.

"Death," she said, loud enough for everyone to hear. The mirror bent and rippled and the misty haze that had surrounded it when Runt had died coalesced.

Seelie, she thought. The mirror flashed an image of green and apricot, and the haze began to dissipate.

Death. The mirror went opaque and reflective again and the fog thickened.

Unseelie. Green, brown and purple.

Death.

She let the haze thicken until it was heavy and swirling. Somewhere safe, she thought. Somewhere quiet. Somewhere the sidhe could not find Elliot and could not harm him. Somewhere safe. Somewhere quiet. She repeated the words in her mind.

"It is time," she said, but she did not glance at Elliot. She couldn't take even the slightest chance that this would not work. He moved forward and put his hand in front of him, as if he would part the curtain to Death before going through.

Safe. Quiet. Somewhere the sidhe could not find him. Now.

The mirror changed, and she saw rows and rows of bookcases, stretching into the back of a dark room. There were piles of scrolls and clay tablets. It reminded her of Bogdana's library, but this place was larger by far. High alabaster windows set into yellow sandstone walls allowed diffused light to shine through. Columns painted in orange, red and bright blue, black and gold held up a high ceiling.

The crowd drew a collective gasp and Astrid heard a commotion behind her. She stayed focused on the Door. Elliot didn't hesitate, but stepped through without a word. The noise behind her was not one only of outrage, but of terror.

She shut the Door behind Elliot and turned to face the crowd, ready for whatever she had to face. The sidhe were frightened, but when they realized that the Door was closed, their terror turned to fury. Yukiko and Red Fawn looked worried. Coyote grinned.

Governor Platt gesticulated and shouted something in another language at Iolanthe, who strode toward the Piper, her goat teeth bared in outrage.

"She has sent him to the Library!" Iolanthe cried.

"She has tricked us!" screamed someone in the crowd.

"Get him back!" yelled someone else.

The Piper allowed the people to make noise for another few moments and then he said, "Stop." He did not shout, but his voice must have reached even the farthest person, because they all went silent.

"We shall not get him back," said the Piper. "He is in a place far from us. And none of us, no matter how fierce, would dare to brave the Library or anger the Librarian."

A murmur of assent went through the crowd.

"We will leave him where he is," said the Piper. "He will die in the Library. He will not trouble us again."

The otherfolk made noises of protest, but when the Piper shifted his weight and swept a look over the crowd, they all quieted.

"It is decided," he said and turned. "Now, Door." He reached his hand out to Astrid, and she was overcome with the desire to place her hand in his large, warm one. But he was merely gesturing.

"You have violated our ways." Now, instead of feeling heat and the disconcerting attraction, she felt the cold sting of fear as he turned toward her. "This cannot be."

"They are your ways," she said, keeping her eyes on his. "Not mine. I am not obligated to follow your laws."

"You were born Unseelie," he said. "The Unseelie obey their people's ways."

"I made the choice," she said. "I chose to deny the Unseelie code. I am no Unseelie."

"Then what are you?" Iolanthe demanded. "You are either one thing or the other."

"I am human."

Iolanthe stepped toward her. "If you are human, then you are ours. You have eaten food in the Seelie world."

"I was not human when I was in Seelie. I was Unseelie then. So your laws regarding humans did not apply to me."

Iolanthe turned to the Piper in appeal.

"She is correct," he said, and Iolanthe opened her mouth to protest, but then shut it.

Astrid then understood something about the Piper. He, surely, had seen her trying out different doors and could have stopped her if he had suspected trickery. He could have stopped Elliot from going through. He was the nearest one to Elliot other than Astrid herself. But he had not. And now, this.

"We are done today," said the Piper. The crowd waited, expecting him to pass down the center aisle the way he had come, but he remained. "Go now."

The otherkind gave him looks as they left, and he watched them go with a placid expression. Santiago, Red Fawn and Yukiko left together, the women talking and Santiago wearing a satisfied look. At last, Iolanthe and the governor left as well, leaving only Astrid, Neil and the Piper.

"Door," he said, and Astrid wondered if he even knew her name. Or was this some strange otherfolk practice where they didn't want to say a name because of its power?

"Do not attempt to bring Elliot Van Dorn from the Library," he said. "The place is dangerous. More so than Seelie and Unseelie. Even if you could enter, you would not be able to exit."

"There has to be a way," said Astrid. She watched the Piper, hoping he would reveal some tidbit of information that might help her. She wasn't going to abandon Elliot to a library, no matter how frightening it might be. "I have to find him."

"Did you not see the fear of the otherkind? They know that the Library is dangerous. I warn you again, Door, you would be trapped there, even with your skills."

Astrid studied him for a moment, and he suddenly seemed so sad, so weary. How old was he anyway? Santiago was thousands of years old, but he retained a snide good humor. The Piper was mighty, but for a moment, she saw something else. And she understood something about him. He had defended her stance that she was not sidhe so that neither faction could gain control of her abilities. It was his way of keeping the peace and balance. That was why he was the arbiter.

He had been the one to take the slaugh back to Unseelie. So he was able to move between worlds also, like her.

"Piper?" she said, and her voice sounded small. "Can you tell me about Doors?"

"I can. It is true that you are not Seelie, Unseelie or human, though human you are, in a way. You are a psychopomp."

The word sounded terrible, like something insane or evil.

"A being who accompanies souls into Death," said Neil from just over her shoulder. She had not felt him move up behind her. Then she understood why he had come, to guard her from the Seelie. Elliot must have asked him to do it.

"The other psychopomps will come for you," said the Piper. "And then, you will get your aspect."

He turned to leave. She understood that he had gone out of his way to speak with her privately.

"Thank you," she said. "For everything."

He turned back to her, and this time, there was a gentleness in the eyes, a slight softening of his sensual mouth.

"I think I hear the sound of wings about you," he said.

CHAPTER 48

THE KETTLE WHISTLED AND ASTRID poured hot water over the powdered hot chocolate mix in her mug. It was too warm outside for a hot drink, but she wanted the comfort of it. She was in Elliot's trailer and Diego and Frieda were gone, taken to the Time Corps house to be with their mother. Cinderella, or rather, Pangur Ban, was alive. She had been Astrid's guardian for most of her life. The thought made her unspeakably happy and also uneasy.

Most of Elliot's things were gone, taken to the house, but she wanted to stay here for a little while before joining everyone at the house. They would talk with her, and then discuss how to get Elliot out. They had probably already begun. But for now, she wanted to be alone.

She had been gone from the human world for a little over a month, and she wondered if her mother had tried to contact her. Her mobile phone was long gone, abandoned in the Seelie world, but Neil had said the Time Corps could get her another one. Even if her mother hadn't called, she decided that she would go see her, even if only for a quick talk at the door. Her mother might not be any different, but Astrid was. She knew the house would look smaller now. The whole world looked smaller.

She would stay in the trailer that night, she decided. And then, Sister needed her at the Time Corps house. The girl was safe and adjusting gradually to life in the human world. Astrid still wanted to attend Columbia, psychopomp or not. She still loved her art.

Runt's body lay in the freezer, and she would take it to Pangur Ban that evening. She wasn't sure what the ritual was for burying their kind, but she would do whatever was required of her.

Elliot's little wire rabbit sat beside the sink. She tied the owl bell over the trailer door so it would jingle when the door opened. It would also protect her from any angry sidhe who might want to pay her a visit. She would pour salt wards later, make knots in cords and string them around. Perhaps she would find a church and get some holy water. For now, she would drink hot chocolate.

When the door opened, she jumped. The man at the door was in his fifties, with graying blonde hair and a tweed jacket with elbow patches. She knew him.

She got up but she did not embrace him. Instead, she studied his face, the lines around his eyes, the changes that age had made to his features. He had aged well, and he watched her studying him with an amused expression. Then he set a bag down at his feet and opened his arms. She hugged him.

"How did you get out? You have to tell me."

"You and the others did it."

"But how?"

"You'll figure it out, just as you figured out how to send me to the Library."

"Why can't you tell me? You said the Time Corps doesn't keep secrets like that."

"If I tell you, then the information forms an unstable time loop. Ask Neil about it. You and the others have to come up with the idea on your own. But you succeed. I wanted you to know so you don't torture yourself and draw a bunch of depressing pictures."

"Shut up. They're not depressing."

"If you say so," he said, and she enjoyed his familiar teasing tone.

"So that's why you came? To tell me we'll get you out?"

"That and I was on my way to your birthdays. I have some stolen library books to deliver."

She reached for the bag, and he did not stop her. Inside were her books, all the books she had received through the years, as well as padded envelopes and note paper, her airline ticket and the tiny sketch pad. There were five one hundred dollar bills in an envelope and the metalurgy book that Elliot had received.

"The information helped me when I needed to find a smith to make the bell," he said.

"How long can you stay?"she asked.

"I have time for a cup of hot chocolate. And then I have to go."

Astrid made another cup and Elliot slid open the window, pausing for a long time to look out at the waves. She wondered if he ever got the chance to surf.

"The Piper said you would die in the Library," she said.

"I might. But that doesn't mean I have to live there."

They drank their chocolate for a while.

"It's time for me to go," Elliot said. He took up his bag and allowed her to give him a last hug and a kiss on the cheek. Then he left.

The owl bell swung back and forth, tinkling over the door.

AUTHOR'S NOTE

I love hearing from my readers. To drop me a note or to learn about my other books, please visit www.heatherblackwood.com.

If you enjoyed this book, please post a review on the retail site where you purchased it.